RUN IF YOU'RE GUILTY

It's the end of the season. Joe Beacon owns some tourist cabins in the California coastal hills, and he's looking forward to closing down for the winter. That's when the weekenders begin to arrive. The businessman and his secretary, the Texas hustler and his young wife, the sensitive artist couple…and son-in-law, Eddie, and his wife, Nancy. He is looking forward to seeing Eddie—it's been awhile. But Eddie is in a strange, confrontational mood. The next morning, Nancy is found down by the lake with her leg caught in a trap, dead from shock. Naturally, Eddie assumes that Joe set the trap, but Beacon knows better than to put traps up during tourist season. But somebody killed his wife—and Eddie is going to make sure that nobody leaves until the killer pays for their crime!

NEVER BE CAUGHT

Three deftly crafted noir novelettes of California crime…

Billy was accused of shooting a man during a robbery, and has been laying low ever since. But when he falls in love with Maria, his cover is blown and they both take off on a desperate run to freedom.

Tony gave up the love of his life when he let pride get in his way. Then he receives Nancy's wedding announcement and rushes to San Francisco to attend with mixed emotions… only to find that she has just died in a car accident. Or has she?

Patrick Reed has been a prisoner of war. When he finally comes home he finds his father in seclusion and his daughter estranged. But it's all a plot engineered by Patrick's half-brother, his wife and her lover to cover the murder of the old man!

James McKimmey Bibliography
(1923-2011)

CRIME NOVELS

The Perfect Victim (1957;
expanded from "Riot at Willow
Creek," *Cosmopolitan,* 1957)

Winner Take All (1959)

The Satyr (1960)

Cornered! (1960)

24 Hours to Kill (1961)

The Wrong Ones (1961)

The Long Ride (1961; expanded
from "The Long Ride,"
Cosmopolitan, 1960)

Squeeze Play (1962)

Run If You're Guilty (1963;
expanded from "Death Trap,"
Cosmopolitan, 1962)

Blue Mascara Tears (1965)

A Circle in the Water (1965)

Never Be Caught (3 novelettes,
1966: Never be Caught, And
Then She Was Dead, Kill Him
Again)

The Hot Fire (1968)

The Man With the Gloved Hand
(1972)

JUVENILE FICTION

Buckaroo (1979)

As Benjamin Swift

Playoff (1981)

As Dewey Daniels

The Martindales' Nightmare
(1981)

"This man can manipulate tension…"
John D. MacDonald

"These slim stories are packed to the gills with
thrills and suspense. This is how sleek crime fiction
is written." Kristofer Upjohn, Noir Journal

RUN IF YOU'RE GUILTY
- - - - - - -
NEVER BE CAUGHT
- - - - - - -

James McKimmey

Introduction by Allan Guthrie

Stark House Press • Eureka California

RUN IF YOU'RE GUILTY / NEVER BE CAUGHT

Published by Stark House Press
1315 H Street
Eureka, CA 95501
griffinskye3@sbcglobal.net
www.starkhousepress.com

ISBN-13: 978-1-951473-28-0

Book design by Mark Shepard, shepgraphics.com
Cover design by James Heimer, jamesheimer.com
Proofreading by Bill Kelly

First Stark House Press Edition: April 2021

Interview with James McKimmey, Part Two
By Allan Guthrie

James McKimmey. Author of seventeen books and more articles and short stories than there are days in the year, James McKimmey is one of the most gifted crime writers of the '50s and '60s. *Cornered, 24 Hours To Kill, Run If You're Guilty, Squeeze Play* - you'll only be disappointed if you don't like fast-paced plots, snappy dialogue, fleshed-out characters or enough tension to snap a bungee cord. Allan Guthrie was lucky enough to speak to James for *Noir Originals*.

Allan Guthrie: In 1957 *Cosmopolitan* published a shortened version of your first novel under the title "Riot At Willow Creek." In 1958 Dell published the longer version as *The Perfect Victim*. How on earth did you manage to sell a first book so successfully?

James McKimmey: When I was in the Army during WWII, I had a good friend named Herb. We stayed together from Fort Leavenworth, Kansas, all the way to Germany where he was killed in action. Herb was a very wise young man. His advice to me about finding success was, "Surround yourself with good people."

AG: The short story is a form you have mastered. For a period in the '50s every issue of *If* included one of your science fiction stories. Similarly in the '70s, *Alfred Hitchcock's Mystery Magazine* boasts a huge number of your crime stories. You've placed just shy of four hundred short stories in your career, and there are plenty more to come. How does your approach to writing the short story differ from that of writing a novel?

JM:
If you love to write
you ain't doing it right;
but if you love to have written,
being a pro's where you're gittin'

Having presented that, I hope I've made two indisputable impressions. (1) I shall never be a poet. (2) Writing is the hardest work in this world, and so the great satisfaction is having done it.

Short stories, of course, usually provide a far quicker return for the effort than does writing the novel, one major reason I seem to have preferred writing them.

A perfect example is one entitled "Last Reunion." I woke up at home on the ranch south of San Francisco and realized that I wanted to write a short story but didn't have an idea in my head. I got in the car and went searching for one. I drove west to the ocean. By noon I found a rustic seafood restaurant built right next to the water. During lunch I was inventing a former WWII infantry captain, down on his luck. Put a guy like that in this restaurant by the sea. Etc., etc…

I drove home fast and started writing. I wrote through dinner. I wrote through most of the night. When I got up late the next day, I typed a final copy and sent it to my agent who sold it to *Cosmopolitan* in three days. *Cosmo* published it within weeks. Days after it hit the stands, my telephone rang.

It was a producer from an anthology TV show, *GE Theater*. He'd like to buy my reunion story for the show. Did I have an agent?

"Yes, sir!" I bellowed.

In the following months, I wrote a new novel. We celebrated its completion by driving to Lake Tahoe for a few days of well-earned rest. I've always been a celebrity fan. And this trip to Tahoe was highlighted by sitting down in Harrah's main casino lounge and finding ourselves a few tables away from an easily recognizable Lee Marvin, with his wife. I had admired this man for some time, a combat veteran of WWII, who'd made it big as a realistic tough-guy actor. We smiled at him. He smiled back. If ever a celebrity seemed open to being approached, it was Lee Marvin that day in that cocktail lounge. We were the only four customers in there.

"I'd like to shake his hand," I whispered.

"Go do it," Marty said.

"He was a Marine sniper during the war."

"He'd be pleased to know that you know that."

"If I went over, he'd probably ask us to join them."

"Did you have better plans?"

"That was a joke!"

"Go ahead. Do it."

But I'd read how much celebrities hated being approached when they were relaxing. And at the rate Mr. Marvin was putting down drinks, I knew he was relaxing a whole lot. I couldn't finally bring myself to interrupt his pleasure.

A few months later, in a TV listing, I learned that *Last Reunion* was being shown the following Sunday night. There was no other information in those days, including who would be starring.

You've guessed it? Isn't that marvelous?

Wasn't it marvelous, to sit and watch my story right there on that television screen starring none other than Lee Marvin. That's what a short story can do for you. Of course, that was the only short story that did quite that much for me. But the history of it rings of the sort of glitter and glamour and personal reward that I love. Perhaps if any of the options on my novels had been exercised, I'd feel differently. But that's how it has personally been.

My only faint regret is that I didn't know that Lee Marvin, when we'd been sitting a table away from him, had been the star of my dramatized short story – they'd obviously filmed the show before we both arrived at Tahoe.

Yeah, it would have been fun, especially if he'd indeed have invited us to his table. But I'll happily settle for the way it all happened, with that short story, any day, any week.

AG: You write fondly about nature and gambling (see *Run If You're Guilty* and *Squeeze Play* for excellent examples). You write about small town America with ambivalence (*The Perfect Victim* through to *The Man With The Gloved Hand*). Are these fair comments?

JM: Although I've never been a true outdoorsman, I've always loved the outdoors. When I was in the Army in Georgia, I found myself in the country on a field trip (with my military buddies, of course) lying on the ground in my bedroll as a cold January rain poured down on us. And then when I was in Normandy, on the way to combat in Germany, it was outdoors in the rain again except we were able to share two-men pup tents for shelter. And I swore I would never again camp out, and I never have since.

But I have enjoyed long walks in the kind of country in which I now live and hope I've reported it with some accuracy in my work.

Gambling has long fascinated me. I recognize the fact that it can be as deadly to some as booze is to others, but it's there. And I've lived in a gambling community for 42 years, so I think I know a lot about it. I have no doubt that it was Ernest Hemingway's involvement in it that attracted me in the first place. I don't glamorize it anymore. But I still get a kick out of walking through a casino. By now, however, it's a rare day indeed when I find myself in a casino.

Ambivalence is right, about my attitude toward small towns. I spent until age 13 living in small towns in Nebraska. Then I found myself in Omaha. Omaha is not a city in the sense of New York City, of course. But it's a city. And I loved being there from the day I arrived. I haven't been back for a very long time, but I still have the very best memories of that city. The small towns, however, have limitations that I simply do not like. I don't like being watched, the way they watch you in small towns. I don't like the community spirit necessary for existence in such towns. I don't like the limited vision that comes with small-town existence. South Lake Tahoe is, of course, a relatively small community. But because of the gambling, because of the world-class resort nature of a very beautiful mountain town, drawing visitors from everywhere else in the world, the basic nature of this place is extremely cosmopolitan. The result is the best of both the small town and the city. I've liked living here.

Your comments were fair indeed.

AG: We've spoken about your crime novels, mentioned your short fiction, and a little while back *Buckeroo* slipped in almost unnoticed. Would you care to tell us more about your science fiction short stories, and your literary and remedial-reading novels?

JM: I got into science fiction because of Ray Bradbury's influence. I found some buying markets, such as *Planet* and *If*. But I never got into it in the fashion of, say, Philip K. Dick. Phil and I corresponded a lot when we were both starting out. I saved his letters, and he had no idea that he would become a sort of icon in the science-fiction world. He was just writing what he felt he had to write, and perhaps there's a lesson there.

I wrote a couple of remedial-reading novels, *Buckaroo* and *Play-Off* as well as some short stories. But I'm such a simple writer that it was no trouble for editors to turn the work into fiction geared for high school students reading at a fourth-grade level. Several of my adult stories landed in the same textbook anthologies.

I really never wrote much with a deliberate intent of achieving literary quality. I think when I really enjoyed writing a short story, and sold it to a target market, was when I later had it picked up in what might be called a literary anthology. An example was a story entitled "The Man Who Danced." I wrote that for and sold it to *Alfred Hitchcock's Mystery Magazine*. Then it was picked up for a college-level text book entitled *Literature 1* which also featured short stories written by all of those writers I'd studied in college, from Steinbeck to Hemingway. I've always been proud of that inclusion.

AG: You mentioned WWII a while back. Did you see combat? If it's not too painful, I'd love to hear about it.

JM: I did see combat in Germany during World War II. I was in the 102nd Infantry Division. But I was very lucky. I was in Headquarters Company of the 405th Regiment, but not in the I & R platoon, which saw a lot of action. And in time, because I'd had some college in my background and seemed a logical choice to the captain of my company, I was sent back to Division Headquarters as an assistant clerk. So we were always well behind those forward rifle companies. For what action I was involved in I did receive two campaign battle stars, the Combat Infantryman Badge and the Bronze Star. I don't believe I earned any of those medals nearly as much as so many of my compadres did, back then. But you notice that I list all of them, which is what happens when you reach 80. You tend to glorify as time goes on.

But I don't mean to say that I glorify war in any manner. These days I often hear people who have never been near battle shout that we should immediately go to war to solve an international situation and shout that anybody who disagrees with them is a traitor. So, in effect, they are accusing me of being a traitor, and my response to that is to say, simply enough – stick it.

AG: Tell 'em, Jim. Back to your crime novels. I'm going to pick out (after much agonising), one or two that stand out for me. *Cornered* (Dell, 1960), *Squeeze Play* (Dell, 1962) and *Run If You're Guilty* (Lippencott, 1963) are three of the best crime novels written in the Sixties. What are your memories of writing them? Do you remember how they were received (both critically and commercially) at the time? And when did you last read them?

JM: Oddly, I don't remember very much about the reception and the writing of either *Cornered* or *Squeeze Play*. I do remember how it went with *Run If You're Guilty* because it was my first hardcover. I always sent two copies of chapters and outline of a projected novel to my agent. One went to *Cosmopolitan* for a go-ahead on the eventual sale of first U.S. serial rights, the other package went to the book publisher, which had usually been Dell, for paperback publication. I got a go-ahead from *Cosmo*. But this time my agent tried a hardcover house, Lippincott, for the books rights. He got a contract there, and I got a letter from the Lippincott editor who'd bought it.

The letter was entirely patronizing, telling me that because I knew only how to write paperbacks, she would, as I completed the book, guide me along the path to successful hardcover publication. Here again came some John D. MacDonald influence in that he believed without a fraction of doubt that a book was a book was a book, no matter hard or soft cover. I had come to the same belief. So, being relatively young and feeling I was beginning to own the world of book-writing and not yet hewing to the rule of putting away smoking letters to be reviewed in the calm of the next day, I fired off a letter to the Lippincott editor.

I told her (a) that my paperbacks had gotten three times what she was paying for this book and (b) that *Cosmo* was getting the serial rights for five times what she was paying and (c) paperback publication in the past had been my choice, not the result of an inability to write for hardcover publication.

Of course, it was a rude, arrogant, nasty letter I never should have written to an old long-established hardcover mystery editor. But her attitude did represent much of the editorial view of paperbacks at that time. Nevertheless, the contract had already been signed and so Lippincott obviously published the final version of the completed novel. But my agent told me that the editor there promised him that she would never buy another book from me. She didn't.

For you now, Al, to tell me that this book is one of three of the best crime novels written in the Sixties puts a special joy in my heart. And I thank you for that.

I hadn't read any of these books for perhaps at least 40 years. But because of your interest, I read *Squeeze Play* a few weeks ago. I'm reading *Cornered*. I'll read *Run If You're Guilty* after that.

AG: I'm interested in how it felt to read *Squeeze Play* after all that time? Also, on the subject of editors, how much editorial input did Dell have?

JM: How it felt to read *Squeeze Play* was as though someone else had written the novel. And, of course, that's true. When you were forty years younger, you were a different man. And the way that man forty years younger than I wrote when he wrote *Squeeze Play* was an interesting discovery.

This older man found faults, of course, mentally rewriting this or that as I read. But basically I was pleased with what I found, in a book written by this younger man. One of my praises for any piece of writing is that it's professionally written. And to my surprise and pleasure, I found *Squeeze Play* to be that, both in construction and word-handling. That probably sounds very egotistical, but I'm not saying it out of ego. I tried to analyze my reaction and it goes this way:

When I wrote *Squeeze Play*, I'd been writing for about 13 years.

When I was attending the University of San Francisco, I wrote a column for the college's newspaper, *The Foghorn*, and I also wrote a column for the *San Mateo Times*. In addition, while I was still in college, I'd started writing and publishing short fiction. I continued writing short stories after college. And then, before I set out on *Squeeze Play*, I'd written and had published six other crime novels, along with a trail of rejections slips for other things that had not succeeded to signal my course for exactly what it had been – writing and failing and succeeding and writing and failing and succeeding, on and on in that fashion.

And along with that had been a lot of study about how other writers had done it. I studied those other writers' work. I read everything I could find written by those same writers about how they'd done what they had done.

On the subject of editors, I had a great deal of revising requested on the first novel Dell bought, *The Perfect Victim*. After that, there was less and less of it from Dell as I wrote succeeding books. There was no input from *Cosmo*. But what was difficult there was cutting the length of the books by more than half. That wasn't involved, of course, in two stories *Cosmo* published as novels, *And Then She Was Dead* and *Kill Him Again* because they were written directly for *Cosmo* at that magazine's length.

AG: The *Cosmo* version of *Run If You're Guilty* was called *Death Trap*. Was that a deliberate homage to John D. MacDonald's 1957 novel of the same name?

JM: It wasn't a deliberate homage to John D. I wouldn't have done that. The problem is that I don't remember whose title that was, although *Cosmo* used more of my titles than anyone else. I don't believe Dell used a single one of my titles. I think it was *Cornered* that I originally called *The Red Snow*. For quite some time I saved every letter I got from an editor, and I saved every copy of the letters I wrote to them. But with the years and moving from place to place, all of that has gone the way of so many things out of one's past. Just the other day I was looking in a mirror, trying to find some small hint of what was there fifty years ago. I couldn't find it.

AG: I think it was Peter Rabe who eventually resorted to calling his Gold Medal novels by the name of the protagonist, since Gold Medal repeatedly shunned his original titles. I wasn't aware that Dell did the same thing. Do you remember any of your other original titles?

JM: *Riot At Willow Creek* was my original title for *The Perfect Victim*. That's the only other one I remember.

AG: While we're still on the subject of Dell, what were the initial print runs?

JM: 200,000.

AG: That's a suitably impressive number.

(originally appeared in *Noir Originals,* February 2004; reprinted in *Paperback Parade*, issue 63, May 2005)

Allan Guthrie is a Scottish literary agent, author and editor of crime fiction. He has authored five hardboiled novels—*Two-Way Split, Kiss Her Goodbye, Hard Man* (republished as *Bad Men*), *Savage Night* and *Slammer*—plus several novellas, for which he has been short-listed for the CWA Debut Dagger Award as well as nominated for an Edgar Award. He also helped launch the first digital-only Scottish publisher, Blasted Heath. Guthrie lives in Edinburgh.

RUN IF YOU'RE GUILTY

- - - - - -

James McKimmey

This work, and all other, past present or future,
Is done with love for MARTY.

Chapter I

He had made love to her with a reassuring fervor. Now she rose, as he lay sleeping. Wearing a blue chiffon negligee over a matching gown, she slipped on pink fur-trimmed slippers. For a moment she stood beside the bed and looked down at his handsome face, illuminated by the pale light of a midnight moon shining through an open window.

The cabin was clean and neat, simply furnished with worn but comfortable Monterey pieces. There was a small kitchenette off the main room, with a four-burner stove and a small refrigerator built below in place of an oven. She bent and kissed his forehead, then straightened swiftly, not wanting to awaken him.

She crossed the plaited rugs scattered over the wood floor and opened the door. The air had chilled, but she was not cold, only refreshed and stimulated. She stepped out and shut the door gently.

There was a row of eight small cabins set well apart in the clearing. They were red frame structures with white trim and newly shingled roofs. Automobiles were parked beside four of them. A hundred yards beyond was a large rustic redwood house with a low shake roof, its slanted surface dusted with pine needles and small fir sprigs blown from the trees. A spacious pine shed, yellow in the moonlight, was on the west side of the house. A white board sign in front of the flagged walk curving to the porch read in neat black stenciling:

JOE'S RETREAT
Fishing   Boating
Cabins

She crossed the clearing. The voluminous singing of twilight birds had been silenced by night and was replaced by a melancholy call of an owl. It seemed a call from the past, and that was what she wanted now: to touch a bit of his past. Her slippers made light stroking sounds against the finely crushed rock which had been packed down in front of the cabins. Heavy plank picnic tables were neatly arranged in the center of the clearing, around a fire-blackened red-brick barbecue pit. The air was cool, and heavy with the scent of fir.

She moved toward a path which led north through the trees and ferns and thick tangles of blackberry bushes. Visible above the dark silhouette of treetops was a thin road snaking darkly down the rock face of the high hill which banked the west edge of the valley. They had come in on it late that morning and entered, she thought, a paradise.

Chiffon swirling, she walked through the woods. The white moon had made the thickly treed area almost daylight bright. Where its rays fell on the tall hill to the east, opposite the rock bank where the road twisted, the moon had turned the stiff, dry October grass into a golden glow.

She passed clumps of Scotch broom and wild violets and rough tangles of oak vines. Once she touched the leaf of a tall nettle stalk. She paused, sucking at the needle stinging spot until the prickling disappeared, amused at her carelessness—he had warned her about them.

She came out of the trees onto the lake and gasped at the beauty before her.

Beneath the yellow leaves of the black locust tree, she gazed at the gray-silver circle of water in the center of which the white moon was reflected in frozen calm. At a small timber dock fifty yards to her left a half dozen gray rowboats floated empty and motionless; the rest of the water was a dark mirror of the star-flecked sky. Near the point where she saw the moon reflected, a fish broke surface and returned with a soft splash. Then she heard the motion near the shore.

She turned and watched a mother raccoon approaching the water, followed by three striped-tailed offspring. At the edge, all four washed particles of food stolen from the garbage can which they had tipped over behind the large house at the clearing.

She stepped forward to see more clearly. Her slipper cracked a dry madrone twig. The mother raccoon turned swiftly, long grizzled coat shining in the moonlight, and growled at her from its shrewd black-nosed face. The growling surprised her. Then, watching the way the animal moved in front of its children to protect them, she was forced to laugh with delight, wondering if *she* had become pregnant tonight.

Following the mother, the trailing animals disappeared into the woods. She moved again, along a bank of ferns. She looked across the water and above. She saw him outlined against the sky, at the top of the cliff.

Neck arched, heavily antlered head poised alertly, long and muscular body tense, he stood on delicate deer legs. She thought of the youth asleep in the cabin and felt a peculiar erotic thrill. She remembered how he had explained the buck: his rampaging, promiscuous runs over the country, leaving so strong a spoor that it could jerk a good dog's head around with a snap, taking doe after doe, until he would finally stop, as this one had stopped now, alone, blowing hard, eyes glazed, oblivious to all the world around him. She shivered with an unexplainable sensuousness.

She moved sideways to get a better view. But detecting her motion with needle-delicate perception, the buck turned his head. He took a half dozen nervous steps, head swinging back and forth as though his long neck was fixed on rockers, then bounded away among the rocks.

She walked along the edge of the lake and saw a trail, its grass surface flattened by night animals and scattered with half shells of acorns, running from the shore into the woods. It was the same trail, she was certain, the sleeping youth had described to her. He had loved to use it to hike into the deep woods and then climb the rock face of the cliff.

She smiled, knowing she was capturing some of his life, and moved onto the trail. She looked up at the sky with its blaze of stars and moon, taking a deep breath.

Then her right ankle felt a quick pain as though it had been struck by a thin knife. A flash of bright light exploded. She flailed at the air, losing her balance, and pitched forward toward the jaws of the trap waiting in loosely sifted soil.

She tripped into it, and the steel whipped and bit hard into her ankle. She started to scream, but choking smothered the sound. Her eyes, wide and dark and white-rimmed, caught the moon's reflection. She twisted and writhed, arms flailing against the biting jaws. She dragged the trap a dozen feet, heart pumping wildly.

Then the hooks of the drag snared against thick brush. *Oh, God!* she thought blindly. She curled around toward her caught ankle like a cat trying to bite its tail, feeling the pain explode within her chest. Then blackness washed over her mind, like a shade pulled swiftly over light. Her slim body convulsed, trembled, then lay motionless in the quiet of the night.

Chapter 2

The morning of the day before was cool. Clouds had formed just before dawn, and now lay in pockets between the mountains, like puffs of smoke from a giant pipe-smoker's lips. Above, a bright sun shone from a sky the color of spring lilac. Joe Beacon, his three night guests already checked out, stepped from the redwood house, lean, hard body clothed in a checked shirt, levis and boots; he'd heard the car coming down the road from the highway. He waited on the porch, a rather short man of forty-seven, with a tanned, weather-lined face that was mixed with a combination of toughness and pleasantness.

He wore a broad-brimmed straw with furled sides over thinning brown hair. He adjusted the hat against his head and watched with gray eyes the blue and cream Ford sedan roll too swiftly down the snaking road. It came to a skidding halt in front of the flagged walk, resting high on its back wheels. There were traces of sand caked around the rear bumper, as though it had been driven over a wet beach.

There were six of them, in their late teens: three boys and three girls, laughing and shouting. It was just eight o'clock. They had, he decided bitterly, been up all night, probably drinking inside some coastal cove across the mountains.

The driver, a tall sallow-faced youth with yellow hair, slid confidently out. He leaned loosely against his car. Joe Beacon could smell the liquor now. "Cabins," the boy said. "Three."

Two of the girls giggled. The blond boy smiled conceitedly. This was what this land meant to him, Joe Beacon thought. Out from the city, away from restrictions, to drink and search out the cabin sign. He controlled his anger and shook his head. "Sorry."

"Sorry? Sign on the road, right? Cabins?" The boy's fingers snapped. "Let's have three."

"I told you I'm sorry," Joe said, his voice turning impatient.

The other two youths climbed out of the car. The driver said, "The sign said cabins on the highway. Now that is what we want. Are you going to say you're sorry again?"

"No," Joe Beacon said quietly. "I'm going to tell you to get the hell out of here."

The boy shook his head slowly. "You're out here all alone. No other cars. Nobody else in sight. You don't talk to us that way."

The three youths stepped forward, hands doubling, shoulders lumping with tightening muscles.

Joe reached up to the ledge of the porch's inner roof joist. His hand opened the carefully wrapped plastic and closed around the handle of the .22. He brought the pistol down and held it loosely.

The three stopped and stared at the gun. The one on the right, a fattish boy with dark hair, paled.

"On your way," Joe said coldly.

The driver wagged his head. "You can't get away with this."

"I'm going to."

"We'll take that gun away from you."

"I won't shoot for your head or belly. I'll shoot for your legs. I'll shoot the tires off your car. Then I'll take my time telephoning for help."

"He's crazy!" the fattish boy whispered.

Joe snapped the safety off the pistol. The fattish boy ducked into the car, followed by the second. The driver remained outside for a few seconds longer, blinking with frustration.

"I'm going to call the police when we get out of here," the boy said, his voice breaking.

"All right."

The boy got back in the car and raced the engine, yelling, "We're coming back! You hear?" The car skidded away. He knew they would not be back.

Ten minutes later a faded red one-ton truck crept carefully down the road. Joe came out of the pine shed where he'd been checking the points of his pickup. The truck came to a halt in front of the house. He walked out to meet the man crawling from the cab. "Morning, Fred."

"Joe," Fred Bell said. He was a balloon-shaped man with a cheery sunburned face who seemed stuffed into his faded blue overalls. He jerked a hand at his truck. "Brought you some eggs, side of beef, bunch of garden stuff. Sure that's enough?"

"That'll be fine, Fred."

"Season's about over, anyway."

"I think I'll hang the closed sign out at the end of the week. I should have hung it out this morning."

"Those kids? I saw 'em going out when I turned in. You have to kick 'em out?"

"That's what I did."

"What were they after? Little hum-de-dum?" He grinned widely enough to expose one missing front tooth.

"It's not funny, Fred. Remember how it used to be?"

Fred Bell nodded, smiling sadly now. "Better than you. I've been here longer, remember."

Joe looked across the clearing, toward the hills rising smoothly to the east. He'd come to Northern California just after the war, with money saved from the jobs he'd had before the Army: ranch hand in Montana, construction worker in Colorado, logger in Oregon, where he'd also trapped and hired out as a hunting guide. He'd come with money saved while he'd served two and a half years in combat as an infantry sergeant. He'd found what he'd been looking for over the years: a large piece of land, 3,500 acres in all.

It was good land, rolling and beautiful, the kind of land that would support cattle. He'd put all his money into the land and cattle, as well as money he didn't own, scratched from a G.I. loan and straight bank loans. He'd made it work. The cattle had fattened, and every year had produced a bumper crop of calves. He'd sweated from sunup to sundown and loved giving every drop of that sweat.

But time had caught up and people had caught up. You had to have a big spread to survive. You also had to have minimal taxes, because the profit margin was too slim to survive any other way. But civilization continued to roll westward. People wanted land to live on. The real estate people were in the business to give it to them. It was inevitable that some owners, attracted by increasing offers, began to sell small chips of their land. When that happened, sections went under the control of townships. Townships meant incorporation and higher taxes. They also meant restrictions demanded by communities not concerned with ranching.

Finally, to defend himself, he'd had to sell too, to make the profit to pay the taxes, to fight the restrictions. Pretty soon he had 3,000 acres, then 2,500 acres. Pretty soon he had too little to support what he was doing. Four years ago he'd had to give up, sell the cattle, keep a thousand acres for himself, and turn to this. He straightened his shoulders. "I tell you Eddie's coming home?"

The sadness left Fred Bell's smile. "That's fine, Joe. When?"

"They might get in today."

"His wife too?"

"I look forward to it. She writes some good letters. I'm anxious to meet her."

"Sure you are, Joe. You tell Eddie to take that girl and come to see us. Molly'll be pleased. We'll make up some homemade ice cream. Remember how that boy used to come over and eat homemade ice cream?"

Joe smiled faintly. "I remember."

He walked into the house, to the large living room. When he'd bought the property this room had not existed. He'd built it himself, extending it from the room that was now the dining room. It was long and sturdy-looking, with thick wooden beams and a wide stone fireplace midway along the south wall. He'd built it for Nita.

The same furniture she'd selected was still here: solid cherry with tough but attractive upholstery. Cases filled with books were still lined across the whole of the west wall—he was the one who'd collected and read them; he'd spent long nights with them since Nita had gone.

Still, the room had changed. Nita had done things that he couldn't or wouldn't do. There had been gay scarves placed on the sideboards; there had been flowers and small vases and knickknacks and figurines, all of which he'd removed when she'd gone. It was easier to clean and maintain that way. It was also measurably colder.

He walked to the long table beside the fireplace and looked at the gold-framed photograph there. The woman in the picture was delicately beautiful with a small nose and wide warm eyes; she was a blonde—you could see that even though the picture was a black and white. He would never forget the exact color of that hair: it was the color of the October grass. The picture was a mute and stony memory of what once was. But the picture in his mind was not. That image was still alive, and sometimes he wished that it would die.

A blue envelope which had come in the mail three days ago was beside the picture. He drew out the letter and reread:

Dear Pop,
I must call you Pop, as Eddie does. He has told me so much about you. (We've been married an entire four months as of next month on the 5th!) And I know that even if you are not his real father he thinks of you in no other way. You can hardly stop him from talking about the wonderful years he spent growing up with you on the ranch. I'm simply dying to see it. And that is what we're intending to do!

Eddie has been working terribly hard at the plant, I guess he's worn himself out. His boss suggested he take a leave of absence and get some rest. I agree.

So we are gassing up the old jalopy and heading north from L.A. in a day or two, all depending upon when Eddie can get his duties switched over to someone else. I can't tell you how excited I am. Eddie has brightened ever so much at the thought of seeing you and the land again. He has, as have I, been truly sorry that we got married so quickly that we didn't even give you a chance to get down here for the wedding!

So until next week sometime, perhaps Monday, we send our love.
                                                                        Nancy.

Carefully, he replaced the letter in its envelope and looked again at the picture of Nita. She had been divorced from her first husband a year when he'd married her. Eddie had been twelve. Even then he'd looked like his mother. He had the same eyes, mouth and nose. Now Eddie was returning. Joe Beacon was glad in one certain sense: he'd grown to love Eddie as his own son during the five years Eddie and Nita had lived with him. But in another sense seeing Eddie again would be like breathing life into Nita, exploding the memory alive, and getting with that all the hurts of the past....

He shook his head. There was no use hiding from the past, though he wanted to. God knows he tried hard enough. But Eddie was coming, bringing a wife. And he ought to be happy. And there was only another week of keeping his gate open to the public, wondering who, besides Eddie and Nancy, would decide to stop.

Chapter 3

At the junction, down the highway, the counterman had opened the coffee shop at seven that morning. He started the grill heating; the coffee was already made and waiting in Silex containers on a row of electric coils. A tall man with a wizened face, his white apron tied around a skinny waist, he rounded the counter and sat down on a stool. He spread the sports section of that morning's *San Francisco Chronicle* and began reading laboriously.

It was a good part of the day for him. Mrs. Gronish, who owned the coffee shop, would not be in until a quarter to nine—and she didn't badger him much anyway, probably less than any of the other countless employers he'd worked for in his 61 years. You could almost always count on practically no business until after nine, when Mrs. Gronish would start taking care of the booths, prepare the breakfasts, and leave him to the uncomplicated task of washing dishes and swabbing down the counter now and then.

On a weekday morning like this they mostly got the delivery men and salesmen and telephone repair people coming this way from the lower Peninsula, ready to have the late breakfast. He couldn't remember having to get anything before nine o'clock for weeks, aside from some donuts and coffee—just for that new sergeant with the sheriff's department, who'd showed up yesterday and ordered a full breakfast. That had made him a little mad, because the other sergeant, the one before, had never come in ahead of ten o'clock, and was a good talker. He didn't like this new one. He'd overdone the eggs to prove it. But probably, he thought, he wouldn't get that sergeant again in weeks.

It was a comforting thought, and he was completely relaxed and lost in his reading when the new station wagon with the sheriff's emblem stopped outside. A short, hefty man got out. He wore a crisply clean, well-pressed uniform; the gleaming visor of his hat was pulled down well in front of his eyes. The leather of his holster was polished so that it glistened against the early sun as he strode toward the neat brown building with its yellow trim.

The sergeant had got all the way inside and put himself down in a booth before the counterman realized that someone had broken his early morning peace. The counterman looked around and stiffened his mouth.

The sergeant drew off his hat and hung it on a hook above his head, which was bald and glistened like the leather of his holster. He picked up a menu and read with deliberate consideration.

The counterman turned back to his paper and bent his head in false concentration. The sergeant had to call to him three times before he got off his stool and ambled slowly over to the booth, wondering why anybody should have to get up and quit the sports section and work up a breakfast before 9 o'clock on the kind of wages he was getting from Mrs. Gronish anyway?

"Didn't hear what you said," he said petulantly.

The sergeant owned massive shoulders and a barrel chest, both of which bulged against the fabric of his uniform shirt. He had small hands. His face appeared nearly cherubic; it was pink and round and without blemish, and his light blue eyes, small and rather close-set, stared out from it with no discernible emotion. The counterman had thought he was older at first, maybe 40. But it was the bald head, he decided. He maybe wasn't even out of his twenties yet. It didn't matter. The counterman didn't like him.

"I said," the sergeant repeated in a surprisingly high voice, "I'll have two eggs, over easy, the hash-browns, bacon on the side, not too well done, and coffee. You can bring me an orange juice while I wait."

The counterman felt stubborn. He knew he was taking a chance with Mrs. Gronish, but he said it anyway: "Too early."

The light blue eyes stared at him without emotion. "What's too early?"

"Breakfast like that."

"What're you talking about? I had a breakfast like that yesterday morning, same time."

"I ain't saying you didn't."

"What changed it today?"

The counterman felt suddenly cornered, and it made him angry. He finally said, "I'll give you donuts or rolls. Which one do you want?"

"I want two eggs, over easy, the hash-browns, bacon on the side, not too well done, and coffee. And an orange juice while I'm waiting."

The counterman pressed his thin lips together tightly. "The grill ain't hot enough. We don't serve this early anyway. Not the whole breakfast." He was beginning to believe it now: that it was the exact rule of the house.

But the sergeant looked down at the menu held in his small hand and poked a square finger at it. "It says here, 'Breakfast served from 7:00 a.m. through 11:00 a.m.' It's ten after seven, right now."

"That menu don't mean anything."

For the first time a faint tightening was visible at the corners of the sergeant's eyes. "What do you mean it doesn't mean anything? It's the menu, isn't it? It's the listing of what you serve and when. What do you mean it doesn't mean anything?"

"The grill ain't hot enough." He was certain of one thing now: he shouldn't have to take an argument like this from anybody, including a sheriff's deputy.

The sergeant looked at the menu again. "When somebody writes out something like this menu, they ought to mean what they say. Who owns this place anyway?"

The counterman sniffed and rubbed his nose with one knobby finger. He didn't answer.

"Who owns this place?" the sergeant repeated.

"Mrs. Gronish."

"Where is she?"

"She ain't in."

"When does she come in? I want to talk to her."

"Ain't no need to talk to her. I got charge here now."

"I want to know why it says something right here on this menu that isn't so."

"I'll take a check on the grill," the counterman said, suddenly giving up.

"If you don't serve breakfast when you say you do, it ought to be changed on the menu," the sergeant said, his blue eyes impassive again.

The counterman walked slowly around the counter and examined the grill with overdramatic speculation. "She just might be hot enough."

"I'm going to talk to Mrs. Gronish," the sergeant said in his high voice.

"I'm getting your breakfast, ain't I?" the counterman said.

"I'm going to talk to Mrs. Gronish," the sergeant said, and studied the menu again.

The counterman cracked eggs onto the grill and slapped down strips of bacon. He'd been too long at this job anyway. At the wages Mrs. Gronish was paying him, when you took away that nice spell with nobody bothering him for almost two hours in the beginning of the morning, it wasn't worth it. He would quit when Mrs. Gronish came in, then go down to the unemployment office and claim he was forced out and try for the compensation that way.

Chapter 4

It was late morning when Joe heard the next car coming through the highway gate. Sunlight flashed against black paint and shining chrome as the Lincoln Continental came into view, rolling majestically down the narrow road with a sureness that indicated its wheel was held by a confident driver. He could see the man's outline now; there was a woman beside him. He wondered if they would pause on the descent to examine the look of the valley with its lake spread out in full view, and the hills rising in back, first green with trees and then golden, and then bluish at the higher ridges? But no matter, he thought. They would be customers. He would take their money. And when they left, the gate would shut behind them, to stay shut for the winter.

The car didn't pause. It came directly to the bottom of the cliff and stopped in the clearing. He looked at the man behind the wheel: a large man in his late thirties whose years had bulked him at waist and jowl. He was handsome despite the excess poundage; Joe could see the press of heavy fatted muscles beneath the man's white shirt. Probably a good athlete at one time, he thought. Now a professional man, perhaps, or a business executive.

The man smiled at the girl seated beside him, a smoothly pretty blonde, at least ten years younger than the man. She was dressed smartly in a pink, lightweight suit, but not overly so or too expensively so. Joe could not take his eyes from her for a few moments—she was beautiful in a way that touched his senses immediately. She turned and looked back at him, coolly at first, then with a shift to curiosity.

She was angry, he thought.

The man, smiling broadly, patted her knee, gave her a look of reassurance, then climbed out and walked briskly toward Joe Beacon, eyes crinkling personably at the corners.

"Saw your sign on the highway. Just what my wife and I have been looking for. Haven't got any gear with me, but it'll just be overnight."

Joe nodded. "I've got some things you can rent."

"Need a fishing license up here?"

"I've got a cover-all license for my property. I'll give you a card with the rules on it. I'll have to ask that you follow the rules here."

"You'll have to ask me just once. Where do I register?" He grinned and called to the girl, "Looks swell, doesn't it, dear? Just what we've been looking for."

She did not answer. The man laughed. "You know how women are when they're traveling. A little rest'll do her a world of good. My name's Victor Day."

"Glad to know you. I'm Joe Beacon." He led the man inside to the registry in the hall, where he signed rapidly and said, "Great spot you've got here, Beacon. Any trout in that lake?"

"I keep it pretty well stocked."

"Wish I'd known about this before. I wouldn't mind doing a little hunting around here either, but all I've got with me is a .22 pistol. But then I don't think you've got much of the big stuff in these hills. It's mainly getting outside. Ever hunted in Oregon, Beacon?"

"I've hunted a lot of places, Mr. Day."

"Been around myself. Went for lion up north a couple of times. Just came from Monterey. Went for pigs down there a couple of seasons back. You don't fool with those. What I'd like to get into one of these days is Cape buffalo. Those are the mean babies. They'll track your scent home and be waiting for you in the kitchen...."

Victor Day went on talking. Joe nodded and listened with a fraction of his attention. He knew the man. He'd met him, in slight alterations, a hundred times. Still, he tried to look interested, at least, but he was thinking about the girl he'd seen in Victor Day's car. Something had happened when he'd looked at her. He felt guilty about it, standing in front of her husband, making an effort to look interested. But he couldn't help the feeling. It had just happened.

The next car rolled in a few minutes past 11 o'clock. It was a Volkswagen, and Joe, returning from carrying a bundle of oak logs to the barbecue, watched it crawl down the steep road like a pale blue snail. The driver was no Victor Day, he thought, and he was certain of that when the small car finally stopped in front of his house.

A small, frail youth in his mid-twenties sat gripping the wheel tightly. He wore a thin mustache which was lighter in color than his dark-blond hair. The mustache had been grown recently, Joe decided, and it failed to accomplish the aging the boy had obviously tried for. He wiped a shaking hand across it, then turned to look at Joe with wide, blue, frightened eyes.

Joe nodded pleasantly and looked at the girl beside the young man. She was a big girl, with a strong, clean-planed face, who wore her light brown hair straight back in a pony tail. She appeared, in contrast to her companion, in complete control. Joe stepped forward and opened the driver's door. "That road didn't bother you, did it?"

The young man blinked slowly, then forced himself to climb out. "Not at all, sir. No, sir."

"Sometimes people are bothered by it. I'm glad to hear you weren't."

"Not a fraction," the young man said, his voice blurring. He coughed to get it going again. "My name's Norris Glenn, by the way. I'm a writer and an artist. This looks like a perfect spot for a few days of soaking up atmosphere and doing a little work. We're on a short vacation. And I hope you might have accommodations for my wife and myself."

Joe nodded and held out his hand, which Norris Glenn grasped weakly. "I'm Joe Beacon. Yes; I think I have a nice cabin for you and your wife. Would you like to come in and register?"

"Delighted," Norris Glenn said and went around the car to help his wife out. On low heels, Joe saw, she stood at least three inches taller than her husband. "This is Rosalind, Mr. Beacon, my wife."

Rosalind Glenn smiled brilliantly. "What a perfectly beautiful place you have here, Mr. Beacon! We were thinking of driving on north and looking in on the Valley of the Moon. But Norris said he'd heard they'd made a perfect tourist trap out of it. Which I'm sure, in this age of commerciality, is quite true. And so, we said, why not just stop out here? I told Norris this was truly nature. And I instantly thought of *Walden*. Do you know Thoreau's *Walden*, Mr. Beacon?"

"I've read a little of Thoreau, yes," Joe said, smiling faintly.

"Yes," she said, "and then Norris said he was reminded of Alfoxden. When Wordsworth and his sister went to visit Coleridge at his Nether Stowey cottage? And then into Alfoxden just three miles away?"

"Wonderful Alfoxden," Norris said. "But I told Rosalind that I was really feeling more artistic at the moment than literary. I thought these mountains just could be the Pyrenees. Arles and Saint-Rémy.

Van Gogh country."

"My husband is wonderfully imaginative, Mr. Beacon."

"He certainly is," Joe agreed. "Come on in, both of you. Maybe you'd like a cup of coffee after you've registered."

"Why," Rosalind said, "how delightful of you!"

He led them inside, where Norris signed his name. Then they went into the large kitchen. Joe poured coffee from a huge pot and sat down with them. "You say you're a writer and an artist, Mr. Glenn?"

"Well, actually—" Norris began. "Actually—"

"Of course, you're a writer and an artist, Norris," Rosalind said positively.

"Well," Norris said, "what I mean is, I actually earn my living as an architectural draftsman. But that's a temporary matter. It's only a job. My real work is my art."

"Yes," Rosalind said, "and it's going to be great art, Mr. Beacon."

"I'm glad to hear that. What kind of writing and art work do you do?"

"Now that's a good question," Norris said, obviously relaxing a little. "I'd say it was quality writing. Quality art work. Wouldn't you, Rosalind?"

"I wouldn't know any other definition for it."

"I see," Joe said. "But I mean, do you write novels or short stories? Do you paint in oil? Or—"

"All of that," Rosalind said swiftly. "Norris has just a number of things accomplished and, I might add, in progress. We have a small flat in San Francisco, and it's becoming virtually a *stu*dio! Norris is terribly prolific, but that's never spoiled his quality. Tell him what you've done, Norris."

"Well," Norris said, his voice assuming a proper degree of modesty, "a poem, four short stories, the first five pages of a novel, thirty-five watercolors, two charcoals, and five oils."

"That's quite a span of work," Joe said. "Have you published any of your writing, Mr. Glenn?"

"Actually," Norris said, gulping another swallow of coffee, "I'm not ready for that."

"Now, dear," Rosalind said, "you'd better explain that to Mr. Beacon."

"What I mean is," Norris said, "I don't think my kind of writing will find the proper acceptance in this day of mundane tastes and commerciality. Maybe I should say *they* aren't ready for the kind of writing *I'm* doing."

"That's it," Rosalind nodded emphatically.

Joe busied himself lighting his pipe. "And your art work? Have you shown any of it?"

"More or less the same on that," Norris said. "I mean, who's ready for it?"

"Of course," Rosalind said. "But tell him about your taking the watercolors and charcoals and oils to class one evening."

"Well," Norris said, modesty going into his voice again, "I'm taking art in this adult-education class in the Marina. The instructor is hardly Picasso, if you know what I mean. But the man does have an astonishingly good critical eye. So I just packed everything along one night and set it up for him."

"Tell Mr. Beacon what he said, Norris."

"Well," Norris said proudly, "he said he'd never seen anything quite like it."

A few minutes after Norris and Rosalind Glenn had gone to their cabin, Joe heard the third car. A hot sun had burned off the last traces of fog now. Morning shadows had almost disappeared. The car was a white Thunderbird. It wheeled through the gate with a loud blast of exhaust noise. The car was not new; he could tell that by the rough sound of the engine. The occupants were a man and a woman; and the man took the narrow road with nearly as much speed as the teenagers had earlier this morning. When the car rocked to a stop in front of his house, he could see that it had been repainted; there were spots where the quickly applied white paint had come off, exposing its original black color. The right taillight had been smashed out.

A tall, lean man with black hair, whose left eye was slightly off-center, knocked his door open with a jarring blow of his hand, then got out, grinning. He was, Joe thought, about 30 years old. He wore levis and a striped sport shirt. His dark hair was rumpled, and his black eyes looked shrewd and failed to match the smile of his mouth. He walked forward with a long stride. The girl, probably no more than 18, remained in the car, looking at the camp with obvious boredom. She was plumply pretty, wearing tight white Capris and a Mexican-styled red shirt which tied in the front and left exposed a portion of her midriff. She had, Joe Beacon noticed, extraordinarily large breasts. She also, he thought, had a vacuous look that could only mean a fairly low intelligence. The girl found him looking at her and instantly smiled back with open seductiveness.

Joe turned to the man, who said in a deep drawl:

"You got a real nice-looking place here, mister."

"Well, thanks."

"We're fresh up from Texas." There was a ring of false conviviality in his voice.

"I see."

The man's voice lowered and took on a conspiratorial tone. "But I got to admit that me and Flo there—that's my bride of three weeks—we stopped down in Vegas. Ever been in Vegas?"

Joe Beacon nodded. He could sense the direction of the approach now. "I've been there."

"Then you know what I mean." The man put out his hand. "My name's Roy Ives. I'd sure like to know yours. You look like a man of the land, and this-here land is sure pretty. I been with the land most all my life myself. This looks like it's good ranchland."

"It was." Joe shook hands with him. "I'm Joe Beacon."

"Glad to know you, Mr. Beacon. What happened with the ranching, anyway?" There was an overdramatic note of concern in the man's voice.

"Taxes, restrictions, a few things."

Roy Ives nodded. "Hard, ain't it? I mean, life's just plain hard sometimes. That's what I was talking about, me and Flo stopping off in Vegas. I had me a little stake, only those people turned me upside down and shook me a few times, and then just scraped up everything that fell out of my pockets. I came out pretty near busted. That's a sad tale of woe you probably heard before, ain't it?"

"One way or another."

The man's dark eyes flickered, but the smile flashed on again. "Well, I ain't asking any favors, Mr. Beacon. Don't get me wrong. I'm just saying that my luck went out in Vegas, and all I was wondering was if you might not have some place other than the regular cabins that maybe Flo and me could kind of use? You know. Cheap. Like a dollar a night or something."

Joe shook his head. "The cabins are ten dollars. They've got kitchens. You can drive up to the junction south of here and buy groceries. Or I've got some things. Bacon. Eggs. Lunch meats. Bread. Canned food. I've also got some venison and a few beef rib steaks. But it'll cost you ten dollars, plus whatever food you need. Nothing to sleep on out in that shed."

"That's too bad. How about the house? Maybe you've got an extra room inside and not so much trouble to put somebody into as the cabins. Like relatives? I'd give five bucks for a room like that in the house."

"I'm just renting the cabins, Mr. Ives."

He watched the friendliness go out of the man's face. The dark eyes hardened. "You want in advance?"

"That's right."

Ives slapped a ten-dollar bill angrily into Joe Beacon's hand.   ,

"You can register in the hall," Joe said calmly.

Ives did, then came out, face hard. Then Joe saw his eyes discovering the Lincoln Continental parked beside the first cabin. He smiled. "Now that's the prettiest damn car I seen all day. Who owns that, Mr. Beacon?"

"One of my guests."

"Don't you know his name?"

"If you run into him while you're here, you ask him."

"Know what he does for a living?"

"No, I don't."

"Well," Ives said, his eyes now gleaming with speculation, "a man owns a car like that, that man must be doing all right."

Ives wheeled his Thunderbird in front of his assigned cabin with a roar. As his wife walked inside with a great deal of motion within the tight white Capris, he paused to inspect again the new Lincoln Continental.

It was past noon when Joe heard the fourth car at the top of the cliff. He came out, instinctively knowing who it was. The 5-year-old Dodge came in sight, and he felt his pulse quicken.

Midway down, he heard the Dodge's horn sound, bouncing down through the valley. He smiled, certain that Eddie was telling Nancy that the cliff was a natural phenomenon which sent out sound as though it were a large loudspeaker.

The car stopped before him. Nancy, thin and pretty, jumped out first. She ran to him, laughing. He put out strong hands to hold her shoulders.

He turned to see Eddie getting out of the car. The boy looked just a bit older, he thought, but not much—he was a movie-handsome boy, with short blond hair and a fair complexion. Yes, Joe thought, he still looked like his mother. Joe felt a tightening of his throat, but then he pushed away the old emotion and tried to enjoy the pleasure of seeing his stepson again, of feeling his stepson's bride hugging him.

"Nancy," he said to her huskily, as the boy rounded the car, "Eddie always had good taste. I see he still has."

"Thank you, Pop," the girl whispered.

Then Joe turned to Eddie and held out his hand. "Eddie, I'm awfully glad to see you. Welcome home."

The boy did not take his hand. "Not my home."

"Eddie," Nancy began.

The boy shook his head slowly, staring at his stepfather accusingly. "I've never forgotten."

Joe's voice turned very quiet. "Forgotten what, Eddie?"

"The way you treated my mother."

Joe's left hand closed slowly: the knuckles whitened. "I tried to treat her as well as I was able, Eddie."

"Don't give me that."

Joe took a breath, smiled tightly at Nancy, then said to the boy, "I'm glad you're here, Eddie. Both you and Nancy. I've got the back bedroom in the house ready for you."

"I'm not staying in that house."

"Eddie, please," his wife said.

"We'll take a cabin," Eddie said, a sarcastic note in his voice.

Joe Beacon nodded, surprised, hurt and puzzled. "All right, Eddie. A cabin would be nice for you. I'll show you where—"

"If it wouldn't be too much trouble to give us the key, we'll find it ourselves."

"All right," he said softly.

The boy turned from them and walked to his car. He kicked at a tire and dust flew out from the inner rim in a small cloud. "Goddam dirt road." He ran a finger hard across the finish of the hood. "Washed this car and polished it, and now look at it." He looked at Joe meanly. "You ought to pave this road."

"Pop," Nancy said, "can't we go inside?"

He led her in, as the boy stared sullenly after them.

Inside, she said, "Pop, I just don't know what's wrong with him. He hasn't been feeling well. And he's been so moody. I didn't expect anything like this."

"It's all right." He touched her shoulder again, wanting everything about this to be right, yet knowing that it wasn't. "I don't know. Maybe just some rest for him. He doesn't seem like himself. But—"

"Pop, what did he mean? About the way you treated his mother? Maybe it isn't any of my business. But he's never really talked about her. You don't have to tell me anything if you don't want to. I know you must have treated her wonderfully well. But he seemed so angry."

"Yes," Joe nodded. But he did not want to tell her. Yet he could see that boy glaring at him, accusing him with his voice and manner, then walking over to kick that tire....

"I'm sorry, Pop. I shouldn't have asked."

"No, you've got a right to that. It was just that Nita, Eddie's mother, had problems. Within herself. She never quite got those straightened out. I did my best, I—"

No, he thought, he didn't want to tell her. But she was waiting.

"Maybe I didn't do my best, not really," he said. "I don't know. When you look back, you see things so much more clearly than you could when it was happening."

"And what happened, Pop? I just don't know anything. I'd like to. Is she alive?"

"No. She was killed. An automobile accident." He felt it coming again, the pain of it, the hard, brutal, hammering pain of it.

"Pop?" He suddenly found a true maturity in her eyes. "We'll talk about it later. When we're all relaxed. I don't want you to have to do that now."

He smiled at her, and knew Eddie had done no wrong in marrying her. "We'll do that." He nodded. "I think everything's going to be fine. Eddie just looked tired to me. That's a long trip driving up here. You two go ahead and move into that cabin and rest a little. And, yes, we'll talk later." He smiled again at her, reassuringly, and gave her a key. "It'll be fine, Nancy. Everything'll be fine."

She kissed his cheek and left swiftly. He was grateful that she'd stopped him, because he hadn't wanted to go on telling her about it. But he would have to, he knew, and he would. And, in the meantime, he had to believe it: Eddie was just tired, and everything was going to be fine.

But a wriggling worry in the back of his mind persisted, and his conscience kept telling him that he was doing only what he had been doing all these past years: pushing away the difficult and trying to take only what he wanted, that which would make it easier and more comfortable, so that he was becoming less with reality, more with the unreality of what his mind wanted out of this life....

Chapter 5

At the junction, down the highway, Sergeant Albert Cole braked his patrol car at a stop sign and looked across to the restaurant. He'd made his morning patrol, just exactly as he'd been instructed to do it when he'd been taken on a dry run over this territory by Sergeant Lew Barnes, now Lieutenant Lew Barnes. It had been a quiet morning, with only three jobs to take care of: a fawn run down on the highway, which he'd removed with the Forestry man; a motorist out of gas, whom he'd driven to the junction; and a complaint from the owner of a small ranch to the north that hunters had been using his property last week end.

He'd written a complete report on the last and had it ready to turn in when he went down to headquarters at midafternoon, after he'd turned over his duties to the next shift. It had been such a quiet morning that he'd had plenty of time to keep remembering that counterman who'd argued with him about serving a breakfast which was plainly printed on the menu. He'd finally got the breakfast, that was true. But why had the counterman argued about it when it was printed right there on the menu?

He wheeled his patrol car across the concrete to park it in front of the small restaurant. He radioed in the information that he was going to have lunch, delivered the name of the restaurant, estimated the exact time he would be in the place, then got out and strode toward the door, hat visor gleaming in the sun.

This time there was a thin, fast-moving, middle-aged woman behind the counter, who wore a flowered red apron and a fine net over hair obviously died jet black. The sergeant hoisted his thick frame onto a counter stool. He picked up a menu and examined it carefully. The woman behind the counter put a glass of water before him and waited. He made his selection, put the menu down and looked at the woman.

"Good day to you, sergeant. Trouble up here?"

He shook his head and said, "No," in his high voice.

"Never saw you before, did I?"

"No," Sergeant Cole repeated.

"Well," she said, "I thought this was Sergeant Barnes' territory."

"It's mine now. Sergeant Barnes is a lieutenant now. He's down at headquarters."

"Oh," she said, nodding. "Well, that's real nice for him. This is a promotion for you, isn't it?"

"I was counting on it anyway," he said somewhat defensively. He'd waited to become a sergeant for three years, and he really hadn't believed he would get it until the day the appointment came through. But there seemed no point in telling that to this woman.

"What's your name?" the woman asked.

"Sergeant Albert Cole."

"Glad to know you, sergeant. Welcome to the country. I'm Mrs.

Gronish."

"You own this place, don't you?"

"That's right."

"What happened to the counterman?"

Her eyes darkened with quick anger. "Quit. This morning. Didn't give me five minutes' notice. Just quit."

"Oh." The sergeant contemplated that, then said, "I'll have the cheeseburger with the potato salad, pickle and coffee. It's called the Gronish Lunch Special on the menu."

"Sure."

"You serve that, don't you?"

"Just like it says on the menu, sergeant."

He removed his hat, so that sunlight from the front window made his bald head gleam softly. He relaxed a bit. "That fellow on the counter this morning didn't want to give me the breakfast I ordered."

Mrs. Gronish had started toward the grill. She stopped and turned around. "He didn't what?"

"I asked for the two eggs, over easy, the hash-browns, and bacon on the side. He didn't want to give it to me."

"Why not?"

"He said the grill wasn't hot."

"The *grill* wasn't hot?"

"He served it finally, but he argued about it. I told him it was on the menu."

"Of course it's on the menu. What was the matter with him, anyway?"

"I don't know. That breakfast was on the menu."

"Then he quit. Without notice." Mrs. Gronish gave one disgusted shake of her head. "The dumb bastard." She went to the grill and started the sergeant's cheeseburger. The sergeant reached down the counter and picked up a newspaper. He felt better now, as though he could handle anything that might happen out here.

After he'd finished his cheeseburger and was having a cigarette with his second cup of coffee, he said, "It seems pretty quiet around here."

Mrs. Gronish leaned convivially against the counter. "Pretty quiet."

"Two or three bars along the highway going north."

"Yeah. Somebody gets a snootful every now and then. I haven't heard of a fight in maybe two years now, though."

"A lot of people hunt around here without permission?"

"Oh, yeah."

"I got a complaint this morning."

"Who from? Burnigan?"

"I wouldn't want to say the name."

"Burnigan, I'll bet. He's a damn nut. He about drove Sergeant Barnes crazy. Don't pay any attention to Burnigan."

He looked at her steadily with pale blue eyes. "If somebody makes a complaint, I turn in my report on it. That's my job."

"Oh, sure," she said agreeably.

"I saw this sign for a camp down the road."

"Where? Joe Beacon's place?"

The sergeant nodded.

"You're not going to have any trouble there."

"He takes in people, doesn't he?"

"Yeah, but he can handle everything by himself. You don't have to worry about Joe Beacon. He wouldn't need any help from anybody."

The sergeant stared at her without blinking. He was irritated that Mrs. Gronish felt somebody was capable enough that he, as a sheriff's sergeant newly appointed, might not be needed. But, he thought, civilians always thought they could handle everything until they got into trouble. Then they needed the law. And he was the law here now, the whole law, and he was going to handle it the way it ought to be handled. Whenever he had to. No matter what it was.

"That was a good cheeseburger," he said, nodding definitely. "Just like it said on the menu."

Chapter 6

In his kitchen, Joe Beacon rechecked his provisions. Still bothered by the way Eddie had handled himself when he and Nancy had arrived, Joe tried now to keep his mind simply on running this business. Eddie was just tired, he kept telling himself. But Eddie was here now. He had a fine wife, that was obvious. And the only thing to do was not worry and take care of the lesser problems, the main one of which was food.

He'd taken a good supply to the cabin where Nancy and Eddie were. Nancy had been grateful, but Eddie lay on the bed, one arm over his eyes, saying nothing. But, Joe thought, that boy wasn't going to starve, at least. Norris and Rosalind Glenn hadn't inquired about provisions yet. He could explain to them that they could drive up to the highway and down to the junction to the general store. But Norris Glenn, he knew positively, was not going to drive that road up the cliff until they left. Flo and Roy Ives had carried in a large sack which looked as though it might contain sandwiches bought on the road. But they would need something later. He was positive the Days had no food with them.

He looked over his supply again, then closed the large freezer door, certain that he would have to drive out and add supplies within a couple of days. Then he sat down at a table near a window from which he could see, because of the way this room extended from the house, the line of cabins, looking peaceful and sleepy in the early afternoon sun. Apparently everyone was inside at the moment, and he wondered, as he always did, who, exactly, the people were who had come in to rent those cabins. Outside, you saw one side of them. But if you could penetrate within the privacy of those walls, you would, he was positive, see another. He knew none of them, except Eddie. After that meeting earlier, he was not sure he even knew Eddie anymore. So they were all strangers. And what were they saying, doing, thinking within the sanctity of those walls, where there was no need for showing a stranger like himself a facade or a mask or an act....?

Chapter 7

Victor Day unscrewed the cap from a bottle of good bourbon and splashed a healthy drink into a glass. He looked at the girl across the room, who sat smoking a cigarette, not looking back at him.

"Drink?" he asked.

She didn't answer.

He sipped from the glass and sat down across the room from her. She continued to stare at some invisible point on the wall, saying not a word.

"Oh, come on, Lynn," he said finally. "Let's not be childish." At last she turned and looked at him with cold, examining eyes. But she said nothing.

Her eyes, he thought; they were beautiful, even when she was angry. And she'd been angry ever since they'd checked out of the expensive motel in Carmel early that morning, when he'd finally realized that she was truly serious about ending it. He'd driven into Monterey, taking the 17 Mile Drive past massive mansions and dramatic sea cliffs, and insisted that they have a comfortable breakfast in one of the Wharf restaurants over a gun-metal ocean. The breakfast had not been comfortable, and she had gone on insisting that it was over. Since they'd arrived here, she'd been silent, just looking at him angrily with those beautiful brown eyes.

It was her eyes, he thought, that he'd noticed first, when he'd found her watching him that first week. She'd sat at her receptionist desk in the Montgomery Street investment company where she'd gone to work ten months ago and watched him across the room whenever she had a chance. He'd been pleased and curious. And though he'd never done any real flirting with other women since he'd married Frances sixteen years before, he'd been too attracted to turn away the impulse to ask her out for a drink one late Friday afternoon.

They'd walked down Montgomery toward North Beach to a small bar away from the jostle and noise of the financial district cocktail hour. They'd sat in a dimly lit booth where Lynn had continued to look at him with undisguised adoration.

He said, "Surprised I asked you out?"

"I was hoping you'd ask me."

He felt suddenly secure and confident in her presence. He'd never been so attracted to a woman in his life. It hadn't been so much an attraction with Frances, not with her rather severe handsomeness and businesslike attitude, but simply a solid, workable arrangement that had gotten them somewhere.

"I haven't made a habit of asking girls from the office out."

"And I haven't made a habit of going out with vice-presidents of the companies where I've worked either."

They talked lightly about nothing in particular, until Victor Day found himself holding her hand over the table, feeling more youthfully assured than he had in twenty years. "A beautiful hand. Perfectly designed, with tapered fingers. A marvelous life line. And—"

"Be careful, Vic."

He looked at her questioningly.

"What is it they say?" she said. "Be careful, it's my hand—or is it my heart?"

"You don't mean that."

"I do."

He shook his head. "You can't feel that way, Lynn. We've barely met."

"I do feel that way."

"But why? I mean—" He didn't know what to say. He was surprised and intensely pleased.

"I saw you that first day, and ... something happened." She looked away from him. "I'm sorry if I embarrass you."

"You don't embarrass me." He gave her hand a comforting squeeze. "I just want to get things straight. I'm married. I have been for sixteen years. I have two young boys. I have a very comfortable home, and I haven't been dissatisfied."

She nodded and met his eyes again. "I'm sorry I've been so unconscionably forward. And thanks for the drink, Vic."

"I just wanted to get it straight, Lynn."

"I have it straight, Vic."

"All I'm saying is that a man just doesn't kick all of that over on a whim."

She made no attempt to hide what was obviously her quick and complete love for him. "I wouldn't ask you to kick all of that over, would I?"

She was renting a small flat on Greenwich Street. He took her home that evening. She seemed helpless in his presence. He'd left finally, exhilarated with the realization that he'd had all of Lynn Marsey there was to have.

But the exhilaration had evaporated the moment he'd walked into his house. It was a large house in St. Francis Heights, which he and Frances had started buying only two years ago. He was now aware that he did not want to lose anything they had acquired after so much work and pressure.

He walked up the white-carpeted stairway and saw light beneath Frances' bedroom door. They'd decided, when they had moved into this house, to make use of two of the second floor's adjoining rooms, to enjoy proximity and yet the comfort of separate sleeping rooms. Frances often had migraines. He was usually blind-weary from his work. It was a sensible arrangement.

He hesitated nervously, then tapped his knuckles against the door. Frances was seated before her dressing table—a tall, thin woman, who bore herself with nearly military stiffness. Right now she was sitting with such starched severity that he was certain that she had, by some rare feminine instinct, already detected that he had been untrue to her. He'd had an odd thought then: realizing how peculiar it was that the straight line of Frances' back could reduce him to nearly a juvenile wariness, when, on the other hand, he could take over a conference table and pulp his male opposition without the slightest loss of confidence.

She turned and smiled at him. "Darling."

"Sorry." He crossed to her and kissed her neck lightly.

"You might have phoned."

"Didn't have a chance. I'm really sorry."

She looked at him through her mirror. "Another woman, Vic?"

He was certain that he flushed. Then he saw the mischievous quirk at the corner of her mouth. "That's it," he said, putting his arms around her.

She turned to him with as much tenderness as she ever displayed. "You can look like a rock sometimes, and yet I think you're as beautifully naïve as the day you were born. I love you for that, Vic."

He held her tightly, relieved.

"What was it, really?" she asked. "Henderson?"

"Yes," he said into her carefully tended brown hair. "Henderson."

Henderson was another but lesser executive with Kensington, Fisher and Brown. He was ambitious, ruthless and a stumbling stone for Victor Day. His presence meant a constant vigil, to make certain of not being tripped by the man's savage drive. A short, florid man with prying eyes, he represented the only obstacle to Victor Day's own surging ambition to head the company one day.

"What did he do this time?" Frances asked, wholly interested.

"I had to head him off at the pass again. The usual. It took the evening."

She put the flat of her palm against his cheek. "Don't think about him now. You won't sleep. You're worth ten of him any day."

He held her tightly, reassured and grateful. "How're the boys?"

"Fine and asleep."

He kissed her forehead softly. "Have I told you lately how much I appreciate my wife?"

"Aren't we being warm tonight?"

"Why not?"

She tipped her face up and met his lips. He could not help thinking how Lynn Marsey's mouth had tasted and felt when he'd kissed her for the first time.

"Sometimes these two rooms are a bore, aren't they, darling?" Frances whispered.

Now Victor Day felt a churning anger. He'd so carefully distributed his time between Frances and Lynn Marsey since then, and now, this morning, Lynn had told him that it was over. He repeated, his voice harsh in the cabin, "Damn it, let's just not be childish, shall we?"

"The one thing I'm not being is childish, Vic," she finally said. "I'm being quite mature, probably for the first time in ten months."

"I don't know what's mature about this. Ten months? That's almost a year. How can you throw a year of your life away? By God, I don't intend to do that."

"I know," she said quietly.

"What's that supposed to mean?"

"It means that maybe I threw away almost a year, but you didn't."

"That's good feminine lack of logic, isn't it?"

"Is it?" She had finished her cigarette. She lit another, with a quick motion. "I'm not talking about the time we've been together. I wanted that and that's all that mattered to me. I presume you enjoyed the time with me. I must have been pretty good, anyway. Because you—"

"Don't start that, Lynn. Just don't start that."

"All right. I'll talk about the time in the past ten months we haven't been together."

He was annoyed and puzzled and angry. "I've given you every minute I possibly could."

"After everything else, yes. After your business. After your wife. After your children."

"I told you from the beginning that a man didn't kick all of that over on a whim. I seem to remember very accurately that you said you wouldn't ask me to!"

She stared at him with steady eyes. "I'm not, am I, Vic? I'm just saying no more. I'm just saying it's the end of the line and the old cliché—you obviously like sleeping with Lynn, but you don't intend to do anything more about it. You have a capable wife, handsome children, and a very efficiently operating home. I've loved you, Vic, but you never loved me. So I'm not asking you to kick anything over. I'd hoped for something else, but I didn't ask for anything else. I'm not now. I'm just saying it's over."

He glared down into his drink. If he could just pinpoint where this had started to break up. But he couldn't. And that was what was particularly infuriating. There had been no special thing. It had just started coming apart about a month ago, and nothing he did now seemed to help. He'd been so certain that bringing her in here would change her mind. Didn't she know what he was risking by taking this extra day?

He tipped the glass up again, thinking how, as they'd driven north from Monterey, he'd decided to take the chance. He had been so certain that this trip would solve all of it. Lynn had a second half of her vacation coming. At home he'd pleaded business again, and then, with great care, set up a meeting at Monterey with one of the company's more important investors, so that it would look all right at the office. Then Lynn had pulled this, and he had to continue the risk.

They had come into a small mountain village. He'd stopped near a service station where he saw a public telephone booth. He'd gotten out without explanation to Lynn and a few minutes later was talking to his wife in San Francisco. He'd told her:

"Frances, I'm in a bind. It's getting complicated down here. But I think it might mean a good chunk of business, so I'm hanging on."

"Really, Vic—aren't you going to make it home today?"

"I might just be down here overnight."

"Well, if it's important, Vic. Business first."

"Call Harvey, will you? So they know at the office? I might not make it there until tomorrow afternoon. How're the kids?"

"Ray's all right. But Billy's grim. He was counting on you to take him to Fleishhacker's yesterday. To feed the silly monkeys."

"Tell him next Saturday. It's a promise."

"I'll tell him, Vic. And good luck."

There was sincerity in her voice. She'd always been behind him, right from the beginning. And that was one good reason why he'd gone somewhere. It might, he thought, striding back to his car, be a good lesson for Lynn.

He drove away, saying, "I called Harvey Freeport to tell him I'll be held up here overnight."

Lynn closed her eyes wearily. "Please, Vic, just drive me back to the city. That's all I want."

"How about my feelings? How about what I want for a change?"

"It won't hurt if you don't get something you want for a change."

"I'm a fighter, Lynn."

"I know."

"Remember how I told you I made up my mind to be president of my high-school senior class? I did it."

"I remember, Vic."

"When the war came along and I went into the Army as a private, I promised myself I was going to be an officer. I was a company commander at twenty-two."

"Yes."

"And when I got back I told myself that I was going to get into the top ten per cent of my graduating class."

"You did it, Vic."

"Yes. And when I started at Kensington, Fisher and Brown, I said I was going to be a vice-president within ten years. Did I make it?"

"You made it, Vic."

"I fight. I'm fighting now."

"That's all right when you have something to fight. But you have nothing to fight now. It's simply over."

But he had not been able to believe that. And when he'd seen the sign announcing the cabins and fishing and boating, he'd decided that would be perfect. Out here? In the country? What could be better? He was a good sportsman, when you came down to it. She'd never seen him against that setting. Sometimes it took the simple, natural background—man in the elements—to make the right impression.

Yet here they were, and she was stubbornly telling him there was going to be no more. He stood up and paced, holding his empty glass with a hard grip. "I never expected it from you, Lynn. I'll tell you that honestly. This isn't anything but pure selfishness on your part, is it? When you really look at it?"

She ground out her second cigarette. "For the past ten months, Vic, I haven't thought about anyone but you. At work, I watched you whenever you were in sight. When you weren't, I thought about how you looked. At the end of the day, I'd go home to a lonely apartment. If you couldn't make it that night, I'd sit and read by myself. Or watch television. And think about you. No family for me to go home to when we weren't together. No other men, when you couldn't break away from your family."

He was remembering now how the lean, taciturn camp owner had looked at her when they'd come, how she'd returned the look with a curiosity he'd never seen her give another man but himself. What, he suddenly wondered, was going on when he wasn't around? She'd slept with him pretty easily, hadn't she? He picked up the bourbon bottle again and splashed himself another drink. He looked at her narrowly. "All right. The rest of this doesn't mean a thing, does it? You said other men. That's it, isn't it?"

"No, Vic," she said wearily. "It's exactly as I'm explaining. With me this was everything. With you, it was a whim."

He laughed sarcastically. "Everything's my fault."

"No. It was my fault for allowing it to happen in the first place. I won't make it messy for you. No tears, you notice."

He looked at her again, suspiciously. At least some tears would have made it more understandable. But she was cool and aloof and kept telling him that it was over. He just couldn't believe that. She'd *loved* him.

"Please, Vic. This is no good. Let's leave. Take me home, will you?"

"We're staying here," he said, "until you come to your senses."

"I've come to my senses," she said. "I'd like to go home, Vic."

"No."

She got up and started for the door.

"Where are you going?" he demanded.

"I think," she said patiently, "we'll need some food, won't we?"

"Oh, yes," he said, feeling a flood of hot jealousy he'd never experienced with her before. "That's right. You'd better go see that Beacon fellow, hadn't you? That's a good idea. I think he'll like that. I think you will too."

She gave him a final look. He was certain he could see contempt in it. She shut the door behind her and he lifted his glass again, feeling it trembling against his mouth as he finished the drink with one thirsty swallow.

Chapter 8

In the next cabin, Roy Ives stood beside the nearly drawn drapes and looked out at the Lincoln Continental, as Flo stared about the cabin with obvious disgust, saying, "This is sure some crummy, crappy place compared to the others we was in."

He didn't answer.

"Hell," she said. "You can take this dump and—"

"Shut up," he said.

She looked at him, surprised. Her voice went into a faint whine, "What kind of way is that to talk?"

"Shut up for a minute," he said. "I'm thinkin'."

And he was. He was thinking how all of this had come about. Flo. And the repainted Thunderbird. And the money that had started all of it, coming from that widow down in Butte Junction, Nebraska. Christ, he thought, smiling tightly, Butte Junction, Nebraska....

Nine months before he'd even met Flo, he'd got tired of Texas and gone up from Fort Worth, driving a beat-up Chevy, heading north, heading anywhere. He went up through Oklahoma and Kansas and finally stopped in a little town on the south edge of Nebraska— Butte Junction.

He'd gone into the town's single café for a T-bone and French fries and discovered a tall, leggy, red-haired waitress. Her name was Irma and she wasn't the best-looking girl he'd seen: her face was long, and she'd done something wrong with her make-up. But he'd liked the way she looked at him when he came in. They talked the same kind of language, he found quickly. So he'd taken her into the beer parlor that night, which was the first night he'd gotten into a fight in that town.

There weren't many girls in Butte Junction. And there were even fewer who felt that it was all right to go into the hall and drink beer and dance to the jukebox. The local boys felt a kind of ownership about Irma.

To get them over it, Ives had to go through seven of them in five days. He got a room in the back of an old house near the center of town, renting it from a nearly blind and totally deaf native who had been county treasurer forty years ago. Sometimes he slept in that room. Sometimes he slept with Irma, in her small cottage down near the railroad depot. He knew, very quickly, that Irma would go anywhere with him, if he asked her. He was the first one, she'd told him frankly one early morning, who could leave her feeling as though she couldn't lift a dish the next day.

But he didn't intend to go anywhere for a while. He was looking for something. After two weeks in Butte Junction, he found it. She was a plain woman named Mrs. Jensen, who had a weary, defeated face and the slump of grief in her shoulders. She'd turned 38 five days after her husband had dropped dead of a sunstroke the summer before, and left her alone in the world with two sons, 10 and 12. Now she was attempting, with little success, to keep the small dusty farm she owned east of Butte Junction going. She'd gotten help from an old man who hired out when he was able. But the old man had developed a severe case of arthritis three weeks before and had to quit.

Roy found out about her one day when he was hanging around the grain elevator. He was waiting for her at the co-op market the next day.

"Name's Roy Ives," he said with his convivial drawl, "and I just come up from Texas. I don't mean to be too forward, Mrs. Jensen, but the boys down at the grain elevator were telling me you run into a bit of misfortune. They said you got a nice farm out east of town, but no help. Now I know I'm a stranger here, and you can tell me to go run up some tree if you think I ain't no worth to you. But I think I know about as much as any man about working on a farm. I like it here, around Butte Junction. And I personally ain't got anything against offering to go to work for you, ma'am, if you think you could use a hand out there."

She'd stood in front of a row of large flour sacks and looked at him suspiciously.

But he smiled widely and said, "I got me a place here in town, and

I'd want to come in nights. You wouldn't have to worry none about my staying out at your place. And I ain't too worried about the kind of wages, on account I like to prove if I'm any worth to somebody first. And, like I said, I heard down at the grain elevator about your misfortunes. And the truth is—I lost my own partner in life, my loving wife Aggie, down in Texas. It was just last spring. I don't know. They was telling me about you and your two boys and your husband gone and all. You could tell me to go on and run up that tree, and it won't hurt my feelings none at all. But I'd be glad to help out, if you think I could."

He waited, smiling apologetically, and gradually her face lost some of its severity. She nodded shortly and said, "You want to come out in the morning and take a look around, I could think about it overnight, anyway."

At first, after he'd gone to work for her, she kept a wary distance. But his quick impression on the two boys seemed to warm her. Pretty soon she began having him in for supper with herself and the boys. After that, she began to ask him to stay after supper, so that they could sit and talk in the living room for a bit.

Ives stopped seeing Irma in public in Butte Junction. But after he returned to his room at night, he would often sneak out and drive down to Irma's place to stay until just before dawn. He told Irma straight out that Mrs. Jensen was trying to get intimate with him and that she was already so jealous that she might fire him if she caught him with Irma, an announcement that turned Irma into a fury. But he promised that he would keep away from her as much as possible and that he had plans—if Irma would just be patient for a little while, he explained, he would take her away from Butte Junction, her deepest desire.

As the months passed, Irma turned dangerously impatient. But finally, after some carefully casual questioning, Ives found out what he wanted to know: Mrs. Jensen had received $5,000 in life insurance when her husband died. She'd already spent $2,000 of it trying to keep the farm alive. Ives was disappointed about that. But the $3,000 that remained, he decided, was better than nothing.

He sat down with Mrs. Jensen in her old-fashioned living room one evening after supper and said, "Now, I ain't got no right busting into somebody's business, Mrs. Jensen. Not anybody's, including yours. But ever since you mentioned about that insurance money the other night, I've been thinking. I've been thinking I want to see you and those boys the best off you can be. I come to like it, working out here.

And those boys—they pure and simple get to me. It's like—I don't know—I was some kin to them. Now that's a fool thing to say, ain't it?"

Mrs. Jensen sat looking at him with warm, grateful eyes and shook her head swiftly. "I don't think that's a fool thing to say at all, Mr. Ives. I think that's a very wonderful thing to say."

He smiled at her gently. "Well, I thank you for that. And you wouldn't want to start calling me Roy about now, would you?"

"I'd like very much to call you Roy," she said, "if you'd start calling me Libby."

He nodded. "I sure will, Libby. And proud to do it."

"What were you thinking about that insurance money, Roy?"

"Well," he said, "it's just this way...."

He talked with deep sincerity and put a touch of humility into his voice. He didn't say directly that he'd fallen in love with her and would want to marry her. Not directly. He did not say exactly that he wanted to be a father for her sons. Not exactly. If she happened to believe those things out of what he said, that was her own imagination working.

What he did say positively was that he knew this farm could absolutely be put on its feet, and that he, Roy Ives, could do it. It would take added investment, of course. It would take giving a good man some substantial money so that he could get into his truck and drive to Omaha and do some good and clever buying of stock as well as of some equipment this farm needed in the worst way. That was where the insurance money came in.

But he didn't come right out and ask Mrs. Jensen to take the $3,000 out of the bank and give it to him. That was her own idea, at the end of the evening, and he could feel her sobbing in gratitude when he came over and put his arm comfortingly around her weary shoulders.

Roy Ives drove back to Butte Junction that night and told Irma to pack. She was on a bus with her suitcase riding toward Grand Island by eight the next morning. At nine, Ives met Mrs. Jensen at the bank, where she drew out the $3,000 and gave it to him and wished him Godspeed. He'd already packed everything he owned into his pickup; he drove fast over to Grand Island, where he picked up Irma. Then they went on to Omaha.

They had a roaring good time there for three days. Then, as Irma lay sleeping early one morning in their hotel room, Ives counted the money remaining. There was just over $2,000. He folded the bills into his wallet, silently packed his things again, and left while Irma slept in contented exhaustion.

Ives cut down through Kansas again, crossed Oklahoma and returned to Texas. He had never given more than a passing thought to either Irma or Mrs. Jensen since.

Then he'd met Flo in Dallas and felt it was probably time for him to settle down a little. Because Flo had owned that good and ample body, he'd asked her to marry him—in fact, that body was just about all that had attracted him about her, but it was enough. They'd driven to Las Vegas, where Ives had bought the secondhand Thunderbird after collecting $5,200 on a quick and wild win on a Sands crap table. They'd spent another high-living week in Nevada, then some similar good living after crossing over the desert to Los Angeles, where he'd gotten into a minor collision which had broken out the right tailight, then down to Tijuana and back again. And finally he was cruising in Northern California on Highway 5, taking the curves at high speed, leaving tire marks on the hairpins, feeling nervous and edgy, impatient for something to happen. Anything.

It wasn't Flo. He wasn't tired of her yet. She'd turned out all right. She was like an animal once she got into bed. It was a fact that she'd kept on flirting with every man who looked at her ever since they'd been married. But that didn't bother Ives. He could handle anybody who tried to pick up her signal. In fact, he'd been wishing lately that some man would, because he hadn't had a good, slam-out fight in a long time. Steam was building inside him, and that was one of the reasons why he was nervous.

The other reason was that he was running out of money. Which was why he'd come in here, because he thought it might be cheap. It hadn't been as cheap as he'd hoped, and he was going to have to figure out something, and pretty soon. And so all of that was what he was thinking, standing there looking past the nearly drawn drapes at the shining Lincoln Continental. The man who owned a car like that wasn't worried about money, he thought. And, again, he felt a hot flash of anger, knowing somebody had more than he. Why is that? he thought. Why the hell is that?

He snapped the drapes all the way shut and turned around. Flo stood looking indignant, saying, "Tellin' me to shut up! Is that the way to talk when somebody's been married only 'bout three weeks?"

He grinned tightly, then reached out and pulled the tied bow free of the front of her red blouse. He looked at her bare, very large breasts. "The only talk I want to hear right now," he said, "is no talk at all."

Chapter 9

As Roy Ives snapped the drapes shut in his cabin, Norris and Rosalind Glenn burst out of theirs and marched swiftly to Joe Beacon's house. Norris was feeling good and free. He'd liked that cabin the instant he saw it. It looked pleasant and clean and just bone-simple enough to give him a true artistic feeling. He was still a little shaky from the drive down—he'd felt dizzy enough for a moment that he'd had to stop the car completely, trying to keep his leg from jerking spasmodically, as he pressed his foot on the brake. But they'd got down all right, and he'd found real confidence just being around Joe Beacon. Usually the outdoors type terrified him. But in Joe Beacon he sensed a compassion that you didn't always find in those fellows. That made him comfortable.

So now all he was truly concerned about was what kind of animals must be running around in a remote spot like this. God knows what there would be, including snakes. But he tried to forget that and just breathe deeply of the fresh, stimulating air that encouraged you to sniff Nature right into your very being. They knocked on Joe Beacon's door, and in a moment he appeared.

"Food?" Rosalind said in her ringing voice. "We just forgot all about food, Mr. Beacon."

"Well, sure." He motioned them in. "I should have told you earlier I had something you can buy. That is, unless you want to drive up to the highway and down to the junction. There's a general store there." He looked at Norris, smiling.

Norris shook his head quickly. "Actually," he said, "I think you've got such a lovely and quaint place here, Mr. Beacon, that I wouldn't think of leaving just to drive to that general store."

Joe Beacon nodded. "That's fine then. I'm glad you like it that much." In the kitchen, he showed them his selection. They made careful, economical choices, and he said, "You say you're on vacation?"

"That's it," Norris said. "And we thought, where can we go? So we thought of the Big Sur. We'd heard that was becoming something of an art colony. But, my God, you should see the roads down there. And we didn't find any artists whatever. So we came back up through Santa Cruz and stopped there for a bit. Then we were heading north again, toward the Valley of the Moon—Jack London, you know, wrote out of there. But I told Rosalind I'd heard they'd made a perfect tourist trap out of it, which I think we might have mentioned. And so we saw your sign and came in. Do you have many artists stopping here, Mr. Beacon?"

"I believe you're the first one."

"Now isn't that something, Norris?" Rosalind said. "To find yourself in a truly wonderful place like this, knowing it's absolutely never been tapped artistically before?"

"Yes," Norris said, nodding. "That's true, of course. But I must say that I've been quite eager lately to meet someone else actively engaged in the arts. I mean, I'll have to admit, Mr. Beacon, that for some reason, although we know a wonderful number of people who *like* art, we just don't know any *real* artists."

"Now don't run yourself down, Norris," Rosalind said sternly. "Remember, it's confidence in your work that matters. It's really all an artist has to count on, in the end."

"Yes, that's so right. But I mean if we only *knew* somebody, Rosalind. Somebody truly great, just to talk to and soak up a little bit of the juices of accomplishment. I'm exploding with creativity. But it's direction. Where do I go? With what?"

"Well," Rosalind said, "while you're out here in this wonderful natural land of Mr. Beacon's, just getting the feeling, why don't you spend a little time working on that movie you've been thinking about? Just work on the script, right on your own confidence. As a kind of warmup."

"Which movie was that?"

"The one where the hero is turned into a mushroom. The girl falls in love with the mushroom. Only it turns out he's a toadstool, and—"

"My God, yes. I should make notes on the movies I'm writing." He turned to Joe Beacon. "It's a marvelous motion picture, Mr. Beacon, ripe with symbols." Then he turned back to Rosalind, saying, "But who in America could do it justice? It would have to be done by Ingmar Bergman. I wouldn't sell it to anyone else. I'd have to take the script personally to Sweden, and—"

"Maybe you should think about getting a Hollywood agent, Norris."

"And have him sell it to *Disney*? They'd make a darling little character out of the mushroom, like a mouse or a dog or jackass or something. I'm not selling out that way."

"You're right, Norris," Rosalind said definitely. "Look what happened to Fitzgerald in Hollywood."

"Oh, God," Norris said, shaking his head sadly. "Well—thank you for the excellent service, Mr. Beacon."

When they got back to the cabin, Norris lay down on the double bed while Rosalind finished unpacking. He saw, as she was removing things from a suitcase, the Henry Miller paperback version of *Tropic of Cancer*. She covered it swiftly with a sweater, flushing faintly, and Norris looked self-consciously at the ceiling. It was actually Henry Miller, he thought, who had been responsible for their coming down this way in the first place.

They had read somewhere that the author lived in the Big Sur. And they had read several favorable criticisms about him in the small literary journals Norris subscribed to, though they hadn't yet examined any of his actual work. There seemed to be quite a flurry about some of his efforts.

So they'd left their small flat in San Francisco and had driven south toward the Big Sur, discussing with mounting enthusiasm how Henry Miller, when you really thought about it, was really the last link with the kind of thing Gertrude Stein represented in the Twenties in Paris. Although neither Norris nor Rosalind cared much for Hemingway beyond the fact that he'd been a Naturalist—he was much too base in much of his work and primeval and savage, spending his life killing all those animals and drinking and shooting up the plumbing—there was Fitzgerald, who had been fair, and there was Pound, who had been terribly misunderstood and wronged, and God knows there was Joyce, if you could get around some of his dirty writing. All of them had been in Gertrude's group.

So it had seemed logical to drive down to the Big Sur and see if they couldn't find Henry Miller and perhaps gain an audience with him. In fact, Norris had carefully typed up his poem and the five pages of his novel and packed them in his suitcase, just in case Mr. Miller cared to look them over.

But they had run into some roads which had turned Norris half sick with dizziness, the fog had come in, and nobody seemed to know Henry Miller anyway. The owner of a country general store in a small crossroads community had said he'd heard that somebody named Kerouac had been around at one time and was supposed to be a writer. But neither Norris nor Rosalind wanted anything to do with him or any of the other Beat writers. They, in fact, considered themselves effective rebels against the Beat influence, with its negations, and instead were searching for the uplift of romantic spirit discovered by the nature poets.

They had found an economical room that night, and then driven back to Santa Cruz the next day. That was where Norris discovered a rack containing the paperbound edition of Mr. Miller's *Tropic of*

Cancer. He'd bought a copy, and found another economical room in a cottage motel on the beach. It had been a warm, sunny day, and Rosalind went clam digging, while Norris set up his easel, feeling more artistic now than literary. He intended to do something substantial that day, while he read a passage or two of Mr. Miller's book between artistic sessions. But he didn't get around to doing anything artistic all day. Instead, he read the entire book.

Over sand dabs and a little Chablis in a restaurant near the boardwalk that evening, Rosalind asked about the book. Norris did not quite know what to say other than it was not entirely what he'd expected. Rosalind started reading it in bed after dinner.

She read with what appeared to Norris to be a mounting grimness. He, of course, had been surprised himself. He had not quite expected anything like that. Still, he was somewhat disappointed in Rosalind's seeming reaction, since he'd felt, after finishing the book, that Rosalind, who somehow always took the initiative in such things, might feel a bit in the mood for capturing that uplifting emotional soaring of the bird they'd been seeking in their marriage of two years. But Rosalind kept looking more stern and angry.

At two in the morning, she turned to glare at Norris, then threw the book violently across the room. Norris managed a smile, and said, "Well, it was rather interesting anyway, wouldn't you say?"

"That," Rosalind said loudly, "is a travesty upon the right of free speech!"

She'd turned off the lights then, and Norris had almost willed himself to sleep when she got up and got into bed with him. Sometime later, after he staggered to his feet, he picked up the book from the floor and carefully put it away in one of the suitcases.

In the following days, they never talked of the book again. Rosalind continued to dig for clams, and Norris painted and sketched quite a wealth of new material. In the evening they ate sea food and discussed Thoreau's *Walden,* which Rosalind was reading to remove the effects of the Miller book. Norris avoided the boats coming in during the day because he could not stand the sight of fresh death in any form, including caught fish, and especially if he were going to eat some of them that night. But by the weekend the fog had come in again, and the coast turned a bitter cold. So on Monday morning, after a final look through a fantastically quaint used-book shop, they decided to head north, where they had found this place.

They had still not talked of the Miller book again. And now Rosalind had just covered it swiftly with a sweater, flushing faintly. And Norris had looked self-consciously at the ceiling. For a few moments, he thought perhaps the book would not again have the effect it obviously had created in Santa Cruz. But then Rosalind came over and sat down beside him.

"Would you like," she asked softly, "for me to recite 'The Newly-Wedded'?"

"All right," Norris said. Rosalind had memorized "The Newly-Wedded" by Winthrop Mackworth Praed before their marriage and had recited it to him on their wedding night. He knew what it meant and instinctively set himself.

When she had finished the recitation, she put her arms around him and hugged him tightly. He hugged her back with a vengeance.

When Norris got up quite a while later, he stumbled out of sheer exhaustion.

"Oh, that soaring of the bird!" Rosalind breathed ecstatically from the bed. "We were so very beautifully close to finding it, weren't we, Norris?"

"Yes," he said, collapsing into a chair. "I really think so."

"Oh, I *know* so," Rosalind said, looking at him in a way that made him certain he'd better get out of the room, at least for a little while.

"I do think so, at that," he said. "I really think I'm possibly quite sure of it."

Chapter 10

In the last cabin being used in the line, Nancy Crayne tried not to worry because Eddie had again lapsed into one of his silent moods. He lay on the bed and had said not a word since they'd come in here. It was the way he'd acted the night before.

On her insistence, they had stopped at a motel in Merced on their way up from Los Angeles, even though Eddie had said that he could drive all the way into the Bay area and into Pop's place that night. She had thought he might rest, but a half hour after they'd gone to bed he'd got up and just sat there in the dark. She tried to talk to him, but he wouldn't answer. He went back to bed finally, and she went to sleep.

But when she awakened sometime early in the morning, she realized that he was not in his bed. She got up swiftly and looked in the bathroom. He wasn't there either. Then the door opened and he came in. He was wearing pajamas, a jacket, and bedroom slippers. He was shivering with the night chill.

"Eddie?" she'd said. "Where have you been?"

"What do you mean, where have I been?"

"Did you take a walk, Eddie?"

"Did I take a walk, Eddie?"

He took off his jacket and the slippers and got back into bed.

"Are you all right?" she'd asked.

"I am tired. It's night, isn't it? I would like to sleep. Do you mind?"

When she was packing, later, he got up wordlessly. He dressed and put their bags in the car, and by the time they'd reached the East Bay and were crossing the water toward Palo Alto, he still had said nothing. But she tried to remain silent, determined not to increase his tension, whatever the reasons for it, by appearing overanxious. She wouldn't even look at him for a time, because it sometimes made him nervous if she stared at him. Instead, she'd looked out at the water, calm and green-blue with flickering whitecaps. Across, she'd seen the west shore with its mud flats and then the profile of Peninsula buildings running along in a solid cluster. They were getting closer to Pop, and that had started an excitement in her.

Because somehow, she was certain, everything was going to be all right when they reached Pop. Eddie had talked so much of him, describing the ranch the way it had been when he'd lived there. He had never talked about his mother. She was certain that his mother was dead, but Eddie had never told her. She was going to ask Pop about it.

Then she found herself looking at him again, as he drew a hand across his forehead and blinked. She wanted to talk to him. But she forced herself to wait until he was ready. She knew how it was to have someone continually worried about you. She knew that more than most.

When she was seven, living with her parents in a small cottage in Bellflower, she'd contracted a strep infection which, turning into rheumatic fever, had scarred the heart valves and left her with a damaged heart muscle.

An only child, she'd learned to hate the constant attention which had inhibited her every motion from then on. That steady parental vigil had ended only when she'd married Eddie, over their protests. They could not, and still did not, believe that she was sturdy enough even to be a bride.

But she was a bride. Eddie's bride. And now she was trying desperately, because she loved him so, to do the right thing at all times. Six months ago he'd begun to get periodic headaches, which no medication seemed to cure. She had known his tendency to be moody ever since she'd met him in a Long Beach amusement park. But suddenly his moods began to cover a wider range. He would become deeply depressed. Then the headaches would begin. When the headaches disappeared, he would shift into high spirits and optimism. She'd tried to talk him into seeing a doctor, but he was stubborn and wouldn't go. But perhaps, she thought, Pop could talk him into it, once Eddie relaxed on that land he'd loved so much.

He rubbed his forehead once more, and she could no longer resist. "Is your head aching again, Eddie?"

He looked at her, angrily, then back at the bridge.

"I don't mean to nag, Eddie. I just want to help."

They came off the bridge and rolled across the overpass above Bayshore Freeway, then moved into a residential section of neat, expensive-looking homes whose lawns had been kept meticulously green through the dry season. He finally said:

"My mother had headaches."

She became curiously alert. "She did?"

He said no more until they had crossed the city and were driving west on Sand Hill Road. He had been sitting tensely erect, his hands gripping the steering wheel as though he feared some impending crash. Suddenly he relaxed. "Look at all those homes, Nancy. This all used to be nothing but land."

"They're beautiful homes, Eddie."

He shook his head. "It'll be years before we can move into anything like that."

"Who cares?" she said, smiling brilliantly now. "So long as we have each other."

"Yes," he laughed. "We can live on love."

"And pale moonlight," she agreed happily.

They talked all the way up to Route 5. And after they had reached the crest, Nancy watched intently as Eddie explained the landmarks. Three miles from Joe Beacon's gate, Eddie was talking again in detail of the good life he'd had on that land. He told her about the rabbits he'd shot, the raccoon that had stolen a bag of fish, the trail he'd favored, the old bobcat that had come in against its instinct and lived secretly in the pine shed for three nights in order to raid the garbage can because it was too old to hunt its natural quarry.

Finally they rolled through the gate and down the road she'd heard so much about.

He was smiling broadly, his eyes bright with eagerness. "This rock cliff," he said, "is just like the Hollywood Bowl. Sound bounces off like it was a big loudspeaker. Listen." He hit the horn, and the sound echoed loudly down the valley. They could see Joe Beacon coming out on the porch of his house and stand waiting for them. When the Dodge stopped in front of the porch, she was the first out.

In that instant, Eddie's mood had shifted; he'd been so impolite with Pop. And once they got into the cabin he'd stretched out on the bed, closed his eyes, and said not a word.

She'd finished unpacking now, and she sat down in a chair and just watched him lying there. Minutes went by, then he rubbed a hand across his eyes. He looked at her. A smile spread slowly across his handsome mouth. "This is nice, isn't it, Nancy?"

She nodded swiftly, feeling a surge of relief. "It's very nice, Eddie."

"I wonder if Pop's got some coffee on the stove? He always kept a big pot going. I could sure use some coffee."

"Why don't we go see?" she asked softly.

They walked back to the house. Joe Beacon opened the door. "Those are real nice cabins, Pop," Eddie said with enthusiasm. "I like what you've done here."

She watched Joe Beacon's eyes warm.

Eddie led them into the house. "You see, Nancy? This is a beautiful house. I'd rather own one of these than ten of those big tract jobs we saw coming in. This is a real house."

They followed, as he strode briskly toward the kitchen. "You still keep a pot of coffee going, Pop?"

"Yes," Joe said, a husky sound going into his voice. "You'll find it on the stove."

"This is great," Eddie said. "Home again. And it's just the way I told you it would be, isn't it, Nancy?"

"Yes," she said, certain in that moment that nothing would ever go wrong now, not ever, not so long as she lived. "It is."

Chapter 11

Joe Beacon enjoyed a pleasant talk with Eddie and Nancy over coffee. He'd again assured himself, after they'd gone back to their cabin, that Eddie was going to be all right. He had to be—because, God, how he'd grown to love that boy.

Those years before Nita and the boy had arrived had been self-sufficient but lonely years. And he had not truly known that until the house had been warmed by them. Then he'd become a husband and father all at once and found the taste of real and honest devotion. The boy had been a springing well of energy, curiosity, eagerness and inventiveness. He'd gotten angry with him sometimes, that was true, but other times Eddie had gotten to him in the heart so much that his throat had ached with it. Then, finally, he'd found his stride with the lad. And, oh, yes, he thought, that had been fine and wonderful.

Now, at first, he'd felt a strangeness in the presence of the boy. The way he'd acted right away—that hadn't helped. And, too, there had been a little time and distance between them. Eddie looked different: leaner, a bit older looking. But that was, he told himself, the natural way of it. Pretty soon it would be like it had been, between them. Being home again, in the country, was going to be the medicine for Eddie. But why, he asked himself, did Eddie need that kind of medicine? Then he shut his mind against that question.

Still, with Eddie back, he'd been thinking of Nita again; thinking of the way it had once been, with everything right and secure, with the future open brightly in front of them, like a good road you could see down, fast, clear of traffic, with the destination obvious, looking safe as walking. Then the road had turned bumpy, and what he'd seen had been a mirage after all. And there had been nothing secure or bright or safe in what he'd thought was going to be the future. And everything was gone, changed, and this was what he had left.

But all right, he thought. It was enough right now. Eddie was here. Eddie's bride was here, and he liked her. The days were moving. The sun, he thought, as he washed the cups and saucers he'd used with Eddie and Nancy, was moving to the west faster. The leaves would be coming off the locust trees pretty soon, and the rains would come. He would have that gate shut against the world then. And there would be privacy in this much of the land he still owned.

With the rains would come the dark, foggy days, and he had always liked them for the cattle—they brought the green the cattle could eat.

But now he liked them only for himself, because time seemed to stand still. There was no sunrise visible, no sun moving across the sky to prove that time was escaping, no sunset. Light just came and hung on evenly, not too much, not too little. And the fog would shroud the land and keep the moment eternal. The grass would grow, and the thistles would grow with it. But you wouldn't notice the growing, until one day you could see the grass was higher, wetting your boots now, and the thistles had become giant, with purple flowers sprung from their centers and the lower yellow-tinged leaves looking like saw-tooth blades. Then the rains would stop, and the grass would show in green-carpet smoothness. And pretty soon, like the thistles, it would dry again. And summer would come back. And he would have to open the gate again, to admit a year's passing.

But don't think of that, he thought. Don't waste a winter in your mind that hasn't happened yet. Hold out now through the close days ahead. Then shut the gate. And hold the land to yourself, the time to yourself; try not to think that time is always going away, that you can never stop it and own it when it is the best time.

Behind him, he heard a voice say, "Hello."

He turned to find Victor Day's wife in the kitchen doorway. She was wearing a simple pale blue dress. She was bare-legged and looked lovely. When she smiled at him, her smile was bright. She looked a little tense, he thought, but the anger he'd detected when she and Victor Day arrived seemed to be gone.

"Hello." He smiled back at her slowly and felt a quick physical reaction. She was a beautiful girl and she undoubtedly created the same response in any male. Moreover, Nita had been gone a long time now, and he'd enjoyed only an occasional time with a woman since. "Is everything all right?"

"Everything's fine. Just the small matter of food. Vic came in on a whim, really. I was coming over here earlier. But I saw that young couple go in to see you. So I took a walk around, down by the lake. It's absolutely beautiful here. I've built up a tremendous appetite."

He grinned. "Good." He opened the large refrigerator and showed her the meats. He wondered where Victor Day had met her and how long they had been married. He wondered if they had children. He was unreasonably sorry that she was married to Victor Day.

She selected the things she needed. He put them in a carton.

"My husband will pay you, Mr. Beacon."

"Fine, Mrs. Day."

She looked at the large coffeepot on the stove. He had just brewed a fresh supply. "That smells absolutely delicious."

"Would you like a cup?"

"I would love a cup."

He seated her at the table and brought her the coffee. He sat down, feeling a free and easy comfort with her.

"Delicious," she said, tasting the coffee. "The way it ought to be made."

"That comes with plenty of practice."

"Do you live here alone?"

He nodded.

"Do you like the freedom of that?"

He smiled wryly. "During the season there isn't too much freedom. Not when I fill those cabins. But I've got it through most of the winter."

"I see. But I was thinking about marriage. Typical female. Always curious about a man who isn't married."

"I was married." He did not elaborate, and she did not pursue it. He said, "My stepson just came in from Los Angeles this morning with his bride. They're in one of the cabins down the line. They're the ones you saw earlier."

"That must be nice for you."

"It is."

She took a pack of cigarettes from a pocket and put one between her lips. He lit it for her, as she watched his eyes. "Do you stay open just through the summer and fall then?"

"I'll close up in about a week, I think."

"Then?"

"Just live here. I don't get rich during the season. So I trap and hunt and fish for food."

"It sounds exciting."

He looked at her with faint surprise. "Does it? I didn't get the impression that you were the outdoors type."

"I'm not. I haven't been, anyway. But I've always liked the outdoors when I've been in it. And I believe people should always learn new things, new attitudes, new capacities. I—" She shrugged. Her smile turned slightly bitter. She'd been hurt in some way, he thought. Recently. And hurt down deep where the hurt was most painful. But she brightened her smile and asked:

"How did you happen to start this place?"

"Necessity," he said frankly. "This was a ranch once. It wouldn't support itself, so I turned to this."

"You don't like this?"

He motioned a hand. "I can't complain. At least, I shouldn't complain."

"But you preferred ranching?"

"Yes."

"Have you always done that? Before you went into this?"

He felt warmed by her curiosity and he talked with an intensity and volume of words he had given to few in these recent years. She listened carefully and said finally:

"I think you're a very kind and warmhearted man, Mr. Beacon. And some of the things you do, the hunting and trapping—I don't understand that, I'm afraid. It takes a certain cruelty to kill, doesn't it?"

"It depends upon how you kill."

"You mean there's a good way?"

"There's no good way to die. That's certain. But killing is natural for the predator. And we're predators, you and I."

"I never thought of it that way."

"The hunters and the hunted. One hides or runs. The other keeps moving forward, looking for the natural kill. God made it that way. So if you kill fairly, you're simply carrying out a natural law."

"How do you kill fairly?"

"So that you don't destroy uselessly. I kill to eat. That's not useless. Not so long as I accept the fact that I've got reason for survival. I think I have. I think any man or woman has. If I'm shooting, I try to kill swiftly. If I'm trapping, I don't leave my traps for long, so that whatever gets into one doesn't spend a long time suffering. I use mostly a small toothless trap that'll only get the smaller animals. It won't get a deer. They'll spring out of it because they've got a smooth, almost fleshless, leg above the hoof. I don't set the trap against a permanent fixing, because if an animal can't move a little it'll start chewing itself out. I hook the trap to a drag, which is a five-foot chain with double hooks on the end. They can go a little way, but they'll keep hooking into brush or bushes. So—" He stopped, smiling apologetically. "Sorry, I get going, and—"

The heavy male voice sounded sarcastically from the doorway:

"Don't stop, Beacon. That's really very good. Quite a lecture."

Victor Day stood in the doorway, eyes hard, face set stiffly.

Joe stood up. He could feel the man's anger. "I'm afraid I've been boring your wife with my philosophy about wild-life."

The girl also stood up. She smiled tightly. "He hasn't been boring me, Vic. It was quite fascinating. And the coffee was delicious, Mr. Beacon."

"Thank you," he said quietly. "Would you like a cup, Mr. Day?"

Day shook his head abruptly. "What I'm interested in is doing some hunting around here. How about renting a rifle, Beacon?"

"I'm sorry. It's the way I told you. I don't allow hunting. Just fishing."

"Not interested in fishing. If you had a good, fast stream I might pick up the limit. But I'm not fooling around with your stocked lake where they'll jump in your hand just because you like to please the tourists. I'm going after a good buck if you'll give me that rifle."

Joe felt his face flush. "Aside from the fact that the deer season ended three weeks ago and you don't have a deer tab, I just don't allow any kind of hunting here. I'm not saying you aren't a hunter I could trust. But this isn't a hunting lodge. I can't afford to allow shooting around here, when I've got guests who aren't interested in hunting. I allowed it for two weeks when I first started this. At the end of the second week I had a man climb that cliff you came down to get here. He started shooting at a spike buck, which happens to be illegal, and all he accomplished was shooting the back window out of the number-four cabin. You see my position."

Day's eyes were dark. "I see your position, all right, Beacon. And I'm still telling you—"

"Darling," the girl interrupted, her voice sardonic, "we owe Mr. Beacon for the food in that carton. Would you pay him, please? Then why don't you relax instead of wanting to go hunting? I think it would be so good for you, just to relax."

Chapter 12

It was midafternoon when Joe Beacon thought he had another guest. He went outside at the sound of the car, and saw that it was a sheriff's station wagon. He expected to see Sergeant Barnes, who occasionally came down for an easy chat. But instead he saw a stranger, a short, hefty sergeant.

The man came forward, looking over the grounds, hunching his broad shoulders.

"Yes, sergeant. What can I do for you?"

"I'm Sergeant Cole," the man said in a high voice. "I've taken over this territory. Mrs. Gronish, up at the junction, told me about you. I came down to look it over."

"Very good, sergeant. What happened to Sergeant Barnes?"

The man looked at him with a steady blinkless stare. "He's a lieutenant now."

"That's fine. I'm glad to hear that. But we'll miss him. He was a good man out here."

"He's in the office now. I'm in charge here from now on. You ever have any trouble in a place like this?"

"Not very often, no."

"How much is not very often?"

He looked at the man curiously. The sergeant appeared solidly impassive. His eyes never seemed to change expression. But there was hostility in his question, delivered in that oddly high voice. "Just what I said," Joe said, some of the friendliness going out of his voice.

"What kind of trouble?" the sergeant asked.

"The usual kind when you run what amounts to a motel." He felt the start of anger, because the man was obviously viewing him simply as the owner of a set of cabins and therefore open to suspicion by the law. Just because sometimes things took place in motels that the law did not approve.

"What do you mean, the usual kind? Shackups?"

The anger had started, all right, but he tried to control it. "People try that now and then, yes. I had some kids in here this morning. A set of them. They were drinking and obviously weren't married. So—"

"I was down on the Peninsula before I came up here," the sergeant said in a monotone. "This place was in my territory, and the man who ran it had himself a turnover about every two hours. I don't go for that in my territory. I shut his door and had the padlock put on. I don't fool around with that."

"Now wait a minute, sergeant. I don't run that kind of place. I think you could find that out by asking around."

"I ask for myself. I don't go by hearsay. Anything I'm asking you now is along the lines of duty. No more, no less. I work for the public, and I'm an officer of the law. I'm here for the good of the community. What happened with those kids? You give them a place?"

"I sent them out of here."

"How?"

Joe rubbed his jaw, staring at the man. "With a pistol, as it happened."

The sergeant's blue eyes narrowed very faintly. He hunched his shoulders again. "A pistol?"

"That's right. They didn't like the idea of being refused cabins.

They threatened to get rough. I showed them the pistol and they left."

The sergeant wagged his head slowly. "What makes you think you can go pulling a pistol on citizens?"

"I don't think it, sergeant. I did it. You have an objection? This happens to be my place you're standing on. I own the land and the property, and it's my understanding I have a right to protect it, along with myself. What do you think I'm going to do? Take a beating from a bunch of liquored-up kids?"

"You got a permit for that pistol?"

"Of course."

"Next time you get into trouble like that, you call the sheriff's office."

"All right. I'll do that. If there's enough time."

"The sheriff's got charge of the law out here," the sergeant said impassively. "I'm a sheriff's sergeant. You call our office when you've got trouble. We know how to handle things. There's an answer for everything, and we know what it is, because we're the law. A civilian isn't the law. You remember that."

Joe Beacon's jaw muscles ridged. The sergeant heeled around and marched back to his car. He drove it up the road and disappeared. Joe turned grimly and went back into his house.

It was just an hour later when he felt the anger return, seeing from his study window Victor Day stride into the clearing and throw that dead raccoon down on the short porch in front of the cabin.

Day, as he threw down that dead animal, felt the bruise at his knee where he'd torn a trouser leg, then rubbed a hand across the scratch at the bridge of his nose. He looked at the animal furiously. The soft-looking fur was bloody and matted. The head rested at an odd angle to the fat body. He shouldn't have gone after it, he knew now, because the thing had scared him. But he had, because he was driven to do something—and what he'd wanted to do was to kill something. Anything. And why not? he thought. The way it was going....

When he'd left Joe Beacon's kitchen with Lynn, he'd felt his temples pulsing with the beginning of his fury. It hadn't just been finding Lynn with Beacon, listening to him with that doe-eyed, innocent look. He'd learned to hate Beacon swiftly, that was true. But it wasn't just finding her with him. It was also because he'd realized, after the first few minutes, that Beacon was one of those who did not respect him. That was the deepest cut.

So he'd let Lynn go back to the cabin alone and had stopped at his car, where he'd removed the .22 pistol from the glove compartment. Beacon wouldn't rent him a gun, and he was, he'd thought, going to have to settle for the pistol. It was illegal to carry it concealed like that, but certain laws, legal or moral, were made only for certain people he'd convinced himself: stupid, weak, inept people. He was not among them.

But then he'd slipped out the magazine and opened the breech to discover no cartridges inside. He'd remembered that Frances had talked him into unloading the gun for the safety of the boys. Irritated, he'd searched the compartment and found the blue and yellow ammunition box. But there were only six shells in it. He'd sworn silently, positive that Beacon would not sell him more, and thought, for a moment, of driving out and buying extra ammunition someplace else. But he didn't trust leaving Lynn behind. She was in a mood now. And he'd seen the way she'd looked at Beacon.

So he'd shoved the pistol and cartridge box into his jacket pocket and turned around to find, with increasing irritation, a tall, lean, black-haired man with an off-centered left eye. The man grinned, examining him with a bright look. "Name's Roy Ives, mister."

Day nodded shortly and failed to give his own name.

Ives kept grinning and said, "That's a nice little popgun you got there."

"Yes," Day said coolly. "If you drive around out here in the country, you need some protection."

"That's right, ain't it? Man can't tell, can he? World ain't safe anymore. That's what I been telling everybody. You can't tell, and it ain't safe."

Day started to move past the man, but Ives shifted his position so that he blocked the way.

"That's a real pretty car, mister. That baby's got enough horses to reach the moon, ain't it?"

"Just about," he said impatiently.

Ives shook his head. "A man who buys himself a car like that, that man must be doing all right. Yes, sir."

Day looked at the Thunderbird parked in front of Roy Ives' cabin. It had to belong to this man, he was certain. On the highway, moving, the car would look good. But parked, you could see it clearly for what it was. Repainted on the outside and probably worn out on the inside. Driven by several owners. Probably wrecked at least once and pounded back together. Junk of what was once a good car. But this man would rather pay good cash for a piece of junk because it had once represented something special.

"It gets me around," he said of his own car, and waited for Ives to get out of his way.

Ives didn't move. He felt himself unreasonably irritated. "If you'll excuse me," he said brusquely.

"Why, sure, mister. Didn't mean to hold you up." Roy Ives smiled with obsequious eagerness, but his eyes remained coldly speculative.

Day brushed swiftly by and returned to his cabin. Lynn was brushing her hair in front of the bureau mirror. She didn't turn around and wouldn't look at him through the mirror. He strode across the room and dropped the pistol and ammunition on top of the bed. Finally she looked at him through the mirror and said, "What are you going to kill, Victor? Me?" Her voice was cool and edged with sarcasm. During the past month she'd tended to call him Victor instead of Vic.

"Let's not be too damn clever, shall we? Let's have a drink and cool off, shall we?"

She turned around, smiling tightly. "I don't need a drink to cool off, Victor."

He angrily splashed liquor into a glass for himself. He tossed the drink down, and felt the warmth flowing through him. She was unnerving him, and that bothered him. The liquor tasted and felt good. "I thought maybe you needed to cool off, after your session with Beacon."

"My God, Victor."

"It didn't take you long to switch targets, did it?"

"I'm not a hunter, Victor. I simply enjoyed a conversation with him."

"Oh, I *know* that."

"Don't be childish, Victor."

He put his glass down. He walked to her and put his arms around her. "I'm not going to be childish. What we're going to do now isn't for children."

She stood unresponding, turning her face away, saying nothing.

"Come on, Lynn," he whispered. He had always wanted her, but never more than now.

She remained wooden in his arms.

Roughly, he fumbled open the top button of her dress.

"I'm not going to fight you," she whispered. "But if you go on with it, it's going to be an animal thing. No soul. No heart. No emotion— not from me. You might do better, Victor, if you just got out of here and bought yourself a nice little prostitute on the way home. She might at least give you the illusion that—"

He spun away from her, face hot. He poured another drink and downed it swiftly. He shook out the shells from the box and loaded the pistol. Without another word, he walked out of the cabin....

Two hours later he slung the dead raccoon down on the small porch in front of the cabin.

He'd run across it a mile out in the woods. He hadn't expected to see a raccoon in the daylight, but this one was just ambling along when he spotted and spooked it. It took off like a cat, and he'd fired quickly. It crawled into the bushes and lay there, not moving. He thought it was dead.

He'd started into the bushes, then it turned around, resting on its back, with its paws held up like a Teddy bear's, watching him. He came in closer to get another good shot at it. It growled and swiped a paw at him. That scared him, and then he was angry because he didn't think a raccoon *could* scare him. He'd jumped back, firing two more shells into it.

But he didn't kill it. It wriggled backward, growling again, flashing those clawed paws in his direction. He'd never hunted alone before. Sweat broke out on his forehead. He pumped the last three bullets he had into that damned animal. It quit moving. But its eyes stayed open, watching him.

He started shaking. He didn't know what was wrong. He'd had nerve in the war, and later. But it was all draining out of him now. He got a thick fallen branch and went with that into the bushes. He pounded at the animal. It didn't swing its claws at him anymore. And it wasn't growling now. It was whimpering. Shaking and sweating, he'd pounded again and again, but he couldn't kill it. At last, forcing himself to do it, he reached down and got hold of a rear leg. Gasping with increasing fright, thinking that it might somehow still bite or claw him, he jerked it out from the bushes and swung it against a tree trunk.

That did it.

Joe came out of his house, as Day rapped sharply on his cabin door. He saw Day's wife open the door and stare down at the animal, frowning.

"Little present for you," Day said, and Joe was now certain the man had been drinking.

The girl shook her head. "What's the matter with you, Vic? Why did you have to do that?"

"I happened to want to do a little hunting, that's all. I'll have a hat made out of that fur for you."

"I would rather you just take it away, please."

Now, Joe saw as he moved across the clearing, Roy Ives had opened his door and stepped outside. Behind him, his wife appeared in the doorway, dressed in those white Capris and red shirt, and, Joe Beacon was certain, not a thing else.

"Listen," Day said loudly to his wife, "apparently you can look like a wide-eyed schoolgirl when that Beacon is talking about killing animals, but when I—"

"When you do it," Joe snapped, "you're breaking the rules. I thought I told you I don't allow hunting on this land."

Day turned around, a mean look in his eyes. He glared at Joe, then at Roy Ives, who ambled over with a smile, then at Flo, standing in the doorway; she smiled at him and shifted her hips; Day watched her for several seconds. Then he looked back at Joe and said:

"So—I'll take him back."

Roy Ives laughed loudly and looked down at the raccoon, shaking his head. "Man, you purely shot the whoop out of that, didn't you?"

"I got him."

"You sure did. Them things can get stubborn, can't they? I had me one near took my eyes out once. Had to kick him in the head and bust out his brains, before he gave up."

"Why don't you just get rid of it, Victor?" the girl said thinly.

"You don't want it?" Ives asked quickly.

"No," Day said, his eyes grazing Joe Beacon's, then returning to look at the smiling Flo in the doorway again. "We don't want it."

Ives could not help but see the obvious interest in Day's expression as he looked at Ives' wife, Joe was certain. And behind Ives' smile, there was a look of cold hatred. He did not hate Victor Day himself, Joe thought, but the man was certainly irritating him. "If you didn't want it," he said coldly; "then it was a waste to kill it, wasn't it?"

"I wouldn't say that," Ives said. "What I mean, me and Flo there, we could use him. I'll just take him out back and skin him, then I'll show Flo how to make the best old coon stew you'd ever want to taste."

"Take him then," Day said.

"Do that," Joe said. "And then I would appreciate it, Mr. Day, if that's the last thing you kill while you're in this camp. I'll repeat it to you— I don't allow any hunting of any kind on this land."

Ives looked fondly at the raccoon, then shifted his eyes toward Joe. "Now that's news to me, Beacon. I didn't know about that no-hunting business. Figured it came with the cabin. Caught me four trout in that lake already. Is that hunting? That's fishing, ain't it?"

"Yes," Joe said, controlling his temper. "And there's a fee for that, in case you didn't know."

"Didn't," Ives said. "I just fixed me up a hook off a plain piece of cord and a good straight limb I cut off. Fish came jumping up to meet me. There's a fee?"

"It's posted on the back of your cabin door and down by the dock at the lake. Per fish."

"Well, by, God. I just missed that, I reckon. See, me and Flo went and ate them already, so we couldn't throw them back anyway. I'm sure sorry about that. Got me a rabbit earlier too. Little bitty rabbit come out of the brush, and I quick rocked him. Along with this raccoon, me and Flo got ourselves well fixed. Set up a couple of deadfalls out there for some other stuff. But now if you don't allow it, why—"

"I don't," Joe snapped. "And take those deadfalls down." He looked at the raccoon again, then at Victor Day. "I don't want any more of this going on. I hope that's clear by now." He turned abruptly and strode back to his house.

Ives watched him go, shaking his head sadly. "Now that didn't put him in no good mood, did it?"

Day pushed past him, motioning Lynn Marsey inside. He shut the door behind them, hard.

Ives shrugged. Then he picked up the raccoon by its back feet. He strode back toward Flo, swinging it back and forth as he walked. "I'm going out back and cut this here up. You want to come along and watch?"

"Hell, no."

Ives' eyes tightened at the corners. "Rather watch other things, huh? Like that fellow who shot this here up and owns that Lincoln Continental? Is that it?"

"Why don't you figure it out?" Flo said.

She shut the door. He walked on, around the cabin. He didn't have to figure anything out, he thought. He'd already figured out everything.

Chapter 13

Rosaline and Norris Glenn had missed Victor Day's return, because an hour earlier they had set out on a walk, north from the clearing. At first, Norris had been nervous and doubtful, fearing that some kind of animal might very well come leaping out of the bushes at them. But Rosalind insisted that all wild animals were really afraid of human beings and that they had nothing to worry about. Norris, carrying a sketch pad in one hand, his pockets filled with drawing pencils, had allowed her to lead him into the woods. Now, in the early afternoon, he had finally relaxed enough to join Rosalind in attempting to name the birds they saw.

"There," Rosalind whispered, as they stopped in a sun-drenched path, looking up at the foliage. "I do believe that's your California woodpecker."

"It's a woodpecker, all right," Norris agreed. "Look at him go."

"It's your California woodpecker," Rosalind said definitely.

"I'll bet it is."

"It is," she nodded.

They moved on. A covey of fat birds fluttered out of a thicket with a great volume of noise. Norris jumped, but then realized what the sound was.

"Quail!" Rosalind said. "Lovely, lovely quail! Can you imagine anyone hunting those birds? What kind of person would do that?"

"A savage," Norris stated.

"Don't you want to sketch them, darling?" Rosalind asked.

"Well," Norris said, "maybe you've got something."

He wiped the surface of a log with his handkerchief and sat down. He closed his eyes. "I'm just going to let it happen. I don't want to look at another quail now, until I get this true impression right from my being."

"I won't say a word," Rosalind promised.

Norris worked swiftly, using a charcoal pencil, and then said, "I think that gets it."

Rosalind looked at the paper. There were five small dark V marks, nothing else to mar the whiteness. She nodded slowly. "Yes. I see. Utterly simple and terribly effective."

Norris smiled with pleasure. "Do you really think so?"

"This is really terribly good, Norris, if I may say so."

He re-examined his drawing. "It just came out. Nothing but the white, and the birds in flight."

"Well, don't forget to sign it. Then let me carry it. I'll be very careful. I just think this might be one you'll want to place into competition somewhere."

Norris carefully signed his name across a bottom corner. "And I wouldn't have gotten it if we hadn't come here. It would just have been lost."

"Which proves," Rosalind said, "the absolute value of being on location, so to speak."

They strolled back toward the camp as the sun edged westward and sunlight came down in shafts on the path in sharper angles. Norris felt the elation of having created and created well. He followed Rosalind with a bouncing stride, watching with pride the careful way she carried his drawing. He started to hum the melody of an old English folk song they'd heard at one of their Bohemian parties when Rosalind came to an abrupt halt, gasping.

Norris froze. "What's the matter?" he whispered.

She slowly lifted a hand and pointed ahead. Norris peered over her shoulder. Ten feet ahead of them, lying across a sun-warmed patch of path, stretched a very large snake.

"Oh, God!" Norris whispered.

"It's a rattlesnake!"

"Oh, dear God!"

"Don't move! It'll coil and strike!"

"What are we going to do?"

Rosalind was silent for a moment, then she said, "Scream!"

She opened her mouth and did exactly that. The sound echoed through the woods. Then the snake lifted its head slightly and wriggled forward. Norris opened his own mouth and joined Rosalind with loud whooping shouts.

He didn't know how long they kept that up. It seemed like hours, though he later realized that it had probably been only minutes. The snake had stopped moving, and again lay motionless. Finally there was the sound of someone running toward them on the path from the camp.

Joe Beacon came into view, and Rosalind, just before he ran directly over the snake, pointed and shouted, "Rattler!"

Joe came to a stop and hopped back with swift agility. Norris saw a pistol in his hand. He then darted sideways, putting Norris and Rosalind out of range, and fired at the snake. The snake wriggled forward swiftly as the bullet bit into its body just behind the head. Joe fired again, and the snake, hit a second time, curled its body, its head twisting in Joe's direction. Norris watched in horror as the snake created a hooking pattern with its body, head bobbing toward the man shooting at it. Then Joe Beacon fired again, and the snake slowly dropped its head and started a series of slow, coiling motions. Joe fired twice more; it was dead.

Face tense, he looked at Norris and Rosalind. "Are you all right?"

"Yes," Rosalind whispered.

Joe moved to the snake and looked at it carefully. He looped it on the end of the pistol barrel and held it up, shaking his head. "It's not a rattlesnake. Just a gopher snake. Sorry I killed it—they do a lot of good. But they look like rattlers, and I didn't have time to do anything else." He tossed the snake into the brush. "Sorry it scared you."

Norris stood there, blinking, hearing others coming up the path now. He plunged into the brush in the opposite direction from where Joe Beacon had tossed the snake and was sick. Then he thought of other snakes, and jumped back to the path. He ran toward the camp. He could hear Rosalind calling. But he didn't stop until he'd reached their cabin. He stumbled inside and fell on the bed. He closed his eyes and saw the snake crooked, with its head darting forward. He was certain that he'd seen the holes in it where Joe Beacon's bullets had torn through. "Oh, God," he moaned.

"Poor dear," Rosalind whispered.

"Oh, God, seeing it *die*. Jerking and coiling...."

"Hush," Rosalind insisted, putting herself down beside him, almost smothering him with her comfort. "Don't think about it."

"Can't help it," he moaned. "Never forget it. Jerking and coiling and *dying*. Oh, dear God ...!"

Chapter 14

From the highway above the camp, drivers slowed at that point of vantage where the ocean was visible across the golden hills and admired the view of the sun, a fiery red circle, as it touched the blue of the Pacific. There was a moment when the circle seemed to be floating atop the sea, fire upon water. Then the sea took it, as yellow and pink and orange rays flared across the sky. Darkness came then, and the night animals left their shelters to prowl for food.

Joe, in the grateful solitude of his house, read and smoked his pipe.

He had found himself still faintly angry at the hunting performed that day by Victor Day and Roy Ives. And he was still slightly exasperated with the Glenns for having sent him tearing down that path to kill a harmless snake; he couldn't really blame them, but if they had not been here it wouldn't have happened. On the other hand, he was grateful that Eddie had seemed, the rest of the day, the Eddie of other days. And that had been worth all the rest of it.

He was feeling those emotions, and he was also continuing to feel the emotion created by the girl, the wife of Victor Day; that one was the one that finally remained with him as he went to bed. He was thinking of her still, of her looks, the sound of her voice, when he fell asleep....

The sound seemed, at first, to be part of a dream. Then he came completely awake, and realized that someone was shouting and pounding on his front door. He got out of bed, grabbed trousers and shirt and got into them as he rushed through the house. He knew now that it was Eddie. The pounding shook the door. Eddie's voice was near a scream.

He threw open the door and looked at his stepson's pale face. "Eddie—what's the matter?"

Eddie shook his head, jerking his shoulders nervously. "Nancy!"

"Has something happened to Nancy?"

Lights flared on in the Iveses' cabin. Then other windows glowed with light. Eddie's yelling had been loud and intense. Roy Ives, wearing trousers and T shirt, opened his door. Then Victor Day appeared in his doorway, hair rumpled, blinking angrily.

Eddie shook his head. "She's gone, Pop."

"Gone?"

Now the Glenns' cabin door opened very slightly, and Norris peered out through the crack.

"I went to sleep," Eddie said. "Early. When I woke up, she was gone."

"Well, but—" Joe began.

"So I got dressed and went outside. I thought maybe she just stepped out for some air or something. But she's not around anywhere. I ran on down to the lake. I called for her. Nothing. Something's wrong, Pop!"

His voice was rising again to a scream. Joe shook his shoulders firmly.

"All right, Eddie," he said. "It's going to be all right." He looked down the line of cabins. Eddie's car was still in place, and so she had not, for some reason, driven away in that. "She probably just took a midnight walk."

"Listen, Pop," Eddie said tensely. "She hasn't got a strong heart. Why doesn't she come back? She could hear me shouting!"

Roy Ives came out and called, "What all's the matter over there, anyhow?"

"My stepson's wife is missing," Joe said. "I think I'd better go out and look for her. Sorry to disturb all of you people this way. But if anybody wants to help, I'd be mighty grateful."

Ives shrugged. "I'll get my damn shoes on. Where'd she go, anyway?"

"We don't know," Joe said calmly. "We'll just have to take a look."

Day shut his door, as did the Glenns. Joe said to Eddie: "I'll get my boots on, Eddie. You stay calm now."

Joe switched on the floodlights which lighted the camp's clearing. As he pulled on his boots and then got two powerful flashlights from a drawer, Roy Ives, in his cabin, put on his shoes. Flo, sitting up sleepily in bed, wearing not a thing, said, "Oh, this is some swell place to stay, all right. Damn old dump of a cabin. People yelling most every time you turn around. Snakes. Damn old raccoon. That stew gave me indigestion. Now we can't sleep worth a—"

"Shut up, Flo. Girl went and disappeared."

"That's what I'd do, if it was up to me. Disappear right out of here."

"Why don't you go back to sleep?"

"Hell, that's what I'm gonna do."

Victor Day, in his cabin, stumbled into the bathroom after he'd shut the door and splashed water over his face. He was still dressed. Lynn had undressed in the bath earlier that evening, then appeared in her robe. She wouldn't let him touch her—wouldn't, just by looking at him coldly, until he was so infuriated he didn't want to touch her. Instead he'd begun drinking again after dinner, and when the liquor had dulled him enough, he'd simply lain down on the couch and fallen asleep—until all that shouting awakened him. He was not entirely sober now, even after the sleep, but he was sober enough to know that coming here in the first place had been a huge mistake. He would correct that in the morning by getting out.

Lynn had got up now. She was dressed in her robe again. He turned around and looked at her with reddened eyes. "Now what's the matter?"

"Apparently something's the matter out there—that boy's wife is gone."

"I think I'm well aware enough of that, after all that goddam shouting."

"Are you going to help?"

He looked at her, then walked past her and put on his jacket. He went out without another word and stood shivering in the cool night air until Joe Beacon came out of his house with Eddie.

The natural light, as the moon grew smaller in its crossing of the sky, was dimming. But there was still a pale glow surrounding the brighter light of the floodlighted clearing. Norris Glenn opened his door a crack again and, dressed now, peered out once more.

"You don't even have a flashlight," Rosalind said. "And you are simply not going, Norris. Don't be foolish."

He wagged his head. "There are times when a man's personal courage is at stake."

"Then I'm going too."

"All right," Norris said with obvious relief, "if you insist."

He stepped outside, forcing himself to walk with his head high to where Beacon stood with Eddie, Victor Day and Roy Ives. Rosalind swiftly tied a kerchief over her hair and came running after him.

"This is very good of all of you," Joe Beacon said. "Did anyone bring a flashlight?"

"I got me a good one," Roy Ives said.

"I have one," Victor Day said.

"We don't," Rosalind said.

"All right," Joe Beacon said, handing Norris one. "Eddie, you can—"

"I don't need a flashlight," Eddie said in a peculiarly tight voice. "I know this land like my own mind. Let's get going. What's the matter that she doesn't come in? What's happened to her, Pop?"

"We'll find her, boy," Ives grinned. "She just liked to take out on a walk, that's all. You can't figure out no woman. You just got to take 'em for what they're worth and then go looking for 'em when they disappear on you. You just know she ain't in no trouble, that's all. You take that from a man from the north. North Texas, boy, right up there from north Dallas, Texas."

Roy Ives laughed, but no one else did. Joe gave quick instructions about the way to conduct the search. Then they all fanned out from the clearing, moving into the woods.

They proceeded separately, except Norris and Rosalind Glenn, who went together down the widest path toward the lake. Norris began trembling almost as soon as he started down the path; he could see very clearly again, in his mind, the way that snake had died. He had been moving ahead of Rosalind, but now he was losing his nerve, hating himself for it, and he knew that Rosalind instantly sensed his growing fear.

"Here," she said. She took the flashlight from his hand and moved resolutely ahead of him, her large athletic body swinging along with strong strides. Norris clenched his hands and followed.

The memory of that snake jerking its head up, twisting and darting in the direction of Joe Beacon as he fired at it, grew in intensity; and Norris, mouth dry, stomach tightening, suddenly felt unable to go on. He stopped and closed his eyes, wishing to God that he had never joined in this thing in the first place. He didn't even *know* that girl. And what business had she to run off in the middle of the night and get lost?

At last he forced his eyes open and could see in the dimming moonlight that Rosalind was no longer in sight. He knew she had gone striding ahead, certain that he was behind her. He bounded ahead, then he saw something dark lying across the path ahead of him. He made a small sound of terror and danced sideways. He ran full into a tangle of vines and tripped to his knees. The vines, as his imagination took over, became dozens of small snakes. He tore himself out of the tangle and plunged back on to the path. He looked at that thing lying across the path, and very slowly his reasoning told him that it was not a snake, but only a broken branch lying there. Yet the limb would not become total reality for him.

He ran down the path. He wanted to call out loudly, but something prevented him. He couldn't give away his weakness to the others by yelling for his wife.

He reached the shore of the lake and spun wildly, searching the dimly lit shoreline. Rosalind was nowhere in sight. He finally froze, trying to get hold of his nerves. Then he heard the sound: a *yip-yip, yip-yip*, high and wild, sounding like the cry of some inhuman thing.

He waited, breathing hard. Then he heard something crashing through the brush. But nothing appeared. There was only the lake resting quietly under the light of the dimming moon.

A fish broke surface, and Norris ran wildly away from the dark water, ran straight away from the water, onto a path. Then he stumbled into something. He fell and smashed his face against dirt and pine needles. When he raised his head, he was staring at a white face, lying not six inches from his own.

His mind jumbled into a paralysis of fear. Her face was marble-frozen in the dying moonlight. He saw one eye, staring up, unmoving. He saw the whole of her, lying there in the unnatural sprawl of what he knew was *death*.

He gasped weakly, and could make no more sound. He could not take his eyes from her.

Joe Beacon knew, by the cry of the coyote, that one was sniffing about nearby and had found something. It was more than knowledge. He also had a feeling. And as he moved swiftly toward the sound of that *yip-yip*, he felt apprehension rise strongly.

Flashlight in hand, he cut down to the lake, then up the trail where he'd placed the coyote's call. The beam of the flash caught the girl first, then Norris Glenn, staring at the light with wide, frightened eyes.

Joe touched the girl's face. She was, he knew, dead. He put a hand out to Norris Glenn. "Are you all right?"

"She's *dead*," Norris managed to say.

Joe pulled Norris to his feet, feeling suddenly heartsick. He'd liked her. He could have loved her. And Eddie....

"You found her like this?" Joe Beacon said tightly.

Norris Glenn nodded, then stumbled away, retching.

Joe looked down at the body, shifted the beam and for the first time saw the trap gleaming as it continued to bite into the dead girl's ankle. "My God," he whispered. Then he yelled, "Eddie!"

He regretted shouting the instant he'd done it, because he should have tried to protect Eddie from seeing her this way. But he was not thinking well right now.

Eddie came crashing through brush. Joe started to break the trap, then Eddie came up. Joe turned, shaking his head, finding no words.

Eddie blinked once, then dove forward, grabbing the trap. He screamed, tearing at it uselessly. Joe closed his arms around him from behind. "Eddie, easy...."

The others were coming now, and Eddie kept screaming, wriggling out of his grasp. The boy went at the trap again, jerking at it.

"Eddie!" Joe said. He grabbed the boy's shoulder, spun him and slapped him hard across the face.

Eddie stared at Joe. Then he looked at the body. He walked around it slowly. Finally he bent and took her left hand in his. He drew the wedding band from her finger and looked at it. He looked up at Joe. Then he put the wedding band back on her finger. He held the hand and looked at it and then let it drop to the ground. "It's cold. Her hand's cold. And stiff...."

"Come on, Eddie," Joe said, and lifted him to his feet. Then the boy stood silently, not moving anymore, just staring at the motionless figure at their feet.

Roy Ives, then Victor Day and Rosalind Glenn arrived. Day and Ives stared at the body. Rosalind saw it, gasped, then ran to Norris. Day said loudly, "What the hell's the matter with her?"

"She's dead," Joe said. "If you'll just go back to the camp, I'll take care of this. I'd appreciate it if you'll stay in your cabins, please."

"Dead?" Victor Day said angrily.

"Man," Roy Ives said, "she is, ain't she?"

They moved away, followed by the Glenns. Eddie stood beside Joe, stiffly but quietly.

"Eddie—" Joe began.

"Can't you get that trap off her, Pop?" Eddie said in a peculiarly high-pitched voice.

"Yes," Joe said. He kneeled swiftly and broke the trap. He took off his jacket and covered her face. He straightened and looked at Eddie again. "I'm sorry, Eddie. It must have been her heart. I don't know how this—"

"Pop," Eddie said, shaking his head, his eyes looking at Joe with an odd expression, "you shouldn't have put a trap here."

Joe Beacon frowned. "I didn't set that trap. You know I wouldn't—" He stopped, looking at Eddie's eyes, and then he knew quite suddenly that words were going to do no good, no good at all.

Chapter 15

Twenty minutes after Joe Beacon's telephone call to the sheriff's office, an ambulance carrying a doctor and two assistants rolled down the road from the highway. Accompanying it were two sheriff's cars; two deputies were in one, a lone Sergeant Albert Cole in the other. Joe Beacon, ringed by everyone from the cabins except his silent stepson, who remained with the body, waited on his front porch.

He watched the thick-shouldered sergeant climb from the car and come striding sullenly forward. The floodlights were still on, illuminating the clearing brightly; but the natural morning light was beginning to appear now. Against the shock of having found Nancy dead, Joe found himself wondering without any real curiosity if Sergeant Albert Cole ever slept so that he would be required to leave his duty.

The sergeant hitched his shoulders as he came to a stop in front of the porch and said in his high, toneless voice, "What happened here?"

"A girl—my stepson's wife—got caught in a trap, sergeant."

The other two deputies came up now and stood behind the sergeant. The doctor and the two medics came forward from the ambulance. "What kind of trap?" the sergeant asked impassively.

"The kind you use for hunting."

"She's dead, is that right?" the sergeant said. "That's the report I got."

"Yes, she's dead."

The sergeant turned to one of the deputies. "Use my radio. Tell them she's dead. She was when we arrived."

"Is that all then?" Victor Day demanded suddenly. He glared at the sergeant. "My wife and I are quite anxious to be on our way."

"Vic," Lynn Marsey said, "this is hardly a time to be thinking of ourselves. After all—"

"Do you want to stay here?" he said angrily. "Stay here, then. I've got an important day coming up."

Joe saw another car coming down the road. It bucked to a halt, and a man carrying a camera got out on one side; another got out on the other side with a small notebook in one hand. Joe Beacon looked back at Victor Day and saw more panic in his face than he had yet seen the man demonstrate. "I'm leaving," Day announced and strode down the steps of the porch. He had reached the glimmering Lincoln Continental, when the sergeant said:

"I don't want anybody leaving here."

Day turned his head around, staring at the sergeant. "What do you mean you don't want anybody leaving here? This has nothing to do with me. The girl's dead, isn't she?"

"Yes, for God's sake!" Joe said harshly. "She's lying out there in the woods this very moment. That boy's with her. Now can't we get this over as quickly as possible?"

The sergeant licked his lips. "I'm a sergeant in the sheriff's office. This is the sheriff's jurisdiction. That's why I'm in charge. I don't want anybody leaving here. Not one person, until I say so. We'll get this done just as quickly as it can be done right. But it's going to be done right. And I'm the one who's going to see that it's done right." He waited, looking slowly around at every face, then said to one of the deputies, "Stay here and see that nobody leaves who was here when the victim died."

"Right, sergeant."

The sergeant nodded shortly to Joe Beacon. "Where is she?"

Joe stepped off the porch and led them through the woods. Eddie Crayne was kneeling beside her body. When he heard them approaching, he turned and looked at them with blank eyes. The doctor, a lean, young-looking man, bent swiftly beside the body. Eddie stared at him.

"It's the doctor, Eddie," Joe said, and helped the boy to his feet again.

The doctor examined the girl, as the sergeant watched with eyes that never seemed to blink. Then the doctor looked up at Joe Beacon. "It wasn't the trap."

"No," Joe said. "She had a history of a bad heart. Didn't she, Eddie?"

Eddie stared at the doctor. He didn't answer.

"She had rheumatic fever when she was a child," Joe explained. "I imagine when she stepped in the trap, she might have panicked. Then—" He shrugged.

Others were coming through the woods: more reporters and photographers from the Peninsula papers. The first flash bulb exploded. Eddie Crayne made a sound and started toward the photographer. Joe caught his arm and held him tightly. "Easy."

"All right," the sergeant said. "You say you imagine she might have panicked when she stepped in the trap?"

"It seems logical."

"I think so," the doctor said, straightening. "If she had that kind of history."

"What we're not going to do here," the sergeant pronounced, "is imagine this or that, or think this or that, just on account of anything's logical. We're going to find out what happened here, just the way it did."

Roy Ives, who had followed the group, looked at the sergeant with bright eyes. "Well, this-here little girl had this bum heart and she's out takin' herself a bitty walk in the woods and she falls down and gets her foot hooked into a four and a half Newhouse like that, she just might go and do what she did, huh? Now that ain't no federal case, is it?"

"Never mind, Ives," Joe said, watching the sergeant turn his impassive stare on Ives. "Let's just try to co-operate and get it over. Is there anything else you need to know, sergeant?" The sergeant hitched his shoulders again and said to the medics, "You can put her into the ambulance now." To the doctor he said, "I want to get your report before you leave." Then, to everyone else, "I want everyone who was in this camp when she died to stay in this camp. I've got a report to turn in, and it's going to be turned in complete."

The medics lifted the body to a stretcher and moved with it carefully through the woods to the ambulance. There, the sergeant asked Joe for use of his living-room and then, coldly, asked Joe Beacon, the Iveses, Victor Day and Lynn Marsey, and the Glenns to wait for him there. He dismissed the other two deputies, radioed to his headquarters that he was going to conduct a thorough interrogation on this case, and then ordered, with mounting authority, the newsmen to remain outside until his investigation was completed. The newsmen argued with him briefly, then most of them left; a photographer and two reporters remained, grumbling, lighting up cigarettes. The ambulance roared up the grade, siren sounding near the top, the sound echoing down across the valley, through the chilly, ghostly morning.

The sergeant drew a clipboard from the interior of his station wagon, then marched inside with it, to eye, one after another, without a trace of emotion that Joe could detect, the group of people staring back at him—including Eddie Crayne, who had not indicated a desire to accompany the body of Nancy down to the Peninsula, and who seemed now only vaguely aware that he was still a part of this world from which his wife had abruptly escaped. "All right," the sergeant said, "is this everyone who was here when she died?"

"I think so," Joe said. He had come to dislike the man's looks, manner, and obviously stubborn desire to follow any line selected. He didn't want Eddie to have to hear any more of this. But the sergeant went on, resolutely:

"And your name is Beacon?"

"Yes. Joe Beacon."

The sergeant turned and looked at the Glenns. Norris sat in a large chair, white-faced and shivering. Rosalind stood behind him.

"Your name," the sergeant said.

"I'm Rosalind Glenn," Rosalind said firmly. "This is my husband, Norris. He's an artist and a writer, who—"

"I don't need that," the sergeant said shortly, and turned to the Iveses. "You?"

Flo Ives sat on a sofa with her legs doubled, mouth pouting, small hands closed in her lap. She still looked sleepy, and Joe Beacon was certain that she'd slept through everything until her husband had brought her out of the cabin after they'd found Nancy. Roy Ives sat beside her, long legs stretched out, a humorless smile remaining steadily on his mouth. "How long," Flo said, "have we got to hang around here like this, anyway?"

"He didn't ask for that," Roy Ives grinned. "He asked for our names. Ives, officer," he said. "Roy Ives, out of Texas. And this here's my bride, Flo. This still don't look like no federal case to me. What it looks like is—"

"And you?" the sergeant interrupted, wheeling to stare impassively at Victor Day.

Victor Day, Joe was positive, had consumed even more liquor since they'd come back from the woods. He stood beside the fireplace, leaning heavily against the mantel, his eyes faintly filmed, his cheeks ruddy. The girl sat in front of him, erect, smoking a cigarette, her face serious and, Joe Beacon thought, dramatically beautiful.

"Victor Day," Day snapped to the sergeant.

"This is your wife?"

"Certainly. What's the meaning of all this, anyway, sergeant? Simply because of an unfortunate accident—"

The sergeant turned to Eddie. "Your name?"

"Edward Crayne," Joe Beacon answered swiftly.

"And it was his wife?"

Eddie looked at him without a word, and Joe Beacon said, "Yes, it was his wife Nancy. And can't you hurry this, sergeant?"

"Who found her?" The sergeant looked from face to face. Norris Glenn made a small choking sound. Rosalind said quickly, "My husband, sergeant."

"How?"

"That poor young man there," she said, nodding toward Eddie, "was shouting that his wife disappeared. So we all gathered outside to search for her. Norris and I went down this path. Only we got separated. Then he just happened to trip into her—"

Norris bent down, shutting his eyes, turning even paler. Rosalind leaned over him and stroked him comfortingly. "Poor, poor dear...."

"She was in the trap?" the sergeant asked Norris.

Norris bobbed his head weakly.

"What part of her?"

"Is this really necessary, sergeant?" Joe said, looking at Eddie again. "She apparently tripped and stepped into that trap. Her ankle was caught. I broke the trap after she was found. But I don't see where—"

"What was she doing out there in the middle of the night?" the sergeant asked.

"We don't know that," Joe answered sharply. "Apparently she just got up and decided to take a walk in the moonlight." The sergeant turned to him directly and stared at him with his pale blue eyes. "How come you had a trap like that out there where somebody could walk into it?"

He took a breath, fighting anger and resentment. This had been coming, and he'd been expecting it. "I didn't have that trap out there, sergeant."

"What do you mean?"

"I didn't set that trap."

"Somebody set it."

"That's obviously true. But the last time I saw it, it was hanging inside my shed."

Across the room Victor Day lit a cigarette. "It didn't walk out there and set itself, did it, Beacon?"

"No, it didn't."

"It was your trap, wasn't it?" the sergeant asked.

"Yes," Joe said.

"And you didn't set it?"

"That's what I said."

"When did you see it last?"

"Yesterday morning."

"Where?"

"In the shed."

"What's the shed?"

"The pine shed, beside the house."

"Somebody had to get it from the shed and out to where it was set."

"That seems to be what happened. The shed wasn't locked." Joe looked at Eddie, who remained standing silently, arms hanging straight at his sides.

"Who did that?" the sergeant asked.

"I don't know, sergeant."

The sergeant looked around the room, from face to face again. "Somebody did that. Somebody in this room."

"Oh, come on!" Victor Day said loudly. "It was your trap, Beacon. I'm sorry the girl died. Nobody wants to be responsible for a thing like that. But don't try to shift the blame on to us."

The sergeant lifted the pencil he'd been using to scratch out his report and pointed it at Day. "I'm asking the questions here." Day looked at the man with disgust, then down at the girl in front of him, as though he were blaming her for every inconvenience of this. He didn't like Victor Day, Joe thought, and he didn't like the sergeant. He didn't like Roy Ives very much either. At this moment, he was certain there were not very many people he particularly cared for. He looked at Eddie and thought: *if only they hadn't come here, and this hadn't happened....*

"Now I'm going to ask one thing here," the sergeant said in his high voice. "I'd like an answer to it. Somebody went out and set that trap. Now who was the one who did it?"

Nobody answered.

The sergeant waited, then went on persistently, "This is for the record, because it's got to be right on the record. Now who went out and set it?"

Again, there was no response, until finally Ives said, "Why don't you go and fingerprint it, officer?"

The sergeant turned his unblinking eyes on him and said, "There's no place on that trap that'll hold a fingerprint. I checked that. But it's my determination about how this investigation is going to be performed. Did you set that trap, Ives?"

"Me? I didn't even know no trap like that was around."

"Day?"

"Of course not!"

"Glenn?"

"My God!" Norris shook his head, looking appalled. "I wouldn't even know how!"

Then Joe saw Eddie look again at all of them, one after another, and turn and walk out.

"Where's he going?" the sergeant demanded.

"I think he's heard enough about now," Joe said. "I don't blame him. My God, this is his wife you're talking about."

"And why go on with this?" Day said. "The girl had a bad heart. Something like this would have happened sooner or later. So what's the point? The trap belongs to Beacon there. This is his responsibility, sergeant."

"And I repeat," Joe said, "that I didn't set that trap."

"Why try to sell that, Beacon? I heard you talking to my wife. What was it? The ethics of killing? You love to kill things in those traps of yours, don't you? Why deny it?"

"If I remember correctly," Joe said tensely, "I saw you bring in a raccoon you'd shot hell out of for no particular good reason. Don't talk about the ethics of killing to me."

"What is that supposed to mean?" Day said, his face turning even more flushed. "You're accusing me of setting that trap?"

"I'm not accusing you of anything. But if you want to know, yes, I think you could have set it."

"Now wait a minute, Beacon! Why would I have done that?"

"How about for ego reasons?" Joe snapped. "You went out hunting with your pistol against my orders, and the reason you did was because you wanted to kill something. Anything. All you could get was a little raccoon. So you killed it. All right. What if you happened to have found that trap in the shed? Maybe you thought you could get a deer with it. That trap was big enough. Maybe you wanted the horns, so you could put them up on a wall at home and tell your friends you shot the deer with a perfect neck shot."

He watched Victor Day hunch his shoulders, then start toward him across the room.

"All right," the sergeant said, putting up his hand. "I'm in charge of the questioning here. I'm the one who's going to say what's what. You stay where you were, Day."

Victor Day, eyes mean, moved back behind the girl.

The sergeant turned back to Joe. "You trap out here, don't you? You owned the trap."

"I've got several traps, yes. And certainly I trap out here. But I would never put a trap in a place like that, where somebody could accidentally step into it. Years ago, when my stepson and his mother were living here, a trap in that place would be all right. We all knew where it was. I had fencing halfway along the lake, so the cattle couldn't get into this part. We didn't have a dog. It would have been all right then. But not today. As a matter of fact, I don't set traps of any kind when the motel season's on. I wouldn't take that chance. Certainly not with a trap that large. I haven't used that large a trap for years."

"All right," the sergeant said. "But you know all about that kind of trap, don't you? It was yours, wasn't it?"

Joe felt his anger burning just below his control. The sergeant had an infuriating way of peering at you, of coming back to the same thought, of pressing with it. "I've admitted that."

"That's a big trap," the sergeant said. "It's hard to handle, isn't it?"

"Extremely. It takes strength. It also helps if you know how to break it open in the first place, to set it."

"So it wouldn't be everybody who could set it then, would it?"

"That's true. I can tell you something else. It almost had to be set by somebody with experience. There was loose soil around where it snapped shut. That means it was buried in the way an experienced trapper places his trap, sifting just a thin layer of soil over it after it's set. It was baited properly too. When you bait a trap like that, you take a coyote dropping and pour a little animal gland oil on it. That attracts any animal. There was a dropping by the trap. I had a bottle of oil in the shed. I checked—it's gone."

"Then why do we keep fooling around like this?" Day said loudly. "You're the only one who knows all that, Beacon. You're the only one who could have set it!"

"That sounds pretty logical if you discount all of your hunting experience, which you happen to have told me about. You've hunted with professionals, haven't you? Most professionals know a good deal about trapping. You could have learned it from them. If you wanted that trophy bad enough—"

"I said I'm handling this," the sergeant stated. He looked at Norris Glenn. "What do you know about setting traps?"

"Not a thing!" Norris said shrilly. "Absolutely nothing!"

"Of course he doesn't," Rosalind said. "He detests seeing anything killed. We both do. It's against Nature."

The sergeant turned to Victor Day. "You're a hunter, are you?"

"Now and then, yes."

"And you're familiar with trapping too?"

Day's eyes tightened at the corners. "I've never used a trap in my life."

The sergeant pivoted slowly toward Roy Ives. "You?"

Ives shrugged. "Naw."

"You don't know anything about setting a trap like that?"

"I wouldn't know too much about that, no."

"Nothing?"

"Not a particle, now I think of it."

"I don't think that's true," Joe said.

He met Ives' eyes and saw them darken slightly. "You put your mouth in pretty good when you feel like it, don't you?" Ives said.

"If this is going to be straightened out for the record, which the sergeant seems to want so much, then we may as well get everything out."

"I wouldn't know nothing about setting that trap, and that's what I said. That's what I mean, Beacon."

"Any man who can hook up a plain piece of cord and get trout out of the lake is a man who knows his way outdoors. A man who knows how to set up a deadfall trap for rabbits knows something about all kinds of traps. You did both of those things yesterday. I saw the way you skinned that raccoon, after Day gave it to you. That wasn't the first animal you've skinned."

Ives rubbed the bottom of his chin with the back of his hand. "I don't know as I like all of that coming from you, Beacon."

"Maybe not. But those are the facts."

"You know how to trap, then?" the sergeant asked him.

"I seen a teeny little in my time, maybe," Ives said grudgingly. "But not no trap like that one got the girl. I never set me up no four and a half Newhouse."

"What's a four and a half Newhouse?" the sergeant said.

"The damn trap, that's what it is. But I seen just one or two in my life, and I never set one up."

"You didn't set this one?"

"What the hell did I just say? I didn't even know there was no trap like that around no place!"

"But you set up your own trap for a rabbit yesterday? You fished? You skinned a raccoon?"

"Sure!"

"Why?"

"Well, goddam it, *food*, man!"

The sergeant stared at him, then looked down at his report attached to the clipboard. He seemed, Joe thought, to be moving everything slowly through his brain. But when he looked up again, no decision was apparent in his expression.

"Well, what is it?" Day demanded. "What are we supposed to do now? The girl's dead. What difference does it make who set that trap? Nothing's going to change anything now. It was an accident, that's all."

"I'm determining this," the sergeant said.

"All right then," Day said. "What's your determination?"

"There ain't gonna be nobody going into the pokey?" Ives said. "You ain't gonna tell us that now, are you, officer?"

The sergeant stared back at everyone. "Somebody set that trap."

"Well, man," Ives said, "we knew that about three hours ago. That ain't nothing new, is it?"

"Now," the sergeant said, "I'm getting a ruling on this from headquarters."

"What kind of a ruling?" Day asked angrily.

"There's going to be a ruling on this," the sergeant said, and Joe Beacon knew that no matter how determined he'd been, no matter what he'd learned, he was now confused and wouldn't admit it; and so there would be more delay in clearing his camp.

"I'm leaving," Day snapped. "Now."

"Nobody's leaving," the sergeant stated, "until I get my ruling on this." He nodded. "I'm going out to my car and radio this in, and then we'll see what's what."

With Day swearing bitterly, Ives laughing softly with an edge of sarcasm, the sergeant marched outside. The others followed; Joe watched them filing out. He could hear the two remaining reporters asking questions and the voice of Roy Ives saying, "Now you ain't got nothing against me answering this-here fellow's questions, have you, officer?" A few seconds later he heard Norris Glenn's voice also answering questions; Glenn seemed to be in a sudden contest with Ives, in the attempt to relate the story.

Why, he asked himself in his living room, had this happened? And who had taken that trap out there and set it, so that now Nancy was gone and Eddie's life was a sudden tragedy? Almost any of them, he told himself. Victor Day certainly could have done it. Ives, more than anyone else, was familiar with traps, that was obvious. Not the girl, Day's wife; he was certain of that. But Norris Glenn? It didn't seem possible that the youth could have set the trap, or would have done it if he'd known how. But Norris Glenn seemed to have an unusual preoccupation with death. And sometimes, he thought, people do peculiar and unexplainable things. And Norris's wife, Rosalind? No; he was certain she'd had nothing to do with it, although she was surely strong-looking. She just might have enough power to have....

"Beacon!" he heard Sergeant Cole calling from outside.

Mouth setting in a grim line, he walked outside, thinking that he never should have opened this camp to the public. He never should have lost so much land in the first place, so that he'd been reduced to this. But who could he blame? Time, he thought; only time.

Chapter 16

"What's the matter, sergeant?" Joe asked, approaching the deputy standing beside his automobile.

"Radio's out," the sergeant said, and peered at Joe as though it were entirely his fault.

"Well, I'm sorry about that. What's the matter with it?"

The others stood nearby, waiting for the sergeant's release of them. The sergeant scraped a boot across the surface of the road, his frustration indicated only by that single movement. "That radio was all right when I came in here. Not a sheriff's car leaves the garage down below without its getting checked out for everything, including the radio. That radio was all right before."

"I realize that, sergeant," Joe said. "I heard you using it."

"Now it's dead. I've got a report to turn in."

"You don't know what's the matter with it?"

"It's dead. It's not part of the training to learn how to fix radios, on account they're supposed to be in perfect shape when they give you your car to check out of the garage when you go on duty."

"That's unfortunate."

"Can you fix it, Beacon?"

"I'm afraid electronics isn't my specialty, sergeant."

"You can't fix it?"

"I'm afraid I don't know anything about it. Why don't you just use the telephone?"

"Where is it?" the sergeant demanded.

"In the hallway, on your way into the house."

Without another word, the sergeant wheeled and marched inside. Joe followed to the porch and waited. In a moment, he heard, "Beacon!"

He stepped inside. The sergeant was holding the telephone in one hand, once again staring at him accusingly. "This doesn't work either."

Frowning, Joe took the telephone and put it to his ear. The line was dead. He jiggled the cradle. There was no answering tone.

"What's going on, anyway?" the sergeant said, his high voice going slightly more shrill.

"The telephone appears to have gone out, that's all."

"And my radio too?"

"Must be a coincidence, sergeant."

"That telephone's supposed to be working, isn't it?"

"Yes, of course. But up here we often lose it. The line runs through the hills. A lot of things can happen to it."

"I don't like this," the sergeant said, petulantly.

"I'm afraid it can't be helped, sergeant."

The sergeant stood staring at Joe for several seconds, then he walked outside again, motioning for Joe to follow. Outside, he said to everyone waiting there, "I'm driving back down to headquarters. The radio won't work, and the telephone won't work, and so nobody is going to leave this place until I get down and turn in my report and get a ruling on this."

"You can't do that, sergeant!" Victor Day exploded.

"Those are my orders," the sergeant said. He turned toward his car.

Then Joe saw Eddie walking down the road from the direction of the highway. His hands were shoved in his pockets. His face was set. His eyes stared blankly. When he reached the sergeant's car, he stopped and looked at Joe Beacon without seeming to see him.

"How are you feeling, Eddie?"

Eddie shook his head, shrugging. "Went for a walk up the road."

The sergeant had opened his car door; now he paused, looking at Eddie with his expressionless pale blue eyes.

"Eddie," Joe said, "the sergeant's going to drive down now. Would you like to go down with him? Are you sure you don't want to see Nancy?"

"See her?" the boy said. "When somebody dies, they're not here anymore. How could I see her? Are they putting her body in a mortuary?"

"Yes. I talked to the doctor about that."

"Wait for the funeral, then; that's all to do now, isn't it?" he said dully. "Unless they're going to cut her open and see how she died."

"I think that won't be necessary, Eddie."

"That's good," Eddie nodded. "I wouldn't like that, even if she isn't in that body anymore." He shrugged again and looked at the sergeant. "Are you leaving now?"

"Right now."

"Then I'll ride just up to the highway, if you don't mind. Then walk back down again. I like to keep moving right now. If I'm moving, then I don't think too much."

"All right, Eddie," Joe Beacon said. "You do that, and try not to think too much about anything. You be careful and come on down when you feel like it. You'll be hungry. I'll fix something for you."

Eddie shook his head. "I'm not hungry." Then he climbed into the sergeant's car. The sergeant got behind the wheel. The two reporters and photographers left. Then the sergeant moved his car forward, heading up the narrow road toward the highway. Joe Beacon stood watching the car leaving, hearing the grumbling of Victor Day as he strode back to his cabin, hearing the others walking back to their respective cabins, tasting the bitterness of hurt for that boy....

In the sergeant's car, as it climbed upward, Eddie was silent for several minutes. When the sergeant said nothing to him, he finally asked, "Did you find out who killed her?"

The sergeant looked at him, then looked forward again. "I'm not done yet."

"Somebody killed her," Eddie said in a toneless voice.

"Somebody set that trap. I'm going to find out who did it."

"How?"

The sergeant again looked at the boy, defensively, then forward again. "It's just a matter of getting the record straight, that's all. Somebody set that trap."

Eddie was silent for a moment, then he said, "Now I lay me down to sleep."

"What?" the sergeant asked.

"That was her prayer. She said that every night." He looked down at one hand, opened it, shut it, turned it over, and then said, "I wonder if she said that before she died?" He looked at the sergeant.

"I don't know."

"Who asked you to open your goddam mouth?"

The sergeant stiffened. A flush of red rose from his collar. "I thought you were asking me."

"How would you know, anyway? Are you God?"

The sergeant started to speak, then did not.

"God knows," Eddie said. "You don't. You keep your damn mouth shut."

"All right," the sergeant snapped.

Eddie scrunched down in his seat and peered out at the rocky cliff they were climbing. Then he looked at the sky. "If I had a big enough cannon," he said, "I'd shoot out that sun. I'd make it black everywhere. Nobody'd have any light then. That'd be all right, wouldn't it? She's dead. Why should there be any light when she's dead?" He turned his head and straightened again. He looked at the sergeant. "Somebody murdered her."

The sergeant said nothing.

"I said something to you," Eddie said.

"I thought you wanted me to keep my mouth shut."

"Not when I'm saying something to you. I said somebody murdered her."

"I'm going to get a ruling on it," the sergeant said. "At headquarters. That's why I'm driving down. My radio went out, and the telephone quit down there. I told everybody not to leave that camp."

"What is telling everybody not to leave that camp going to do? I told you: Somebody murdered her."

The sergeant rolled the car through the gate at the top and stopped beside the highway. "It wasn't murder. It was that somebody set the trap. She happened to get into it. So it was accidental, I think. Only somebody set that trap. So I'm going to wait for the ruling."

"What good will that do? Will that bring her back?"

"No, but—"

"What's a ruling? Does that mean you're going to arrest somebody and send them to the gas chamber?"

"I said I thought it was an accident."

Eddie nodded. "I knew that. I knew you wouldn't arrest anybody. But somebody murdered her, and nobody's going to pay for that, are they?"

"Not that way, no."

"Wrong," Eddie said. He pulled a pistol from under his jacket and held it just below the dash and pointed it at the sergeant.

"What are you doing?" the sergeant demanded.

Eddie stared at him. A single car went by, fast, then the highway was quiet again.

"What are you doing, pulling a gun on me?" the sergeant said.

"Give me the gun from your holster."

"What's the matter with you, anyway? I'm not giving you my gun."

Eddie's voice rose. "I'm telling you to get that gun out of your holster and put it down between us. Do it now!"

Swiftly, the sergeant did so. Eddie picked up the gun and continued pointing the pistol at the sergeant. "All right."

"You fixed my radio, didn't you?" the sergeant said.

"That's right."

"And the telephone?"

"I cut the line, all right."

"Why?"

"Because somebody killed my wife. They're going to pay for that."

The sergeant shook his head slowly, his mind whirling.

"See," Eddie said, "you're going to drive on when I tell you to. Then I'm going to close that gate and put the closed sign on it. Then I'm going down the road where I put the dynamite. I got that out of Pop's shed, see? I carried it up and planted it. While you were in the house, just talking and not doing anything about arresting the person who killed my wife, so he could pay for what he did. When I get back down to it, I'm going to blow the dynamite. And that's going to plug the road with rock. And nobody's going to come in. Nobody's going to go out. Not until I find out who killed my wife. What you're going to do, you're going to drive on down to your headquarters. You're going to tell them down there it was just an accident. You're not going to come back here. Because I'm going to do this all by myself—you couldn't and didn't do it. And when I find out who was guilty, I'm going to shoot the son of a bitch through the head. If you don't do what I say, then I'm going to kill anybody at all, because somebody killed my wife. Do you understand now?"

The sergeant's high voice reduced to a whisper. "You can't do this."

"I'm going to. And you do just what I say. When you hear that dynamite blowing, you don't even slow down. There's a quarry not far from here. Everybody'll think it's the quarry. You drive down and do everything just the way I've told you to." Eddie looked at him for a moment longer, then got out of the car, shut the door, pocketed both guns and motioned for the sergeant to drive off.

The sergeant, mind still whirling with the sudden turn of events that he could not yet understand, paused, then pressed down on the accelerator. His car sailed down the highway. He didn't look back.

Eddie stared down the highway until the sergeant's car disappeared. Then he walked to Joe Beacon's white sign. He kicked at it until the post was loosened in the ground. He pulled it out with a savage jerk. He carried it back to the gate and shut the gate. He lifted the metal "Closed" sign hanging on the back and hung it on the front, so that it faced the highway. Then he chained the gate shut and locked it with a padlock which had been hung on the back section of the gate. He walked back down the road a dozen yards toward the camp and threw the sign into the brush. Then he went on down the twisting road, out of sight of the highway, a muscle shivering beside his mouth.

The sergeant was five miles down the highway when he heard the muffled sound of an explosion. He stared at the highway ahead, blue eyes unblinking. He didn't slow down.

Joe Beacon was walking back toward his house when he heard the explosion and felt the concussion. He whirled, looking up at the rock cliff, then ran to his pine shed where his pickup and Jeep were. He threw open the double end doors, vaulted into the Jeep and sent it, tires spinning, up the cliff. He climbed swiftly, taking the short, hooking curves with abandon. Then, finally, out of sight of the camp, he slammed his foot against the brake pedal and came to a skidding stop in front of Eddie Crayne.

Eddie stood in front of the rubble which was still shifting and rolling a little; behind, the road had been demolished and the exploded rock now blocked the passage to the highway. Joe's pistol was in Eddie's hand again.

"Eddie!" Joe Beacon said, jumping from the Jeep.

"I blew it," Eddie said in a peculiar toneless voice. "I left the house down there when that sergeant was asking questions. I picked up your pistol from upon the roof joist on the porch. Then I cut the phone wire back of the shed. Then I went into the shed and packed a box with some of your dynamite. Those reporters asked what I was doing, and I said I was minding my business and figured they could do the same." He nodded and pinched his nose. "I came up here and set the dynamite to blow, then I went down again. When I came back with that sergeant, I took his gun off him and told him what I was doing and told him to go down there and report what happened to Nancy as an accident. I warned him I'd kill somebody, anybody, if he didn't do what I said. Then I took down your sign on the highway and locked the gate and hung the closed sign on. I came down here and blew the road. That sergeant, he isn't coming back. Nobody's coming down here now. That gate's locked and the sign says closed. Nobody's leaving, either."

"*Why*, Eddie?"

"Didn't that sergeant say that whoever killed my wife had to be somebody who was down in your house when he was asking questions?"

"He was talking about whoever set the trap, Eddie. But—"

"Same thing. Whoever set that trap was the one who killed my wife. All those people are still down in the camp. They're not leaving. Not until I find out who killed her."

"Eddie, listen to me. You can't—"

"I have already. You get behind the wheel of that Jeep, Pop."

Joe stood motionless for a moment, looking at the boy's eyes, then he got back into the Jeep. Eddie jumped into the back section, pointing the pistol at Joe Beacon's head.

"Drive down, Pop."

Joe began the descent, feeling a cold prickle of apprehension. This was his fault, he thought. He should have known Eddie was coming apart....

"Pop," Eddie said coldly.

"Yes?"

"Did you kill her?"

"I didn't kill her."

"Somebody did."

"Somebody set the trap, Eddie."

"I didn't like the way you treated my mother."

"Eddie, listen to me. I—"

"Just drive. Put this car in front of the house and then sit there behind the wheel until I tell you what to do next." Joe listened as

Eddie started whistling an odd tune. Then he heard Eddie laughing. Then he heard the boy swearing bitterly. And finally Eddie was silent. And that cold prickle of apprehension became the feeling of reality: Eddie was pressing the cold muzzle of the pistol directly against his neck.

Chapter 17

The explosion, followed by Joe Beacon's wild ride up the cliff, had brought everyone outside. When the Jeep reappeared, they all came forward. Norris Glenn was pale and held Rosalind's hand tightly. Roy Ives frowned, stepping ahead of Flo, who looked honestly irritated, what with too many things beyond her understanding happening too rapidly. Victor Day, face red, looked visibly shaken and nervous. He marched ahead of Lynn Marsey, saying angrily, "What the hell's gone wrong around here?"

Eddie stood up in the back part of the Jeep with Joe Beacon's pistol in his hand. "Get out of the Jeep, Pop."

Joe got out.

"What the hell does he think he's doing?" Day said, nearly shouting.

"He's blown the road," Joe said quietly.

"Blown the road?" Day yelled.

"Shut up," Eddie said softly.

Day stared in amazement, then realized that the boy was holding a gun. He closed his mouth, and fear spread into his eyes.

"I think we'd better do as he says," Joe said.

"What did he blow the goddam road for?" Roy Ives said.

"I didn't ask you anything," the boy said. He stared at Ives. "I blew it so nobody leaves here. Not until I find out who did it."

"Did what?" Ives asked.

"Killed my wife."

There was an immediate silence. Everyone stared at Eddie. He pinched his nose again. He nodded.

"Somebody killed her," he said positively. "And it was one of you. I'm going to find out which one." He moved the pistol up and down and looked at all of them. He said to Lynn Marsey, "Come over here."

"Now wait a minute, Eddie," Joe said.

"I want her," Eddie said.

Joe shook his head. "I don't know what you've got on your mind, Eddie. But leave her out of this."

"Don't argue with him, for God's sake!" Day said. He motioned a hand at Lynn. "Do what he says!"

Lynn walked over to the Jeep, and Eddie hopped off it to stand behind her. He pointed the gun at the small of her back. "Somebody killed my wife. I'm going to kill somebody else's—this woman right here—if you people don't do what I say!"

"Eddie—" Joe said, moving toward him.

Eddie shook his head. "You get back, Pop. I don't trust you any more than I trust anybody here. I'll pull this trigger, and I mean it. You keep away from me, all of you." He watched them for several seconds, then he said, "You've got three guns I know about besides this pistol, Pop. A twelve gauge Marlin. A Browning. And that Winchester with the scope. I want them all and your ammunition. Have you bought any new guns?"

Joe shook his head. "No."

"You better not lie to me."

"All right, Eddie."

"Go get the guns."

Joe walked toward his house, and Eddie said to the others: "Anybody else got a gun?"

Nobody answered for a tense interval, then Victor Day said, "Yes! I've got a pistol!"

Ives looked at him angrily, shaking his head. "Why didn't you keep your mouth shut, mister!"

"Shut up!" Eddie snapped. He looked at Victor Day again. "Where is it?"

"In the cabin."

"Which cabin? And where in the cabin?"

"Number one. On top of the bureau."

Eddie motioned with his gun at Rosalind Glenn. "Go get it and come back carrying it by the barrel."

Rosalind swallowed, then lifted her chin and started toward the cabin. Norris started to follow her.

"Come back here," Eddie said.

Norris stopped, looked after Rosalind desperately, then returned.

Rosalind came out with the gun, carrying it by the barrel.

"Put the pistol in the back of the Jeep," Eddie ordered. Then he called, "Get those guns out here, Pop! I'm watching the house and the windows. If I see anything going wrong, I'll squeeze the trigger and this woman gets a slug through the spine. I wouldn't mind. Somebody killed my wife, didn't he?"

Joe came out of the house carrying the guns. "Easy, Eddie."

"And if anybody else has a gun, he'd better tell me right now."

"I haven't!" Norris yelled in a quivering voice.

"You?" Eddie said to Roy Ives.

"Hell, no, boy. I'd had me a gun along, I'd got me more than a little ol' raccoon." He looked at a shaken Victor Day, smiling, then back at Eddie. "Why don't you just relax now? All of us here, we're real sorry about what happened."

"Shut your mouth," Eddie said.

Joe approached with two shotguns and a rifle.

"In the Jeep," Eddie said.

Joe put the guns and the rifle in the Jeep, then added the ammunition from his pockets.

"Now," Eddie said, "I want your car keys. All of them."

"That ain't going to do you no good," Ives protested. "You blew that road shut. What's the good of—"

"I told you to shut your mouth. Throw your keys in the Jeep." Ives did so.

"One set?" Eddie asked.

"That's all I've got. It was one set come with the car."

Eddie looked at Victor Day. Day's hand plunged into a pocket and came out with his key case. He threw it into the Jeep.

"One set!" he said, jerking his head. "My wife didn't bring hers! I just had one set, I tell you!"

Eddie looked at the Glenns. They each produced a set of keys and tossed them into the Jeep. Norris missed his throw and the keys fell on the ground. He jumped forward, picked up the keys and finally got them into the Jeep.

"Let's have your keys for the pickup, Pop," Eddie said.

Joe placed his truck keys in the Jeep.

Eddie turned his eyes toward Roy Ives. "I want you to take out the plugs of your car and that Lincoln, plus that Volkswagen." He nodded positively. Then he said, "Haven't you got more than one set for the truck, Pop? You gave me just one."

"I lost the other set a few weeks ago."

Eddie shook his head. "You're lying to me."

"I'm not, Eddie. I—"

Eddie said to Norris Glenn, "You go get the plugs out of the pickup in the shed."

"I'll do that," Ives said, starting for the shed.

"No, you won't," Eddie said. "I wouldn't trust you."

Ives came back reluctantly, shrugging. "What do I use for tools?"

Eddie, moving Lynn Marsey with him, stepped closer to the Jeep and got out a small tool kit from under a front seat. He tossed it to the ground in front of Ives. "Get busy, and then you," he said to Norris Glenn, "take a wrench and get the plugs out of that pickup."

Norris opened his mouth and managed, "I don't know how!"

"Well, go watch him do it with the cars and learn how!"

Everyone waited silently while Ives removed the plugs from the Thunderbird, the Lincoln Continental and the Volkswagen. Then Ives handed the tool kit to Norris Glenn. Norris bounded to the shed and disappeared. He was gone a very long time. Finally Eddie called:

"What's going on in there!"

Norris came out, face greasy, sweat glistening on his forehead. He held up four spark plugs. "I couldn't get the others off!"

"Let it go," Eddie snapped. "All right. Now we're going to stay right here, in this camp. We're going to stay in this camp until whoever killed my wife starts thinking hard about what he did. Then he's going to get nervous. Nobody kills without its getting into his conscience. Then he's going to start sweating. When he starts sweating, he's going to start getting scared. Real scared. You see the way the crushed rock is spread around this camp? It goes all through here and around the cabins and the house there, and it runs up to about ten yards from the trees circling this place. You can all use that part where the crushed rock is and the house and the cabins. But the first one who puts his foot out of that circle, he's going to be as dead as my wife is. I don't care what you do, so long as you don't try anything funny with me and you don't try to get away. Because the one who tries to get away, that's the one who starts sweating and getting scared. That's the one who killed my wife. Now I'm going up the road. There's a little ledge up there where I'll have a good, clear view of this camp. I want you all to stay out here in plain sight until I get up there. Then you can do what I've said you can do."

Eddie looked at everyone to make certain they had understood him. Roy Ives said, "What happens if somebody goes and makes a try for getting out of here?" He stared at the youth with cold, appraising eyes.

Eddie met his stare and said calmly, "I'll shoot him through the head." He nodded again and said to Lynn Marsey, "Get in the Jeep, behind the wheel."

"Eddie," Joe said, "leave her here, please."

"Goddam it!" Victor Day said. "Leave it alone. Don't fool with him. Let him do what he wants to do!"

"Into the Jeep," Eddie said to the girl.

She got into the Jeep, behind the steering wheel.

"Do you know how to shift it?" Eddie asked her.

"No."

"Tell her, Pop."

Joe Beacon did. Then Eddie hopped into the back part with the guns. He held the pistol pointed at the girl's head.

"You do what I say," he said. "Because otherwise—" He shrugged and said to Lynn Marsey, "Back up, turn around and then go slow up the road until I tell you to stop."

The girl shifted into reverse and backed the Jeep. Then she moved forward, swinging slowly in a circle, and started up the grade with the gun pointed at the back of her head and Eddie looking back at the unmoving group standing in the camp.

Sergeant Albert Cole turned in his car to the garage, and in a high monotone delivered the information that some juvenile had played a prank on him and cut out his radio. "Fix it," he ordered, and then walked woodenly into the new, large hall of justice and records. In the anteroom of the sheriff's offices, he stopped and gazed at the office now occupied by Lieutenant Lew Barnes, whom he had replaced in the country. His mind kept turning slowly, repeating the scene with Eddie Crayne, that explosion sounding again and again in his head, and yet there was no answer to anything. None.

Finally he forced himself to walk into Lieutenant Barnes' office and stand at attention, the report in his hand.

"Oh, there you are, Al. How did that work out up there?"

Sergeant Cole placed the report on the desk of the lieutenant. "I got it all down here."

Lieutenant Barnes, a lean, athletic-looking man in his early thirties, saw the empty holster at the sergeant's belt. He looked at him curiously.

"I lost it," Sergeant Cole said.

"*Lost* it?"

"I was driving up out of that camp, and I thought something went wrong with a tire. My radio went out—they're fixing it up in the garage right now. And I thought maybe it was bad luck, and a tire went out too. So I stopped to check it. Then I thought I heard a rattlesnake. I crawled down some rocks there, and I had the .45 in my hand, and I tripped. It fell out of my hand and went down there under some rocks. I can get it out, but I wanted to get down here with the report. I'll go back and get it. I'll get another one from Jack. Meantime. But I'll get mine back. It's all right."

Lieutenant Barnes continued to look at the sergeant curiously. "You thought you heard a rattlesnake, and you got out and lost your pistol in the rocks. Did you find the rattlesnake, Al?"

"There wasn't any rattlesnake."

"You look a little tired, Al. You didn't have to go out on this thing this morning. It was ahead of your shift, you know."

"Anything happens in my territory, lieutenant, I want to know about it. That's my responsibility."

"Don't call me lieutenant, Al. For Christ's sake. I think you ought to relax a little."

"I'm relaxed," the sergeant said tensely.

"All right, Al. Just go at it easy, that's all." He looked down at the report and scanned it swiftly. "Tough break, having something like that happen right at the start. When I was up there, the worst I ever had happen was a fifteen dollar robbery of the general store. The girl's heart just stopped, was that it?"

"That was it."

"And you couldn't find out who set the trap?"

"No, sir."

The lieutenant looked up at him again. "How's Joe Beacon's boy taking it?"

"His stepson?"

"Yes."

Sergeant Albert Cole looked above the lieutenant's eyes. He stared at an imagined point on the man's forehead. "Not so bad," he said.

"Well, that's good, anyway. I don't think I'd take it too well. If something like that happened to my wife, I think I'd want to take care of whoever set the goddam trap."

The sergeant kept staring at the lieutenant's forehead and said nothing.

"Are you feeling all right, Al?"

"I'm feeling all right. Yes, sir."

"Goddam it, Al. Relax. Don't call me sir."

"All right," the sergeant said tonelessly.

"I'm not trying to get on your back. I just want you to relax."

"I'm relaxed."

The lieutenant nodded. "Good. So how do we wrap this up? Should we keep on it? Try to find out who set that trap?"

Albert Cole closed his hands tightly, then forced them open again.

"It was an accident, that was all. Somebody set the trap. Only the trap didn't kill her. It was her heart. I'd call that an accident."

"We can send one of the detectives up there, Al."

The sergeant was silent for a time, then he said, "I think it was just an accident. It wouldn't do any good to send a detective up there, would it?"

"I guess not." The lieutenant spread his hands. "And so that's it, as far as we're concerned." He examined the sergeant again. "Why don't you take off now, Al? Go home. Get some sleep."

"I might do that."

"Don't worry about things, Al."

"No, sir."

"Don't call me sir, Al."

"I won't, lieutenant."

Eddie told Lynn Marsey to stop the Jeep at a point in the rock road where there was a small craggy lip on the side facing the camp below. He nodded her out of the Jeep and put down the pistol. He picked up the Winchester and loaded it. The sound of clicking metal carried loudly down the side of the cliff.

He looked down and called, "All right. Do what you want. But don't try to leave that clearing!" His voice skipped down with sharp clarity.

He sat down on a small shelf of rock, body protected by the lip, and smiled slightly. He lifted the rifle and squinted through the scope, letting the telescopic circle track slowly over the oval-shaped area of the clearing created by the crushed rock. Then he suddenly stretched his legs out and turned on his back, pointing the rifle at the sky. He looked at the girl and grinned. She stood there silently.

He shut one eye and looked through the scope again, aiming the rifle at the sun. "If I could hit it, I'd shoot it out." When she didn't answer, he said, "Didn't you hear me? I said if I could hit it, I'd shoot it out."

"Shoot out what?" she asked quietly.

"The sun!" His grin disappeared, and he opened his eye and looked at her. "What's the matter with you? Don't you understand?"

"I'm afraid not."

"That's because you're stupid, then. You're pretty, all right. But you're not as pretty as Nancy was. She's dead, do you know that?"

"Yes," she said softly.

"But you're not, are you? You're happy about that, aren't you? That she's dead and you're not."

"I'm glad I'm alive. But not that she's dead."

He laughed with a humorless snort. "Oh, I'll bet. You're pretty and she was pretty. But she was prettier than you. Only she won't be now, will she? They'll put her in the ground, and pretty soon she won't be pretty anymore. The worms'll fix that, won't they?"

"Please," she said. "It doesn't do any good to think that way."

"Do I want you to tell me how to think?" He lifted the rifle again and pointed it directly at her. "I'll put you where Nancy's going if you get smart with me anymore."

She shook her head slowly. "I don't want to do that."

Slowly the anger went out of his eyes. He grinned again, then turned himself over on his stomach and pointed the rifle down at the clearing again. He laughed. "Goddam all the world and the sun and all of them down there. One, two, three." He nodded again and squinted through the scope. "You can go now," he said in such a quiet voice that she could not understand him.

"What?" she asked.

"I said you can go now."

"Back to the camp?"

"Yes."

She looked at him a moment longer, then turned carefully and started down the road. Behind her he said: "What would your husband feel like if you were dead now—like Nancy?"

She stopped. She shook her head, not looking back at him. "I don't know."

Eddie considered that, and then he said, "I don't know either. You'd have to be dead, wouldn't you, before anybody would know that?"

"Yes," she said quietly. "I think so."

He nodded and smiled. "Go ahead."

She again moved down the road, walking stiffly, carefully. He watched her moving away from him. He lifted the rifle again and pointed it above her at a small cloud in the sky, looking at the white in the scope. He couldn't put the sun out with this rifle. But it was a good big-game job, with enough wallop and accuracy to take care of almost anything on this earth. He adjusted the scope for wide vision, and then brought the rifle down. He found her head and put it in the cross hairs and followed her with her head right there, bisected in the scope. Oh, yes, he thought. His smile widened. His finger tightened on the trigger....

Chapter 18

As soon as Eddie had commanded Lynn Marsey to drive out of the clearing and up the road, Victor Day strode into his cabin, shut the door and crossed the room to open his bottle. He drank straight from it and shook his head, then went to a window and slid the drapes partially open. The front of the cabin, the way he was looking out, faced away from the rock cliff. The Glenn couple had disappeared. Only Joe Beacon and the Iveses were left. Joe stared at the Jeep traveling upward. Roy Ives walked lazily to a picnic table and turned and sat down on a bench, hands shoved in his pockets, as he stretched his legs out. He looked toward the cliff with squinted eyes. Flo stood midway between him and their cabin, her back to Victor Day.

And Victor Day, feeling the liquor burning down into him, not able to feel its new effects fast enough, swore silently and bitterly. It was all going wrong, and he didn't understand how his luck could have turned so fast. He was thinking of the way Lynn had looked when she'd turned that Jeep around and driven slowly away with that insane kid: frightened but obviously in control. And he was thinking of how Beacon had looked at him then, with scathing contempt.

All right, he thought. To hell with it. This was all Lynn's fault anyway. She was the one who'd got him into this. Goddam the day he'd ever laid eyes on her. Practically puffing him into bed, then quitting on him when he had all that steam up, and now this.

He stood there, fury pounding through him, remembering how, after that stupid sergeant had questioned them in Beacon's house, he'd come back in here with Lynn and said, "By God, what do you think this is going to do to my reputation! They've even got pictures! When Frances finds out about this—!"

And Lynn had said softly, "Poor Victor."

"You listen to me," he'd said viciously. "We got into this thing together, and you're going to help me get out of it. We didn't go down to Carmel together. Do you understand? I simply needed some papers once I got down there. I telephoned you and asked if you'd bring them down from the office. You took a bus down and gave me those papers. Only you weren't feeling well, and I didn't want you to have to ride a bus back. So I was driving you home, only you got very sick. We saw that cabins sign on the highway, and you were too sick to go on. To keep out of complications, I simply registered us as Mr. and Mrs. Victor

Day. The reason for that was because naturally I was concerned for your health as a trusted employee. And I sat up all night, by your bedside, and—"

And she'd said, with a bitter smile, "Poor, poor Victor."

Now she was in the hands of that kid, somewhere up that cliff, and to hell with her. He was the one who was in the real jam. She wanted to fool around with a married man? She was getting what she deserved. But he had roots. A home. A family. And how was he ever going to hide this from Frances? If only he'd never met Lynn. *Damn her*, he thought.

Then he didn't want to think of her anymore. The liquor was helping to calm him now, and he no longer wanted to think of anything. As he was finally able to stop the wild spinning of his brain, he felt again a strong thrust of sexual desire. He was looking at Flo Ives standing out there, looking at the swell of her buttocks in those Capris, the insolent angle of her hips.

She turned and walked back toward her cabin. Then she saw him in the window looking out at her. She stopped. A slow, meaningful smile spread across her mouth. He stared at the dramatic thrust of her very large breasts. She lifted her chin a little.

The desire became a tight ache, and he snapped the drapes shut. He turned around and crossed the room and returned to his bottle.

Outside, Joe Beacon, with Roy Ives seated just behind him, stared up at the cliff, his hands opening and closing. The Jeep stopped. He could feel the sweat prickling in his hands. If he had only seen the way it had been going with Eddie. If he'd only prevented this from happening, somehow....

"That's your boy, huh?" Ives was saying.

"He's my stepson."

"He's some stepson, ain't he?"

He didn't want to answer. He didn't want to know what was happening. He didn't want to look up that cliff and see what he was seeing. All he wanted, at this moment, was to erase everything and go back. Back to the way it had once been. When Eddie was a boy. When there had just been Nita and Eddie and himself alone out here. Those were golden days, he thought, when the world was his.

He could, in that moment, remember exactly how it had been. The hard, self-willed labor of every day, rewarding him with a comfortable sense of weariness and accomplishment. Day upon happy day, one fitting against another, so that the time passed with such smoothness that he'd never noticed it was going. One day like another was the good thing. Enough for him. And when each day closed, it was the evening that he really liked. One evening like another. So that when he came home in the last light of the day, sometimes walking, sometimes in the Jeep, sometimes riding the horse he'd eventually given up when he opened this camp, he'd known that he wanted nothing else but what he had.

Winters, he could smell the fir burning in the fireplace, coming out of the chimney into the crisp air, or the rainy air, or the cold wet air after a heavy rain. And he could feel the relaxation from his work loosening his body, so that he would be thinking of Nita before he saw her, thinking of the moments later in that night, when they would be in bed together. And then Eddie would be calling to him, coming out to meet him. And he would come inside, with the boy's hand in his, feeling more love than he'd ever known before, smelling with hunger-sharpened senses the good food Nita had always known how to fix. And what, he had asked himself in those days, would he have wanted more out of his life? Nothing.

Still, he should have learned many long years before he did, that that kind of perfection was never quite real, never permanent, never owned by any mortal man long enough to call it his own, and he hadn't owned anything, really. He'd only been given a taste, a short rental on it, and that had weakened him, knowing how good things could be. Then it had started slipping away from him. And he should have seen that coming then, as he should have seen this coming now. The same thing, all over again. Nita. Eddie.

"I said," Roy Ives repeated behind him, "that's some stepson, ain't he?"

"He's disturbed." Now the girl was getting out of the Jeep. He could see the pistol in Eddie's hand, steadily pointing at her. What is the matter with her gutless husband anyway? he thought. Letting her go that way? But then, he thought bitterly, what had he been able to do himself? What was he doing right now?

"Disturbed, hell," Ives said. "That son of a bitch's crazier than a rabied skunk on a hot day."

"Damn it, Ives!" Joe exploded, whirling around. "Just keep quiet for a minute, will you?"

"Hell," Ives said, "you were goddam near as loco as he is when you gave him every gun you had. That was every gun you had, wasn't it?"

He met Ives' stare. He thought of the carbine he'd left in a closet. No, he hadn't given Eddie all of his guns. He'd kept the new carbine, because he knew the boy didn't know about that one. But what was he going to do with it? Fire at a boy he'd loved with an intensity surely as great as though he'd been the boy's real father? Maybe do something with it, he thought. If he had to. But the one thing he wasn't going to do was let Roy Ives know he had it. If Ives got that rifle in his hands....

"Well?" Ives said.

"I had to give him every gun. Because if anybody does anything now that pushes him a little further—"

"They get their head blown off. You ain't telling me anything, Beacon. I seen a guy once looked like that in the eyes. He was so goddam squirrelly it took—"

"Shut up, Ives." Joe turned back toward the cliff. He watched the girl start walking down the road now. He clenched his hands again. "Just shut up."

Ives lifted his feet, crossed his ankles, and then let his heels drop hard to the ground. He'd seen Victor Day in the window of his cabin, staring out at Flo. He'd seen Flo stop on her way back toward their cabin. He'd known exactly what she was doing: smiling slowly, asking with that smile to come and get it, you rich bastard; come and get some of it, just because you've got the money and the car and the clothes. Oh, yes. That's what she'd been doing.

And he'd known what Day, the yellow son of a bitch, was thinking. Day was thinking he'd like a little of that slut material. Grab it white hot, right from slumsville, just because he was who he was, and forget about her crooked-eyed Texas bastard of a husband. Oh, yeah? Ives thought.

Then he forced all that out of his mind and put it away to handle later, and looked up at the cliff, where the girl was walking down the road; that crazy bastard of a kid was lifting a rifle now, aiming it, almost like he was tracking the girl with it. Ives grinned and said to Beacon:

"I had me a gun, I could shoot that son of a bitch off there like I was shooting me a old bird off some telephone wire."

The girl stopped. She seemed to wait, frozen. Then she started down again. By God, he thought, the kid is pointing that rifle right at her, all right.

"But you, Beacon," he said. "You had to give all your guns away to that whirly brained bastard."

"I'm telling you for the last time," Joe Beacon snapped, "just keep your mouth shut, Ives!"

In their cabin, Rosalind Glenn had collapsed on the bed. Norris was pacing in a circle, seemingly not aware of where he was. Rosalind reached out toward him. "Norris, Norris," she said, tears starting down the sides of her face, "what are we going to do?"

He ignored her.

"Norris, Norris," she moaned from the bed, stretching her arms out to him.

Finally he stopped pacing, and yanked out his drawing board from a corner. He sat down with it under a lamp, hunching, and began drawing with charcoal.

"Norris," she said. "Look at me, won't you, Norris?" He shook his head with irritation.

"*Norris!*" she called impatiently.

"Oh, for God's sake!" he yelled back at her harshly. "Just cool yourself off for a minute, will you? I'm *drawing!*"

Rosalind stared at him in amazement. Tears welled up in her eyes again. She pushed herself up, staring at him in disbelief. Then she fell back and put her hands over her eyes. "You never talked to me that way before! Never. Never in our whole marriage!"

Then there was the sound of a powerful rifle exploding.

The drawing board flew out of Norris' hands. He threw himself across the room, onto the bed. He went into her arms. And then they lay there quivering, pressed together toe to toe, hip to hip, knee to knee.

Smiling with satisfaction, Eddie Crayne lowered the rifle. The girl had frozen when he'd fired. He'd shifted his aim just before he'd pulled the trigger. He'd rested the barrel of the rifle on the rock ledge before him and sighted a glass insulator on a telephone pole fifty yards from Joe Beacon's house. He'd squeezed the trigger, felt the kick and watched the glass fly apart, glinting in the sun as it exploded. This rifle was all right, he thought. If one of them made a try for getting out down there, he could place his shot just where he wanted it.

In the head, he thought. In the head....

Chapter 19

When the rifle exploded, Joe ran in the direction of the girl, toward the edge of the clearing. Eddie called down, "Far enough, Pop."

Joe stopped, realizing that the girl hadn't been hit, that Eddie had instead fired at and hit the glass insulator. He felt his stomach quiver as he watched the girl start down again. When she reached him, he took her arm and looked at her pale face. "Are you all right?"

"Yes." She nodded slowly, her voice a whisper. "Scared. But I'm all right." He watched her eyes search the clearing, obviously for Victor Day, who was not in sight.

"Do you want to go over there and sit down?"

"Yes," she said weakly. "Please."

He led her over to the picnic table, where Ives slowly got to his feet, grinning without amiability. "That ought to've scared hell out of you, huh?"

"Ives," Joe said, "why don't you go over to your cabin and see how your wife is doing?"

"That's a good idea. A man ought to be concerned how his wife's doing at a time like this." He looked at the girl, and then at the cabin where Day remained inside, and then grinned; he ambled easily toward his own cabin.

The girl looked up toward the cliff where Eddie waited.

"I don't think," Joe said swiftly, "he'll do anything now. Not unless somebody tries to do what he's told us not to do."

"I'm not going to do that," the girl said.

"No," he said. "And I hope nobody else does. But—" He shook his head and motioned a hand uselessly. "I don't know what to do about him. He—"

"What about that sergeant?"

Joe shook his head again. "Eddie told me he'd ordered him to go down and report what happened to Nancy as an accident. He told him not to come back, on the threat that he'd kill somebody, anybody...." He spread his hands. "Still—he's the best hope we've got right now. I just hope to hell whatever he does he does right."

"Yes," she said softly.

"I'd better see how the Glenns are doing."

She nodded and looked at her cabin, her mouth tense. "And I'd better go back to my cabin and see my husband. That's the thing to do, isn't it? When you've been scared badly? Go to your husband? For comfort?"

Sergeant Albert Cole drove his own car, a two-year-old Plymouth, into the drive of his neat, unimaginatively designed, uniform, Peninsula tract house. He walked inside through the garage, the newly issued pistol in his holster now. His wife, he knew, would be in the kitchen. She always started the ham-and-bean soup about now on this day of the week, and he could smell it as he walked in.

She turned around from the stove, a small, rather unattractive woman who had given him two children, both of whom were at school right now. "Thought you ought to be coming about now."

He nodded listlessly.

"Got the soup going," she said. "Just the way you always like it. Want to taste it?"

He shook his head. "No."

She looked at him closely. "How'd that go up there? Everything all right?" She seldom asked him about his work, because he'd told her when he'd first gone to work as a deputy that he didn't want to mix his work with home life. But she always knew when something had gone wrong.

"Yes," he said miserably. He kept trying to work it out, and all his brain would do was to stop. And so he hadn't worked anything out. Not a thing.

"I'll bet you've got indigestion again," she said. "You always do when you worry."

"I'm not worried about anything," he said loudly in his high voice.

"Maybe you'd better take some Tums."

"I don't want any Tums."

"Alka-Seltzer then. Take an Alka-Seltzer."

"I don't want any Alka-Seltzer."

"Maybe you just need sleep."

"I don't need anything," he said. "There's nothing wrong with me."

"Why don't you take an aspirin and get some sleep? I'll pick up the children myself, and we won't make a sound when we come back. When you wake up, you'll feel fine. You'll want a whole lot of that ham-and-bean soup then."

He stood unblinking, waiting until she put two aspirins in his hand and gave him a glass of water. He took them, then walked forlornly into their bedroom. He took off his gun belt and then his uniform. He sat down on the edge of the bed in his underwear. The manual of instruction which had been given him the first day of school, when he first went to work as a deputy, lay on the nightstand. He liked to pick it up and read it before he went to sleep. It was his favorite reading, and it had never failed to give him a secure sense of satisfaction.

He picked it up now and lay back with it. But all he could see was what his imagination created. He kept seeing that camp, that road, that kid holding a gun, and all those people down there in the clearing. His head had begun to ache, all right, and he didn't see why the aspirin didn't start working faster. He looked at the manual and tried to force away all the visions of that camp and how it might be right now. He turned to the index and read everything there. There wasn't one thing to cover this. He stared at the manual and then, swearing bitterly, threw it across the room. It was letting him down, that manual, and it never had before.

When Lynn Marsey walked back toward her cabin, Victor Day finally opened the door. He stood in the doorway and waited for her grimly. When she came in, she said, "Thanks so very much, Victor, for all your help. I'll be eternally grateful."

"What could I do?" he demanded, shutting the door. "That kid's crazy. He was armed. What could I have done about that?"

"Nothing, Victor. Not a thing."

He walked to the bureau and poured himself another drink. "That goddam Beacon," he said. "He should have known that kid was going to snap. The whole thing's his fault. He set that trap. Does he think he's kidding anybody about that?"

Lynn sat down on the edge of the bed. "Would you mind giving me a small portion of what's left in that bottle, Victor? I think I could use it, if you wouldn't mind."

He looked at her angrily and then splashed another drink. He carried it over to her.

"Thank you very much, Victor."

He stood above her and said, "You know Beacon set that trap, don't you?"

"I don't think he did." She drank; she put the glass down. He felt the liquor dulling his brain, knowing that he was getting drunk now. He moved his eyes, examining the good lines of her body. He knew that body so well. "You don't think Beacon set that trap?"

"No. I don't."

He sat down beside her, heavily. "Who do you think did, then?"

"I don't know." She would not look at him. She stared beyond him. "Ives?"

"I wouldn't know."

"Me?" he asked roughly.

"I didn't say that, did I?"

"I didn't say you did. But you don't think Joe Beacon did it, you say?"

"That's what I said. I don't think that."

"And that," he said, whispering with his anger, "is because you've switched from me to him, isn't it? No love. That's something you don't know anything about, isn't it? You talk about love, and you're talking about something you don't know anything about, aren't you? You're interested in Beacon for just one thing. You—"

"Don't, Victor," she said.

He smiled at her with meanness. "What's the difference? Beacon? Me? What bull in any pasture? Right? What do you care?" He reached out and unbuttoned the top button of her dress. "Isn't that right?" He opened her dress and looked at her firm breasts. He put a hand hard against one of them. She closed her eyes. "How can you tell the difference?" he asked, the biting desire intensifying. "One hand like another? One...."

He felt her hand whip hard across his face. His head snapped back with the force of the blow. Her eyes were open now, just barely, staring at him with dark hate.

He staggered to his feet, glaring at her, livid with fury. He finished the remainder of his drink and lurched across the room, pushing outside to take long, angry breaths, seeing nothing at all for a few moments.

Joe, outside the Glenns' cabin, called to them. They had not appeared since the sound of Eddie firing that rifle; he was worried about them. He called a half dozen times, and finally he could hear a muffled whisper behind the door: "Be careful, Norris. Be careful!"

Then the door opened just a crack and he saw Norris' eye peeking out, large and round and frightened. "What's going on out there?" the young man asked in a trembling voice.

"It's all right," Joe said. "He just fired a rifle at an insulator."

Slowly the door opened. Norris moved slowly onto the short stoop in front of the cabin, followed by Rosalind who stopped in the doorway and looked around the clearing nervously. Norris sat down on the porch stoop and shook his head.

"I think," Joe said, "as long as we try to keep calm and be careful, this is going to work out. I'm sorry about it, but there's nothing I can do right now. The boy may change his mind and forget this, if we don't push him. I think that's the thing to do right now. Just live with this."

Norris nodded, without looking up. Rosalind stood in the doorway and said, "You'd better get inside, Norris. We'll lock the door again, and—"

Then Joe Beacon noticed that Norris was watching something. He turned and saw a small lizard coming off a tree trunk. It raced from the tree, across the ground, heading straight for Norris. Norris' eyes widened even more. His body turned rigid.

"It's just a lizard—" Joe Beacon began.

But Norris leaped up, dove off the porch, ducked and grabbed a rock. He dove forward again, to slam the rock into the speeding lizard. He did a good job. The lizard lay smashed. Norris, breathing hard, stared down at it.

"*Norris!*" Rosalind gasped.

Norris continued to glare at the lizard. Then he turned abruptly and marched back into the cabin. Rosalind peered inside at him. "Norris! *Why?* One of nature's creations!"

Joe Beacon heard Norris' voice coming out, hard and ringing with tough authority: "Please, just shut up! I'm drawing!" Shaking his head, Joe Beacon walked back toward his house.

In the Iveses' cabin Roy paced for a time. Flo sat disinterestedly, watching him.

"By God," he said. "I had me a gun, I'd fix him."

"You ain't got a gun," Flo said. "So what happens? We wait around until that crazy comes down and shoots us all to death?"

"You worried about that?"

Flo shrugged. "Hell, no. I ain't never been scared of nothin' in my life. You?"

Ives shook his head. "I ain't ever been scared either. Like to know when if I ever was. Not me."

"So—what happens next?"

"We wait."

"For what?"

"For me to figure this out."

"You gonna go after that kid?"

"Maybe. Only that ain't all I'm figuring out."

"What else then?"

He pulled the drapes apart slightly. He looked out at Victor Day's Lincoln Continental gleaming in the early afternoon sun. "I'll tell you when I get to it."

"Well," Flo said shrugging and standing, "you keep figuring. I'm gonna grab a shower and something to eat and get me a nap. This all wore me out."

"Yeah," he said. Joe Beacon had gone by, returning to his house. Now Victor Day came outside. Ives watched him lurch to the side of his large car and lean against it. Getting drunk, Ives thought, good and drunk. He nodded, his eyes gleaming. That's all right, he thought. And he's mad about something too. Why? His wife? Or was that his wife? There was something wrong there, Ives was certain. He could always smell it out somehow when something like that was wrong. He turned as Flo headed for the bath. "Come here."

"I'm grabbing me a shower," she said.

"Later." He snapped the drapes completely shut.

"I ain't had a shower since early this morning."

"You take them showers all the time."

"Makes me feel good. Good and relaxed."

"Come over here one time, and I'll get you relaxed."

"My mamma said it was godly I should take plenty of baths and showers."

"Come over here. I'll show you another way to get to heaven."

Flo giggled. "You think you're somethin' about that, don't you?"

"Don't you?"

She came over to him. "You ain't so damn bad."

"I'm better than that," Roy Ives said. His hands slid under the blouse she was wearing. She pressed against him, beginning to breathe hard. "You bastard," she whispered.

Minutes later, as they lay on the bed with Flo's eyes closed and her clothing removed, Roy Ives moved away from her. She opened her eyes and looked at him. "What's the matter?"

"I got to thinkin' about that kid up there."

"Come *on!*"

"I ain't got it no more, Flo."

She stared at him, her face turning pink. She sat up. "What the hell did you start somethin' for if you can't finish it!"

Roy, still dressed, also sat up and shrugged. "We'll get it later."

"Yeah?" Flo said angrily. She got up and flounced across the room. "Maybe we will, maybe we won't!" She slammed the door of the bathroom behind her, and in a moment Roy could hear the shower running. He stood up and slowly combed his hair. He stepped outside, leaving the door half open behind him.

He ambled casually over to the Lincoln Continental, against which

Victor Day was still leaning.

Victor Day looked at him, straightening, wishing to get away from the man instantly. Damn everything, he thought, including this smiling jackal.

"That boy still up there?" Ives asked, smiling.

"I haven't looked."

"I reckon he is. He went and snapped good, didn't he?"

"That's obvious," Day said, speaking carefully around the tendency to slur his words.

"Well," Ives said, "none of this would of happened if that trap hadn't gone snap and the girl died in it. Wonder who set that?"

Day started to move away, but then he saw, through the half-open door of Ives' cabin, Flo stepping out of the bath. There was a large yellow towel wrapped around her. Her bare legs and shoulders gleamed under the ceiling light. She saw the open door, then looked beyond, to find Victor Day staring at her over the shoulder of her husband. Day brought his eyes away and said to Ives, "I don't know who set that trap, Ives. Who do you think it was?"

Ives gazed across the clearing, as though meditating. A small smile remained on his mouth. "Just don't know. Can't figure it." He looked down at the car and rubbed a hand lightly over its gleaming finish. "Sure love this car of yours, mister."

Day looked back into the cabin. Flo met his eyes, smiling seductively, not moving out of sight a step. She rubbed her hands slowly against the towel, from breasts to belly.

"What?" Victor Day said.

"I said I really love this car of yours. You got to be getting ahead in life to own a car like this. That's a fact a man would have to be as crazy as that kid up there to miss."

Day nodded, compelled totally by Flo who now removed the towel from her body, and stood gleaming and bare. She stared back at him, then began to dry one breast with the towel, then the other. Victor Day's throat became dry. Finally he tore his gaze away to find Ives staring at him with dark, mean eyes.

"Yes, sir," Ives said softly. "If I was the man who had me this-here car, I'd know I was doing so damn well I'd be nervous every minute, watching to see if somebody wasn't going to take some of that which I had right off of me."

In his neat, quiet tract house, Sergeant Albert Cole suddenly got out of bed. His wife had driven out and picked up the children and brought them back; he'd heard them coming in. He dressed swiftly and buckled on his holster with its new pistol. Then he walked quickly through the house. His wife and two children were in the kitchen. He didn't speak to any of them and walked toward the garage.

"Where're you going, Al?" his wife called.

"Out."

"But—"

Then he was in the garage, getting into the Plymouth. He shot it backward out the drive, then hooked it around and whipped down the street, fast.

He drove until he reached Sand Hill Road, there he turned and really pushed the accelerator down, speeding west, toward the hills lying in a bluish silhouette of peace beyond.

He'd made up his mind.

There was nothing written down on this for him to do. He couldn't bring himself to report the situation as it was, because how would that stand him in the department as a brand-new sergeant in this territory? Letting them know that he didn't know what to do? So— now he was going to do something. By himself. It was all very clear.

Go in by himself, he thought. Get that kid. Shoot him right out of there, if he had to. But get him. That was the only thing to do, he told himself, and hunched his shoulders a little. His blue eyes stared impassively forward. He passed the green fairways of a new golf club, stretching away from a California-modern clubhouse which had collected more fast-drinking members than had the greens. Farther out a pair of teen-aged girls atop a pair of riding horses came out of the gate of a recreation park and glanced at his car with a sweeping aloofness ignited at birth. The edges of fashionable, horse-loving Woodside began now. Trees clustered more thickly. The road tipped upward. He saw nothing but the blacktop being gobbled away with the speed of his car. He'd made up his mind. And he felt the first peace of mind that he'd felt since that kid had ordered him to go on and then exploded that rock behind him....

Chapter 20

The twelve-by-twelve room in the northwest corner of Joe Beacon's house had become, after Nita had gone, an all-purpose room. In the winters he generally kept the long living room closed off to compress the propane heat and used this room, instead, as a living room. He had put a couch in it, a television set, a comfortable easy chair, and an old roll-top desk. He was sitting in the easy chair now, because it faced a west window and gave him a direct view of the distant image of Eddie, whose head, shoulders and glinting rifle were visible over the rock ledge behind which the boy waited. The carbine was in his hands.

He lifted it and looked along the short barrel at Eddie. The carbine had enough power, he thought. But it didn't have the long-range accuracy, with the cut-down barrel. He'd bought it for short-distance, quick shooting. And he'd bought it for animals, he thought—not his son.

He brought the rifle down, shaking his head. He couldn't try it, not that way. He got up and carried the rifle back to the closet just beside the front door, thinking: If it comes to it, I'll use it. I'll have to. But not now—I can't try that now.

He returned to his study and his chair, and then he heard somebody rapping lightly on the front door. He called, "Come in." He heard the door open and then the tapping of high heels. He stood up. "In here."

He knew, before she stepped into the room, who it was. He was glad she had come. Her face was still pale, and she was still frightened, he knew. She had gone to Victor Day, he realized, hoping for some kind of comfort; but Day had given her nothing; he was sure—he could see that in her face.

"I wanted to come," she said simply.

He nodded. "Sure. Sit down, please."

She sat down on the sofa, just beside his easy chair; he sat down again, beside her.

"I've been watching him up there," he said. "That's all." And no, he thought, he couldn't tell her, nor any of them, about the carbine.

"Yes," she said. "And it's worse for you. I know that. You know him. Love him."

He stared at the outline of the boy. "Yes. I know him. Love him. When he's Eddie, that is. But I'm beginning to realize how much that boy, right now, is somebody I don't know. I'm hoping that whatever snapped him out of reality will snap him back again. Are you still frightened?"

"Not so much now," she said. "Not in here. With you."

He looked at her quickly. "I'm sorry about this."

"Why should you be? It isn't your fault. I—" she put a hand lightly on his arm—"I'd like to call you Joe. I'd like you to call me Lynn. First names are better right now, I think. It's closer, and I'd feel less scared."

"Yes," he said. "Sure. But don't say this isn't my fault. It is."

"I know you didn't set that trap, Joe."

He saw the certainty in her eyes. "No," he said, "I didn't. But that isn't what I meant." He looked upward again. "I know what he can do. I don't mean to frighten you anymore. But it's always best to know the truth. Then you know what to be afraid of. That mind up there in that boy's head—that doesn't belong to the Eddie I know. I know that now. But the rest of him, that's the same right now. He's got a good rifle in his hands. And he knows all about using a rifle. I've seen him pick off a fast-moving jack rabbit at two hundred yards with a single-shot bolt-action twenty-two. The rabbit jumped out straight across his vision, and he got the rifle up and hit it in the flank. He had a spare cartridge in his left hand, and he jacked that first casing out and reloaded and caught the rabbit in the head while it was still moving. He did it in three seconds flat."

He was silent for a moment, staring out the window grimly. Then he said:

"That's a Model Seventy Winchester he's got now. It's a bolt-action repeater. He's got five cartridges in the magazine, and I figure he's got one in the chamber. With that rifle he can jack the bolt in less than a second. It's a three hundred magnum, and it's got a two and a half to eight variable scope mounted. He'll have the scope screwed down to two and a half from where he's sitting, and he's got a large enough field of vision that he can bring down anything he sees moving out of this clearing. I hand-loaded that ammunition, and it's loaded to maximum pressure. That means whatever he shoots is going to be blown to bits." He shook his head. "And what have I been doing about it?

"I've been sitting here, philosophizing, hoping somehow he'll come to his senses and put that rifle down and come walking down here to apologize for this." Joe Beacon slapped his right hand against the arm rest of his chair. "Philosophizing! Telling myself that that boy sitting up there with that rifle is just another symbol of life. Because there's always something like this, in everybody's life, every minute. He's the sword hanging by the thread, and the man under it doesn't know when the thread is going to break and the sword is going to fall. He's Disaster. And there's always Disaster, waiting for everyone. Sickness. A car wreck. A plane crashing. A boat sinking. A slip on the stairway. Going broke. Getting fired. A million things. And always, the biggest of them all—death. And all Eddie means is that we've got Disaster—reduced to one thing right now: Eddie and his rifle. One of us might have died, anyway, today or tomorrow. Maybe by tripping on our shoelaces. Philosophy. Rationalization. And to hell with that. To hell with me for ever letting this happen!"

"Joe," she said softly, touching his arm again. "How can you blame yourself? How could you know what was going to happen?"

He rubbed his jaw angrily. "I'll tell you. I'll tell you about Eddie's mother. Her name was Nita. She was a beautiful woman, and I met her one day at an open house at a ranch down the road. She was a friend of a friend, and the friend told me that she'd just had a bitter divorce. She'd gotten it in Reno, and she'd come to Saratoga to live with Eddie. I went down there one day. She had a little cottage. I don't know. She was more than attractive to me. Something happened that had never happened before. I couldn't think of anything else but her. I simply found that I worshipped her. I finally asked her to marry me, even though I was certain, somehow, that she wouldn't. But she did. I brought her and Eddie here. We had a marvelous time. Until—"

He took a breath, forcing it out, in a way he'd done with nobody before. He'd thought maybe he was going to have to with Nancy. But now Nancy was dead. And so he said:

"Good years, and then it started going wrong. Little things. One day she accused me of deliberately breaking and throwing away a small vase she'd brought to this house. I'd never even seen such a vase. She began accusing me of being interested in other women. I wasn't. Once she disappeared with her car, leaving Eddie with me. She didn't come back for three days. I didn't know where she was. When she came back, she wouldn't admit having made the trip. Then she would admit it and tell me stories of the men she'd been with during those three days. I was furious, and she seemed to enjoy that. She got more specific, about having slept with this man or that man, telling me exactly what they had done. Only then I realized that the stories were changing and that she must have been inventing them—or that she actually didn't remember exactly what happened. I sat down with her one day and told her that she'd have to get medical attention. She was infuriated. Then she begged me not to think there was anything wrong with her mentally. She'd just taken a little trip, just to get away, and nothing at all had happened. She'd told me all those things, she said, just because she'd thought I didn't love her."

He took another breath, was silent for a moment, then went on:

"She was all right for a time after that. I was willing to forget everything if it would get back to the way it had been. Then the whole thing started again. She began saying peculiar things, doing peculiar things. And one day she left again. I tried to trace her. I checked with everyone. Finally one of her friends told me where she thought Nita was. I drove there. It was a cheap motel on the outskirts of San Jose. Her car was parked by one of the cabins, and as I drove up a man came out of that cabin and got in her car and drove away. I walked over and slammed the door open, and Nita was sprawled on the bed. There was a bottle on the nightstand. She was lying there nude, and the bed was obviously—used. She saw me, and she began to laugh...."

He fell silent again. Lynn put her hand against his. "Joe," she said softly.

His strong fingers closed around hers. "I went home. She didn't come back. And I didn't want her back. I heard about her, now and then. Heard that she was doing wild things. But I just concentrated on bringing up Eddie. Then one day I got a telephone call. She was dead. I identified her body. The police gave me the story. She'd gotten drunk one night with a man who picked her up in a bar in San Francisco. He'd driven away and put the car up to a hundred miles an hour on the Skyway. There wasn't much left to identify, but enough."

He held her hand in the silence. Finally he said:

"The reason Eddie and Nancy came up here was because Eddie had worn himself out. His boss suggested that he take leave of absence and get some rest. When he got here, he acted peculiarly. He wouldn't come in the house at first. He was surly with me. He got over it quickly enough. But it should have been the signal to me. I don't know how much Nancy really knew about his mother. I should have told her. I might have found out more about how Eddie had been. That way— maybe none of this would have happened. Somehow—"

"Joe," Lynn Marsey said, "you can't blame yourself for everything."

"But I do. Because I've been hiding from things. If something goes wrong, I turn my back. If something comes along that I don't like, I close my eyes. I—"

"Joe," she whispered.

He turned to her. He moved an arm, put his hand behind her, and she came to him easily. He kissed her and felt her lips softening ... then she pushed away from him, turning away swiftly. She stood up and walked across the room, facing away from him. At last she turned and said, "As long as we're checking souls, you'd better give me a chance— so you know the kind of woman you were kissing."

"Lynn," he said, "I had no right to—"

"I wanted you to. I'd like you to do that again. But you might as well know what you were getting."

"You're married. I know that. But—"

"No," she said bitterly. "I'm not married."

He stared at her in surprise, but at the same moment he felt a quick relief. "You're not married?"

"No," she said harshly. "Oh, I came here and went into a cabin with Victor Day. That's quite true. But I'm not Mrs. Day. Mrs. Day is in the family home in San Francisco with the Days' two sons, thinking her husband is on a business trip to Carmel. We were in Carmel, but not on business. I'm a receptionist in his firm. I have, to be candid about it, been sleeping with him for the past ten months."

She came back across the room. She picked up her small bag and got a cigarette from it. She lit the cigarette swiftly and snapped the match into a tray. "Do you like that?"

"I'm glad you're not married to him. But the other—no, I don't like that."

"Tawdry, isn't it? And now here I am, in your house, asking you with my eyes, expression, any way I can, for you to kiss me again. I am as promiscuous as a female cat. I am—"

He stood up and put his hands on her shoulders firmly. "Don't do that. I only want to know one thing. Do you love him?"

"Now?" She shook her head. "No. I don't love him. I didn't want to come here, to the cabin. I was finished in Carmel, and I told him that. But he insisted."

"Did you love him?"

"Yes," she said, her voice softening. "I thought I did, anyway. But now I don't know what happened to me. At first, I was so completely involved that I didn't care about what was right or what was wrong. I didn't care what rules I was breaking or he was breaking. I just had to be with him, any way I could. But somehow I was wrong about all of it. About a month ago—it just came apart for me. All of it."

He stood holding her, watching the hurt in her eyes. "Something happened."

"Not some big, specific thing. We had dinner at my place one evening. We had Martinis, and he drank an extra one or two. We had wine with dinner. His wife had taken his children down to Southern California that week end, and I guess he was feeling truly free. After dinner, he sprawled on the couch, and he just asked me to—" she looked straight at his eyes "—make love with him. Just like that. In a dirty voice. And suddenly I could see all of it for what it was. I didn't mean very much to him, not really, and I knew that suddenly. I simply told him that I wasn't feeling vulgar at the moment. He got quite angry. But I didn't seem to care anymore. I knew—I could suddenly see us for what we were—that all we did was drink, eat, make love. Like rabbits. Do you see?"

"I don't want to see that. I only want to know that it's over being like that."

"Oh, yes," she nodded. "It's over being like that. It was then, really. He became angry. I wasn't. Just sick to my stomach. I told him it was all booze and sex and nothing else. I told him we never even talked together. Not real talk, between two human beings. I asked him if we couldn't, for a change, just talk. He was still angry, but he seemed to calm down. He asked what I would like him to talk about. I told him anything, anything at all. So he started talking about a man named Henderson in his company. I knew Henderson was an ambitious man, and I knew he would like someday to have Vic's job. But I'd never known before that Vic had been bothered by it.

"He talked for thirty minutes about Henderson, vilifying and crucifying the man. Then, when he seemed to know what I thought of seeing this side of him, he stopped. He got up and he was quite drunk. He left very angry. When I saw him the next time, he asked me why I'd ever brought up Henderson in the first place? And that was the beginning of the end. I'd seen too much of him, and I didn't like what I saw. He'd shown more of himself than he'd wanted to, a smallness in his character, something deep down and permanent, something that weakened him all the way through. And there it all went. But he was stubborn about ending it. I was a nice toy for him, a fine little ego prop, and he'd gotten used to having the toy—he didn't want to give it up. But he has to now. Because I've finished with him. But take a look at the lady. Here, now, with you—"

He drew her to him again and kissed her again, long and carefully and gently. Then he held her, not wanting to think of her time with Victor Day, not, for once, wanting something out of the past—but only this new and present feeling. He held her and felt the pressure of her arms in response. Then he looked out that window, above the fragrance of her hair and the feel of it against his face, up to where Eddie was waiting, and the moment cracked apart.

He saw, coming down above Eddie, just appearing over the rocks where the road had been blown, clambering slowly down, down, apparently alone, pistol in hand: Sergeant Albert Cole!

"My God," Joe whispered. He took his arms away from Lynn and turned to stand watching tensely. "That damn deputy! He's come back alone. If Eddie sees him...."

Then he saw the sergeant duck behind a rock. In a moment he rose slightly and aimed his pistol at the boy.

"*No!*" Joe whispered. "*The goddam fool ...!*"

A rock came tumbling down from where the sergeant crouched, his movement having dislodged it. Eddie, like a frightened wildcat, wheeled and fired upward. His throat tight, Joe saw the sergeant's pistol jerk. But his aim was off. The sergeant ducked again, and Eddie fired at him twice more, screaming.

Joe Beacon wheeled, ran through the house, and burst outside, shouting, "Get out of there, sergeant! Get the hell out of there!"

Eddie's voice echoed down, a wild, tearing sound: "Yes, by God! Out of here! Do you hear me? And don't come back! I swear it–I'll start firing down at that clearing ...!"

"Do what he says!" Joe Beacon shouted. "For God's sake, just get out of here!"

High above, crouched among the rocks, the sergeant stared down at his pistol. He'd missed, and that kid had almost got him. He'd removed his hat before he'd started down, and small beads of sweat now gleamed on his bald head. What to do now? he asked himself painfully. What to do?

Then that kid was screaming at him again, and he heard Joe Beacon's voice coming up at him, over and over. Finally he started crawling backward, keeping rock between himself and that insane kid. He crawled by inches, the sweat increasing and starting to stream down his face. But he didn't change his expression. His eyes remained impassive as he moved out of sight and out of range of that kid.

He went faster now, and returned to his car waiting where he'd left it, in front of Joe Beacon's gate. He got inside and sat there, staring out at the highway, watching without expression the curious stare of the occasional driver passing with a high whine of speed.

What to do? he asked himself. He didn't know. He just didn't know.

Chapter 21

When the shooting had stopped, Joe stared up at Eddie, who again had fixed himself into his watching position. What is going on in Eddie's mind? he asked himself. That damn stupid deputy. Had he pushed Eddie too far? So that at any moment now, Eddie might....

He put that thought out of mind and turned to survey the line of cabins. Roy Ives was coming forward. Victor Day had come out and leaned loosely against the side of his cabin, obviously drunk. He glared at Joe Beacon with filmy eyes. There was no sight of the Glenns.

"That boy's a real squirrel, ain't he?" Roy Ives said, stopping beside Joe.

"If that deputy stays out of here," Joe said, "maybe—"

"Maybe it just don't matter," Ives smiled tightly. "Maybe he goes all the way loco, anyway. Maybe he just starts shooting down here, and then—"

"We'd better hope he doesn't. We'd better hold on here as calmly as we can."

"Then she'll just blow away, right?" Roy Ives shook his head. "You got a great belief in things turning right, haven't you, Beacon?"

Joe met the man's eyes, then moved on, toward the cabins. When he neared Victor Day, he saw the man wheel drunkenly, go into his cabin and slam the door behind him. He went on to the Glenns' cabin and rapped on the door. There was no response. He called to them, trying to keep his voice reassuring, explaining the shooting. There still was no answer, and he was certain they had become too frightened to respond. He went back in the direction of his house, out of which Lynn Marsey appeared. He met her and said, "You can stay in my house, can't you?"

Her mouth and eyes looked strained. "I think I'd better go back to him."

He shook his head. "No."

"Yes," she said. "I can't just—you know. I—"

"Don't go in there," Joe said. "He's drinking heavily."

"I know. But—" She shrugged and smiled wanly and moved on, toward the cabin where Victor Day waited. He watched her going away, hating to see her go. Then he turned and looked again up the cliff, where Eddie waited with his rifle.

She did not want to return to that cabin and Victor Day. But there was nothing else to do now. He was, as Joe Beacon had said, drinking heavily. But she could handle him, she was certain, and she could not bring herself to remain in Beacon's house, announcing her sudden switch—she couldn't do that.

And so she had to go back. And perhaps he would drink himself senseless. And she would try to think about Joe Beacon, the new one, puzzled and surprised by the overpowering feeling she had for this man, which she could not trust. She'd felt a similar feeling for Victor Day in the beginning. And now this. Like the female cat she'd described to Joe Beacon. She didn't trust the feeling, no matter how strong; she didn't trust herself.

She approached the cabin, hoping that Victor Day had gone inside and fallen on the bed, hopelessly drunk, so that she could sit alone, to search within herself for the deep and real reasons for what she was feeling. Was it simply the rebound from the emotional well she'd been submerged in for these last few months with Victor? Was it simply the result of having been forced by that boy, with the chilling look in his eyes, to walk in absolute terror along that road until the rifle explosion had stopped her, then coming down to be greeted by the blessedly welcome sight of Joe Beacon? Was it gratitude? Or was it simply the instinct of the promiscuous, the desire to switch beds and love mates, so that....

She came into the cabin and saw that Victor had not passed out at all. There was a bottle and glass in his hands, and he was pouring fresh fuel for his building desire to become blind drunk. But he was not that way yet. And when she saw the look of his eyes, she lost confidence that she could control him. His eyes were drunken, filmy, unreasonable in their expression.

"Well, well," he said, making a great effort to form his words. "The harlot returneth. How was it? Did it suit the hungry lady?" He laughed harshly. "But there aren't any ladies in this room, are there? Speak up. Any ladies present?" He shook his head and put the bottle down hard. "Not in this room. I guess not. No ladies whatever."

"You're getting very drunk, Victor."

"Oh, that is good to know," he said. "I am getting very drunk, she says. Now that is news, isn't it? I have been drinking steadily, by the bucketful, and the lady—check that—the beautiful, hot, nymphomaniac female in this room says that I am getting drunk. I wonder why you think that I'm getting drunk?"

"You can't hurt me anymore, Victor."

"No," he said, shaking his head slowly, a loose and nasty smile on his mouth, "that is a physical impossibility now, isn't it? Too much conditioning, right? But you like that kind of conditioning, don't you? So—let's go to bed, shall we?"

"Please don't make this more difficult than it is."

"Come on," he said, lurching toward her, his voice rising. "If we're passing the love around, let old Victor have a little again, shall we?"

He grabbed for her. She dodged him. He stumbled and fell to one knee. But he was now between her and the door.

"Victor—don't."

He pushed himself up slowly, staring at her. "You're going to let old Victor have some of that again, by God. You're going—"

There was a hard rapping against their door. Victor blinked and turned slowly around. The rapping continued. He threw open the door. Joe Beacon was there. She let her breath out gratefully. Joe had heard. He was stopping it.

Joe *had* heard the loud sound of Day's angry, drunken voice. He had waited until he could wait no more. Then he had come over fast and knocked on the door. Now, as he stared at Victor Day weaving in front of him, he found that he could hate the man with ease.

"What do you want, Beacon?" Day said thickly.

He made up his mind swiftly. He had to get Lynn out of there. And he had to do something about all of this. There was no use going on just waiting for something to fix it. Something had to be figured out; something had to be done.

"I think," he said, "we'd all better get out here and talk about this. It's five-thirty. It'll be dark shortly. We've got to work something out."

"Do you mean you haven't already, Beacon?" Day said meanly. "Do you mean the great outdoor man hasn't already been able to figure out a single goddam thing to stop this?"

Joe walked down the line and knocked on the Iveses' door. He asked Ives to come out and bring his wife. He could hear her protesting as he moved on to the Glenns' cabin. Again he knocked several times. Finally Norris opened the door a crack and peered out. "I'd like you and your wife to come out to the table, Mr. Glenn. We're going to have to talk about this."

Rosalind said from within, "We're not going out there, Norris!"

"Oh, yes, we are!" Norris said, suddenly swinging the door open wide. "Yes, sir, Mr. Beacon. Right away!"

A few minutes later, all of them met at the picnic table. Joe talked to them quietly:

"I've been hoping that the boy would just simply forget this, come down, and then it would be over. But he's not forgetting it. I thought that deputy might be the answer. He only made it worse. So we've got to figure out something."

Victor Day stood beside the table and said, "Like what, for God's sake?"

"I'm open to any idea anybody has," Joe replied.

"Well," Roy Ives said, sitting carelessly on the edge of the table as Flo sat sullenly on the bench beside him. "I figure if we could get somebody up back of him, why, all that man'd have to do is rock him in his head."

"You can't do that," Joe said, trying to keep his voice calm. "In the first place, you'd never get out of this circle."

"Christ," Roy Ives said. "He shoots off that popgun. Maybe he likes the noise. Maybe he ain't going to shoot nobody. Maybe he's bluffing. He wants some attention up there."

"He's not bluffing."

"That's what you say, Beacon. We ain't heard too much out of you that's done us any good so far, have we?"

"Maybe he's right," Victor Day slurred. "I don't know where you get the idea you're the last word, Beacon."

"I know him," Joe said.

"Yeah?" Roy said. "Then how come you let him get us into this?" He laughed shortly, then stood up. "I figure I might be right. He's a squirrel, all right, but he might be bluffing." He strolled carelessly toward the east edge of the clearing away from the table.

"I'm telling you, Ives," Joe said. "Don't push him."

"You stay where you are, Beacon," Ives said, as he moved. "Don't worry none about it. He ain't gonna do nothing. You watch." He looked up toward Eddie, visible to him now, and grinned. "He's touched up in the head, that's a fact. But he ain't gonna shoot old Roy Ives, now is he?"

"Ives—" Joe Beacon began.

But Roy Ives kept moving toward the far boundary created by the crushed rock. He was within a yard of the end of that crushed rock, moving casually, when Eddie's rifle cracked. A bullet whined down to smash into the rock with an ugly tearing sound just a foot ahead of him.

Ives stopped, and Joe could see his face freeze. He stood there for a moment, motionless, then he turned and came back. His smile returned, but there were fine lines of tension around his eyes and mouth. "He ain't bluffing," he said shortly.

Norris Glenn had again begun trembling visibly. Victor Day's face had paled noticeably beneath the flush of his hard drinking. He glared at Ives. "If you don't know what the hell you're doing why do you fool around like that? What's the matter with you?"

"Well, now, I'm sorry about that, Mr. Day," Ives said quietly. "I thought you said maybe I was right, maybe he was bluffing. But now we know he ain't. So you just know how goddam sorry I am—"

"All right," Joe said. "That ought to prove it. Just don't push him anymore."

"Don't push him!" Victor Day said loudly. "You've said that enough, Beacon. But what are we going to do about it?"

"I have one idea. The light's fading. It'll start getting dark in a few minutes. Maybe I can convince him that the floodlights have cut out— a short somewhere. Maybe he'll buy that. Then a couple of us can try to get up to him and take that rifle away from him in the dark. Ives? You and I could try that."

"Sure," Ives said darkly. "Anything to get that squirrel off there."

Then the voice came down to them, clearly, as though issued from a loudspeaker: "About time you turned on those floods, Pop. It's getting too dark."

Joe took a breath. Ives smiled and said softly, "Just like he was reading your mind, huh?"

Beacon stepped out to face the boy above. The sun was behind Eddie now, and the sky in that direction was a fiery red, so that there was visible no more than the black outline of him, rifle up. "Eddie," Joe shouted. "Those lights, they've shorted out."

"I want those lights on!" Eddie screamed. "Now! And don't try to tell me they're not working. If they're not working, I start shooting!"

"Eddie—!"

"Now! *Now!*"

Roy Ives laughed without humor. "Great idea, Beacon. But she didn't work, did she?"

Joe Beacon, frustration doubling his hands, walked grimly to his house. He turned on the floodlights, then came back to the picnic table to listen with building irritation to the sarcastic voice of Ives saying:

"We're just plain in trouble, ain't we? And there ain't nothing to do but wait that boy out. Maybe he'll go to sleep up there. Just doze off. Rifle falls out of his hand. A big eagle swoops down and flies off with the rifle. Then—" he motioned a hand toward the cliff and looked at

Victor Day with dark, gleaming eyes—"a whole passel of United States Marines comes busting right down that hill. Hallelujah."

Chapter 22

Nobody laughed at Ives' humor. They remained silent until Joe asked, "Any other ideas?" There was no response, and he spread his hands futilely. The Glenns returned silently to their cabin. Victor Day sat down loosely on a bench beside the table, looking at no one. Joe met Lynn Marsey's eyes, and said, "If you and Mr. Day would care for coffee, you can get it in my house. I'll be over there in a little while."

Lynn nodded quickly, obviously relieved. She said, "Thank you very much, Mr. Beacon." She looked briefly at Victor, who continued to sit there, saying nothing. Then she moved off toward Beacon's house. Joe Beacon said to the Iveses:

"You two like coffee?"

Roy Ives shook his head. "Coffee makes me nervous. I mean to grab me a little nap. Ain't nothing else to do, is there? Take a snooze. See what happens. You comin', Flo?"

"I'll be in," she said, and Joe saw her staring with obvious interest at Day.

Ives, he thought, must have seen it, too; the man grinned, but there was a hard look in his eyes. He strolled casually to his cabin, shut the door behind him, and Flo remained where she was, smiling at Victor Day. Joe turned and walked away, toward the cabin Eddie and Nancy had used. He had a single idea left, and it wasn't much. But he had to do something, he thought, anything.

Finding himself alone with Flo Ives at the picnic table, Day turned his reddening eyes on her. She smiled more widely and said:

"Ain't this an awful thing to get into?"

"Yes," he said thickly.

"I don't know as Roy minds so awful much. He likes something to happen. He don't care. Roy, he's not scared of one damn thing. But for a nice fellow like yourself, with a big car like you got, you ain't used to something like this, are you?"

"I can handle myself," he said, looking at the thrust of her breasts. She was wearing a simple red and green Mexican dress now, with white moccasins. She was barelegged; and he was positive, in his slowly revolving mind, that she wore nothing at all but that dress and shoes.

"Oh, I don't doubt that," Flo said. "But I mean this ain't right for a nice fellow like yourself to get caught up in something like this. More Roy's style, I reckon. Me—I ain't scared either, not really. But I don't like it, particular. I mean, I ain't scared. But I get excited. I feel all funny when I get excited. Do you know what I mean?"

He looked at her eyes and listened to the words carefully. He nodded.

"I feel all funny that way right now," Flo said, almost whispering. "I guess I ought to get up and move around a little and see if it don't go away. I was looking over there at that pine shed. I was wondering what was in there." She stood up. "I think I'll go take me a look." She looked sideways at him, her glance sliding over him so that he could almost feel it. Then she moved away, with a heavy swing of her hips, in the direction of the pine shed.

He sat there loosely, feeling the tension fight against the dulling effects of the liquor and then finally concentrate into a tight, nearly unbearable knot of desire. He licked his lips and watched the girl turn past the corner of the shed. She would be going in the back door, he thought. He watched the windows. No lights came on. She didn't come out. He stood up, looking at the Iveses' cabin. The door remained shut. The drapes were tightly pulled. Ives was, he assured himself, asleep.

Carefully keeping his balance, he moved toward the pine shed, forcing himself to walk, not run.

In the house, Lynn Marsey poured coffee for herself and waited for Joe Beacon in his kitchen. She'd had enough of Victor. She wanted no more of him. Ever. And it no longer mattered what anyone thought of anything. She was going to remain here, in Joe Beacon's house, until this ended one way or another.

In the Glenns' cabin, Rosalind lay on the bed again and watched Norris sitting beneath the lamp, his drawing board on his lap, face tense as he drew. "Oh, Norris," she pleaded. "Come and comfort me."

He did not.

"Norris," she said. "How could I ever have felt the world was romantic? It is not romantic. It is cruel and base and terrible!" She turned her head, looking at him.

He did not respond.

"Norris," she said. "I mustn't talk that way, must I? Life *is* beautiful! It must be! Why else do the birds sing? Why else do the flowers bloom? Come to me, Norris. Whatever you're drawing, that can wait, can't it? Come to me, and put your arms around me."

She waited, watching him, trembling with hope. He did not look up.

Joe Beacon stood in the cabin once used by Eddie and Nancy, and felt his throat go tight. He could smell Nancy's perfume in here. If Eddie had come back in here and that had touched his senses, it would have been enough to have started this. Just that alone.

Grimly, he shook off the emotion—it was remembering Nita too, he knew—and began a methodical search. Perhaps Eddie had already suffered lapses like this before. Perhaps Nancy had not wanted to tell him the entire truth. And perhaps there was some kind of medication. If there were, then perhaps he could get it to Eddie somehow, and calm him.

But he found no such medication. He found only the possessions of two young people who had not been married long and who had come to stay a short time with him. He felt desperately sorry for the girl. Dead. And all left behind. Now a body. And not even her own family knowing that she was dead yet. And Eddie up there now. Sick of brain, but his son just the same...

He shook his head quickly, angrily, looking around. Her dresses were in the closet. Eddie's jackets hung beside them. Her cosmetics were carefully placed in a traveling case on the vanity. In the bath were Eddie's toiletries. There was Eddie's robe across the bed. The girl's purse was on the bureau. Beside it was a camera, a new Polaroid. He remembered that. She'd written him about using money saved before she'd married Eddie to buy that camera for his last birthday. She had been joyful to have given him something he wanted so much. A *world living*. A *world ended*. And all because somebody had set that trap....

He looked again at the camera. Something was trying to get out from his subconscious. *Something....*

He walked across the room and picked up the camera. He re-examined it, his mind turning, remembering back through the years. Suddenly he opened the camera's back. A picture had been taken, but not removed. He peeled it away and looked at it, frowning....

When Victor Day rounded the corner of the shed, he lurched straight to the small back door and pushed it open. Light from the floods spilled through the elongated shape of the doorway to illuminate Flo Ives standing against the side of the pickup. She looked at him, smiling.

Day kicked the door shut and walked to her. Only light from two small windows broke total blackness now. He didn't need light. He didn't need to see her or hear her—all he wanted was to do what he was going to do.

He reached for her skirt. She swiftly unzipped it and helped him pull it over her head. She was bare except for her shoes, which she kicked off.

Day forgot everything else. He put his hands on her. They sank to the floor, and his world turned slowly with the alcohol, his senses drumming. She wriggled under him, willing, eager, ready. Desire became all of his consciousness.

But suddenly she was slipping from him, skidding away, as light from the doorway splashed down on them. He slowly came to reality, while the girl kept scrambling back, her face full of panic in the glare from the doorway.

Day hitched himself up to his knees and turned to find Roy Ives in the doorway, a tight, mean, savage smile on his mouth.

"Now, Roy," Flo said, reaching for her dress. "It wasn't nothin', Roy. You know that!"

Ives closed the door and stood with his back to it. He switched on an overhead light, a single dim bulb. He stared at Day still frozen on his bare knees. He said, "Get your dress on, Flo."

"We wasn't really doin' nothin'," Flo protested, slipping on her dress, then her shoes.

"It sure looks that way."

"Listen, Roy," Flo pleaded. "It wasn't my fault anyway. I—"

"Shut up," he said thinly. He nodded at Day. "You're gonna get your ass whipped, you know that, don't you?"

Victor felt sobriety returning fast. He looked at Roy's lean frame. Ives looked skinny. He must outweigh him by fifty pounds, at least. He tensed his muscles.

"I'm just tellin' you that," Roy Ives said. He touched the end of his nose with the palm of his hand. "But you better pull up your pants first."

Victor wrenched himself to his feet. Roy Ives came forward with unbelievable swiftness and chopped him so hard on the chin that he was tumbled feet over shoulders all the way across the interior of the shed.

It was not a fight. It was a swift, methodical butchering. Day never got off one good swing. He was tangled in his trousers to the end. And when the end came, Roy Ives was not breathing hard. Victor Day lay supine, almost senseless, his face a bleeding pulpish caricature of itself.

Roy Ives stood over him, spraddle-legged. He shoved Day's limp body onto its side with his foot and pulled out Day's wallet. He took out the money and counted it. There were five hundred and eighty-five dollars in currency. He dropped the emptied wallet back on the slack body. He folded the money and shoved it into his own pocket.

"Down payment," he said.

Eyes opening between rapidly swelling puffs, Day looked up in pain, defeat and fright.

"Me and Flo, we're getting out of here about now," Ives said softly. "But I ain't done with you." He shook his head. "You wasn't really married to that blonde broad you got in the cabin, huh? Uh-uh. You got a wife though, huh? And this ain't gonna be good, is it? Shacking up with some broad like that blonde one. What with the girl in the trap and all that publicity. Now this, with Flo. She's my wife, man." Ives drew a shoe back and carefully kicked it into Day's temple. Day gasped weakly, as his head jerked. "And," Roy Ives went on softly, "she ain't but eighteen. That makes it rape in this state, don't it? Man ought to know, if he's got any sense, what age he's raping in what state. But you ain't got any sense, have you?"

Ives bent down. He grasped Day's shirt front and jerked him up. The terrified, slitted eyes stared back at him.

"Me and Flo, we're going out now. And we're just leaving that T-bird right here. Dog, anyway. And if that kid up there ain't shot you through the head, we'll be looking you up later, mister. To see if you can't maybe buy ol' Roy and Flo there one of them Continentals. And maybe some other stuff. And maybe grease the palm with some more cash money. Otherwise—" Roy Ives shook his head.

He let go of the shirt, and Victor Day's head bounced on the floor. Ives straightened and said to Flo:

"We're getting out of here."

Flo shook her head worriedly. "That kid up there—"

"Hell with him. Money in my pocket now. We're getting out and we're gonna have some fun."

"How do we get out, Roy?"

"Run for it."

"I'm scared."

Ives' eyes looked at her, hard and bright within their tightening sockets. "That ain't all you are, is it? You also got some real round heels, huh?"

"Roy, listen to me," Flo whined. "It wasn't—"

"Shut up. We're leaving. Anything we leave behind we can get later.

None of it worth a crap anyway. So you listen careful, you hear? We walk out that door, real easy, and go around the shed heading back for the cabins. We're out of sight of that kid then. He'll be looking for us to show up on the other side. You do that. You go out walking natural. Only I'm going out the opposite way. I looked it over. It's the shortest distance I got to clear to get to them trees. Then it's good-bye to that kid."

"Maybe good-bye to us too," Flo whimpered. "What happens to me?"

"He'll be going for me, not you," Ives said. "Soon's you hear him shooting, you break off and run straight to your right. Head right for the trees. He won't even look at you. Just me. And that'll draw him off that ledge. And we go out."

"I *can't*."

"You better. And you better do it fast. You can run good. I seen you do it. And if you run as fast as you fell down on the floor with this—" Ives' mouth thinned. He kicked Victor Day's ankle, hard. "You're gonna do it, that's all."

Ives opened the door of the shed and stepped out without looking back to see if Flo were following. She was. They walked at an even pace to the back end of the shed, turned the corner and were out of sight of Eddie waiting on the cliff.

They stopped. Flo, blinking with fright, whispered, "Roy—"

He shoved her on, roughly. Reluctantly, she kept walking to the north and came into Eddie's sight again, moving in the direction of the cabins.

At the same moment Roy bounded in the opposite direction. He ran with long, leaping strides. Two seconds passed before Eddie, waiting for him to appear from behind the shed in the other direction, caught his movement. Then Eddie saw him and sighted him through the scope.

But Ives, timing his run, zigzagged, dove forward and somersaulted. The bullet smashed into crushed rock a foot behind him. Eddie, standing, making a low animal-like sound, sighted the flashing figure again. Ives came out of his somersault, rolled to his feet, and went on at top speed. The second bullet missed. Close. But Ives was fast, and he'd estimated his chance accurately. He was gone, into the woods.

Eddie, his sound turning into a high-pitched moan of fury and frustration, came running down the road, intent upon one thing: to destroy this man who had now demonstrated his guilt. He did not even see Flo, who moved in a fast, breast-jouncing run to the moonlit trees to the east.

Far above on the highway, before Eddie's rifle had cracked the first bullet after Roy Ives, six sheriff's cars had rolled to a stop by the gate. Lieutenant Lew Barnes climbed out of one of them, followed by a defeated-looking Sergeant Albert Cole. "Goddam it, Al," the lieutenant said, "what got into you that you didn't report this before?"

The others got out of their cars, swiftly, and came forward toward them. Sergeant Cole hunched his shoulders and said, "He told me not to."

"Well, he's crazy. You knew that."

"There wasn't anything to cover it, the way it happened."

"Yes, and that's why you should have hightailed it down and told me what was going on! What the hell did you think you were doing, taking this long before you—"

They heard the first shot.

"Christ," the lieutenant said. "Let's go. Fast!"

Joe Beacon was still in the Craynes' cabin when that first shot sounded. He plunged outside, just in time to see Roy Ives disappearing into the trees. He saw Flo running swiftly across the crushed rock to his left. He sprinted forward. When he reached the cabin nearest his house, he saw Eddie coming down the road at high speed, rifle flashing in the moonlight.

"Eddie!" he shouted.

Eddie snapped off a shot in his direction. Joe dove to the ground, the bullet whining over his head. Then he scrambled up and ran for the house and that carbine.

And Eddie went on, because he was not interested in Joe Beacon—he simply did not want to be stopped. He ran straight into the trees where Roy Ives had disappeared. There was not as much moonlight as there had been the night before, but enough. He would find Ives. He would shoot him. Through the head. Because Roy Ives had killed Nancy. He knew that now. He plunged through the underbrush, hearing the sound of someone ahead circling to his left. He would get him. By God, he would get him.

Ives, in his circling to the left, crossed paths with a frightened Flo. "Come on!" he whispered furiously. He yanked her with him, moving away from the camp, then switching back in the direction from which he'd come.

"Roy," Flo whispered. "We ain't gonna make it!"

"*Move!* We drew him off there. Now we shake him and go out!"

Flo moaned and kept running with her husband. Then he stopped her. They crouched silently, while Ives listened. Eddie was moving in the direction Ives had been going originally, before he had switched and come back this way with Flo. He could tell that by the sound. "We're gonna circle back now," he whispered. "Go right back in the direction where he was sitting up on that cliff. Make the highway direct. He ain't gonna look for that. Do it quiet!"

He jerked Flo up and they moved on, more silently now, around to the south, then west again. They stopped a second time, and Eddie's sound was well behind them now. They moved forward, wriggling and bounding through the brush, making very little noise.

But Flo dropped to her knees, as they were approaching the cliff just to the left of the road snaking up the rock. "I'm run out of gas, Roy," she moaned. "I can't—"

"Get going!"

Again he yanked her to her feet and pushed her on. They started climbing now, and then Flo tripped, crashing through dry brush. The sound echoed back. Roy Ives swore savagely and lifted her to her feet. Ahead was the rock, rising steeply. There was one gap of pure rock they would have to pass, but then, if they stayed to the left of the road, there were enough trees and brush to hide their exit all the way up.

Flo was gasping now. Ives moved ahead of her, climbing. He was leaving her and she called to him, loudly. He swore again and stopped. He turned around, watching her trying to scramble after him. He could hear something else now: Eddie, who, having heard them, had reversed his direction and was coming back after them swiftly, crashing through the trees.

Ives looked down at Flo. She pushed herself up, reaching out to him. He looked at her breasts heaving with her heavy breathing. She'd been breathing like that in the shed, when he'd kicked that shed door open and found her with Victor Day. He bent down and drove his fist into her head. She tumbled backward.

He started climbing again swiftly. He was free of her now, and he could really move. That kid would never get him. Never....

He reached the span of open rock. His feet and hands churned as he climbed. He had almost reached cover above when the bullet whined up from the trees below. It tore through the base of his skull, and when the body finally came to a sprawled stop beside Flo, there was little of his head left.

Joe came running up, with the carbine. He saw Eddie standing in a patch of moonlight coming down between the trees. He heard the crashing sound to the right, then he saw Sergeant Albert Cole coming in, gun in hand. Eddie stood motionless and limp; and the rifle held loosely in one hand, the butt resting against the ground. The sergeant saw Eddie, stopped and lifted his pistol. Joe raised the carbine, fast, pointing it at the sergeant only feet away, yelling, "No!"

The sergeant seemed not to hear. He aimed his pistol at the boy. Joe's carbine cracked, and the bullet snapped the pistol from his hand. The sergeant turned his eyes on Joe Beacon as though coming out of a dream, and then he looked down at his empty hand.

Joe walked to Eddie and said, "Give me the rifle, Eddie."

Eddie nodded and handed the rifle to him willingly. "Shot him through the head."

The sergeant picked up his own pistol and came over. Joe said, "Put that pistol in your holster, sergeant. Eddie, you stand here with the officer. Do what I say, will you?"

"All right," Eddie said. "I'm all done, anyway. He's dead. That's all I wanted."

Joe climbed ahead to the two figures lying there. He looked at what had once been Roy Ives. Flo was regaining consciousness. When she saw the body, she began howling. He grasped her arm firmly, lifted her to her feet, then gently but firmly moved her away.

Chapter 23

The rest of the sheriff's people came in, climbing on foot over the exploded rock; one of them was left with Roy Ives' body until a stretcher could carry it out. Eddie was handcuffed. Flo continued to howl. Then Joe went back with them to his camp. There, Lynn Marsey and the Glenns appeared; they were told what had happened. Norris, looking strangely calm, sat down and curiously watched Lieutenant Barnes direct the now-relaxed Eddie to be seated in a chair in the center of the large living room. Nobody knew where Victor Day was. Joe Beacon volunteered to repair the telephone line Eddie had cut. When he went out to the shed to get the tools to do it, he found Victor Day lying on the floor there. He called for a deputy, and they half carried him inside, where he was put to bed. Lynn Marsey, with an impersonal coolness, washed and medicated his beaten face.

Joe repaired the telephone line and checked it. Then he returned to the clearing. He went into the cabin Eddie and Nancy had occupied, picked up the camera and picture he'd discovered earlier, and walked back to the house. Flo had also been put to bed, and her howling had stopped. Lieutenant Barnes, with a baleful-looking Sergeant Albert Cole standing beside him, asked Joe to explain again everything that had happened. He did so, then the lieutenant turned to Eddie, who sat silently, almost cheerfully, in the chair in the center of the room.

"Do you know what you did, son?"

"Yes," Eddie said calmly. "I killed him. I'm not sorry."

The lieutenant look at Joe. Joe stepped in front of the boy. He held the photograph before Eddie's eyes, not wanting to do it, but knowing that he had to. "Look at this picture, Eddie."

Eddie looked at the picture and blinked slowly.

"Do you know who took it?"

Eddie shook his head, his eyes frightened.

"It's a picture of Nancy, Eddie," Joe Beacon said determinedly, holding it steadily in front of the boy's eyes. "Just before she went into the trap."

"Get it away from me!" Eddie said, his voice rising.

"I know how it was taken, Eddie," Joe Beacon insisted. "The camera was set up just in front of the trap. A wire was stretched across the path and hooked up to the shutter mechanism. Whoever set up the camera, Eddie, set the trap. I found the camera and the picture in it in your cabin. I remembered how you used to set up a camera and a flash gun with the traps you set so that if an animal missed the trap, you got his picture anyway. You set the camera up, didn't you, Eddie? On the same trail where you used to trap? And you were the one who set the trap."

The room was silent. Everyone stared at the boy. Eddie's eyes shifted. He looked down at his knees, frowning. "That night," he said slowly, "I couldn't sleep early in the evening. I went out with the camera and set it up. Then I went back to the shed and got the trap and set that. I came back to the cabin, and Nancy and I talked. Then we—" he gripped his handcuffed hands together tightly—"I went to sleep. When I woke up, she was gone. So I went outside and I couldn't see her. Then I heard her, down by the lake—just a gasp, just barely, and I—" he swallowed with difficulty—"I went down there where I'd set the trap and found her. Then I picked up the camera and the wire and went back to the cabin. I sat down and thought about it, and I couldn't believe it. I didn't believe it. Then I went out and yelled that she was gone ... gone...."

He shook his head once more, and something shifted in his eyes again.

He sat straighter. "He killed her. That Ives. So I killed him. Shot him through the head. I'm not sorry. He killed Nancy, didn't he? So I killed him."

Joe turned from the boy, face grim, feeling an ache deep inside that he was certain he would never lose. He felt Lynn's hand going into his.

"Sorry, Joe," she whispered. "I'm so sorry."

Chapter 24

At the first light of dawn, a caterpillar bulldozer was brought in by the sheriff's people from the highway. The rock which blocked the road was pushed away. By one o'clock that afternoon everyone but Joe Beacon had left the camp. He stood beside his house, watching the last car leave, knowing that more than people had gone this time; it was something else—a piece of his life, so that he would have to put something else back in now, to replace the missing part....

Nancy Crayne's body was shipped south for burial by her family. A preliminary check on Eddie's sanity was made. A hearing would be held, but there was no doubt that he would be placed in an institution.

Albert Cole was demoted from sergeant immediately and put back on a routine patrol. He seemed to remain impassive, so that even his new partner could not detect his true feelings beyond being repeatedly irritated by the man's dedication to the rules. But inside, Albert Cole felt a roiling, savage determination to regain the rank he had lost. He was certain he could do it; he had even been promised by Lieutenant Barnes that if he handled himself well for a time, he would again become a sergeant. But late at night, lying in his bed, staring sleeplessly at the ceiling, he would find a return of that nagging worry that again, some time, somewhere, he would be faced with something that was not in the book, and he would not know what to do. It did not seem to him, in that dark moment, fair. Not fair at all.

Two days after he was killed, Roy Ives was buried by Flo in a cemetery south of San Francisco. Flo had sobbed hysterically and steadily during those two days, then bought the cheapest burial she could with the money taken from Ives' pockets, the bulk of which had come from Victor Day's wallet—Day made no effort to reclaim the money. Roy Ives was buried at three o'clock in the afternoon, then Flo drove the Thunderbird to the cheap motel she'd rented. She repaired her make-up and put on fresh clothes. Then she walked down the block to a bar to pick up her spirits. After five drinks, she was sitting with a tall, lean man who explained that he was a logger from Washington. Flo drank four more drinks with him, then took him home to her cabin. He reminded her a lot of Roy. Two days later she went north with him.

Victor Day's wounded face gradually returned to its normal appearance. But during the next days at home, he did not speak to his wife. She did not speak to him either. They simply existed in an icy vacuum. The children were sent off to their mother's parents. Then one evening Victor walked across the room and dropped to his knees before his wife. He begged her forgiveness. She gave it, finally, saying with a cold, warning note in her voice:

"But never again, Victor. I warn you. Never again."

"No," he said, and he could not help actually sobbing with gratefulness. "Never again."

When he returned to their flat in the city, Norris Glenn finally showed Rosalind the charcoal he had been working on during their tense wait in the cabin in Joe Beacon's camp. Rosalind stared at it in horror. It was a sketch of a dying woman. She knew immediately that it was Nancy Crayne dying in the trap. She looked at Norris in astonishment. "It's awful, Norris. An absolute refutation of all of nature's beauty. Destroy it! I beg of you, Norris. Destroy it immediately!"

But Norris, who had developed a new and sturdy confidence, did not. Instead, he showed the drawing to his friends, one of whom insisted on arranging for it to be hung in a North Beach saloon. The day it was displayed, a customer offered five hundred dollars for it. Norris took the offer, then did another, depicting a crushed lizard. That one had a similar commercial success. He started a third drawing, and Rosalind, remembering how intently Norris had watched them bringing Roy Ives' body in from the woods, knew what it was going to be. She begged him to go back to his drafting job. She begged him to give up art entirely. She waited, terrified, for his response. He looked at her, hard lights gleaming in his eyes, and said, "Ridiculous." He went right on drawing.

It was three weeks before Joe Beacon saw Lynn Marsey again. He had spent that time re-examining his life. He had known, when his examination was done, that time indeed changed everything, that it always would, and that there was no use looking back anymore. His ranching days were done. Now he had this camp. He could make much more of his life, as well as this enterprise, if he tried. He was going to try, he knew. Because he was done with turning his back on things, refusing to admit the realities that kept coming.

On a bright, cool day she came, driving down the winding road. He heard the car and waited on the porch. He had only to look at her face, when she stepped out and came to meet him, to know that she would stay here if he wanted her to. He wanted her to. It would be better than it had ever been. He knew that.

THE END

NEVER BE CAUGHT

- - - - - -

James McKimmey

NEVER BE CAUGHT

The town of San Lupe lay under a yellow January sky, cooled by a sea breeze from the coast seven miles away. The boy and girl sat silently in the old convertible on a quiet residential street dominated by a very large white frame house with rococo trim. Into the quiet came the distant sound of the whistle of a train speeding toward Los Angeles eighty miles south. The boy—tall, blond and extremely slim—was looking at the white house. The girl—strikingly pretty, with a fragile, pale face, black hair and very dark eyes—was looking at the boy. At last she said:

"I'm sure it'll be all right, Billy."

"Oh yes."

"She just wants to talk to you."

He rubbed his chin with long fingers. He was handsome, she thought. He was intelligent, warm and loving. He was twenty-two, six years older than she. He was more than anything she could think of. She could only feel, and know through that, that she loved him. What else was love? she asked herself. And she had felt it from the instant she'd gone into the small truckers' café on the highway for a coke and seen him behind the counter.

He turned to smile at her. It was a fine smile, she thought: an infectious curve of the mouth, showing even white teeth, making her heart pump faster and her inner self melt. Oh, God, she thought, I do love him.

"We'd better go in," he said, looking at his watch. "It's four-thirty."

"Yes." She took his hand. "She'll love you, as I do."

He slid from behind the wheel and came around to help her out. They walked toward the large house. And she knew, because of the way he had spoken, because of the look of his eyes, that he was very nervous.

The interior of the house was high-ceilinged and furnished sparsely with durable furniture. There was a fireplace in the sprawling living room. Over its mantle was hung a large oil painting of a man in his forties. He had thick, loosely brushed hair, graying faintly at the temples. His face was angular, dark, and strong-looking. His eyes stared forth unafraid and commanding.

"That was my father, he died when I was two months old," the girl said, then led the youth across the room and down a mahogany-paneled hallway to a closed door. "She wants to see you alone."

"Sure," he smiled, but the smile was no longer easy.

She rapped lightly on the door and opened it. He went in alone.

Elizabeth Nivero's office was awesome in its simplicity. The walls were white plaster and held no pictures. Black beams ran across the ceiling. The floor was stone, and French doors looked out upon a sweeping garden of small palms shadowing a trimmed lawn which was circled by a giant hedge. There was a single gold brocaded chair placed in front of a massive baroque desk. Behind the desk sat Elizabeth Nivero, perhaps fifty-five, he thought, extremely small, extremely handsome, with olive skin and white hair. There was authority in her stiff posture and in her black eyes, so piercing and steady that he stopped midway across the room, feeling her power.

"Sit there," she said in a soft, husky voice that nevertheless carried the force of her personality.

He sat down in the armless gold chair, spotlighted with the pale yellowish illumination of the late winter afternoon coming through the panes of the French doors. He felt alone and stripped of defense in her steady examination of him. But he found nothing to say and waited silently until she spoke:

"Billy Marsh?"

"Yes, ma'am."

"How old are you?"

"Twenty-two."

"That's what Maria told me. She's sixteen. She has a year and a half more of high school to finish. She's a child."

He started to reply, then he did not.

"All right, Mr. Marsh," she said. "I've known you've been seeing her. Ever since it started, about six weeks ago. You've never come here, have you? You've always met her somewhere else."

Again he did not know what to reply.

"You thought I'd interfere, didn't you?"

"Yes, ma'am."

"All right. Keep giving me straight answers like that."

For the first time, he began to relax. He smiled at her, but she did not return the smile. She removed a cigarette from a pack on her desk and put it between her thin lips. He immediately drew a packet of matches from his shirt pocket. But she lit the cigarette with a flat silver lighter before he could lean forward. He slipped the packet back into his breast pocket, flushing slightly.

"I'll tell you why I haven't interfered," she said dryly. "It's because I decided when Maria was born that I would never allow myself to restrict her freedom. Maria is my only child. Nevertheless, I resolved that I would never become overly protective about my daughter. Do you understand, Mr. Marsh?"

He had grown to love Maria swiftly. She was kind, sweet, humble and devoted to him from the instant they'd met. But he had been very certain that one thing about Maria which might be a fault was the fact that she had obviously been overprotected. But he said, "I think so."

"Then you'll also understand why I wanted you to come here today. It's not that I'm trying to interfere with a twenty-two-year-old man spending so much time with my sixteen-year-old daughter. It's not the fact that you happen to be employed as a counterman in that truckers' café on the edge of town. It is simply that I feel I have a right to know who you are, where you come from, what you're doing here, and what you intend to do with your life. Since you haven't given me the respect of coming here before now to tell me these things, I've asked you to see me today, so you can. I repeat, Mr. Marsh, I'm not trying to interfere. I'm simply trying to meet my responsibilities as a mother. Am I clear?"

His voice was very quiet. "Yes, ma'am."

"Where do you come from?"

"Los Angeles."

"Did you graduate?"

"Yes. I had a year of college too."

"Where?"

"Pasadena."

"What did you take?"

"Art."

"You want to be an artist?"

"I don't think so. I thought so then. I don't think so now."

"You decided to be a counterman in a truckers' café instead?"

Again he flushed faintly. "I just haven't decided yet. I have that job for a living, that's all."

"You're twenty-two years old, but you don't know what you want to do yet. Is that it?"

"Yes," he said softly, feeling resentful.

"Do you love my daughter?"

"Yes." Now his voice had turned firmer. He sat straighter.

"You think you love her."

"I know I do."

"What does your father do?"

"He's dead."

"Your mother?"

"She lives in Los Angeles."

"Does she work?"

"Yes," he said. "Well, I mean—not right now." Her questions were coming fast, and he could feel his palms dampen.

"What do you mean, not right now?"

"I mean she did. She doesn't now."

"How does she live then? You don't make enough to support her, do you?"

"She had insurance, from when my father died."

"He had a good amount of insurance then, didn't he?"

"Yes, ma'am. A pretty good amount."

"What did he do for a living?"

"He was a carpenter."

"You lived in Los Angeles all your life? Then you came here. Why?"

"I just happened to like it here."

"You mean you came through and just happened to like it?"

"Yes, ma'am."

"Just like that."

"Well—we, I mean, my family and I drove through here once, when we came down from San Francisco, and we—"

She watched him carefully. "Down? Your home was in Los Angeles, I thought."

His face suddenly turned hot. "I mean, yes. But we took this trip *up* to San Francisco. Then we went down, coming back."

"I see." She inhaled, then turned her cigarette out against an ash tray, watching him steadily. "Are you nervous, Mr. Marsh?"

"No," he said swiftly.

"I thought you were. But if you were honest about all of this, about your background, and yourself, and this love you say you have for my daughter, then you wouldn't be nervous, would you?"

"No, ma'am. I wouldn't be. I'm not."

She continued to stare at him, then she looked down at her desk. She shifted a paper. "All right, Mr. Marsh. I imagine Maria's waiting for you."

"You don't mind then?"

"Mind what, Mr. Marsh?"

"My seeing Maria?"

"Not so long as you handle yourself with complete propriety. Not so long as you be very careful about your intentions. Not so long as you keep everything absolutely in the open. If you get any ideas more serious than you have so far—such as marriage—I trust you'll talk to me. Otherwise—" She slid another paper before her eyes. "You may go, Mr. Marsh."

He left the room, shutting the door carefully behind him.

When he had, Elizabeth Nivero lifted her telephone and dialed. A male voice responded: "Sheriff's office."

"Let me speak to Carl Miter, please."

Moments later a hard, nasal voice said, "Miter here."

"Elizabeth, Carl. I'd like to see you, if you have a moment."

He was there in twelve minutes, tapping gently on her door.

He was a bantam-sized man with slightly bowed legs. He wore Levis and a matching denim jacket. He carried a worn black western hat and moved casually across the stone floor, his dark motorcycle-styled boots clumping.

"It's so good to see you, Carl."

He smiled and took her hand, then sat down on the gold chair, crossing his legs.

Now her eyes lost their warmth. "Have you heard of a Billy Marsh? Works out at Rudy's Café. He's been seeing Maria."

"I wondered how long you'd let that go on."

She drew out another cigarette. Miter leaned forward and lit it for her. She said, "I thought it was something that would die by itself. The one thing I've learned about Maria is that you don't handle her any way but carefully. I've been trying to do that, hoping she'd forget this. But she hasn't. Now I've got to do something about it. But I don't want to make any mistakes."

Miter dusted a palm across a boot. "You want me to handle him?"

"Not unless we have to do it that way. But I want you to check him. I had him in here, questioning him. I don't like his looks. I don't like the way he answered. Woman's intuition, perhaps. But I think he's in trouble. He seemed flustered, especially when he was telling me where he came from. First he said Los Angeles. Then San Francisco. I'd like you to find out where he really comes from. If you have to travel, do it. Fly, take the train, take your truck. Anything. But track that boy's background down. I think he came here to hide. I think he's a cheap, rotten opportunist as far as my daughter is concerned. I want you to handle this for me, Carl. Quickly."

He nodded, eyes glistening behind the steel-rimmed spectacles.

"You say it, Elizabeth, I do it. I always did." He grinned and stood up. "Don't you worry now."

"Thank you, Carl," she said, some of the anger fading from her voice. "You're very kind to me."

"Just you don't worry now," he said, and ambled casually from the room.

The youth rolled his convertible into the drive-in. "Hamburger and shake?" he said to the girl. She nodded, and he got out to give his order. It was cooler now and light was fading. A thousand yards away on the by-pass cars were speeding north and south on Highway 101. Two hamburgers and two milkshakes were placed in a cardboard holder. The boy carried them back to his car. They sat eating, sipping the milkshakes.

"Aren't you happy, Billy?" the girl said finally.

"Sure."

"It went perfectly, didn't it?"

"Absolutely."

"She didn't object to you. She isn't going to interfere."

"That's what she said."

"Then everything's all right, isn't it?"

He smiled at her. "Everything's always all right, if you want it to be. The world turns rosy, everyone loves each other and we all live in a paradise." But his eyes were hard.

He tossed the empty containers into a refuse can and backed with a high whine. He swung the car around and drove swiftly through the sleepy downtown section. Then he went out of town, down a narrow blacktop, past an orange grove. He turned on the radio full-volume, laughing, and took a sharp turn onto a country road, tires squealing. He finally stopped in the quiet of a small wood, cut the engine and turned the radio down low.

"You really don't understand me, do you, little one?"

"I try."

"Why?"

"Because I love you."

"As simple as that? No strings?"

"No strings."

He put his hands on her shoulders. "That's the way love should be. No strings."

"Do you love me that way?"

"Yes," he said very softly. "I do."

Then all of his worries, tensions, nervousness seemed to disappear. He kissed her carefully and tenderly. He was aware of nothing else for a long number of minutes, until the voice of an announcer broke through the radio music. She did not hear it because she was lost in her love for him. But he heard it, the first words, and got the radio snapped off, because he'd heard all he needed.

Twenty minutes before, Elizabeth Nivero's telephone rang atop her desk. She lifted it to hear: "Carl, Elizabeth. I don't think I'm going to have to make any trips to check that kid."

"Why not?"

"I went through the old teletypes. Should have caught it before. Blame myself. But you get so many of these things. It happened over a year ago. It wasn't hot when he showed up here."

"*What*, Carl?"

"He's from San Francisco, and we just checked the description with them up there on the phone. He's wanted, all right."

She could feel her face stiffen, a small tremor go into her hand holding the telephone. "Maria's with him right now."

"Hang on, Elizabeth," Miter said. "His name isn't Marsh. It's Lang. The sheriff's getting everything coordinated right now. I'm going out myself, just as soon as I hang up. Maria'll be fine. We'll have that son of a bitch behind bars in minutes. I'll phone you."

"Carl," she said tensely, "what is he wanted for?"

"A killing," Carl Miter said simply and hung up.

Billy Lang heard the truck approaching. Maria was no longer in his arms. She was staring at him, saying, "Billy, what's the matter? You're white."

"Maria, you've got to believe in me. You've *got* to!"

"But I do, Billy."

"No matter what."

"Of course," she said positively.

"Somebody's driving in here," he said. "Whoever it is, if they ask for me, keep their attention. Tell them we ran out of gas, that I walked back toward town."

"Billy—"

But he was out of the car, running. He disappeared behind a tree, just before the pick-up came into view around a curve and skidded to a stop. Carl Miter sat behind the wheel for a few moments; the aluminum housing of the living unit built over the flatbed and cab gleamed softly. Then he got out, a rifle in one hand. He came toward the convertible. Maria watched him in surprise.

"Carl? What's the matter?"

"Where is he?" Miter wheeled slowly, searching the woods.

"Who?"

"Billy-boy."

"We—ran out of gas. He walked back toward town."

Miter's eyes switched to look at the radio; it was silent.

"What's the matter, Carl? Is something wrong?"

"Yeah," Miter nodded.

Now she saw him coming from the trees, loping with high speed toward Carl Miter, who was faced away from him. Miter saw her eyes looking behind him. He turned. But before he was halfway around, Billy's hand sliced flatly against his neck. Miter grunted and tried to bring up the rifle. But the boy hit him again, with a closed fist. The rifle went out of Miter's hands and his legs loosened, his eyes glazed. Again a fist came up in a long, looping arc; there was a dull crack as it struck Miter's jaw. Miter tumbled heavily to the ground and lay motionless.

"Billy!" the girl said. "What's happening?"

"Stay there," he snapped. He emptied the ammunition from the rifle, then swung it by the barrel against a tree trunk, smashing the stock. He ran to the pick-up, jerked the keys from the ignition and threw them into the brush. Then he ran back to the convertible, vaulted in and started the car. He left the woods with a roar.

"Billy—?" the girl began.

"No questions," he said. "Not now. You've just got to believe in me. We're going. Will you? With me?" His blond hair was tumbled over his forehead, as he bent against the steering wheel. "Maria, will you? *Please*. I love you!"

"Yes," she whispered, eyes frightened, her hands held tightly together. "Anywhere. With you, Billy!"

The sheriff's office was neat and well arranged. There were metal files, a glassed gun cabinet, a map of the county on a wall. The sheriff sat behind a large metal desk. His name was Monty Case, a large man with a fleshy, pleasant face, dressed neatly in a lightweight suit. Elizabeth Nivero sat stiffly in a straight-back chair, watching him. Carl Miter stood to her right, eyes savage behind his glasses. His left cheekbone was bruised; there was a small piece of tape on his chin.

"I'm sorry, Elizabeth," the sheriff said.

"It was my fault," Miter said coldly. "I never should have—"

"Don't blame yourself, Carl," she said. "You found him anyway."
She turned to the sheriff.

"Do you have his parents' address in San Francisco?" she asked.

"Yes," the sheriff nodded.

"I'd like to have Carl for a while," she said. She looked again at the tough, pocked face of Carl Miter. "We'll take the truck. With the dogs. He'll head for home."

"Elizabeth," the sheriff said, "We're doing everything humanly possible."

"May I have Carl?" she said.

"Yes, of course. But—"

"This is my daughter he's kidnapped!" she said harshly.

In San Francisco the air had turned chill. The sun had set and darkness was coming fast. Home-going drivers rolled bumper-to-bumper up the incline of Twin Peaks. At the top, occupants of a half-dozen parked cars were watching the lights of the city turning on. Down the east side of the hill a station wagon came to a stop in front of one of several very neat white houses built only inches apart. The driver, a strong-looking rather short man, reached in back and picked up a newspaper and a six-pack of beer from a collection of fishing gear. He got out of the car, moving with the natural ease of an athlete.

He was climbing the steep stairway to his door when a voice stopped him. He turned and looked at two men crossing the street from a police car. He felt the apprehension immediately.

The taller of the two led the way up the steps and said, "Ernest Lang?"

"That's right."

"I'm Inspector Ford. This is Assistant Inspector Johnson. We missed you where you work. We talked to your wife on the phone. She said you ought to be along about now."

Ernie Lang rubbed his chin with the back of a hand. "I'm not in trouble, am I?"

"Not you."

"Billy?" he said softly.

"We'd like to come in, if you don't mind."

Ernie Lang's powerful shoulders shifted. "All right." He motioned them into a quiet, somber interior. A woman rose slowly from a chair. Ernie Lang smiled at her. Her shoulders were slumped wearily; she looked, he thought, older than her forty-four years.

"This is Inspector Ford and Assistant Inspector Johnson, Anna," he said. "My wife, Mrs. Lang."

"How do you do?" the inspector said. "We talked on the phone, I think."

"Yes," Anna Lang nodded. "Please sit down, won't you?"

They all seated themselves in the old, comfortable living room; and Ernie Lang said, "Did you find him?"

The inspector's voice was crisp. "He turned up down the coast in San Lupe. He's been working down there for the last six months in a truck café. He was using another name—Marsh. About six weeks ago he started going with a young girl down there. The girl's mother, a Mrs. Nivero, finally got suspicious. I gather she's one of the important people there. She had the sheriff's office check and a deputy ran into an old teletype on your son. He tried to pick him up. The boy was parked in a wood with the girl. He disarmed the deputy, knocked him out and took off. That happened this afternoon. The sheriff's office phoned that up to us. So the boy's with the girl. We don't know where. We'd like to. Has he contacted you, Mr. Lang?"

Ernie Lang shook his head, meeting the inspector's steady gaze. "No."

The inspector nodded. "If he does, you'll let us know?"

"Yes, of course."

"There's an APB on him. But it won't concern us unless he shows up here. He might do that, you know. So I'd like to know all I can. I wasn't familiar with his case, and I haven't had too much time to check it. A robbery and a shooting, wasn't it? A little over a year ago?"

Ernie looked down where he had placed the beer carton. The beer was warming now, and there was going to be no relaxation this evening. "That's right. He and another boy, Pete Howells, were accused of robbing a bar on Noe Street. Billy was driving his car. He parked in front of this bar. It was a Monday night. There weren't any customers in the place, just the owner at the bar. The Howells boy went in and showed a gun. He took a hundred dollars. Then he ran out. The owner had his own pistol under the bar. He picked it up and went to the door and fired after Howells. Apparently that's what happened, anyway. Howells was wounded, but the owner was hit in return. He died before anyone got to him ..."

The inspector waited politely, then he said, "And the boys?"

"They both went home. We didn't know what happened at first. But the Howells boy had been hit. I guess he didn't know how seriously until he got home. He finally told his parents. They phoned us. I talked to Billy in his room. He said it had all been Howells' idea. He said Howells just told him he wanted to buy some cigarettes in the bar and to wait for him. Then he came out running. The owner followed and started shooting. The Howells boy fired back and Billy drove off. He said he had no idea the Howells boy was armed or intended to rob the place. I believed him. I still do."

"Apparently he didn't think anybody else would."

"No," Ernie Lang said quietly. "I told him we'd have to phone the police. He said he wanted to get dressed and asked me to do it. I left him in his room. When I got back, he was gone through a window."

"And the Howells boy had another story?"

"Yes. He was taken to a hospital. He said he'd never intended to use the gun. He said he and Billy had just wanted a little money. They'd planned it together, he said. But when he came running out, and the owner fired, Billy grabbed the gun and fired back. He wasn't talking too straight, when he told the story. He was hurt pretty badly, running a high fever. Then ... he died."

"That's the way it hung up?"

"Yes."

"He's been gone about a year and you haven't heard from him in that time?"

"Not until now, through you."

The inspector stood up, and his assistant got up with him. "If he should try to contact you—"

"I'll let you know."

After the police had gone, Ernie Lang looked at his watch. "I think there's time for me to get on a train this evening. I'll see if I can get a reservation. I'm going down to San Lupe."

Fifteen minutes later he was driving down Twin Peaks. His wife sat silently beside him. Finally he said:

"Whose fault was it, Anna?"

She shook her head slowly.

He went on, "I loved that boy. I still do."

"I know," she said quietly.

"Now, Anna. I didn't mean it that way. That he was all I loved. You and I—"

"Oh, yes. You and I. Maybe this isn't the time to say it. But I'm going to, anyway."

"I've always been loyal to you, Anna."

"I know that. But love?" She shook her head. "You loved Bea. I was just her roommate. Bea was the pretty one. The boys always loved

Bea, including you. But not Anna."

"Don't talk that way."

"When you married Bea and she died giving you Billy, you felt you had to turn to me, didn't you?"

"Damn it," he said, flushing.

"You wanted a mother for him. I was it."

"Damn it, Anna. You've no right—"

"I'm sorry. I'm done now."

They were approaching the station. He stopped the car and turned to her. She smiled at him sadly and said:

"I don't want you to punish yourself. Don't, Ernie. Just go down there, do what you can, the best way you can."

"Yes," he said softly. "If Billy should—"

She nodded. "I'll tell him where you are."

He sat looking at her for a moment longer, then he kissed her, clumsily, and was out of the station wagon with his bag. He moved toward the station, a wide, strong, graceful man who looked as though he were bearing more burden than he should.

An hour earlier, Billy Lang had stopped the convertible. He had driven inland, using country roads, then doubled back, toward the coast. Now they were in rocky coastal country, parked on a road little more than a path. Trees were thick, bent by a sea wind. There was a small stream running below. Billy opened the glove compartment and drew out a service-station map. It was five minutes before five; there was enough light left to read the map.

"About fifty miles north of San Lupe," he said softly. "A mile from some town called Tiller. Then Dunston up the line, about another mile." He looked around. The surface of the ground was pure rock which sheared off abruptly, down to the creek running below. "They figure we're winging out of here." He shook his head. "Not yet."

"Billy—" the girl said.

He looked at her. Then he smiled. "Now don't worry. It's going to be all right."

"Tell me what happened, Billy."

"I will." He took her in his arms and held her tightly. "But I've got to figure this out first. If I don't, it's over. And that means it's over for us. Don't you see that?"

"I'm trying."

"You've got to believe me. There won't be any more, if they catch us. Do you want that?"

"No!" she said swiftly.

"Then believe in me, little one. I'll explain pretty soon. Everything. All right?"

"Yes," she whispered. "Yes ..."

Billy left the girl in the car and walked across the fields to the small town named Tiller. The air was cooling rapidly, and he moved fast, checking his watch. He stopped at the outskirts, standing on a knoll. The highway by-passed the town, to his right. The main street offered a dozen stores. He could see them from where he stood. At the far end was a surplus store with a gaudy red and black sign announcing the fact. There was a five-and-ten midway down the block. He rubbed his jaw. They'd broadcast their descriptions everywhere by now, he was certain, but this was a chance he had to take.

He walked down the knoll and into the town.

He went swiftly down the street to the surplus store. The owner was short and heavy, with a fringe of grey hair around an otherwise bald head. "Yes, sir?"

"Those jackets over there. How much?"

"Honest-to-God Army fatigue jackets. I'd say I was maybe the only place in the state, maybe in the country, that's got those kind of jackets."

He followed the man across the store. He bought a jacket; he also bought a second-hand civilian hat: a grey snap-brim. While he was waiting for change, the owner said, "Staying in town, or just heading through?"

"Heading through," Billy said. "I've been hitch-hiking. But the luck isn't so good. There's not a bus station here, is there?"

"The nearest station's over at Dunston. Next town up."

He put on the jacket and hat and returned up the block to the dime store. It was 5:25 now. A lone girl was checking receipts at the front when he came in. It was a self-service store, and the girl glanced up at him, then at the clock above the door. She looked annoyed.

He walked through a metal turnstile and moved casually, searching the counters. He glanced back at the girl when he reached the cosmetics section. She was engrossed in her counting. He found a bottle of red hair dye and slipped it into a jacket pocket. There was a display of kerchiefs. He took one and slid that into a pocket. He checked the girl in front again. She had not looked up. He neared a display of eye glasses. He touched them idly, until he found a pair that seemed to have no correction. They followed the dye and the kerchief.

The hands on a wall clock read 5:30. The girl called back, "Closing time."

He removed a cardboard suitcase from a shelf and walked toward the front. He put the case on the check-out counter.

"That's all?" the girl said, fingers hovering over the register keys.

"That's all," Billy said.

Minutes later he was returning through the fields, but it was almost dark when he reached the convertible. The girl turned swiftly, saw him in the fading light, and held out her arms to him. He got in and held her. "That's done. Now we'll have to wait for a little while, then we're going to walk to the next town. Are you cold?"

"Not now," she whispered.

"Good," he said softly, breathing the clean fragrance of her hair. "Maria—I'll tell you now. About what happened."

"Yes, Billy."

He told her, the way he'd told it to his father. When he'd finished, she said:

"But you didn't do anything, did you? I mean, it was the other boy. Billy, if you really didn't do anything, wouldn't it be better to give up?"

His hands closed tightly on her arms. He stared at her with angry eyes. "Then what? Do you think anybody's going to believe me? I ran around in this neighborhood, when I was a kid. There was always trouble. And who did they go after? Billy Lang. Every time. They never would listen to the truth. Oh, that was small stuff. But I was never guilty of anything, any more than I am now. But this isn't small stuff. This is a murder, and they want me for it. And so what happens if I give up? I'll tell you. It won't matter that I didn't do it. Because they have to have somebody. And I'm the one. And what'll happen then is that there won't be anything left of you and me. Do you want that?"

"Oh, no, Billy," she whispered.

He put his arms around her again. "Then we've got to run. And not be caught. And then, pretty soon, it'll all die down. We'll find a new place to live. We'll be together. What more could we ask?"

"Nothing, Billy. That's all I want. Ever."

"Good," he said gently, smiling now. "Good ..."

They walked in the dark to the town called Dunston. Maria was wearing light, thin-soled shoes, and her legs were scratched by the brush. But they made it finally to the outskirts, and Billy knew he'd handled the car all right. Before they'd left, he'd released the handbrake and let it roll down the cliff into the trees near the small creek below. It had made some noise, crashing. But nobody had heard that, he was sure, and who was going to look for that car there?

She was shivering with cold when they stopped, looking at the lights of the village ahead.

A chill breeze had come up now, and he should, he thought, give her the fatigue jacket. But the jacket was to help fool them, and he couldn't.

There was a small shed a hundred yards behind a house at the edge of town. He waited to hear if a dog barked, but there was no sound. He directed her into the shed. In the dark, he kissed her and whispered, "Wait here. I won't be long."

Then he moved on, into town.

Street lamps reflected the moisture in the air, so that a halo circled each one. Billy looked down the central avenue. Most of the shop windows were lighted, but the stores were closed. Open were two bars, the waiting room of the bus station, and what he was looking for: a small, cheap-looking hotel midway down the block. He was wearing the Army jacket, the hat, the glasses and carrying the cardboard suitcase. He strode down the sidewalk toward the hotel and looked at the lobby from the street.

It was ancient and small. A clerk wearing a light, checked sports jacket with wide lapels bent over the desk, reading a paperback. There were two tattered-looking chairs in front of the desk. What appeared to be a self-operating elevator was just beyond. Opposite that, further back in the lobby, was a narrow stairway. The lobby opened to a short hallway, which led to an alley. He walked in.

The clerk looked up without interest. Billy smiled and said, "Have you got a room for not too much?"

"Five dollars the cheapest."

Billy shrugged. "I'll take it."

The clerk tapped the registry, stifling a yawn. Billy signed, "John Morgan, 2252 Noriega, Watsonville." The clerk slid a key to him across the desk. "Second floor. Turn right from the elevator."

"Sure," Billy said. "Only I'm going to get myself a beer first."

The clerk had returned to his reading before Billy reached the street. He moved back in the direction of where Maria waited in the shed. He saw a single Los Angeles newspaper left in a rack on the way. He put it inside his jacket. Then he went back to Maria.

They left the shed and traveled through the town on near-deserted streets. When they reached the alley which ran back of the hotel, he guided her into the shadows. "The back entrance is right up there, where that little light is. I'll go around to the front now. You can see the desk from the back. Give me about two minutes, then open that door a crack. When I move my hand like this, go in and up those stairs. Here's the key. Are you all right?"

"Yes," she said softly.

Then he was gone.

She went down the alley to the door and waited, shivering with the cold. Her throat felt scratchy, and her heart was beating fast. She kept thinking of her mother and how she'd never really disobeyed her about anything important before in her life. Little things, yes, but nothing big. And she could hear her mother's voice right now, ordering her to give this up and come home.

But she was not, and she stood there, her back against the brick of the building. Down the block she could hear the laughter of men drinking in a tavern. The alley was dirty, littered with garbage cans.

She turned and opened the door a fraction, and saw that Billy had entered the lobby and was talking now to the clerk. He pointed outside to the main street, so that the clerk was looking away from the back. He made a motion with his other hand, and she went in.

She ran light to the stairway and up the steps. There was a worn rug runner. Someone had scratched on the wall an obscene word that careless cleaning had not removed. There was a smell of age and old men and cheap wine, and she moved quickly to leave it. She went down the hall, inserted the key into a lock, and stepped into the room, shutting the door against all of that.

But she had not left it. She switched on the bare bulb in the ceiling, whose dimness could not hide the fact that the room, with an iron-framed bed and a worn easy chair, was as tawdry as every other part of the hotel. She walked slowly to the bed and sat down.

He came up seconds behind her. He locked the door behind him. His face looked tense. He examined the room swiftly. "This'll be all right. You did great." He drew the newspaper he'd picked up earlier from his jacket and scanned the front page. Then he opened the pages, one after another. On the eighth page he found it: a short story; there was no picture. His eyes narrowed as he read, then he slammed the newspaper into a rusting wastebasket.

"Is it about us?" she asked.

"Mostly me. And they never tell the truth. Never!"

"Billy—"

Suddenly his face softened. He smiled at her, and that smile made her forget everything else. "Listen," he said. "I'm sorry. It's just—" He walked to her and lifted her gently to her feet. "It's no good for you. I know that. But it'll be all right pretty soon. I swear it."

"But what are we going to do, Billy? Where are we going?"

"I've got an idea. I've been thinking about it. My dad. I mean, he's really something. He believed me about what happened. I know that. Oh, he wanted me to turn myself in. But he didn't understand how it was then. He will now. See, they're saying things, in that newspaper, and probably in the others too. Like you don't want to be with me. Like I forced you. That isn't true, is it?"

"No, Billy."

"Well, you see? But that's how it gets, and my dad'll understand. So we're heading north tomorrow. We'll go up to San Francisco, on the bus. We can make it. Then I'll call my dad. He'll help us, because he'll understand how it is." He opened the cardboard suitcase. "See? I got this hair dye in that other town. That's for you. And this kerchief. We'll get on that bus separately. And nobody'll recognize us. When we get to San Francisco I'll call my dad."

She nodded slowly. "Whatever you say, Billy."

Ernie Lang stepped off the train in San Lupe at 7:30 the next morning. A morning fog had cooled the town to a chilly wetness. He walked to a cab and said to the driver, "Do you know a Mrs. Nivero?"

"Sure, but she's out of town."

"Then take me to the sheriff."

"Sure."

When Ernie Lang walked into the sheriff's office, a deputy told him to wait in the outer room. He sat listening to a woman delivering reports to cruising patrol cars. A few minutes later, a fleshy, neatly dressed man came in through the front. The deputy spoke to him in a low voice. The sheriff came over and said, "Sheriff Case, Mr. Lang. Would you like to come into my office?"

He led him into the office and said, "Sit down, please."

Ernie Lang put his suitcase down beside the chair and sat down. The sheriff eased himself into his own chair. He looked weary, with dark marks under his eyes.

"Any word?" Ernie asked.

The sheriff shook his head. "We're working, but, no—nothing. Why did you come down, Mr. Lang?"

"I had to do something. It was all I could think of."

The sheriff shook his head. "We're working, but, no—nothing. What kind of a kid is he?"

Ernie looked beyond the sheriff, through a window which faced the neat shrubs and trimmed palms in front of the building. How many times had he asked himself that question? And what had he determined? Only that he really didn't know. He simply knew that Billy was his son, and that he loved the boy. "I guess I don't really know, Sheriff," he said honestly. "I mean, at first, he's just a boy. Then all of a sudden he's thirteen, fourteen. What you thought was just an uncomplicated kid turns into something else. A mask comes down. You're not sure anymore."

"Well," the sheriff said, "I've got two of my own. I'm not so sure I know what makes them tick anymore." He got out a cigar from a shirt pocket and twirled it slowly in his hands. "I talked on the telephone to San Francisco last night with Inspector Ford, after he'd talked to you and your wife. I guess I've got the story. But I need to know more about your son. I want to know what we're up against. Aside from that shooting, has he ever been violent?"

"Violent?"

"Has he got a temper?"

"Well, yes."

"He can blow pretty good, in other words."

"He has, I suppose. But—"

"Did he ever hurt anybody—not mentioning that shooting?"

"Not without provocation. I mean, if you're implying that he stood around in dark alleys and leaped out at people—"

"I'm just trying to get this straight, Mr. Lang. I've got a deputy, Carl Miter. He trailed the boy around town when we knew he was wanted. He figured he was out in this parking spot. The kid was. He worked Miter over pretty good and pretty fast. Miter never knew what hit him. And he's no pushover."

"Billy was probably scared. Sure, he learned how to brawl on the streets. He's coordinated and fast. I'm sorry it happened, but I—"

"I'm not blaming you, Mr. Lang. I'm just saying that we want your son, and pretty badly. He's got the girl with him."

Ernie shook his head. "I can't believe he'd force a girl to go with him, if she didn't want to go. He's made some mistakes, but I don't think he'd make that kind."

"I don't think so either," the sheriff said. "I think the girl's in love with him. I think she's going along because she wants to. But that doesn't help anything. It sure as hell doesn't help her mother."

"I can understand that. I meant to see her. I wanted her to understand that I'm just as anxious as she is to see this thing stopped. But she wasn't there."

"No," the sheriff said. "She's not there."

He looked at the sheriff, caught by the sharp tone of his voice.

"You may as well know, Mr. Lang. Mrs. Nivero isn't a woman to sit still over a thing like this. She and Miter, the deputy, took off last night in Miter's truck. That truck's equipped for traveling, and Miter's carrying three hunting dogs and enough guns to supply an infantry squad. They headed your way. They're looking for your son, Mr. Lang."

Ernie frowned.

"You'll have to look at it this way," the sheriff said. "Elizabeth Nivero can be dangerous if she's crossed. Your son crossed her. She loves that girl tremendously. Now—the girl's run off with your son. She means to find your boy if she can, with Miter, and stop him. Any way they have to."

Ernie's face was hot with anger now. "Well, who the hell is this Miter? Doesn't he believe in the rest of the law in this state? How come he's taking it on this way? Aren't there county jurisdictions anyway, so that—"

"Take it easy, Mr. Lang. Elizabeth Nivero's the big power in this community. Her husband died right after Maria was born. He'd started a lot of things. Elizabeth decided to finish them. There were some tough interests around her, and she had to defend herself. Sometimes she had to step on people, to keep moving. She did it through Carl Miter."

"All right," Ernie said tensely. "They've taken the law into their own hands, in other words."

"Miter is the law, Mr. Lang. In this county, anyway. And if he and Mrs. Nivero should catch up with your son somewhere else, who's going to worry too much about what happens then? The kid's a murder suspect. He ran off with Mrs. Nivero's daughter."

Ernie Lang nodded slowly, letting it come to him.

"What are you going to do, Mr. Lang?"

"I'd like to stay in contact with you, if you don't mind. I'm going to phone my wife and have her drive down here. I don't think Billy's going to try to contact me. He never has, when he was in trouble. Do you know a decent place to stay?"

"The Palms Motel is okay, about five blocks down the street. They've got phones."

"I'd appreciate it if you'd let me know when you find out anything."

"It's like I said. I've got two of my own."

By ten-thirty that morning, fifty-one miles north. Billy Lang sat in the bus station at Dunston. Dressed in the Army jacket, glasses and hat, he looked across the waiting room at Maria. He'd gone out of the hotel at nine, into a J. C. Penney store. There he bought a pale blue dress and a pink sweater, telling the clerk they were presents for his mother. Then he'd gone down the street to a five-and-ten, where he'd bought some toilet articles; he'd stolen a set of hair curlers. He went back to the hotel, where Maria had finished dying her hair. She put her hair up quickly then.

Now they were in the bus station. Maria, the kerchief arranged to show some of the red hair, sat alone in the new dress and sweater. She did not look at him; she sat motionless, hands on her lap. In one of those hands, he knew, was the ticket for San Francisco. In his own hand was a ticket for Oakland. He would, when they'd traveled far enough north, get his fare changed to San Francisco.

The minutes crept by. A man in a shiny black suit got up and got a cup of chocolate from a vending machine. A baby lying in the lap of a very plump woman suddenly began crying loudly, then stopped just as abruptly. A bus rolled up beside the station. Five passengers stood up and waited until the boarding call was made through a crackling loudspeaker

Maria got on two people ahead of him and sat down midway through the uncrowded bus, alone. Billy sat down five seats behind her, across the aisle. A hundred miles north, he got up and joined her. She took his hand and held it tightly.

"How're you doing?" he asked, grinning reassuringly.

"Fine," she whispered.

"Good," he said. "We're doing it now. We're doing it just great."

The motel room Ernie Lang had rented in San Lupe was neat, efficient and clean. He sat down on one of the twin beds and put in a collect call to Anna in San Francisco. When she'd accepted it, he said:

"I talked to the sheriff down here, Anna. They don't know anything yet. Billy hasn't—"

"No," she said. "He hasn't called."

"I don't think he will."

"But there were some other people here, Ernie. A man and a woman."

"Mrs. Nivero?" he asked softly.

"Yes. And they—she and that Miter—they're looking for them,

Ernie."

"The sheriff told me. What did you think?"

"She's angry, Ernie. And the man's dangerous, I think."

"Yes." He took a breath. "You wouldn't want to drive down here, would you, Anna? Right away?"

She was silent for a moment.

"I'd like to have you with me."

"Of course, Ernie," she said quickly.

"I'm at the Palms Motel in San Lupe. Be careful, Anna. And—bring my pistol, will you?"

"All right, Ernie. I'll leave right away."

When he'd hung up, there was a tapping on his door. He opened it to a casually smiling young man wearing an unpressed sport coat. "Name's Rogers, Mr. Lang. Reporter from Los Angeles. Sheriff Case said you were in town. I'd like to talk to you, if you don't mind."

Ernie motioned him inside, and the young man said, "Trouble with reporting crime in a state like this is there's always too much. We don't have room for all of it. But this one caught my eye. It's the girl mainly. Human interest. I don't know how much space we can give it, but I'm interested, Mr. Lang."

Ernie looked at him and did not like him; but he waited, trying to be patient.

"You want him caught, Mr. Lang?"

"Certainly, I want him caught."

"Mind if I sit down, so I can take notes? I'd like to have something to phone in before noon, if you don't mind." The reporter sat down and lit himself a cigarette. "You really wouldn't mind seeing him picked up then?"

"It's for his own good. There isn't anything to be gained running."

It was just past 12:30 that afternoon when the telephone rang. He answered and Sheriff Monty Case said, "We found his car near a little town called Tiller, about fifty miles north in the county. I'm going up there. If you want to come along we'll pick you up on the way out."

Ernie left a message with the motel to give to Anna. An hour and half later he was standing on the rocky coastal ground, looking down at the smashed convertible resting against the wind-bent trees near the small stream. There was a flurry of activity by the sheriff's people around the car. The sheriff stood gazing down with cool eyes. Beside him stood Tiller's constable, a skinny young man wearing blue jeans and a plaid sports shirt, who said, "George Hobert's boy found it. He came down along the creek, then told his pa, and George phoned it to me."

"Well," the sheriff said, "we know where he was anyway. I'd like to use your place, Tim, while we get started checking. There's not much more we can do here."

Ernie Lang rode with the sheriff into Tiller, where the young constable led them into a small office on the second floor of a building on the main street.

Three uniformed deputies and two detectives had followed. The sheriff said to all of them, "Just start checking. Any place and every place."

When they had gone, the sheriff said to Ernie Lang, "I talked to Carl Miter on the phone before we left San Lupe. They were heading back down in this direction. They talked to your wife."

"Yes," Ernie said. "I know."

"Well, they'll probably be here in about three hours."

He began using the telephone then, and Ernie listened without really hearing, as the time passed. He studied, without caring, the furniture of the small room. There was a faded oak desk, four wooden chairs and a wooden file case. All of it looked as though it had been purchased from a second-hand shop. Finally the sheriff said to him, "Your wife coming down?"

"Yes. I left word at the motel for her to get in touch with your office in San Lupe. She ought to get there about four o'clock, I think." He looked at his watch. It was now 3:00.

"What do you think, Mr. Lang? Is he around here, or did he take off?"

"I don't know what to think, Sheriff."

The telephone rang. The sheriff answered, listened and hung up. He said to Ernie, "That was Smith, one of my detectives. He just made a check on the bus station at Dunston, the nearest bus terminal. Nobody there remembers a couple matching the description. That's the only transportation they could buy out of here—there isn't a train stop around here."

"They could hitchhike," Ernie said. "Or he could have stolen another car."

"Yes," the sheriff said. "We're covering the highways. But it's too bad we don't have enough men to put a block on every country road around here. Still—he might have ditched that car of his yesterday. They could have gone a long way in that time."

Then the dusty office was silent until a squat, florid-faced detective named Corbin walked in. He said to the sheriff, "I think I've got something, Monty. Girl on the counter of the dime store remembers a kid matching the Lang boy's description. He came in about closing time and bought a cardboard suitcase. She thought he was wearing an Army jacket of some kind and a hat. But her description matches the kid's otherwise."

The sheriff sat more alertly behind the old desk. "Just went in and bought a suitcase? How many places around here could he stay—with the girl?"

"The motels up near the highway, I guess. I don't think there's a hotel in this town."

"Get somebody on the motels. And radio Smith from the car to start checking around Dunston. Motels, hotels, whatever they've got. What kind of Army jacket did the girl say?"

"She didn't. She said it just looked like an Army jacket, that's all."

"He hasn't been in the Army, has he, Mr. Lang?" the sheriff asked.

"No."

"Well, he might have picked that jacket up anywhere. Stolen it, maybe."

"I noticed a surplus place down the street," the detective said. "I'll check it."

The detective left, and the sheriff said, "Just how smart is he, Mr. Lang?"

"He's got an IQ of 130."

"Well, he beats me by fifteen." He got out a new cigar and tore off the wrapper. "I wish to Christ he were dumb."

At four-five the sheriff handed the telephone to Ernie. "Your wife's in San Lupe, Mr. Lang. At my office."

Ernie took the telephone and said, "Hello, Anna. How are you?"

"I'm fine, Ernie."

"Could you drive over here? They'll tell you how to get here. If you're not too tired."

"I'm not too tired, Ernie. They found his car?"

"Yes."

"Anything else?"

"Not much. They're working."

"I'll come right over."

An hour later he saw the station wagon stop below on the street, just ahead of the sheriff's car. He went down and opened the door for her. She looked tired, but he was glad to see her. He thought of kissing her; but he didn't. "I'm glad you came down."

She got out. "If you wanted me, Ernie, I wanted to come. Any more news?"

He shook his head, and then saw the camper coming fast down the street. It stopped behind the sheriff's car. Mrs. Nivero got out quickly and went into the building. Carl Miter followed, pausing to look cooly at the Langs; then he went inside.

"Mrs. Nivero?" Ernie asked wearily.

"Yes," Anna said. "And Miter."

"We'd better go up."

They went up the dust-covered stairway to the small office on the second floor. When they reached the doorway, Elizabeth Nivero was saying crisply, "Where'd you find the car, Monty?"

"Little way out of town, Elizabeth."

"What else have you found?"

"Not much," the sheriff said. "I guess you've met Mrs. Lang already."

Elizabeth Nivero turned and saw them for the first time. "This is the boy's father, Elizabeth."

Elizabeth Nivero met Ernie's stare coldly. She turned back to the sheriff. "Don't you have *any*thing, Monty?"

The telephone rang and the sheriff picked it up. He listened and finally said, "All right. We'll be right over." He put the telephone down. "We've got something now. Smith just checked a hotel over at Dunston. Apparently the boy stayed there overnight. With the girl, I guess."

He got up and left the room. Mrs. Nivero, eyes dark and flashing, followed, accompanied by Carl Miter. Ernie touched his wife's arm and said softly, "Let's go, Anna."

Ten minutes later they were in the small lobby of the Dunston hotel. The detective, Smith, said to the sheriff, "The clerk told me the kid came in and bought a room last night. Said he was wearing glasses, but everything else matched. He was alone. But I went over the room. I think the girl was there too. She probably sneaked in the back way. I found this." He held out an empty hair-dye bottle. "Looks like she dyed her hair red. There're marks on the sink. And I found a couple of strands of hair on the pillow up there, before she'd dyed it." He looked at Mrs. Nivero apologetically.

"When did they leave?" the sheriff asked.

"The boy walked out this morning a little after nine. The girl apparently got out the way she came in."

The second detective, Corbin, had come in. He said to the sheriff, "I checked the surplus store. He bought a fatigue jacket and a hat, all right."

"I want to see the room," Mrs. Nivero said thinly.

"Elizabeth—" the sheriff said.

"If you don't mind."

"All right," he said, sighing. Then he said to Smith: "You might check that bus station again. Try the new descriptions with them." He looked at Mrs. Nivero again. "All right, Elizabeth. We'll go up."

Ernie Lang followed them and stood at the door as Mrs. Nivero walked slowly around the room. The bedclothes were mussed, and there was impression on the old mattress. She bent down and saw another fine hair on the pillow. She snapped her hand across it, then turned around. Her face had paled. Ernie said, "Mrs. Nivero—"

"Get out of my way," she said viciously.

He stepped aside, and she went swiftly down the hall.

"I can't blame her," the sheriff said softly.

Ernie's jaw muscles flickered, then he went with the sheriff back down to the lobby. They were going outside when Smith came back down the street and said, "With the glasses, fatigue jacket, hat, they remembered the kid this time at the bus station. The girl too. She was wearing a kerchief and a sweater and a blue dress. There's a Penny store just down the street. I checked it on the way back. The kid bought the sweater and dress this morning. They got on the bus separately, the ten-forty."

"Where were they headed?" the sheriff said grimly.

"The boy bought a ticket for Oakland, the girl one for San Francisco."

The sheriff looked at his watch. It was now 5:43.

"I checked that too," the detective said. "The bus was on time. They both went to San Francisco. They got there at five-twenty. They got off and disappeared."

Ernie Lang seated Anna in the station wagon, then walked up to the sheriff's car. "We're going back to San Francisco, Sheriff. I appreciate all of your cooperation." He looked up the street, at the parked camper. Carl Miter had gone into a small café moments ago; Mrs. Nivero sat stiffly in the cab.

"Well," the sheriff said, "they'll be at work up there." He looked ahead at that camper. "And I hope the law there finds them, Mr. Lang. I truly do."

The sheriff's car rolled away. Carl Miter came out of the café carrying a coffee carton and wrapped sandwiches. Ernie walked on up the street to the camper. He looked in at Mrs. Nivero, as Miter got behind the wheel.

"I just wanted to tell you that I'm sorry, Mrs. Nivero."

She stared straight ahead, silently.

"I think I know where you're going now," Ernie said carefully. "I can understand how you feel about it. But he's my son just as much as the girl's your daughter."

She turned to stare at him with hating eyes. "Are you trying to protect him, Mr. Lang?"

"I'm just interested in seeing this stopped."

"He stole my daughter."

"She's with him, yes. But—"

"He kidnapped her, Mr. Lang. And he's going to be caught."

"Are you going to San Francisco?"

"We're going wherever he is," she said. "And you'd better do that too, Mr. Lang. Because if we get to him first—" She motioned a hand, and the pick-up leaped away.

Ernie Lang walked slowly back to his station wagon. Anna said quietly, "They're going too?"

"Yes," he said, starting the car and moving it down the street. "I know how she feels, but—"

Anna's hand rested gently on his knee. He saw the concern in her eyes. She had never touched him in that way before, and he felt a sudden warmth toward her.

"Well," he said, speeding up, "We're going too. Because they're not going to—" He shook his head, his face hardening. He picked up the overpass that curled around onto the highway leading north. He pushed down the accelerator and held it there until he saw the camper ahead. He swung into the lane the camper was travelling and came up behind it. He put the truck just a hundred yards ahead of them and drove steadily, keeping it there.

In San Francisco, in a small Tenderloin hotel, Billy surveyed the room. It was better than the one they'd had the night before, he thought, but not much. Yet, he'd bought sandwiches at the bus depot when they got off; they weren't hungry now. And at least, in the city, they hadn't to sneak around like they'd had to do last night in Dunston. He'd simply registered them as man and wife under the first name that came to mind. He paced about, gingerly, feeling his nerves singing. Finally he stopped and looked at Maria.

She sat forlornly in a chair. She'd begun coughing on the bus, and it had irritated him. Now she was coughing again, but this time he felt concern. He sat on the arm of her chair and placed his face against her forehead. "How do you feel?"

"I'm all right, Billy."

"Your forehead feels like it's burning up."

"It isn't anything. I'll be fine."

"I'm going to phone my dad now. Only I don't want to use the phone in here. I'll go down and I'll get some cough medicine. Everything's going to be all right now. They never picked up a thing on us. As far as they're concerned, we're in Mexico. In a few minutes I'll be talking to my dad, and he'll help us. I know he will. Then everything'll be fine. Don't you want to get into bed?"

"Yes, I think so."

"That's right," he said gently. "You do that. And I'm going down now. You just relax. It's excitement, that's all."

He left quickly, so she could undress and get into bed. He took the elevator down and stepped into the cool evening. He paused, looking along the garish Tenderloin street. The first time he'd been home in all of these months, he thought, feeling his anger starting again, and he'd had to sneak in like any common criminal. *Why?* he thought, swearing silently. Why?

Again his nerves were singing. He saw a neon cocktail sign of one of the many bars along the street and moved toward it. One drink, he thought—he could use that right now.

He walked into the bar and sat down at the far end, below a television set. A half-dozen other bored-looking customers sat drinking, looking up at the screen, where a cartoon was playing. A waitress had been reading a newspaper, and now she was getting drinks for a couple at a table. Billy ordered a bourbon and slid the newspaper before him. The story was on the front page: a copyrighted interview with his father, datelined San Lupe.

He read it swiftly, realizing with sudden shock that, being local, he was more important news here. He read, blinking rapidly. He came to the question, "Do you want to see him caught, Mr. Lang?" And the answer, "Of course, I do." And then he closed his eyes, feeling a pulse hammering in his temples. He was breathing hard now, and, with effort, he got control of himself and carefully pushed the newspaper back to where it had been.

His drink was placed before him and change made. He started to pick up the glass, but he couldn't steady his hand enough to hold it for several seconds. Then finally he drank, slowly returned the glass to the bar, and sat staring at the arrangement of bottles ahead of him.

It was several minutes before he realized that the cartoon had changed to a local news program on the television set above.

He looked up to see a photograph of himself, one taken years ago at the Juvenile Hall. He touched his eye glasses, then the brim of his hat. He looked sideways to see six pairs of eyes staring up at that screen.

"Another?" the bartender was asking him.

"No, thank you," he said quietly.

He got up, as the camera returned to the newscaster. He walked out with an even pace, hearing the smooth voice saying, "Law officials have traced Billy Lang back to San Francisco. He and the young girl are known to have gotten off a bus in this city not more than forty minutes ago. The girl was wearing a blue dress and pink sweater. Her hair has been dyed red. The boy is believed to be wearing a disguise of glasses, hat, Army fatigue jacket ..."

He was outside. He looked in both directions, then moved swiftly toward an alley. When he reached it, he bounded down it, running hard....

In the bar a thin man with yellow hair motioned to the bartender. "That kid who just went out of here, Harry."

The bartender looked at him. "Yeah," he said softly. He turned and lifted a telephone.

Billy followed alleys for blocks, then looked back. His heart was pounding wildly. He stood now at McAlister Street, with Civic Center in sight. He removed his hat and shrugged out of the fatigue jacket. He threw them into a refuse can; the glasses followed. It was getting cold now, but he couldn't afford to wear that jacket any longer. Damn him, he thought, thinking of what his father had told that reporter. *He wants me caught.*

He looked across the street and saw a telephone booth. He trotted across, between cars, and stepped into the booth.

In the hotel room, Maria heard the telephone ring. She hesitated, lying in bed shivering. Then she picked it up. "Yes?"

"Listen, Maria, and get it straight. My father sold me out. You get the hell out of that hotel room. And get rid of that sweater! Go out, and fast, and down to Market Street. Get on a Number 5 bus going west. I'm at McAllister Street. I'll get on the bus when I see which one you're on. And don't you phone anyone or tell anyone, or I'll—"

"Billy!" She had begun crying now; shivering with chills, tears streaming down her face.

His voice suddenly softened. "Listen—I'm sorry. I just got excited."

"Billy, I love you!"

"I know, honey. It's just that they're looking for us here now. Can you do what I asked?"

"Yes," she said in a small voice, "I can do it, Billy."

He walked down the street toward the Market Street intersection and waited at the bus stop. Small crowds kept collecting, then dispersing as the buses came to a stop. Finally he saw her. He boarded, paid his fare, then stood in the aisle as the bus moved on. She was in back, sitting near the rear door. Twelve blocks later, he sat down behind her. He whispered, "Don't look at me. Get off the next stop after I do."

He rode in silence then, until the bus neared the University of San Francisco. He pressed the buzzer and got off. He watched the tail lights of the bus moving on and saw ahead the outline of the college buildings, which included the tall spires of St. Ignatius rising into the cold night sky. He could feel the cold, bitterly. He moved in a trot now, toward the next stop. She'd gotten off there and was waiting.

He came to her quickly, and they stepped back into the shadows. He took her hand, and he could feel her shivering. "I heard it in a bar on television," he said. "They found out we came up on that bus. They showed a picture of me. And I read a story in a newspaper. My dad went down to San Lupe, and he wants me caught." He shook his head, tense with anger. "He never loved me. Never! My mother? She's dead, see? When I was born. And that was why my father always hated me. The woman I called my mother—she wasn't. Oh, she put on an act, but she didn't love me either. Now they all want me caught." He shook his head again. "Now when things started going right for the first time in my life. Now when I finally found you!"

"Billy, I love you."

He nodded, eyes bright. "Sure, and they're not going to ruin that. Are you cold?"

"I'm terribly cold." She went into his arms, pressing her face against his chest, coughing again.

"I've got to get a car somewhere." He looked up at the church. "You go up there. Act like you're worshipping or something. And help me figure out where to go, will you? Because we've got to go somewhere and not let them ruin everything. You know what to do inside a place like that, don't you?"

"Yes," she said, "I know what to do."

He waited until she'd disappeared behind the church doors. Then he went to the corner and turned right, walking toward the houses of the neighborhood. He walked block after block on the slanting streets, looking into cars as he passed. There was fog coming in now, adding more bite to the cold, but he moved fast to keep warm. They're not going to stop us, he thought viciously. Not now.

Then, down the incline of a street, he saw a new Chrysler stop in front of a large house. A tall man got out carrying what was obviously a sacked bottle and walked to the door, weaving. Billy waited until he'd gone inside, then he hurried down the street. He stopped beside the car and could see, by the illumination of a street lamp down the block, the keys in the ignition. He looked up and down the street, then at the house where the man had disappeared. Light showed through slanted Venetian blinds. He got into the car, carefully released the emergency brake and coasted away from the curb.

When he'd turned the corner below, he switched on the headlights and started the engine. He hit the accelerator, feeling a surge of new confidence with the power. Then he braked to a normal speed and drove back to the church. He parked the car and ran up the steps to step inside. He saw her kneeling in one of the pews. He went down and took her arm, saying, "Let's get the hell out of here."

As he drove away, she was coughing again. He found the heater controls and turned it on. "That guy who owns this was drunk. I could see it when he went into his house. If he just knocks himself out now, we're safe. Did you think of anything in there, in that church?"

"Yes," she said. "I prayed."

"Prayed!"

She looked at him with wide eyes. "For us, Billy."

"I mean about where we can go!"

She blinked, then said, "There's a place up in the Sierra. A friend of my mother's has a summer house there at Fallen Leaf, outside of Lake Tahoe. I was there twice. I remember where they kept an extra key, and they never use it during the winter."

"Good," he said, eyes brightening. "About two hundred miles. We'll make it while it's dark and ditch the car when we get there. Then we'll be all right."

It was just after midnight when Carl Miter's camper, followed by Ernie Lang's station wagon, came off the Skyway into the heart of San Francisco. Ten minutes later both cars were parked near police headquarters. Five minutes later the four of them—Miter, Mrs. Nivero, Ernie and Anna—were seated around the desk of Inspector

Ford, who was saying:

"We traced them to the hotel. It was on the same block where the boy went into the bar. Found the sweater the girl had in a bureau. When the boy heard that telecast, he took off. Apparently he phoned the girl at the hotel. And she got out of there. We checked transportation. They got on a Number 5 bus. The driver didn't recognize them at the time. But he did when we talked to him. He remembered the girl wasn't dressed for the cold. Neither was the boy. He says the boy wasn't wearing glasses or the hat. He'd got rid of the Army jacket too. He thinks they got off the bus the way they got on. Separately. He doesn't remember the boy getting off, but he does the girl. She got off at the University of San Francisco. "So—" He shrugged.

"Well?" Elizabeth Nivero said sharply.

"That's the end of it. We've been checking around that neighborhood all night. We don't have a thing."

"Maybe he stole a car," Carl Miter said.

"The only report we've had on one missing was two hours ago. That was forty blocks away from that area, and we already picked up the kid who stole it." He shook his head, grimly.

"What about *his* house?" Mrs. Nivero said, looking at Ernie Lang.

"We put that under surveillance as soon as we knew they came up here. But that's a point, Mr. Lang. He might try to contact you now."

"I'm sure he won't," Ernie said. "But—"

"Might pay all around if you and your wife would go home now— just in case he calls."

Ernie looked at Mrs. Nivero; he felt his wife's hand touching his. "All right," he said reluctantly. "If you'll contact me the minute you hear anything."

The inspector nodded. "And do the same for us, please."

Billy drove the large car up the curving mountain road. They had passed Strawberry Lodge now, and would be going over the high elevation at Echo Summit soon. There was snow bordering the road, its whiteness caught in the spread of the headlights, but he had listened to the car's radio and learned there was no new snow expected and that it had only fallen at this higher altitude; the road was clear all the way over the pass. He had also heard on the radio that they had found out which hotel they'd used in San Francisco, the fact that they'd used that city bus, and that they had then lost them. There had been no other news on them, and now the San Francisco stations were fading as they drew further away from the city. All right, he thought, maybe they'd gotten away cleanly. He should, he knew, relax a little, thinking that. Unless that filling station attendant remembered him, where he had to stop for gas in Sacramento.

They'd crossed the pass now, and he rolled the car swiftly down the grade. There was moonlight; stars were reflected in the large oval of Lake Tahoe, which was surrounded by tall pine trees. There were the orange runway lights of the small airport, and the multi-colored lights of the motels lining the highway which ran along the south shore. Beyond swung the white shaft of a casino spotlight.

The anger, the resentment, fired by his nervousness, still pumped through him. When they got to the lower highway, he suddenly wheeled the car off on a small residential road. He killed the lights, and they sat there, in the soft moonlight. He held his hands doubled against his legs to keep them from shaking.

"Billy," she said, "what is it? Is it me?"

He swallowed and gradually got control again. "No," he said softly. "Not you, little one. Never you." He turned and put his arms around her. "How do you feel?"

"A little better, I think. The car's been warm."

He held her more tightly and felt the bitterness melting. Only themselves, he thought. That was all that counted. It was more than he'd ever had, and it was, he told himself, all he wanted. Maria. Himself. Together. "I love you, little one," he whispered. "Would you marry me? Now?"

She tipped her head up and stared at him in surprise.

"We could," he said. "Nevada's only miles away. We could keep on driving. Carson City can't be far. Get married. Then come back up here. I heard they're open all night down there." And now he knew, this was the most important thing of his life.

"Married?" she whispered.

"Will you?"

She nodded. "Yes …"

Ernie Lang had dozed in the living room chair, but he had not been able to bring himself to go to bed. He'd insisted that Anna do that, and she was now sleeping in their bedroom. When the telephone rang he picked it up immediately.

"Inspector Ford, Mr. Lang. A fellow living out near the university got up a half-hour ago and saw his car was gone. Chrysler, current model. He gave us the license number. Five minutes ago we got a report from Sacramento. They stopped for gas. The attendant didn't remember the license number of the car, but the car matched the description of the one stolen. There was a girl with the boy. They match the description of your son and the Nivero girl. So we're pretty certain they went through Sacramento, heading east, about three hours ago. Do you have any idea where he might be going, Mr. Lang?"

Ernie Lang was completely awake now. "No, I don't."

"Mrs. Nivero and Miter have started off. How about you, Mr. Lang?"

"Yes," he said quietly. "I'll be going too. Thank you, Inspector."

Passing the stretch of motels on the south edge of Lake Tahoe, Billy saw a sheriff's car with Californian license plates coming in their direction. They met and Billy held his breath. But the car went on, disappearing in his rear-view mirror. He let his breath out. It was dangerous, he knew, trying this. But he had to do it. If they were married, then Maria would be truly his. Nobody could change that then, no matter what happened.

He looked at her beside him, small, tender, but very real. Yes, he thought, feeling a moment of bursting elation. Yes ...

They crossed the state line into Nevada. There was a glittering display of casino marquees, and then they were beyond the lights, moving over the eastern pass of Spooners Summit, coming down the wide, sweeping grade toward Carson City.

When he drove into the heart of the small, antique capital, he saw a wedding chapel off the main avenue. He parked in front of it and looked at his watch. It was a few minutes after one A.M. He turned to Maria. "Ready?"

She nodded, wide-eyed.

They went into the small ante-room of the chapel. A buzzer sounded somewhere in back. They waited and looked at the simplicity of the small room beyond which was dominated by a plain-looking altar. A woman crossed through that room and smiled at them. "Yes?"

"We'd like to get married," Billy said simply, and once again his nervousness was returning, full-force.

"Certainly," the woman said. "It's twenty dollars. I'll phone the minister for you. He'll be here right away. May I have your license?"

He felt a quick surge of anger. "Don't we get that here?"

"You'll have to get it at the courthouse."

"You mean we have to wait until morning?"

"They're open all night. It's just down the block and across the street. Why don't you go pick that up, while I phone the minister?"

Billy nodded, relieved.

They walked the half block to the courthouse, then went inside to a brightly lit marriage-license office. They stood at the counter, while a business-like woman with gray hair made out the application.

"Name?" she asked.

Billy's throat tightened. He could feel the quivering in his legs now. Would they ask for his identification? If they didn't, he could give them a wrong name. But if they did …

He rubbed his hands down the sides of his trousers. The woman looked up at him impatiently. He would, he decided, tell the truth:

"William R. Lang."

"Driver's license, please?"

When they walked out of the courthouse, back toward the chapel, he thought: we'd better run now, because if that woman remembered anything from the newspapers, she could …

"Billy?" Maria said. He looked down at her. It was cold here, and she no longer even had the sweater. But the simple blue dress revealed her fine, well-molded body. He loved her, he thought, mentally and physically. "Are we really going to be married now?"

"Yes," he said.

Her hand tightened against his. They walked into the chapel. Fifteen minutes later the certificate was in his hand. He drove back through town and returned up the grade toward Lake Tahoe. He put his arm around her, driving through moonlight coming down on the rocky cliffs. He pulled her close, feeling her against him. "Mine …" he whispered.

When they reached Tahoe, Maria explained how to get to Fallen Leaf Lake. Again, Billy drove the length of the south-shore community. This time he noticed a large sporting-goods store near where the highway junctioned with another and then ran north along the west edge of the lake. He slowed, passing the store, and made up his mind what he was going to do. Then he went out the west-shore highway until he reached the sign that pointed to Fallen Leaf Lake. He turned onto a narrow, winding road.

A half-mile in, he saw sand across the road, obviously washed down from some snow-melting day in the past; there were no tire marks on it. "Good," he said softly.

He drove on until his headlights picked up the smooth, clear water of the lake. The moon now was high and small, showing over the high rugged peaks on the other side of the water. He traveled along the east bank, just below heavy clusters of pine, among which were scattered summer cabins.

"Right up there, I think," Maria said. He stopped when he reached a wooden sign that said, "Joseph Norris." Maria nodded and said, "Yes. Up there, on the hill."

He turned the car into a short parking slot, turned off the lights and got out. The freezing high-altitude cold stung his face and hands. He hurried, helping Maria up a steep wooden stairway. She was shivering again, and she'd started coughing as soon as she was in the biting air. When they reached the cabin, a large yellow-pine structure with an aluminum roof, she controlled her coughing and said, "Under that rock over there."

He rolled the rock away. There was a key in the sandy soil, wrapped in plastic. He unwrapped it, walked to the front stoop and opened the door.

The front room was as cold as the outdoors. In the moonlight coming through the open doorway, he saw ghostly pieces of furniture. The windows were draped. He walked to a lamp and turned the switch; there was no light, and he knew the electricity had been turned off.

"There're probably candles," Maria said. "And maybe some canned food. I'm so cold, Billy, and hungry."

"Sure," he said smoothly. He was feeling better. It looked all right here, he thought, and he had only one thing more to do before he closed off the world.

He found candles placed in holders over a fireplace. He asked Maria to shut the door, then lighted them. The yellow flames suddenly brightened the interior. He carried one of the candles through the house to the kitchen. He opened cupboard after cupboard. There was no food. He looked in the three bedrooms. There were no blankets. He could find no heat registers. He came back to the large front room. "I'll get food, little one. I have to go out now and do something."

"Don't leave me, Billy," she said. "Not now."

"It won't take long." He looked at the fireplace skeptically; if he started a fire there would be smoke from the chimney; but he knew she could not stand this cold. "I'll build a fire for you first. There must be some wood here."

"They kept it stacked behind the kitchen."

He found wood piled along the side of the house and carried a dozen logs in. He built a fire, and in a few minutes flames were leaping up the chimney. Heat began dissolving the cold of the room. "See?" He pulled a couch across the floor, placing it directly in front of the fire.

"It's going to be fine now. I'll be back in a little while, and everything's going to be perfect."

"Billy, don't leave me. Please."

"I have to, little one. But don't you worry." He put his arms around her and felt her body pressed against his. He didn't want to go. But he had to, he knew. He led her to the sofa. "Just lie down here, in front of that fire." She did, and he bent over her, touching her forehead with his lips. It was burning, he realized. There was an unusual shine to her eyes. But she would be all right now, he told himself—with some rest, and the heat. "Don't you worry. I just have to do this one thing, then I'll be back. Close your eyes, little one. Think of us. Remember— we're married now." He kissed her; her mouth was hot, responsive, loving. He made himself straighten finally and touched her cheek tenderly, then left.

He drove back along the narrow road to the highway, and returned, on that, to the main road in Tahoe where he had seen the sporting-goods store. There was no other traffic in sight now. He rolled the large car into the parking area in front of the store, and saw that the parking area went entirely around the large building. He drove around to the back and stopped. He waited in the moonlight. A single car passed on the highway. It was quiet, and the store was dark. He could see a rear entrance, with a small window beside it.

He got out and ran to the back door. It was locked. He examined the lock. It was above the handle, the kind that could be opened from the inside. He lifted a rock from beside the building, paused, then tapped it against a pane of the small window. Glass splintered and fell with a light cracking sound. He put his arm through the pane, feeling toward the inside of the lock. His fingers touched the lever. He turned it and the door came open. He went inside, swiftly, shutting the door behind him.

He walked through the store toward the front, where light from a street lamp dimly illuminated the interior. He saw what he was looking for: a gun counter. He selected a .38 pistol, then found ammunition for it, which he put into his pocket. He was returning toward the rear when headlights flashed through the store.

He heard the car rolling into the parking area, and fell, just as a spotlight swept through the room, its white shaft swinging over him.

He lay flat, teeth gritting together. The spot was cut and the headlights disappeared, as he heard the car going around the building. He got up and ran low, to the broken window. He saw a sheriff's car stop just behind the Chrysler. A lone deputy sat there for a few moments, playing his spotlight at the large car. Then he turned it on the door of the building. Billy drew back, watching to see if the light found the broken window. It did not and went out.

Carefully, he looked out again as he heard a car door opening. He saw the deputy walk slowly toward the Chrysler in the glare of his car's headlights, a flash in one hand, the other held gingerly over a holstered pistol.

He stopped beside the door and pointed the flash at the registration. Billy, his pulse pounding wildly, nearly blind with a vicious fury, slowly opened the door. Then he ran toward the deputy, holding the pistol by the barrel.

The man turned, right hand clawing for his pistol. Billy swung his own gun with hard, brutal strength. The deputy had failed to jerk his pistol free when the butt struck the side of his head. He stumbled sideways, blood spitting from his temple. Billy swung again, this time full against his face. There was a crunching sound, and the deputy sat down clumsily, staring at Billy, his face turning crimson. Billy looked at him with bright, glazed eyes. Then he swung the pistol again, deliberately, smashing the man's face again. The deputy fell backward and lay supine, his face pouring blood.

Billy ran to the patrol car and shut off the lights. Then he went back to the Chrysler. He rounded the building, compelling himself not to do it too fast. But there was no traffic on the highway. He swung onto it, turned north at the large intersection, and opened up the engine. He had to skid to make the Fallen Leaf turnoff.

He stopped just beyond the place where the sand had washed across the narrow road and doubled in his seat, gasping against the clutching of his stomach. He could not find his breath for a moment, and gagged, then gradually he felt himself unlocking from the tension. It was not what he'd done to that deputy; not that at all. It was that he'd almost been stopped from coming back to Maria and all that waited for him with her. Oh no, he thought, breathing again with a long shuddering breath. It wasn't what he'd done to that rotten deputy....

He drove on again, watching the sides of the road. He'd seen garages built flush against the road when he'd driven out of here. He found one, a half-mile from the house where he'd left Maria. He got out and examined it. It was locked with an outside padlock, and he could see through a small window that it was empty. He returned to the car and got a tire iron from the turn, then returned to the door. He fitted the iron inside the loop of the lock and levered it down until the lock snapped. He threw the lock into the brush. Then he opened the doors and ran the car inside.

He went on foot back toward the house, carrying the pistol, feeling better. He climbed the steps to the doorway, called softly to Maria and let himself in. He put the pistol on a table and walked to her.

"Are you all right?" he asked gently.

"Yes. It's warm now. Are you?"

"Oh, sure," he said, sitting down, putting his arms around her. "I couldn't get the food tonight. But I will tomorrow, first thing."

"It's all right, Billy."

"You'll be fine now. You'll get some good rest. You'll feel great in the morning."

He kissed her and then lay down with her. Rest, yes, he thought. But not for a little while now.

"I love you," she whispered, and again her lips were responsive.

"Yes," he whispered back, feeling her pressed against himself, thinking of the way he'd swung that pistol into that deputy's face, the blood spurting; the emotion took his breath away.

"Billy, *Billy* ..." she gasped.

It was all that he'd ever wanted, spiraling above anything he'd ever known or felt or even dreamed about: a whirling emotion, building, building ...

Ernie Lang, with Anna beside him, drove into the station in Sacramento at four-thirty that morning. He saw the camper parked beyond the pumps. Elizabeth Nivero and Carl Miter were talking to a tall youth wearing a blue windbreaker. Ernie got out and walked over to them. Mrs. Nivero looked at him with contempt. Carl Miter smiled faintly, without humor. "The kid's father," he said to the youth in the blue jacket.

The youth looked at him, then down at the oil-marked cement.

Ernie asked the youth in the jacket. "You think he was heading east?"

"That's the way the car was pointed."

"I'm simply trying to find out as much as I can," Ernie said, holding his temper.

"Well, I told the cops all I know. That kid came in here and gassed up and took off. That's all I know." He walked off.

Miter had moved off toward a telephone booth. Lang looked at Miter in the booth, and was certain the man was more alert, with the phone at his mouth. A minute later he came out and said, "He went east, all right."

"How do you know?" Ernie asked, tensing.

"They found this sheriff's deputy up at Lake Tahoe. Beat up bad. They figure he might not die. Deputy came to long enough to say what happened. He saw this car behind a sports store and went back to check. Billy-boy was inside, picking himself up a pistol. He came out and gun-whipped him. The deputy got the license number. It checks with the car that was stolen in San Francisco. He just about killed that deputy. And he's armed now. Pretty sweet all around, isn't it?"

Ernie felt the blood draining from his face, listening. There was no doubt about it now, and he couldn't fight it any longer: Billy was dangerous and getting more that way.

"Let's go," Elizabeth Nivero said, her face mask-like.

"Please listen to me for a moment," Ernie said.

She had started toward the truck. She stopped and stared at him again. "Why?"

"I want to see this stopped just as much as you do. I think we should stay together. Do what we can, putting together what we know about them."

Elizabeth Nivero turned away.

"Now wait a minute, Elizabeth," Carl Miter said pleasantly. "Maybe he's got something."

Mrs. Nivero stopped and looked at Miter in surprise.

"What I mean is," Miter said, "maybe Lang here might have a better idea about where Billy-boy's heading than we do."

Mrs. Nivero came back, staring at Ernie, forgetting everything now, he thought, but the thought of getting to his son. "Do you have an idea where he's going?" she asked harshly.

"No," Ernie said honestly. "I don't. I don't think he has any particular place in mind. Lake Tahoe—we've never been there together. I don't believe he's ever been in Nevada. How about your daughter, Mrs. Nivero?"

"She is with your son, Mr. Lang, because she's being forced. This has nothing to do with her."

"Well, that's probably right," Carl Miter said. "But maybe he got her to think of some place they could hide. That's a thought, anyway."

Ernie Lang watched Mrs. Nivero and was certain he saw her expression change.

"Mrs. Nivero?" he said.

She shook her head abruptly and returned to the camper.

Miter shrugged. "Just got to keep on going, I guess."

"Yes," Ernie said grimly, "And I'll be right behind you."

Miter smiled. "Can't stop that." He clumped across the concrete and got into the truck. Ernie returned to his station wagon. He wearily told Anna what he'd found out, then followed the camper onto the highway, heading east.

It was just past seven o'clock when Carl Miter drove over the high-elevation pass. Coming down toward the lake valley, the large circle of Lake Tahoe was visible, a pale, misty blue in the early-morning light. The higher peaks surrounding the basin were white-tipped with snow. Miter came down the grade fast, saying, "They're right behind us, Elizabeth."

She nodded. "Lose them then."

"Just as soon as we get down where those houses are. Regular streets down there."

"Yes."

"All right." He looked at the trailing station wagon in the mirror. "You figure she'd remember that place, Elizabeth?"

"I'm sure of it. We were there together twice. She knew they closed it for the winter."

They came into the community, approaching the large intersection where the highway split. There was a post office, two large supermarkets and several smaller shops. "Where's this Fallen Leaf Lake?" he asked.

"North, on Highway 89. About two or three miles, then you turn left. There's a sign."

"All right. I'll come back to it." He turned right, following Highway 50, going away from 89. "You don't want to turn this over to the sheriff up here, do you, Elizabeth?"

"No."

He nodded. "Good. Just hang on now."

He made a hard left turn, jamming the accelerator down. He drove into a residential avenue, fast, turned again, then speeded up once more. In the sudden surge of speed, the station wagon went out of sight behind. He turned again, then zig-zagged at high speed through the neighborhood. He knew, minutes later, that he'd lost them.

He drove back toward Highway 89, grinning. "Do you want to reach back there and bring up that pistol, Elizabeth?" She did that, then they were beyond the community, turning at the Fallen Leaf sign. He looked at the rock and trees and heavy brush growing on either side of the narrow road. "Yeah," he nodded. "I'm glad we brought those dogs."

Futilely, Ernie Lang searched the neighborhood for the camper. He traced back over a half-dozen streets and gave up. "My fault," he said bitterly. "I was half-asleep when he pulled away."

"Do you really think they know anything, Ernie?"

"I think Mrs. Nivero thought of something. I saw it in her eyes, in Sacramento. This proves it."

"What are we going to do?"

"Sheriff's station up here," he said. "That's all we can do now."

A uniformed officer was standing at the counter of the substation when Ernie walked in and explained why he was here. The officer nodded. "The sheriff came up from Placerville. But he's sleeping right now. We were working all night."

"How about the deputy that was injured?"

Muscles flickered along the man's lean cheeks. "He'll live." He looked at Ernie with unwavering eyes. "We got something else on your son, in the last hour. He and the girl got married in Carson City."

"Married?"

"Walked straight into the courthouse and bought a license, then got married. Woman who runs a chapel down there heard the descriptions on the radio after he came back up here and worked over Harry."

Ernie was silent for a long time, then he said, "There's a good chance he's still around here then, isn't there? If he came back in this direction?"

"Pretty good. We covered the highways going out of here, after we found Harry. They're only two main highways running out, plus two running up to the north shore. If he's going to hide now, I'd say he's got a better chance around here. Better than trying those main highways."

"I followed a deputy from Southern California up here. The mother of the girl's with him. They're hunting for my son. I think they'd like to find him before anyone else does. The deputy's armed and he's got dogs in his truck. I think they figured out a place those kids might go. They lost me when we got here. On purpose. Miter's the man's name. He's driving a blue camper, with an aluminum housing. License is LVA-389."

The deputy nodded. "We'll look for the camper too, then." He stared at Ernie with those steady eyes. "We'd like to find your son as much as anybody else would, Mr. Lang."

The sun was rising, casting full daylight on the surface of Fallen Leaf Lake. The water, where it was deep, was as blue as the sky was now; at the edges, where it was shallow, it was as clear as perfect ice. Carl Miter drove along the narrow road above the water until Elizabeth Nivero said, "Up ahead now, about a half-mile."

Miter cut the engine and let the car roll to a stop. He got out, unclamped the rifle from the seat and rested it against the truck. Then he buckled on his pistol belt. He picked up the rifle again and went around to the back, where he opened the door of the dogs' compartment. The red wide-jawed pointer leaped out first. Next came the small foxhound, then the third dog: a black animal, part Doberman, part Weimaraner. The dogs ranged around the camper, sniffing. Miter motioned up the road, and they ran ahead of him silently.

When he reached the bottom of the steep stairway he snapped his fingers. The dogs stopped and waited for his next command. He looked up at the house with the aluminum roof. Smoke curled from the chimney. He grinned and loosened the pistol in its holster. Then he waved toward the house, and the dogs leaped up the stairway.

Inside, Billy stood frozen, certain he'd heard the sound of an automobile minutes before. The stolen pistol was in his hand. Maria, seated on the couch before the fire, stared at him tensely.

"Billy—" she began.

"Shut up," he whispered. Then he heard something running out there. He went to the drapes of a front window and moved them slightly, just in time to see the dogs bounding toward the house and Carl Miter appearing up the last steps of the stairway. He slashed the pistol into the window, and fired. The pistol kicked in his hand, and Carl Miter sprawled into the brush beside the stairway, then crawled fast, back down the bank.

Billy whirled, ran across the room and jerked Maria to her feet. "Move!"

She ran with him through the house, out the back door. Behind the house there were trees and heavy brush; above that was gray mountain rock.

"Hurry up!" he snapped savagely, going into the brush. He looked back and saw the red pointer loping toward them. He lifted the pistol and fired twice. The big dog tumbled to lie trembling on the ground. Then they were in the cover of the brush. Maria was breathing hard already, choking back coughs. He pulled her ahead until they found a small walking trail. He forced her to run along it, steadily, knowing that the trail was taking them in a circle around the south edge of the lake.

Finally they stopped and Maria stood gasping. "Listen," he whispered. Behind there was no sound. "All right," he said, eyes bright. "Let's go!"

Behind, Miter came cautiously around the house with his other two dogs. He saw the big red dog lying ahead, still trembling. He hurried to it and bent down, seeing the blood pouring from a large wound in its chest. He stared at the dog, loving it as much as he'd ever loved anything in his life. Then he drew out his pistol. He put the muzzle to the dog's head, his face like stone, and pressed the trigger. He stood up slowly and looked toward the brush growing away from the house. He motioned a hand, fury and acid in his mouth. The two remaining dogs bounded ahead. Carl Miter followed.

Sheriff's cars, with those of the highway patrol, ranged through the mountain community. Heavy snow had been late in coming, and the lower slope of the ski run going up the peaks to the south was still brown rock; the tramway and rope tows were unmoving. Dozens of seasonal shops and refreshment stands were closed. Traffic on all roads was light. The casinos on the Nevada side of the line were half-empty. A graying highway patrolman drove slowly along Highway 89, following the route of his regular weekly run. He'd stopped at Pope's Beach, where the marsh had frozen and the waves of Lake Tahoe made a white icy froth against the sand. There was no one there. He'd driven on to Baldwin Beach, which was also deserted. Now, he turned into the Fallen Leaf turn-off. He drove slowly until he saw sand washed across the road.

He stopped and got out. He knew that the sand had come down since his last patrol, and he examined the tire tracks in it carefully. Then he went back to his car and drove on, watching carefully. He knew the look of everything here, minutely, and just as he was nearing the lake he stopped again. He stared at a garage, knowing something was wrong. Then suddenly he knew what it was: there was no padlock on the doors. He got out and opened the doors. The Chrysler was inside. He checked the license and registration. When he came out he was certain that he heard voices further on.

He drew out his pistol and walked on ahead, cautiously. When he rounded a bend he saw the camper with its aluminum housing shining in the sun. A small man in boots and western hat was ordering two dogs into the truck, face twisted with anger. Then a gray-haired handsome woman came around the camper and looked at him.

"What's going on here?" the patrolman asked.

Carl Miter told him.

Fifteen minutes later the area was alive with deputies and patrolmen. The bulk of cars had moved on to the south edge of the lake, to the parking area of a closed commercial lodge. Men had been sent into the brush surrounding the area. Others were slowly checking the homes built around the lake. And now the county sheriff, a small man with neat features and a gentle voice, was looking at Carl Miter and Mrs. Nivero with hard eyes, as Ernie Lang stood beside him. The sheriff said to Miter, "Where did the dogs lose them?"

"Over there," he said motioning toward the west. "Around that falls over there."

The sheriff looked in that direction, where craggy mountains rose toward primitive wilds. Then he said to Ernie Lang, "Does he know how to handle himself outside?"

Ernie nodded grimly. "I taught him quite a bit about that."

The sheriff turned back to Miter and Mrs. Nivero. "All right. We'll do our best. If you want to help, fine. But from now I'd appreciate your cooperation."

"He's a monster," Mrs. Nivero said. "He's got my *daughter*."

"I know that," the sheriff said. "And if you'd called us in instead of trying to take him alone, maybe we'd have your daughter back now. I'd advise you to work with us from now on." He turned to Ernie. "We're not going to take any chances with him, Mr. Lang. We can't afford to."

"I understand," Ernie said quietly.

"If you want to help too—"

"Yes," he said. "I will." He looked at the condemnation in Mrs. Nivero's eyes, then he walked back to Anna, who waited in their car for him.

Billy, urging Maria on, had followed a shallow stream, up, from the falls. They'd gone into the water, green and translucent as it rushed over gray rocks past banks thick with stiff brush and tall pine. They'd come out of the water three hundred yards upstream, feet wet and freezing; Maria was visibly trembling, white, her eyes feverish. They'd found a wooden bridge, which crossed the stream below a very small lake shimmering in the morning sun, its surface moving slowly forward as it fed the stream.

"I can't go on," Maria said.

"You've got to!" he snapped and pushed her ahead roughly. They went on, climbing up along a rocky walking trail, passing a yellow tree, cut and fallen, its bark and branches stripped, on past dry marsh-like grass, until at last the trail disappeared to a nearly indefinable path; only the wilderness was beyond this, Billy knew furiously. And then he saw it, just visible beyond the trees and brush: a cabin.

He half-carried her toward the structure. He saw instantly that it was new, well-built and constructed for nearly complete privacy. The windows were shuttered, and both doors, he found, were locked. There were several logs lying nearby. He picked one up and lugged it to the back door. He rammed it against the wood again and again, until finally the lock broke and the door flew open.

The interior was compact and fully furnished. There was a living room, a bedroom with a bed neatly made up, and a small kitchen. He tried a light switch, and, in surprise, saw a ceiling light go on. He then noticed electrical heating units were built in the walls. He turned all of them on, and heat flowed out from the reddening coils. He went into the kitchen and opened three cupboards there; they were filled with canned food.

He came back to Maria, eyes gleaming with triumph. "You see? It's all right now! Food, heat, everything we need. Listen, you go get into that bed." He motioned his pistol toward the bedroom, and she moved weakly in, removed her wet shoes, stockings, then her dress. She got into the bed. And he paced around the living room, feeling the elation. When he went in to the bedroom to look at her lying there, even her coughing did not irritate him. "Hungry?"

"Yes," she managed.

He brought her a tin of corned beef, crackers and a can of fruit juice. "There's soup too. I've heated some for you. And you're going to be fine, little one. Just fine!"

She nodded and ate hungrily, and he went outside again. He carefully examined the way they'd come in. Then he opened a shutter on the side of the cabin facing that way.

He returned to the living room and sat down beside the window where he'd opened the shutter. He looked through the trees toward the small path they'd used to get here. He did have it figured out, he thought—as long as they didn't find this place today. But if they did

...

He checked again to make sure he'd fully reloaded the pistol after they'd come out of that stream. He had. He removed his shoes to let them dry in front of a nearby heater. Then he put the pistol safety off, in his lap. He leaned back, eyes bright and wary, watching. No, he thought, he didn't want anyone coming up here now. But if someone did—that was all for him …

The winter day faded into a brief twilight, then darkness came swiftly, stopping the search. The sheriff said, "That's all we can do until tomorrow." Mrs. Nivero, the strain showing in her face, walked back to the camper. Carl Miter said, "We'll just lay over right here, then." The sheriff looked at Ernie Lang. "You look pretty tired, Mr. Lang. Better get some sleep."

Ernie nodded. "We'll drive back to Tahoe and get a motel. When it's daylight—"

"Yes," the sheriff said. "We'll go at it again."

Ernie got into his station wagon and drove slowly out of the area. "Ernie," Anna said, "maybe they'll just give up tomorrow. They can't last in this cold."

"Yes," he said without convincement. "And then?"

"I know he's done wrong, but—"

"We've got to face it, Anna. He's my son, and he's yours too, because you tried to make him that. But we can't forgive him forever. We've got to understand what it is he's gotten to be. And I know what it is." His jaw muscles hardened. "He's a killer, Anna—a killer."

Lights from the lodge, which had been opened on the sheriff's request, gleamed softly above the lake. Two patrol cars were parked in front of it, and the overnight detail was inside. There was another car at the mouth of the road leading into Fallen Leaf, where a deputy sat watching the road. Nearer the water, down from the lodge, Carl Miter's camper caught the reflection of a rising quarter moon. He sat on a back step of the entrance to the sleeping quarters inside. He said quietly, "I remember when I got that red dog. He was two months old. Got him from Jerry Koonz. Jerry said he was out of the best pointer stock he ever seen, and I paid a hundred and seventy-five dollars for him." He touched the brim of his hat. "But I used him for everything. Birds. Rabbits. Coons. Coyotes. Everything."

"I'm sorry, Carl," Elizabeth Nivero said from the bunk inside the truck. "It was a nice dog."

Miter stared into the darkness of the trees beyond. His rifle was propped against the truck beside him. "You wouldn't want some coffee, would you? I could go up there to the lodge. They probably got some going."

"No, thank you, Carl."

Miter listened for any sound at all. There was none except the distant roar of the falls. Almost all of the animals had left this high altitude when the cold had come, he knew, and they wouldn't come back until spring. He touched his hand again and thought of how that dog had looked with the blood flowing out of its chest. The anger simmered inside of him. Then he thought of the girl out there somewhere. She didn't even have a sweater, as far as they knew. *That bastard*, he thought; *he's killing her*. And, he guessed, Elizabeth must be thinking about that right now too. He tried to reassure her, saying:

"I wouldn't worry too much, Elizabeth. That's a funny thing to say, everything considered. But they maybe found some place to keep warm. Too many cabins around here to check in one day. And if they didn't, this cold's going to bring them in anyway. You could look at it that way."

"She didn't do it, Carl," Mrs. Nivero said thinly.

"Do what, Elizabeth?"

"Marry him because she wanted to."

"Well, you're probably right about that."

"I know that! He threatened her, Carl. That's the only reason!"

He nodded and said, "Yes, but you just try to lie there and get some rest, Elizabeth. Try not to think too much now. Just get some rest."

She said no more after that, and he sat, not minding the cold because the fury inside of him was enough to warm him. Where is he? he thought, putting a hand against the chilled steel of his rifle. *Where is he?*

Moving down from the small cabin at the edge of the wilderness, Billy Lang went into the water of the small stream. He came out just above the falls, and climbed over rock, then through brush, without sound, until he had reached the edge of the lake. He stopped there, in the protection of the trees, and looked across at the lights showing from the lodge. Then he saw the soft gleaming of the camper's housing below the lodge. His eyes narrowed. His heart began pounding faster.

But he forced himself to go on with what he had to do. He moved away from the direction of the lodge and the camper, along the lake. He'd been certain he'd seen it when he and Maria had circled around this way, escaping from Miter. But in the dim moonlight he could not see it. He began to lose confidence swiftly, as he moved. Then, at last, he saw it in the water, floating motionlessly: a small rowboat.

He looked back toward the lodge. It would be hard to see him from there. But maybe they had others posted along the lake. His mouth felt dry, suddenly imagining dozens of eyes watching him. The bitter cold even seemed to reduce in intensity, as nervous perspiration beaded on his forehead. Then he fought off the fear, knowing that he had to do this.

Cautiously, he went down to the edge of the water. He pulled the rope holding the boat and brought it in toward him, inchingly. When he had, he removed his shoes and lay down in the boat. He untied the rope. Then, using his hands as paddles, working slowly, the cold of the water making his hands stiff, he moved the boat out into the smooth water.

He took it out seventy-five yards, trembling now. Then he brought his hands out of the water and tried to move his fingers. When he could, he drew out the slip of paper he'd written on before he'd left the cabin, and put it on the bottom of the boat. Then he took from a trouser pocket Maria's dress. He put that on top of the note. Finally he removed his shirt, trembling even more with his upper body protected only by a T shirt now. He put that with the dress. Then, holding his breath, he went over the side, into the icy darkness of the water, swimming slowly in the bitter cold for the shore.

The search resumed at daylight. Ernie Lang got out of his car and walked to Carl Miter's camper. He did not look at Elizabeth Nivero. He said to Miter, "When you were working your dogs yesterday, how far up and down that stream did you go?"

"You figured he went into the water?"

"He might have, to cover the trail. He knew you had the dogs."

"I figured all of that, Lang," Miter said. "I went up two hundred yards on that stream, then down past the falls, all the way to the lake. Those dogs didn't pick up a thing."

Just then there was a call from a deputy standing near the lake. He pointed toward the boat floating beyond. Ernie and Miter went down to the water, and the sheriff emerged from his car to join them. The deputy said, "That boat was tied up yesterday. I'm sure of it."

"All right," the sheriff said. "There's a couple of boats stored in back of the lodge. Let's get one of them down here and take a look."

The deputy paddled a boat out and rowed the derelict in. When both boats were beached, the dress, shirt and note were handed out. The sheriff read the note aloud in a grim voice:

"You who find this, tell them we'll never be caught. Come to God, if you want to find us now. Or to the bottom of this lake. Billy Lang."

The sheriff looked first at Elizabeth Nivero, then at Ernie.

"No," Mrs. Nivero said. "No!" Her voice rang over the water, and she thrust a hand at the note. Then her knees buckled. Carl Miter caught her and, despite his small size, lifted her easily. She was moaning now, and he said, "I'll take her back over to the truck." He moved off with her, carefully, gently.

Ernie, mind stunned, watched them. Anna, beside him, took his hand. Then he looked at the sheriff, blinking.

The sheriff shook his head apologetically. "I don't know, Mr. Lang. I don't know."

Ernie stared at the dress, then at the shirt. "Maybe they really didn't do it," he said.

"Maybe not," the sheriff said. "But he was running into nowhere. If the girl loved him that much—"

"Yes," Ernie said, still stunned. "Yes."

"We'll get some people in to search the lake. But it's deep. It could take a long time, and we still might not find anything." He shook his head again. "I'll keep some of my men searching around here, just in case. I'm sorry, Mr. Lang." Ernie, his wife beside him, walked slowly back to his car.

They sat for a long time, saying nothing. Then finally he said, "Is he really gone, Anna? In that water?"

"If he is," she said hollowly, "even that would be better to know."

"It was a terrible thing," he said. "I couldn't think anything at first, then suddenly I was glad. Because it was over!"

"Ernie—"

He laughed bitterly, eyes stinging. "Christ, but man is an animal, isn't he?"

"No, Ernie," she said. "Much more."

He crossed his arms against the steering wheel and leaned his head against them. Finally he said, "No."

Anna watched him and saw him straighten.

"No!" he said again. "I told you last night—there's no use hiding from anything anymore. I don't think he killed himself and took that girl with him."

"Why, Ernie?"

His voice was cold: "Because I don't think he'd have the guts."

Ernie Lang removed his pistol from where he'd placed it on a rear seat, and slipped it under his belt beneath his jacket. Then he got out and walked grimly in the direction of the falls beyond.

As he did, Carl Miter saw him moving away from the area. He said to Mrs. Nivero lying inside the camper, "Elizabeth, you're going to be all right, now, aren't you?"

She lay staring at the ceiling of the housing. She didn't answer.

"Elizabeth," he said, "I've got to leave you here now, and you just try not to think about anything." He reached inside and patted her hand, then, his pistol strapped at his waist, he left the camper. Ernie Lang was well ahead now, walking up the road toward those falls, but Carl Miter followed swiftly.

The road passing the falls rose steeply, made a half circle around the rushing water, then followed the stream, which flowed below. The road had once been blacktopped for a stretch of perhaps a half mile, but that was cracked and broken now. Ernie examined the rushing water as he moved upstream. He'd asked Miter how far upstream he'd taken his dogs, and Miter had said two hundred yards. All right, he thought; maybe Billy went further, knowing Miter had his dogs. Maybe he kept himself and the girl in that freezing water for a longer time, just the way he might have swum that lake last night, because he was tenacious and shrewd and because he was never going to give up until he was stopped. And if he had done these things, and if he were still alive, he was going to be stopped, Ernie thought—he was.

He reached a gray-timber bridge built over concrete supports which spanned the stream. There was a small lake just beyond the bridge, which fed the stream. Ahead, the road narrowed and swung past the lake, then rose toward the wilderness beyond. Hopeless, he thought. They could have gone anywhere. Anywhere ...

Then he saw, where the road narrowed into a trail, a piece of white cloth. He went forward and picked it up. It was a handkerchief, small, with lace edges; there was an old-English M embroidered on one corner.

He looked upward, where the trail wound higher into the mountains. He thought, then, he heard something moving behind him. He whirled, hand on his pistol, but he could see nothing. The woods were silent, with only the sound of the stream running under the bridge behind him.

He turned back toward the trail and moved on, putting the handkerchief in a pocket. The climb became steeper. He went past a fallen yellow tree, its bark and branches stripped. He climbed past marsh-like grass, and then the trail narrowed to a very small path.

Where it did, he saw a woman's comb. He picked it up. He looked around, through the trees, and then saw the cabin resting a hundred yards beyond, barely visible.

He bent down again, re-examined the comb, then he started through the brush toward the cabin, moving low, keeping himself out of sight. Twenty-five yards from the structure, using the brush as a screen, he saw that the front windows were shuttered, except for one.

He pulled his pistol from his belt again, then started making a slow, careful circle of the house. He found all of the other windows shuttered and the back door closed. He came out of the protection of the brush and ran to the back of the cabin. There was a meter near the corner. It was turning.

He took a long breath, then he moved silently along the wall to the back door. There, he stopped and listened, hearing nothing but his own heart beating for a few seconds. Then he heard voices. First the girl's, very faint. Then the other one, growing louder. He knew that voice. He licked his lips, then called:

"Billy!"

The voices stopped. There was not another sound. Three seconds went by. Four. Then a gun exploded inside the house. A bullet ripped through the door. He heard a scream of rage, as he slammed back against the wall. "Billy!" he called again, and another bullet tore through the door.

He pressed against the wall beside the door, and now he was certain that he could hear running through the house, then the door in front slamming open.

He kicked at the back door. It flew open, tumbling the chair that had propped it across the floor, and he went in fast. He saw the front door was open. He could hear the sound of crashing through the brush beyond. He went through the house, pausing only long enough to see the girl in the bedroom, her face drawn and white, eyes staring at him in terror. Then he ran outside in time to see his son scrambling upward along a gray-granite cliff. He plunged after him. And when the boy had nearly reached the top he shouted, "Far enough, Billy."

The boy turned, his back against the rock. His eyes were wild, his face twisted. "No!" he screamed. He pointed his gun at Ernie and fired.

The bullet whined past Ernie's left arm, ricocheted, and screamed through the air.

"Billy!" he shouted. "Listen to me!"

"Damn you!" the boy howled, and suddenly he was coming back down, firing his pistol. Ernie dropped flat, bullets skipping into the rock on either side of him. He stared at his son descending, the gun kicking in the boy's hand. Then he lifted his own pistol, sighted and fired.

The gun flew out of the boy's hand as his arm jerked outward. The impact of the bullet half-turned him. The boy fell to one knee, staring at Ernie with savage hatred. He put one hand to the blood coming out of his chest and fell to his side. He was still watching Ernie Lang, mouth moving silently.

Ernie ran to him. "Billy—"

"*Damn you!*" the boy whispered, then he rolled back, to lie with his eyes open, quite dead.

Ernie knelt beside him. He touched the boy's cheek with a trembling hand, eyes stinging again. "God," he whispered. Then he staggered away. He put a hand against a tree trunk to steady himself, and was sick; and then finally he turned around to look again at the boy lying there.

He did not hear Carl Miter approaching, until he'd stepped directly in front of him, grinning. "Yeah," Miter said. "I lost you there at that house. Then that kid came flying out. I didn't even have time to get off a good shot, before you got in the way. But you took care of him real good   "

Ernie Lang swung with a burst of vicious strength, knocking the small man rolling in the brush. Miter came to his feet immediately, spraddle-legged, brushing a hand along his chin. "Now, wait a minute, mister—"

Then Ernie Lang's strength disappeared, and he slipped to his knees. "Get the sheriff," he said raggedly. "For God's sake, just get the sheriff."

Miter stared at him for a few moments, then he said, "Is the girl in the house?"

"Yes."

Miter nodded, then turned to look at the fallen boy again. His mouth twitched at the corners with a smile. "All right, Lang," he said to Ernie. "You get yourself up and take a look at her. I'll get the sheriff."

AND THEN SHE WAS DEAD

The *employé de bureau* handed me the letter across the desk when I went down at mid-afternoon. I sat with it in the lobby and looked carefully at the familiar handwriting. The letter was addressed in care of the State Department, Washington; there was a San Francisco cancellation mark. It had been forwarded through my European office, and had caught up with me here in Biarritz. Feeling my hands tremble I opened the envelope and read through delicate tissue:

"Mr. and Mrs. Lawrence Rollins announce the wedding of their daughter Nancy Ann to Dr. Curtis Cornell on Tuesday, the sixteenth of January ..."

I stopped reading that and read the message handwritten across the bottom: "For your information." There was a slashing underline beneath it. I sat back, closing my eyes. It was not the message I had wanted.

I walked around to a small bar called The Circus, which faced the sea and ordered a brandy flip. With the drink before me I got out the wedding invitation and reread it. I put it back in my pocket. I wondered who Dr. Curtis Cornell was, then I didn't want to think about who he was. I wanted only to think about Nancy, the only girl I had ever honestly loved, who was now marrying someone else.

The sun finally came out and shone down at such an angle that I caught a reflection of myself in the glass: tall, lean, short-clipped brown hair, a neatly dressed 27-year-old courier off duty, trying to pry some fun out of a 30-day leave by lounging about a French Basque resort off-season, drinking a brandy flip without feeling flip, served by a chill-eyed waiter who had labeled me a lesser American government clerk the first day I had walked in, now feeling the bitter pangs of knowing that Nancy Rollins was about to become the wife of someone else. I hated myself.

I had met Nancy's father two years before. I was a junior attaché with the U.S. Department of State in London. Then, as now, I was taking leave. I'd been in Paris for six days; on the seventh I wanted to fly to Munich to investigate the Bavarian country. Then, as now, it had been cold. Drizzle had turned a November Paris into a gray, wet capital. All flights to Munich, which was closed in, had been cancelled.

I stood beside a rather short but sturdy-looking man wearing a black raincoat and Homburg. I was showing my credentials to a clerk, arguing to get on a plane to Frankfurt where I could pick up an overnight Pullman to Munich.

The man glanced at my credentials, while the clerk stubbornly pointed out that all manifests were full. The man said, "You can come with me, if you care to."

I turned and looked at him more closely. He was in his mid-forties, I guessed. He was impeccably dressed, down to black shoes polished to the luster of patent leather. But there was nothing delicate in his appearance. He had a square tough face, with pale blue eyes which stared straight through me. He was perhaps six inches shorter than I, but there was a bearing about him that removed any feeling I might have had about size advantage. I visualized him, for a moment, in a Marine combat officer's uniform leading his troops into fire—I later found out that he had been an infantry colonel with a long World War II combat record. "Fine," I said. "How are we going? Flap our hands and levitate?"

"They're giving me an Air Force plane. I've got to be in Frankfurt this evening."

I gathered up my bags and followed him outside. We got into a Jeep, which hurtled us toward his waiting plane.

"My name's Anthony Kirk," I said. "Who do you have to know to get yourself a plane like this? The President?"

"It helps."

I examined him again. He somehow looked familiar. "I didn't catch your name."

"Lawrence Rollins."

"Oh. I see. I'm sorry, sir. I didn't mean to be snappy with the Assistant Secretary of State. I'm very sorry about that. Being in the Department myself. New and young, I mean."

He didn't answer. As soon as we were in the plane he opened his briefcase and began going over papers.

I didn't bother him again until we were circling Frankfurt. We exchanged a few sentences while the plane was coming in to land. I left the plane with him, lugging my baggage.

Waiting for him in the cold, foggy afternoon were two women. The older was as tall as Rollins, rather thin, expensively dressed, with a good-looking but somehow lack-luster face. She appeared aloof and faintly irritated. But at the same time you felt that if her veneer were to crack slightly she would become swiftly frightened, or suspicious, or emotionally upset in some other way, so that you would see an entirely different woman.

The other was not over twenty-one, with certain features resembling both Rollins' and the older woman's. But this combination had produced a stunning beauty the older woman did not have and a warmth you could not find in Rollins' appearance. She was small and black-haired and I fell out of step with Rollins as we approached. I did not remember seeing a girl who had struck me with so much impact. I picked up my pace again and then we were stopping before them. I didn't intend to go on until Rollins had introduced me.

He obliged crisply: "My wife, Mrs. Rollins. My daughter, Nancy. This is Mr. Kirk who's with our department in London."

I smiled first at Mrs. Rollins, who dismissed me with a curt nod of her head, then at her daughter, who did not dismiss me with her look. She smiled back at me slowly and with, I was certain, invitation. She said:

"How nice to meet you, Mr. Kirk."

She held out her gloved hand. I held it perhaps seconds too long. "It's entirely my pleasure. Are you staying in Frankfurt long?"

"A few days," Nancy Rollins said. "While Daddy slaves."

"Yes," Rollins said. "And you're probably anxious to get a reservation on that train, Mr. Kirk. Mr. Kirk is on his way to Munich."

"How wonderful," Nancy said. "Because that's where we're going next."

"Yes," I said. "Everyone should see Bavaria in the winter. But I'm wondering if I wouldn't be missing something by not seeing Frankfurt first, as long as I'm here."

"I think," Nancy said swiftly, "Frankfurt might be tremendously interesting to you, Mr. Kirk."

I stayed over, and got a small room near their quarters in the new wing of the Frankfurter Hof. I called Nancy that evening, and we had a sea-food dinner at the Brückenkeller. We quickly discovered that we were both from San Francisco. She was 21, had just graduated from Stanford and had a desire to become a painter. I told her that I was 25, had graduated from the University of San Francisco and had a great desire to have fun.

We proceeded to have fun. Nights we danced and drank beer in cellar halls and, days, carefully searched our way through the city. The Rollinses tolerated my time with Nancy with a cool resignation. After four days, Mrs. Rollins and Nancy left Lawrence Rollins with his affairs in Frankfurt, Bonn and West Berlin and took a compartment down to Munich. I rode along in a sleeper. In Munich, Nancy and I again danced, drank cocktails and tried out the restaurants. Her mother shopped.

Then, on Nancy's insistence, we got into a rented Karmann Ghia and drove down to Bad Tolz and over to Tegernsee. Mrs. Rollins spoke to me sparely and accomplished a convincing façade which indicated that, for all good purposes, I was not even in her presence.

But Nancy and I were becoming increasingly aware of our own presences. The air was bitterly cold in Bavaria, the mountains heavy with snow. But together, skiing, hiking, skating, we felt nothing but warmth. I knew that something had happened to my emotions that was far more serious than a simple infatuation for a girl who had been handy to romance while I enjoyed my leave.

My time ran out, and I had to report back to London. Nancy saw me off at the Munich airport. I kissed her there, long and hard. And though I'd certainly kissed her before in those last days and nights, I had not felt before what I felt then. A few hours later I was back in my small flat in London, wondering if I had not imagined the whole thing.

Proof that I hadn't came in the form of Nancy's letters. They arrived every day, first from Munich, then from Frankfurt, then from Paris, where she and her parents spent a week. They shifted from gay, coquettish notes to serious letters investigating the emotion she was feeling. Then the Rollinses took the boat-train through Dieppe, and I met the boat at Southampton. Nancy came running down the plank. I caught her in my arms, and she hugged me and looked at me with shining eyes.

She whispered, "I could barely stand being away from you. God, I love you, Tony. Please. Love me back, won't you?"

I was both startled and pleased. "Any man would love you, Nancy. I—"

"I *do* love you, Tony. I don't know how it happened. But it did. And I don't care about anything else. I'll sleep with you. I'll marry you. I'll do anything in the world for you. But love me the way I love you, darling. Please!"

I knew, as we rode the train back to London, that Mr. and Mrs. Rollins were well aware of the completeness of Nancy's emotional involvement. They sat stiffly silent across from us as Nancy clutched my hand tightly and looked back at them with defiance. It had been talked about, I knew. The Rollinses were taking it, I was certain, with bitterness.

When the cab from the train pulled up in front of the Cumberland, the hotel the Rollinses had selected, Lawrence Rollins asked to speak to me alone in the bar. I told Nancy I would telephone up for her.

I sat with Lawrence Rollins over a whiskey. He talked quietly, holding me with his penetrating eyes.

"I don't wish to be trite, Mr. Kirk, but Nancy is an only child. Mrs. Rollins and I love her deeply. She is very intelligent, loving and talented. I happen to be an art expert, Mr. Kirk, and I know that my daughter could be an excellent painter. I'd like to see her try. I'd also like to see her mature a little more before she settles down and marries somebody."

He hit that last word with emphasis and stared at me. I waited for him to go on.

"I'm resigning my position next month, Mr. Kirk. I'm going to return to San Francisco with my wife and daughter. I've been a very busy man all of my life. I haven't been able to spend the time I've wanted to with my family. I would like to do that now. I can afford to do that, because my various financial efforts have grown and my investments have paid off to the extent that, at middle-age, I don't have to work anymore. I doubt that it's news to you that I'm a wealthy man."

I could feel my face turn warm. "I haven't concerned myself with that, Mr. Rollins."

"Nancy tells me you come from the Mission District."

I knew I was visibly flushing now. The Mission, as we both knew, was not the most fashionable neighborhood in San Francisco. All of the obvious implications were driven into Rollins' inflection when he made his statement.

"What do you want, Mr. Rollins?"

"I'll tell you what I want. I'd like you to go on living the way you were living before I was kind enough to give you a lift to Frankfurt. I know you, Mr. Kirk. You are a bright, unresponsible young man with a glib tongue and too damn much cockiness. Women obviously like you, and there are a lot of women in Europe. Take advantage of them, but don't take advantage of my daughter. She's not for fun, Mr. Kirk. Break it off with her and immediately. And go on with your life. You're a good man for us over there, but you're no good for my daughter. I think you were right to be thinking of the Courier Service. I think I can do something for you there. What do you say, Mr. Kirk?"

I tossed off my own drink. "I'm wondering what happens when an insignificant State Department employee tells the Assistant Secretary of State to go to hell."

His mouth whitened slightly at the corners, but he reacted in no other way. He waited, watching me.

"I suppose," I said finally, "you know how Nancy feels about this?"

"Yes. But it's a bit of immature fantasy on her part, and she'll know that in time. I don't intend to see her hurt before she comes out of it." He motioned a hand impatiently. "What's your answer?"

I stood up. "I've got a date with your daughter."

I called her and she came down immediately. We had dinner at a restaurant I knew on Jermyn Street. I didn't tell her what Lawrence Rollins had said to me. After dinner we walked to Piccadilly, because Nancy wanted to see it. We walked the bright-lighted sidewalk, hand in hand.

"I love you," she said.

"Immature fantasy. You'll know that as soon as you get home."

She laughed. "You're so silly, Tony. I truly love you. Does that frighten you? Am I being too swift?"

"Of course not. I—" I didn't know what to say.

"Is that a prostitute over there, Tony?"

I shrugged. "Possibly."

"Do you come over here often and use them?"

I looked at her quickly and laughed. "Seven or eight times a week, yes, but no more than that."

She pressed my hand tightly. "Don't joke about it, Tony. I don't want to know anyway, really. I'm already viciously jealous. But I'd rather, I think, it would be a prostitute than someone you loved. I couldn't stand that at all—unless it were me, of course."

"That's the kind of talk that could lead to trouble."

"I wouldn't mind."

"You would when you woke up and found it all to be an immature fantasy."

"Where in the world did you get that phrase? It's absolutely foolish. I know exactly what I feel and what I want."

"What do you want? Right now?"

She stopped and looked up at me with clear, guileless blue eyes. "Anything you want, Tony."

"How about a half and half somewhere, for the hell of it?"

"Yes. Or we could get a room."

"Nancy, listen—"

"Don't you see? I don't want to push you into something you don't want. I don't want you to think I'm rushing you to the altar. I just want you to know how much I love you. I would gladly go to a hotel with you, right now."

"You will. And it'll be your own hotel and your own room. A man can only stand so much, and I need rest tonight because I've got a large day at the office tomorrow."

"Tony, Daddy's planning on flying us home in two days. What's going to happen to us?"

I shook my head, trying to get everything straight in my mind. "I don't know, Nancy."

"Do you love me, Tony? Please tell me honestly. Do you?"

I looked down at her, small and beautiful, so desirable that if I'd had less reasonability I would have taken her and gone off somewhere across the world where nobody, including her father, could tell me that I was no good for her. "Yes," I said, "I love you, Nancy."

I kissed her in the blazing garishness of Piccadilly Circus, then I signaled for the first cab in sight and took her back to her hotel. She held to me tightly in front of her room and whispered, "Do you really have to work tomorrow, Tony?"

"Yes."

"Can't you possibly get off?"

"Can't, no."

"Could we have lunch then?"

"I'm backlogged from my leave. I'll need to work through. Let's make it cocktails. Then dinner. Five-thirty?"

"I'll die waiting to see you."

"The Ritz bar?"

"I'll be there," she whispered. I kissed her again, and she went in swiftly.

That was the last time I saw her.

I did not sleep that night. I walked back and forth in my flat, unable to stop thinking about the way Lawrence Rollins had looked at me in the Cumberland bar or about the things he had said. The resentment built. He'd had no honest right to say those things, but he had taken the right anyway. I'd been an orphan since my mother died in the cheap duplex in the Mission when I was fifteen, and I had not taken words like that from anyone since.

Near dawn I sat down and wrote the letter. It was short and direct:

Dear Nancy,
I have thought all of this out as the sun starts up, and I can only say that somehow we got too serious. I think it would not be good for you to become too serious about someone like me. I am too much a

freedom-loving fellow, and nothing seems to help that. I wish you would fall in love with someone who deserves you, and I don't think I am the one. It was a lot of fun, and I'll always remember it. I hope, when you get home, you'll think back and remember how much fun it was, but how great a mistake it would have been to have gone on with it. I'm sorry I can't make that date at the Ritz, but I think it's best if we close it out right now. Give my best to your father.

TONY.

As I sealed it, I felt a perverse kind of satisfaction, knowing that Lawrence Rollins had not expected it to be so easy; I was showing him a kind of character he did not believe I had. In the near-dawn I delivered the letter to the desk of the Cumberland and asked that it be sent up to Miss Rollins as soon as she ordered breakfast.

A month later my transfer to the U.S. Diplomatic Courier Service came through, and I went to the Continent.

In the months following, carrying pouches like mail sacks, checking invoice against pouch, moving from country to country, never knowing what I was carrying, there was more than enough time to think about why I had broken off with Nancy. Pride? I knew there was pride involved. I was sensitive about my background, against Lawrence Rollins' position. He had taken full advantage of that sensitivity. And had I felt closed in by Nancy's quick and total love? I knew there was that too. I had wanted my fling with what had once appeared glamorous and adventurous. I had been selfish about that.

But I had found no real glamour, no real adventure. I was simply performing a job which, if you did not care for planes or trains or ships, was no more satisfying that servicing cars in an American gasoline station—because there was one definite drawback: loneliness. I stayed nowhere long enough to make friends. The girls I met were brushing affairs, a small night's adventure, with no real meaning. As the loneliness tightened and the glamour paled, I knew, at last, just how much I loved Nancy Rollins.

But there was pride again, and somehow I could not write to tell her that I had made the very largest mistake of my life. I could not bring myself to mail the letter even after I had finally written it.

Still, as I made my last tour before this leave, I made up my mind that if I found the leave as lonesome, as unrewarding, as I expected, I would finally sit down and write the letter and actually send it. My last tour took me from Bonn to Geneva, then to Rome, Athens, Cairo, Addis Ababa and Nairobi, traveling day and night. Then I staged with another courier, like a no-thinking relay runner, rested a day, and flew to Kembapa in Uganda, to Modadiscio and up to Aden. From there I went to Lagos and on to Monrovia, Dakar, Casablanca, Nice and Paris, and back to Bonn. It was a trip to inspire an armchair adventurer. But I was a U.S. Courier, and I was bored with the job.

I left on leave with relief and came to Biarritz. It was here that I knew I would finally send my letter to Nancy begging forgiveness and here that I prayed that she had not learned to love someone else and had perhaps married him; it was here that I had received, at last, the message from her, which I had hoped, in those first seconds, would be my second chance. It was not.

There was an art showing in the Villa La Titania. I walked over, simply because I'd decided earlier to go. There were few viewers, and I made my way slowly along the wall-hung drawings, etchings, watercolors and oils.

A non-impressionistic etching by a young French artist whose work I'd seen earlier in Paris finally caught my eye. I bought it. Newlyweds could always use a good etching.

Bitterly I walked back toward my hotel, thinking that I couldn't purchase wrapping materials for it until Monday, day after tomorrow. The gift would arrive late, because the wedding was to be on Tuesday, just three days away. That thought tightened me inside. I remembered more vividly how Nancy had looked that last night in Piccadilly Circus, looking up at me with clear blue eyes. I remembered the taste of her lips, exactly …

I went up to my room in the Plaza and poured a fourth of a glass of cognac. I sat down beside my window and looked out on the gray, depressing day. If I had only done something. If, even only weeks ago, I had only tried. But it was too late now. Too late …

I felt myself tensing again, after the momentary relaxing with the cognac. I bent forward, pinching my chin, considering. I had money. Not a great deal, but enough, because I'd had expenses as a courier and almost everything else was put away. But was it madness to try it?

No, I decided suddenly.

I telephoned the railway station and tried my bad French with too much excitement to be understood, then switched to English, which the clerk knew as well as I. I made my reservation, then telephoned Paris. They had nothing. But perhaps there would be a cancellation.

The next morning I boarded the 9:30 express out of Biarritz. I arrived at the terminal in Paris at 4:55 that evening. A French train was on time, and I knew luck was with me. I got a room in a small hotel near the terminal and telephoned Air France. The next flight left the next day, and I was hoping for that cancellation. There was none. I slept fitfully, then appeared at Orly early, full of determination. Again my luck was good. There was a last-minute cancellation in the economy section. At 12:40 that noon I was belted into an outgoing Air France Boeing 707 jet.

The plane came down at Los Angeles at the Inglewood field at five past six that evening. I was back in the United States for the first time in four years.

In the Southern California twilight, I took a limousine from the old terminal. The super-modern architecture of the giant new airport south of Santa Monica came in sight with its skeletal mushroom in front and the long, sleek terminal building taking in and spilling out a vast swarm of travelers. I checked my baggage for my flight, knowing I had been gone a long time.

I walked beneath a low light-bright ceiling, down a long tunnel running to United's waiting planes, and rode an escalator up to field level. I had a quick drink in the bar, because I was feeling butterflies as I neared Nancy. Then I walked into the blue-furnished waiting-room and through the final tunnel to the plane. The plane went up with a high whine. I stepped into San Francisco's International terminal at eight twenty-five.

What emotional reaction I might otherwise have felt for returning to the city where I had grown up was minimized, almost destroyed, by my single desire to see Nancy again. I again rode a limousine, onto Bayshore, then into the city on the new vastly complex Skyway leading directly to the heart of town. I saw the giant splash of lights, but I didn't think, because I could feel that knot of excitement, which had begun in Biarritz, become nearly overpowering. I didn't know what I could hope to accomplish. But I was in movement. I was going in the right direction.

I got out at the terminal in the center of town and cabbed the short distance to the Sir Francis Drake, a block off Union Square, where I got a room. I had planned, on the flight over, to telephone. Now I decided against that. I would simply go to her house.

I sent the bellboy down with the etching to have it gift-wrapped and a small card attached, then had room service pick up my best suit. I showered, shaved, and the suit came back. I dressed swiftly, and the bellboy returned with the wrapped etching. I tucked it under my arm and went down and got a cab.

It rolled swiftly up Russian Hill. The cabbie stopped us before a fortress-like house, gray and brooding in the moonlight. I again felt that resentment I'd felt the afternoon I'd sat across a table from Lawrence Rollins in the bar of the Cumberland Hotel. But I pushed that feeling aside, sent the cabbie on and climbed the steps to the arched doorway. I pressed the chimes button.

I waited, feeling my smile freezing. A maid wearing a black uniform opened the door. I tried to liven my smile. "I'd like to see Miss Rollins, please."

She stared at me, looking surprised and confused, as though she might start crying in a moment. "Miss Nancy?"

"Miss Nancy, yes. Miss Nancy Rollins."

"Come with me," she managed. I followed her down a high-ceilinged hallway to a large Victorian living room. A man seven or eight years older than I was seated on a sofa. His hands were folded together, his jacketed shoulders slumped. He turned his head, face grim, and looked at me.

"This gentleman," the maid said in a wavering voice, "asked for Miss Nancy."

Anger flickered in his eyes. He stood up, taller than I, considerably heavier, his dark slim-tailored suit looking tight on his awkward-looking frame. He glared at me and said:

"What kind of a bad joke is that? Nancy's dead!"

I stared at him. The maid, a dim shadow at the edge of my vision, disappeared. The man had accused me of a bad joke, and I was just as certain that he was the one who had delivered it.

"Who are you anyway?" he asked angrily.

"Tony Kirk. She can't be dead."

"She is," he snapped. "We were to be married tomorrow—" The anger seemed to flow out of him. He sat down weakly and put his palms against his eyes. "What are you doing here? I've heard about you. She was done with you."

He'd been the one she had selected in my place, and now he was telling me that she was dead. He was Dr. Curtis Cornell, and I hated him. "It isn't true," I said hoarsely. "She can't be dead."

"Yes," he said, "for God's sake."

"When?" I asked, my voice rising. "How?"

He wagged his head uselessly. I turned to see Lawrence Rollins coming into the room. He stared at me, a stunned look in his eyes.

"What are you doing here?" His voice was harsh; there was no welcome in it.

"I got a wedding invitation." Then I said foolishly, "I brought this present." I put the etching down and shook my head, dazed now.

Rollins put his hand on Dr. Curtis Cornell's shoulder. "You'd better go home, Curtis. Get some rest, somehow."

Cornell got slowly to his feet. He said to me, "Why are you here? I tell you she was done with you!"

"All right, Curtis," Lawrence Rollins said. "Try to get some sleep."

Cornell moved out of the room, large and shuffling.

"You'd better come with me," Rollins said. I followed him down a hall. He paused in front of an open door. I saw, seated in a shaded sitting room, Nancy's mother. "It's Tony Kirk, Ona," Rollins said wearily. "He happened to come."

The aloof, irritated, handsome face I remembered was twisted with grief. Tears streamed down her gaunt cheeks. She looked at me, and slowly her mouth shaped the words, "Get out of my sight."

He led me on to his study at the end of the hallway, explaining that she was not herself. The study was very large with dark paneling upon which were hung a variety of original art: paintings, etchings, drawings. Other art objects—figurines, vases, from a variety of cultures—were scattered about on small, heavy tables. There was a large drafting table in one corner where Rollins obviously examined his collection. Shelves of art books were at one end of the room, opposite the side where Rollins' large dark teak desk rested in front of a broad window through which I could see the lights of the Marina where the Bay touched the north edge of San Francisco. You could see the orange lights of the Golden Gate Bridge, and the white lights of Alcatraz, then, closer, the moving lights of automobiles running along the boulevard by the water.

"Sit down," he said, motioning me into a leather chair. He himself into his own chair, showing the grievous defeat I now felt.

"She can't be dead," I insisted.

"Didn't you see the newspapers?"

"I just got in."

"She's dead."

"When? How?"

"I gave her a Porsche for her birthday, just before Christmas. She was driving it down to Pacifica yesterday. She was going to have lunch with girlfriends on the beach." He lost his voice and sat staring dully at the surface of his desk.

"What happened?"

"There're a couple of sharp curves. She didn't make one. The car rolled down a long grade. Somebody saw the fire. When they got down there, she was—" He shook his head once, and sat saying nothing.

I tried to make myself see it. I couldn't. "No," I said softly.

He got up and paced in front of the broad window. He looked at me, with pink marks of anger in his cheeks. "Why didn't you honestly buck me that day in the Cumberland bar, Kirk? She loved you! If you'd wanted to marry her, why didn't you? If you had, this wouldn't have happened!"

I looked at my clenched hands, hating myself for not having done exactly that.

Rollins stared at me accusingly. "You were too damn touchy! Where do you think I came from? From the slums, by God. My wife's father was a hard-working carpenter. You never thought of that, did you? Now look what's happened. She's dead!"

Finally he slumped back into his chair.

"I can't believe that," I said stubbornly.

"You'll have to."

I sat in the deep silence. Finally I said, "I want to see her room— where she lived."

He shrugged defeatedly. "Upstairs. Take the stairway down the hall. First room on the left. Don't bother her mother."

The room was bright, with white antique furniture. It was the room both of a girl and a woman. A large yellow stuffed elephant, worn with the years, sat upon a small child's rocker. Her cosmetics were neatly arranged on the vanity. Her perfume came to me, and I felt the pain hit, like a sharp, too-low blow to my middle ...

I walked slowly around the room, touching things, finding a completeness of her I had not known before. There was a well-worn photo album. In it I found pictures taken when she was a child. There was one of her in a short-skirted dress when she was thirteen, not yet the woman I had known, but with the same guileless eyes looking brightly at the camera, the smile nearly the same, different only because an eye tooth was out of alignment.

I remembered a day in Bavaria when we had sat beneath a bright sun beside the lake at Tegernsee and she had told me how sensitive she'd been, as a young girl, about that tooth. But she had been stubborn and refused a brace; later, she had gone to a dentist and had the tooth removed and replaced with a plastic one, in perfect alignment. I could hear her warm, liquid voice as she asked me if she were less appealing for having exposed an intimacy like that.

I closed the book and opened her closet. Her dresses, suits, coats hung in careful order. I found the dress she had worn the last night we had been together in London. I closed the door swiftly and left the room. I couldn't take that anymore.

I returned to Rollins' study knowing I could never accept it until I had seen final proof. "I want to see her."

Deep lines in his face seemed the work of an artist who had wished to age him far beyond his years. "For God's sake, Kirk. She's a *char*."

The word bit into me, but I shook my head stubbornly. "I want to see her."

He finally gave me the address. I walked out of the large house and took deep breaths of the chill night air. The mortuary was a few blocks away on Green Street. I walked slowly, knowing I had to go there, but not wanting to go too fast—seeing her would end it.

I got there too quickly. A tall hushed-voiced man with the traditional dark suit and solicitous manner listened to me, frowning a little. He was not certain. The funeral was to be closed coffin. Would I mind if he checked with Mr. Rollins? I waited while he telephoned Rollins. He nodded gravely when permission had been given and led me to the room.

I felt light-headed in that room. It seemed uncommonly hot. Sweat prickled on my forehead, yet I felt chilly suddenly. I looked down at the refrigerated drawer.

What was in it was a black travesty, a fire-darkened rudeness, its teeth grinning up at me. Those *teeth*, I thought. I felt something like a soft blow at the back of the head, then the room tipped abruptly. I tried futilely to hang on to a thought that something was very wrong ... then I woke up lying on a couch in another room.

The tall man in the dark suit looked down at me worriedly. There was a young man standing behind him. They had obviously carried me here after I'd passed out. The tall man said:

"I was afraid, sir, that could happen, what with—"

"I'm all right now." I sat up. I felt no bruises. He must have caught me going down. I closed my eyes for a moment, remembering my last thought before fainting. I rubbed the back of my hand across my mouth. I knew now what I disliked so much about this place: associations of other deaths and that ever-present, too-heavy, over-ripe reminder of them—the smell of *flowers*. I stood up.

"Are you sure you're all right, sir?"

"I'm all right."

I walked swiftly back to the Rollins mansion. The maid let me in. I went down the hall to Rollins' study. He looked up at me, blinking.

"That isn't Nancy!" I said harshly. "She told me about an eye tooth being removed and replaced with a plastic one. All the teeth on that corpse are intact!" My voice was rising. "That plastic tooth would have been destroyed, don't you understand? That can't be Nancy!"

"All right!" he said, staring at me with too-bright eyes. "Sit down, Kirk."

I sat down slowly, staring back at him.

"That isn't Nancy," he breathed. "Nancy's alive."

It was like coming out of a nightmare. I let out my breath. The weak feeling had gone out of my middle now. I felt strength pouring back. I watched him and knew, now, that he was indeed carrying a burden, but it was not the burden of Nancy's death. "All right," I said. "Explain."

He opened and closed one hand over his desk. "All right. I'll explain. But you'll have to know how it started—everything." He stared down at a clenched hand, grimly. "When I came back after that European trip, I resigned my job as Assistant Secretary of State. I promised my family I would give them all of my time. I did, for a while. But I've been an active man all of my life. Doing nothing was making me nervous. The government approached me with a project. I'd already been cleared for top-secret information. I'd publicly resigned my post. They thought I was in an excellent position to work on an intelligence project. I agreed to do it."

"Yes," I said. "But where is Nancy, for God's sake?"

"I'm getting to it," he said roughly. He rubbed a palm angrily down the side of his face and went on. "I should have stayed out, but I didn't. It was a special project, to break up an international forgery ring. My contacts were Secret Service agents. I met them secretly over a period of months, and coordinated the effort."

"What kind of forgeries?"

"High-level documents. Fictional letters, supposedly sent from the President to his various top-level personnel, along with letters which were supposed to have been written in confidence by the Secretary of State, the Attorney General, the Secretary of Defense, all of the high-post people. The documents gave an exact reversal to this country's stated foreign policy. If a public statement were made to the effect that this country supported a given small country, a supposedly confidential document would turn up in that country indicating that the United States was ready to sell the country out. A scattering of these documents had been showing up in Africa, South America, Asia and Europe."

He sat silently, then motioned his hand, saying:

"I should have told them to get somebody else, but I've always believed intensely that propaganda is the real area of offense and defense in a cold war. I went into it, hard. I used the privacy of this office and studied minutely all of the examples of these forgeries given to me, along with the various pieces of intelligence that had been so far collected. The bulk of the material was coming out of the Far East. Our people were certain that it was coming out of Communist China."

After the relief of knowing Nancy was alive, I felt a chill of apprehension.

He rubbed the side of his face again. "These documents were done expertly. But after I'd studied them carefully I knew they were done by one man, a superior craftsman. I finally noticed something on all of the best documents. It was simply a small black speck. On the first examinations I'd thought those black specks were simply bits of ink accidentally flung from the pen of the signer. But I finally put them under a strong microscope. I found that what looked like a speck of ink was really a minute intertwining of two Chinese symbols. Even the people who were smuggling the documents had obviously missed it, once the documents had left the hands of the forger."

"And?"

"There are several collections of Chinese art in the city. I'd studied them before. I went over them again and found what I was certain I'd seen before. I found it on an ink scroll, that same symbol, only large enough on this scroll to be seen easily with the naked eye. It was the formalized signature of a young, fairly obscure Chinese named Wu Lang. He hadn't gotten much notice, because he was almost entirely a craftsman, not really a creative artist. But he was a perfect crafts-man. I knew he had to be the prime source of those forged documents. With an artist's ego, he hadn't been able to let go of his best work without a signature."

Rollins opened an ivory cigarette box, got out a cigarette and put it between his lips. His match trembled. He said:

"I turned over my information to the intelligence people. They traced Wu Lang to Hong Kong, where he was living in obviously new wealth. He was put under surveillance. That was when we started breaking the ring. They used a complex chain of contacts. Each contact had a small share of the procedure of getting the documents from Wu Lang to their ultimate destinations, so that no one knew anyone else. By working backward and forward, using the intelligence reports sent to me, I began to collect enough data that I could piece together the entire picture. I was the only one in our intelligence system who knew the full facts of that operation."

"But what has this got to do with Nancy?" I said impatiently.

"You've got to understand all of this, Kirk. Now listen to me, will you?"

His nerves were obviously ragged, and mine were getting that way as I waited for him to go on. He finally did:

"I realized there was currently developing a large concentration of material pointed at South America. Certain forgeries were intercepted along the line by our agents, then put back into the line, so that the ring wasn't aware of the surveillance. All these documents were aimed at proving that the United States was actually selling out certain South American countries. All of these particular South American countries happen to be in a state of flux regarding absolute loyalty to us. Unloading these letters on various high governmental personnel in these countries might have a heavy effect of swaying judgments, so that we could lose the faith of these countries just a fraction enough that they might swing completely away. The majority of the documents were post-dated January 19th. That's just four days away."

I listened to that, and watched him shredding his barely smoked cigarette into an ash tray. His hand was trembling even more now.

"Somehow they found out about my involvement in this," he said. "There was a leak somewhere. They've got her."

"Nancy?" I said, tensing. "They've kidnapped Nancy?"

He banged a fist down against his desk and took a long quivering breath. "Goddamn them anyway!"

Now I knew. I felt an empty sensation. "Why? What do they want? What have you done about it?"

"I haven't done anything about it," he said raggedly. "I couldn't. Minutes after the police telephoned and told me Nancy had been killed, somebody else called—a man using a falsetto. He told me the corpse found was not Nancy. I still don't know who that corpse was. But Nancy's alive. They let her speak to me on the telephone. She said, 'I'm all right, Daddy.' I said, 'Have they hurt you?' And she said, 'No.' It wasn't a recording, I'm sure of that—she answered me. The man using the falsetto came on again and warned that if I exposed to anyone at all that it wasn't Nancy who was found in that burned car,

Nancy would indeed die. Then I was told they would contact me again, and the line went dead. The call was fast. There wasn't a chance to try to trace it, even if I'd been able to."

"Have you heard from them again?"

"Tonight, just before you arrived. They want me to prepare a false report to be turned over to Washington. The project is going on as scheduled. But because of the false report, the Secret Service agents are going to close in at the wrong place. Tomorrow afternoon they want me to be downtown at Mason and Ellis. At three o'clock I'm to stand at the southwest corner of that intersection. They'll pick me up. I'm to tell no one about this. But I'm telling you, Kirk. And I'm also telling you that this is Nancy's life!"

"What happens then?"

"They're to take me to see Nancy, wherever she is. They're going to examine my false report to make sure it's done well enough. They'll give me certain names to use in that report, because they're willing to allow a few sacrifices among their own people. These victims will be at a certain place they'll name, so that when the federal people come in for the arrest it'll look good. But the documents won't be there. They'll be delivered to South America on schedule. When the interview is finished, I'm to be driven back to the pick-up point and released. I'm to turn in the false report to Washington and then wait three more days to catch up with the dates on those documents. At that time, if I've done everything as they've instructed, they'll release Nancy safely."

I looked at his eyes. "Will they?"

"No," he said. "They'll kill her."

I leaned back in my chair, trying to find a calm, even against that knowledge. Lawrence Rollins, who might have been effective with someone other than his daughter involved, was not now going to be wholly reliable. I could see that.

"Don't you understand?" he exploded. "It's air-tight. Everyone but the two of us thinks Nancy's dead. I can't go to the police. I can't let Curtis Cornell know my daughter is still alive. I can't even let her mother know!"

"All right. But I know."

"Yes," he said, visibly trying to regain his control. "Alone I couldn't have done anything. With you, maybe there's a chance."

I know that I was calm enough now to be reasonably objective about this. I had to be objective, or it was going to be the end of Nancy. "Do you have any idea where the leak was?"

"They obviously know enough to be fairly certain that I had sufficient information to destroy their operation. But I was the only one who knew I had that much. I hadn't delivered that fact to Washington yet. But there was a leak somewhere along the line. I think they simply used reasoning and decided I knew everything. They're right. But the only thing that matters now is that we get Nancy out of this!"

"Were these documents going to be collected at any single place, so that you'd planned to have them confiscated at one time?"

"Yes. They were bringing them, one after another, by ship to Los Angeles. They were to be delivered by car to a house down the coast, in Malibu Beach."

"Did you have all the people involved identified?"

"No. It's basically a Chinese Communist operation. There're several Chinese involved. But there're also occidentals working for them. The only certain thing I know was that they'd set up that house in Malibu for the delivery point. They planned to take the documents from there down over the Mexican border, to Tijuana, then south, to be delivered to the proper points in South America." He shook his head. "You've got to give all you've got to this, Kirk, and not make any mistakes. You've had experience as a courier. You've learned how to keep your eyes open and expect a certain amount of danger. You were sent a wedding announcement. Nancy loved you once. There's a reason for your being here. Let's hope they don't get suspicious about you. Are you willing?"

"Yes," I said. "Of course."

"This is my daughter, Kirk, and if you don't do this right, I'll kill you, so help me!"

I met his stare. I liked him no more than I had from the beginning. But we both loved Nancy, and it was going to have to be this way.

"Where are you staying?" he asked.

"The Sir Francis Drake."

"All right. I've been working this through my mind. Tomorrow morning, rent a car. Drive the car into a parking garage at Mason and O'Farrell. It's called The Downtown Garage. It's a 9-story self-park place. The parking tiers are open at the sides. Park as low as you can where you can still see the intersection down the block where I'm going to be picked up. At three o'clock, when I'm picked up, you check the make and color of the car I get into and the direction it's headed. Then you get into your car and down that ramp. There's a 10-mile speed limit, and you have to give your ticket out coming down. But do it as fast as you can. Then get behind that car I'll be in. Stay behind and follow. But follow only in traffic and stay far enough behind that you don't give yourself away. Otherwise you kill Nancy. Do you understand?"

I nodded.

"If the car I'm in hits any kind of open stretch where you can be seen following, give up. Instantly! That's an order, Kirk."

I nodded again, and he said:

"I just hope to God you can hold your end up. I'd rather have Curtis Cornell helping me. I'd rather have any dozen other people helping me. You were a cocksure smart-aleck when I met you two years ago, and I have a feeling you haven't changed. But I can't bring anyone else into it, not even my Secret Service contacts, because I don't know where that leak was. So I'm stuck with you, and it's my daughter's life involved, and I will, I repeat, kill you if you don't do this right. Now leave me alone, because I've got to get that report ready for them."

I left him, walking down the high-ceilinged silent hall into the chilled night.

I don't know how I got through that night.

In the morning I walked into a car-rental booth in the hotel and ordered a 1961 Oldsmobile. I put it on the Skyway and tested its speed and pickup. It was all right.

I drove to the garage and up a tightly circling ramp to the second deck. There was a slot open near the exit ramp. It was what I wanted.

I locked the car and went downstairs. Pick-up time for Rollins was 3:00. It was going to be a long wait. I began walking to ease the tension.

It was a cool day, and the sky looked gray and threatening. I walked until I was hungry. Then I had a sandwich at the counter in Original Joe's. I walked again. Finally I returned to the garage, paid my charges and went up to the second tier and my car.

At five minutes before three, I started the engine, then got out and stood looking down. People flowed across the intersection a block away. At two minutes before three, I saw Lawrence Rollins walking up from Market Street. He was neatly dressed with a gray flannel suit and dark hat. He stopped at the corner and stood ramrod stiff. I had my checkout ticket in my hand; I could feel it grow limp with the moisture coming from my palm.

At a minute past three, an off-white Chrysler rolled east on Ellis and stopped in front of Rollins. A back door opened. Rollins climbed in.

I slid swiftly into my car, then shot it down the exit ramp. I took the circling descent with tires shrieking, jammed the ticket into the hand of the attendant at street level and plunged the car into the O'Farrell Street traffic, hearing the attendant's protests fading behind.

I cut into the right-hand lane, then turned south at the next intersection. I went down a block and stopped at a red light, searching for that off-white Chrysler. I couldn't find it.

The light turned green. A cable car rolled to a halt behind me. Other cars piled up behind it. I gunned the engine, then purposely killed it. With the ignition off, I tried to start the engine. The cable car's bell clanged. A horn sounded, against the general reluctance San Franciscans have for sounding horns. I did not want to be conspicuous. But I had to find that Chrysler.

I found it. It was double-parked a half-block to my right. It moved ahead. The light ahead of me turned red again. I turned on the ignition and started the engine. The Chrysler crossed in front of me. I counted three dark-suited men in the car, besides Rollins. One was driving. The other two were in back on either side of Rollins. He was now wearing very dark ski-type sunglasses. I was certain he was blindfolded under those glasses. My light turned green. I pulled out, turned left, and followed the Chrysler, leaving three cars between us.

The Chrysler rolled at an even speed, stopping carefully at traffic lights, then moving ahead, neither too fast nor too slow. They did not, I was certain, want to draw attention.

We crossed Market Street, passing another large lot in construction. There was a right turn at Mission, moving us in a southwest direction. The traffic, with buses and automobiles, was heavy but smooth-running. The Chrysler moved back to Market Street, where it turned left and headed for Twin Peaks, one of the many hills in the city. I followed carefully, staying several cars behind.

Then we climbed the curving grade leading up Twin Peaks. I lost sight of the Chrysler momentarily. But I picked it up again when we reached the crest. At the top there was a hard wind, and it was perceptibly cooler. Traffic had become lighter. I stayed a little further behind as we began a descent into the neighborhood district of the west-central part of the city. The traffic increased, as we moved into the afternoon shoppers. The Chrysler turned right, onto Sloat Boulevard. It headed west, toward the beach.

We crossed 19th Avenue, and the traffic was sufficient to give me good cover. I felt a tight knot of tension in my stomach as I followed. I was somehow certain I was going to be able to follow that Chrysler all the way to Nancy.

After we'd curved around the north edge of Fleishhacker Zoo, the Chrysler turned right on the Great Highway. It was the old beach highway. But I saw now, just beyond, that a new freeway had been built and was taking all of the fast traffic running past the ocean. The Great Highway had been turned into a residential avenue. It was absolutely empty of traffic, except for the off-white Chrysler and my rented Oldsmobile.

I followed for a block and saw a head turn back in the Chrysler. I turned off into a driveway, swearing bitterly, and stopped.

My hands gripped the steering wheel until they ached. I watched the car move away from me, down the silent street until it turned out of sight far down the avenue.

I drove back to my hotel, went up to my room and sat down futilely. It had been a fine idea, but it had not worked. I poured a drink, feeling myself trembling with frustration.

Then I waited. That was all I could do now. Wait.

At 6:20, after an eternity, my telephone rang. Lawrence Rollins said, "I wonder if you could get over here, Mr. Kirk? My daughter's funeral is tomorrow morning. This is a hard time for all of us. I would appreciate your company, if you could make it. Perhaps you could help me catalogue that collection of prints I was showing you—just to pass the time."

"Certainly, Mr. Rollins."

I knew he had phrased his words carefully in case his telephone had been tapped. I went down and drove to Broadway, then walked up the steps to the arched doorway. I stepped into a grisly sham. Relatives and friends had clustered into the large Rollins living room. There was the grim bleakness that comes just before any funeral. I could hear a loud sobbing across the room. Mrs. Rollins was there, circled by a sympathetic quartet of very old women. Lawrence Rollins, looking shaken and nervous, came across the room in my direction. Then Dr. Curtis Cornell appeared out of the crowd and moved with him. As they neared, I could hear Cornell saying:

"I tell you, Mr. Rollins, I don't care for seeing him here."

"It's all right, Curtis. I asked him to come."

Cornell stared at me scornfully. He reminded me of a plump, overgrown child wearing a man's suit. He seemed almost to be pouting, and I knew that I should not be overcritical, since grief produces peculiar reactions in certain people. But I couldn't help disliking him intensely. He said:

"If you're here because you were asked, all right. There's nothing I can do about that. But Nancy wouldn't want you here, I can tell you that. And I don't care for your being here either!"

"Just relax, Curtis," Rollins said, his voice almost snapping. "This is difficult for everyone."

"I'm simply making the point," Cornell said petulantly, "that Nancy was marrying me."

I forced myself to say nothing. Rollins put his hand on Cornell's shoulder and turned him toward Mrs. Rollins. "Go see Ona, Curtis. She needs your comfort."

Cornell moved reluctantly away to join Mrs. Rollins. I followed Rollins down the hall to his study. He closed and locked the door behind him.

Then he said tensely, "Were you able to stay behind?"

"No."

He took a half-dozen steps across the room toward me, as though he were intending to hit me. His eyes darkened with fury. He was breathing hard. Finally he slumped down behind his desk. "What happened?"

"I stayed back of you until you got out by the beach. They turned onto the Great Highway. We were the only moving cars on it. I had to give up."

He wagged his head forlornly.

"Did you see her, for God's sake?" I snapped impatiently.

"Yes," he breathed.

He said it with so much defeat that, for one panicked moment, I was certain that she was no longer alive. Then he said:

"She's alive. But—" He shook his head and bent forward, putting his hands against his face.

"But what!" I demanded.

"We don't have her, damn it!" he exploded. "If you'd only been able to stay behind!"

"I followed your orders. Now tell me what happened, or can't you get hold of your nerves!"

The insult seemed to straighten him. He drew his hands from his face and stared at me darkly.

"After I got into their car, they drove half a block down and stopped. They made me bend down and pasted adhesive over my eyes. Then they put sunglasses over that. We drove for a long time. Then we finally stopped, and they ordered me out of the car and up some steep steps. I was inside somewhere—I wish to God I knew where!"

"Then?"

"I'd made up my mind to do one thing when and if they took that adhesive off my eyes. I bent my head when they took it off and looked at my watch. It was exactly four-thirty-five. Then I looked up. Nancy was sitting across that bare room, bound and gagged, staring at me. I tried to get to her. But they wrenched me around. One of them stuck on the adhesive again. They pulled me out of there, warning me that if I tried anything I would be shot instantly. One of them had a pistol in my side from the moment I was picked up until they let me go." He took a long, shuddering breath.

I sat silently, feeling the same frustration he was feeling. He'd seen her, just across a room. Now we'd lost her. "What happened then?"

"They led me somewhere else in the building. I was seated in a chair and asked for my false report. It was checked and given back to me. They gave me the list of names of the people they're willing to sell out. Then I was led back to the car, and we drove again for a long time. My mind was a blank after seeing Nancy. They finally told me to take off the sunglasses and adhesive. We were back at the intersection where they picked me up. I got out, and the car disappeared in the traffic. I was in the same room with her, Kirk! And now ..."

He had given up, I knew. I also knew that was the last thing we could afford. There was a small bar built between shelves. I got up and poured him a brandy. He shook his head. "Drink it," I said.

He finally took the glass and lifted it with a trembling hand. He drank. It seemed to help him. He put the glass down and straightened. "That was our only chance, Kirk. We're not going to get another one."

"Yes, we are. Because we're going to make another one."

I saw a faint sign of hope flicker in his eyes. I said to him:

"Here's the license number." I handed him a paper from my wallet.

"It won't help anything. They'll be stolen plates."

"All right. Then we'll do this some other way. There were three men in the car. You saw them when you got in. Did you get anything out of that?"

"They were disguised."

"How?"

"Putty. On the nose, cheeks. Two more mustaches, one a short beard. Probably false. Enough change that I'd never recognize them without those things."

"Their voices?"

"Only one of them spoke. He used that same falsetto I heard on the telephone."

I forced myself to think as clearly as I could, because panic and defeat were going to get us nowhere. "I know this town, Rollins. You know it. I know where that car you were in traveled up to the time I had to give up. I want you to remember everything you heard, smelled, felt. Was there a window open in the car?"

"Yes, but—"

"Work with me, Rollins! You don't like me. All right. I don't like you very much either. The only thing that matters is Nancy!"

He opened his mouth, then closed it. Finally he nodded.

"Could you feel the car turning?" I asked.

"I tried to keep track of that. But there were too many turns."

"What else could you feel?"

"Climbing." He seemed to come more to life. "I could feel that. I could hear the engine sound going stronger on a climb. We must have climbed not long after I was picked up. Then the pressure went off and the engine sounded quieter—we must have been going down."

"You went over Twin Peaks, about ten minutes after you were picked up. Then you came down on the other side." I was trying to give him confidence by building my own enthusiasm. "Try to remember everything—right from the point they picked you up."

He leaned back, closing his eyes. "Cable car bell. Right away."

"You crossed Powell Street, in front of me. There was a cable car behind me."

"Then a loud noise. Hammering sound."

"Crossing Market, toward Mission. There's a building under construction at that intersection. Air hammers. After that?"

He shook his head, but he was working now, I was certain. "Whistles."

"What kind of whistles?"

"Police."

"On the corners. Traffic cops. About every other block. But the downtown area is the only area they use them. You felt the climb then, didn't you? After you'd left the sound of those whistles?"

"Yes. But something before that. Peculiar sound. Like bowling balls rolling down a lane."

I thought back and nodded. He'd got the sound exactly. "Electric trolleys on Market Street. Then you went up Twin Peaks."

"I could feel the climb—gusts of wind coming in through the window, and cold."

"You were at the top. Then you went down. What do you remember after that?"

He sat for a long time with his eyes closed. "I smelled the sea."

"Maybe 19th Avenue, going toward the ocean on Sloat. After that?"

He opened his eyes. "What good is this doing, Kirk? You were behind us up to that point. It's after you lost us that matters."

"Do you have a city map?"

He reached inside his desk and drew out a street map.

I spread it on his desk. I picked up one of his stub-pointed pens. "You smelled the sea. Then what?"

"I don't know!" he snapped.

"You went along Sloat Boulevard for a long time. From 19th past 47th. There's a slight curve when you pass the zoo. Then you made that sharp right turn onto the Great Highway. Could you feel that?"

He closed his eyes again. He was once again concentrating. "The sea smell got stronger. Then, yes, I felt a turn. Something else. Tires whirring."

"Fast traffic on the freeway above." I drew a line down the Great Highway, moving north. "Then I know you turned again, down the street."

"I felt it after a while, yes. A turn to the left. Then another turn. Very close. To the right. And something else. A loud hissing sound."

I lifted his telephone and called the bus company, running the line on the map to the point where I thought they'd turned left. I asked for the bus routing in that district. I got the information and hung up. "A number 7 bus goes west on Noriega and turns left on the Great Highway. You heard air brakes. So you made a left, then a right, a block apart. And you were still heading north. What then?"

He sat frowning with concentration. "I don't know. I don't think we turned for a long time then. Stopped several times. There're probably stop signs along there. Then we made a turn. Right. I'm almost certain of that."

"Where?"

"I don't know!" He gripped his hands. "I heard something." He shook his head. "A sound like small birds chirping."

I looked at the map. The Great Highway ran into Golden Gate Park at Lincoln Way. You had to turn either left or right. He thought he'd turned right. Birds in the park? Possibly, I thought. I drew the line along Lincoln Way, bordering the park, heading east again. "Then what?"

"Straight for a time. Stops and starts. I heard something kicking up under the car once. Then the sea smell disappeared."

"You were heading east then, away from the ocean. How about the traffic?"

"It got heavier." He shook his head again, angrily. "Confused after that. I think we got away from traffic. A lot of turning. Not sharp. But steady."

I studied the map. "You could have turned into Golden Gate Park. About Seventh Avenue. Maybe you went through the park. That road makes a steady curve around to the Panhandle or Arguello."

"But which one, if that's right?" he said, opening his eyes again. "This isn't going to work, Kirk. It was all start and stop after that and too damned much turning that I could never remember."

"Traffic?" I asked stubbornly.

"Yes. A lot of traffic. But we could have been going any direction."

"Remember anything you can."

He took a breath. "We climbed and went down a lot. I remember that. Low-gear climbing and hard braking."

"In the direction of The Presidio then. Then into your own neighborhood. Right here. Russian Hill."

He lit a cigarette and nodded slowly. "It felt like that kind of climbing. Then we went down. I—" He was trying, I knew, but it was like searching through a jumble of sounds and smells that must all have nearly fused together now.

"Anything," I said.

"Cable running," he said finally. "Very loud."

Again I studied the map. "The bottom of Russian Hill. Near the water. There's a cable car terminal at Hyde. You'd get a very loud cable sound at a terminal. Did you get a sea smell again?"

"Yes," he nodded. "A very strong fish smell. It came and went."

"Crab pits. Fisherman's Wharf. You must have been traveling east now. All the way across the city and back. It took you an hour and thirty-five minutes. That's about how long it would take to make a trip like that. What then?"

"Buoy sounds," he said. "I kept smelling the sea."

"Around The Embarcadero, along the piers."

He sat silently for a very long time. I waited. Finally he said, "Peculiar smell then. Like oil. Maybe gas. I don't know. Then a lot of turning. We climbed again. Very steep climbing."

"Somewhere on Telegraph Hill. Could you hear the buoy sounds yet?"

"Yes. We stopped. I climbed a steep stairway on foot."

"All right." I circled Telegraph Hill. "She's somewhere on Telegraph Hill, somewhere in a house that has a steep stairway."

"For God's sake," he said bitterly. "Half the houses there have those kind of stairways. And how many square blocks is that? What good will that do? We've narrowed it down to a hill. But there're seven hills in this city. Maybe we're in the wrong section entirely!"

I folded the map and put it in my pocket. "It's something to work on, isn't it?"

He wagged his head. All of his strength was leaving him now. I told him:

"I'm going to follow this route and see if it checks."

He stared dully at nothing, a tired, defeated man. He said in a hollow voice, "You take no chances, do you hear? You check that much and no more without my permission. And be at the funeral tomorrow morning at ten o'clock. It's the church at the top of Nob Hill."

On that ironic note I left. He was ordinarily a good man. I might have, even against my initial dislike for him, admired him in time. But right now he was crumbling, because someone had found his Achilles heel. I thought, as I drove away, that I had the same vulnerability. Having left my attempt at enthusiasm behind, I felt a cold fright go through me. The people who had Nancy were playing for high stakes. They were professionals. I felt like a naked, unarmed man in a jungle, powerless while the girl I loved had been tied to a stake, to be sacrificed to the gods in less than three days.

I drove to the point where Lawrence Rollins had been picked up. Then I began following the route I'd drawn out on the map, checking my time as I started. I left a window open. It was cold now, the air damp and cutting. I could not, at night, get the same impressions Rollins had during the afternoon. But there might be something, along the way, that would help prove we had chosen a reasonably accurate route.

There was no construction work as I crossed Market Street. There were fewer cops using whistles as I went up Mission. It was colder climbing Twin Peaks; the wind was blowing very hard at the crest. I could smell the sea again as I came down on the other side and followed Sloat Boulevard to the Great Highway. As I drove toward Lincoln Way, I could hear, as Rollins had described, the whirring of tires on the freeway above.

At Lincoln Way, at the edge of the long strip of Golden Gate Park, I pulled to the curb. It was here, if he had been accurate, that Rollins had heard a sound like small birds chirping. Light traffic rolled by. I listened. I finally heard it.

I got out of the car and crossed the street. I saw an old Dutch windmill in the park. When the wind caught the blades, they turned with a squeaking sound.

I went back to the car and drove east. At 34th Avenue, fine sand had been spread over recent street-repair work. It kicked up under the car. Rollins had heard that. I was going in the right direction.

I cut through the park to Arguello, then started the route I'd marked out on the map in the direction of The Presidio, around to Russian Hill. As I moved toward the Bay, the climbing and descending produced exactly the low-gear work and hard braking Rollins had described.

I drove down to Hyde, approaching Fisherman's Wharf. The cable-car terminal was there, along with a very loud cable sound. I drove through Fisherman's Wharf, past the crab pits with their heavy fish odor, onto The Embarcadero. I had been tense with concentration, and it was only after I got onto that broad avenue that I was suddenly aware that a car was following me.

I intended to shake it, and swiftly. But I did not want to ruin my timing. I drove southeast, along the piers, approaching the base of Telegraph Hill. There I took a hard right into the warehouse section. The lights stayed behind me.

I stopped. The lights of the car behind slowed; then the car moved on, passing me, and turned right. It was a blue and white Chevrolet sedan, occupied by one man. It went slowly west. I was suddenly aware of a peculiar smell here. It was the kind of smell that remains when a gas line has broken. It was what Rollins had described. And I was now very certain that I had been right—I was circling Telegraph Hill, and that was where Nancy was.

The Chevrolet turned again, down the block. I figured the driver intended to loop around and pick me up from behind again. I pulled away, tires spinning. I made a fast, skidding run around to Broadway. I slowed there, driving carefully through the brightly lit North Beach thoroughfare, to Columbus. I cut off at Grant, then started the steep climb toward the top of Telegraph Hill. I stopped just below Coit Tower. I had lost whoever had been following me.

I checked my watch. The run had taken an hour and twenty-eight minutes, just a few minutes short of the time Rollins' ride had taken. She was here, I was certain. Somewhere. But where? And who had been following me? And had I come close enough to her that I'd put her life in even more danger?

I took a long breath. I needed time to think. I didn't want to be seen here. I drove back to my hotel.

I thought of telephoning Rollins to tell him that I was certain now of Nancy's being somewhere on Telegraph Hill. Then I remembered his careful wording when he'd telephoned me—whoever the people were who had Nancy they were thorough and efficient; they might very well have his telephone line tapped. But he should know, I thought, that I had been followed.

Then I knew that telling him these things would help nothing. He was not effective now. This was up to me. And I could not make any mistakes.

I poured a drink and ordered dinner sent to my room. I tried to relax for a few minutes.

Then I spread the map out and carefully circled that section of Telegraph Hill where I was certain Nancy was. It was a small area on the map, but hundreds of people lived within those few square blocks.

In frustration I undressed and got into bed. But my mind wouldn't stop. There had to be some way. Then, very late that night, it came to me. One idea. It was a very simple idea, which would probably lead me nowhere. But it was the only one I had.

In a bright, sunny morning I drove to Civic Center. I parked at the west side of the library, then walked swiftly into the gray, ancient building. I took the elevator to the second floor and looked down on the side where I'd parked my car. The blue and white Chevrolet moved slowly down the block, then parked a half block from my car.

Stomach knotting, I was certain of one thing. I'd lost that car the night before. But it was behind me again. They knew who I was and where I was staying, and the driver had been waiting to pick me up as soon as I left the hotel.

Call Lawrence Rollins, I told myself. Then I thought again: he can't help.

I went into the reference room and asked for a city directory. Using that against the map, I started going down the street listings, checking the names following each address in the area I'd circled. Chinatown was at the bottom of Telegraph Hill. There was a heavy Chinese population running up Grant Avenue toward the hill. But I did not think there were many Chinese in the area I was checking. And Lawrence Rollins had said this was basically a Chinese operation.

I found two oriental names: Grace Sing and Roy Miyako. I was certain that Sing was Chinese. But Miyako sounded Japanese. I telephoned a gift shop in Chinatown from the reference desk. The proprietor said Miyako was Japanese, Sing Chinese. At least I had narrowed the slim lead down to a single target.

I had never cared for funerals. This one, I knew, was not going to make a devotee out of me. I sat far back and looked forward at the casket resting before a huge bank of altar flowers. When the words began, I tried not to listen. I tried not to hear the sobbing of Mrs. Rollins surging steadily behind the words. I tried not to look through the crowd at Lawrence Rollins, slumped in his place like a wax dummy too long near fire. I tried, instead, to concentrate on wondering who was in that casket. Had they deliberately murdered her for this purpose?

Then Dr. Curtis Cornell stood up like a stunned bear and went weaving forward to put his outstretched hands on the lid of that casket. I thought, in one bad moment, that he was going to tear the lid open. But a young man came up swiftly and led him back to his seat. My mouth felt parched. I could not help listening to the words rolling from the altar. I began to believe, because it was such a realistic sham, that it was indeed Nancy who was going to be dropped into the hole prepared for her at the cemetery.

Finally it was over. I saw Lawrence Rollins rise, turn unsteadily, and collapse. A cluster of people formed around him. He had, I knew, felt the reality too much.

When they had revived him, I pushed my way out, took fast gulps of that thankfully cool air, and got into my car, knowing there was no use trying to talk to Rollins now. I went down the steep grade of California Street, leaving the church and the sight of that damnable casket. I drove too fast, then I slowed. The blue and white Chevrolet stayed behind me. I stopped in International Settlement, now a quiet avenue of shops, and strode swiftly on foot up from Pacific to Broadway. An insignificant-looking figure in a gray business suit followed. He was the man from the blue and white Chevrolet. When I reached Broadway, I ducked into a restaurant.

I passed the bar and went back toward the rest rooms. I went out the back door. I ran hard and fast then, and jumped into the rear door of another bar a quarter of a block down. It was dark here, and I had trouble getting my eyes used to the gloom. I ordered a bourbon and soda, drank a quarter of it and walked out to the Broadway.

I walked down the block, then turned into a street which tipped up at an angle of 45 degrees. I climbed it, glancing back as I moved. I knew I had shaken the man who was following me.

I went up Telegraph Hill to Union and Kearney, then rounded the area just below Coit Tower, to the north side. I checked house numbers. The house listed under the name of Grace Sing was down the block, a pale yellow frame house built like a wooden matchbox placed on one narrow end. I saw it from the profile, and looked at the way the front wooden stairway led up the outside from an open garage. Its back was almost flush with an earth bank. There I could see another wooden stairway running from the bottom to the second floor. Lawrence Rollins had climbed a steep stairway.

A figure appeared out of the front door of that house. It was a woman, small, beautifully clothed, extremely pretty and obviously oriental. She came down the front steps gracefully and quickly, looking neither right nor left, nor at me. She went into the garage and backed out a small imported station wagon. She wheeled it down the street in the direction of the Bay, away from me.

I lit a cigarette, cupping the flame against the sea wind, then started down the street. Halfway down the block, I tossed the cigarette away and ducked between two houses up from the pale yellow one where the oriental girl had come out. I went behind the house next to the yellow one, following the bank. I knew now I should have informed Lawrence Rollins what I'd intended to do; I could use help now. And I should have had him supply me with a gun.

But I couldn't turn back now. I ran swiftly to the bottom of that skeletal wooden stairway moving up the back of the yellow house, knowing I could be seen only from that house itself. I reached the first step and looked up at the back door on the first floor and the window beside it. Then I started up the back stairway.

At the first landing, I bent low and went to the frame of the window. Inchingly, I moved my head until I could look inside with one eye. I looked into a kitchen. The high sun, which appeared to be moving into clouds and a possible mist to the west, sent in enough light that I could see an old gas stove, a new refrigerator, a yellowing sink and a shining chrome-frame kitchenette set. There was no one there.

I pulled back and stood against the pale-yellow siding, sweat prickling on my forehead. I measured the way the stairway moved up to the next landing. I would have to pass the window I'd just looked into, to make the climb. But I was, I knew, going to have to do it.

I carefully rechecked that kitchen. It was still empty. I went up the stairway to the second floor, ducking as I reached the second landing. There was one window here, very wide. I moved to it across the plank, landing on hands and knees. I stopped just short of the window.

Then, holding my breath, I brought my face close to the glass and moved until I could see inside.

In the middle of an otherwise empty room sat Nancy.

Seeing her was like looking through time and space, to discover again what you were certain you had lost. Even bound and gagged, she was more beautiful than I had remembered. The sunlight came through the window and gleamed against her dark hair. I felt my heart pounding. I stood up.

Her eyes widened. She stared at me. I was ready to smash the glass between us. Then she wagged her head in the direction of a door behind her. I ducked down, looking with one eye through a corner of that window.

The door opened. Two athletically built occidentals came in. One was blond with a deep tan. The other was pale and very dark-haired. They were strong. They lifted Nancy from her chair as though she were weightless and moved her out of the room. The door shut behind them.

I heard a car rolling up to the house on the street side. I went down the stairway to the first floor and the corner of the building. A large black car was pointing up the street. I saw Nancy being escorted swiftly into it by the two men who had taken her from the room. A fat driver with dark glasses nodded as the door closed behind the three of them. The car jumped forward and disappeared up the street.

I did not even get the license number. I stood at the back corner of that house, frustration pouring through me. I had been so close ...

I knew there would be no use trying to go after that car. I moved silently back across the porch and again looked into that kitchen. It was still empty.

I put pressure on the window, pushing up with my fingertips. It wouldn't give for a few seconds, then it went up an inch with a snapping sound. I leaned back against the siding and waited, listening. I could hear nothing.

I pushed the window up halfway and reached inside along the wall. I could touch the bolt of the door. I slid it open, then opened the door and stepped into the kitchen. I looked around the room. There was a rack of knives near the stove. I took out a butcher knife. If there were anyone in this house, I was going to get out of him exactly where Nancy had been taken, even if I had to cut it out of him.

I moved into a large living room expensively furnished in rich modern furniture. There was a feminine tone to the room, as though it had been furnished and decorated exclusively for a woman.

I searched the room and a small bedroom and bath on that floor. Then I went upstairs. There were two rooms here, one overloaded with furniture, the other empty except for the chair Nancy had been sitting on. There was no one in the house.

I took a long breath, then started a more careful search of the furnished room on the second floor. They had obviously moved furniture out of the room Nancy had been in, perhaps to prevent her from identifying anything, perhaps for effect. But it had all been piled in this room, once a guest bedroom, I imagined, now overstocked with television set, desk, bookcases.

Everything was feminine. I looked through the books and found an old high school yearbook. I found Grace Sing's name and her picture. She had grown into a far more beautiful girl, I decided, thinking of the oriental girl I'd seen walk out of this house.

I discovered another photo album and a diary recorded years before. She was apparently a member of a wealthy Chinese family.

I went downstairs again, and searched the bedroom there. This was obviously the bedroom she used. There was a very long closet filled with expensive clothing. On top of a bureau was an uncashed check. It was written by a savings and loan company with a Chinatown address. There was a withholding statement attached. She did not appear to need money, but she obviously held a job.

I went to the telephone in the living room and looked up the number of the company. I told the company's PBX operator:

"This is Mr. Grange. I'm with Pacific American Insurance. May I speak to Miss Grace Sing, please?"

A polite voice told me, "She's on a two-month leave right now, sir."

I kept my voice calm and business-like. "I wonder if you could tell me where I might find her then?"

"I'm very certain, sir, she was planning a cruise. To the South Seas, I believe. I think you'll find her home address in the phone book, but I doubt that she'll be there."

I hung up. I knew her home address, all right. And she was not here. But I'd seen her only minutes ago. That meant she had not sailed yet. But when was she sailing? Did that mean they were taking Nancy aboard a ship?

I went out the back way swiftly, putting back the butcher knife, and estimated the position of that house resting below Coit Tower. I returned to the street and climbed to the top of the hill. I stopped near the top, hoping that no one would return to that house while I was using up those minutes. I used a public telephone and called Lawrence Rollins. I told him curtly:

"I'm on Telegraph Hill. I've seen Nancy, but I haven't got her. Meet me at Coit Tower. Bring a pair of binoculars and a small pistol I can carry. And hurry."

"What have they done to her, Kirk!"

I hung up and went up to the base of the tower stretching up into the air now turning gray with cooling mist. I crossed to the north side and looked down. I had, from here, a good view of that house, front and back. There were chrome-decorated binoculars for tourists fitted upon metal posts embedded in a concrete wall surrounding the parking area. I put a dime in one. A whirring sound began. The lenses cleared. I swung the glasses until I found the pale yellow house. The garage door remained open; no car was in it. There were no cars on the street in front of the house. They had not come back by car, and I knew they had not had enough time to return on foot.

All right, I thought, as the time ran out and the lenses blackened, hurry up, Rollins....

As I waited, I examined the view. The Embarcadero ran below in a semi-circle. I could see the faces of the piers extending into the steely water of the Bay. There were a half-dozen ships at their berths. Was one of them preparing to sail for the South Seas? And was the Chinese girl planning to be aboard? With Nancy?

Lawrence Rollins arrived in five minutes, his large car rocking to a stop. Minutes before, two sailors had driven up in a convertible and were now looking out across the city, a dozen yards from me. Another car with Nebraska plates arrived just behind Rollins'. An older couple got out and stood staring around. Rollins strode over.

"What the hell is going on, Kirk?" he whispered. He looked pale and ill and very frightened.

Keeping my voice down, I told him everything I'd learned and done. I pointed out the pale yellow house below. He stood tensely, staring down, his mouth moving but with no sound coming out. Then he turned and said in a hoarse voice, "You've bungled everything, damn you! You had her! You let her go!"

"Never mind that now," I said bitterly. "That isn't going to do any good."

"No. Because she's probably dead. She is because you disobeyed my orders! They must have known you'd found her. Why else did they take her out of there?"

"I'm positive they didn't know I was there. But one thing I am sure of—somebody's been following me. He was behind me yesterday. Then again this morning. I lost him the last time on Broadway."

Rollins stood staring down at that yellow house. He didn't answer. He didn't seem concerned about what I was telling him.

"Didn't you hear me, Rollins?" I said. "I've been followed."

"She's dead," he whispered.

I took hold of his arm. "You knew, didn't you? That I was being followed?"

"All right," he snapped. He looked at me with angry, accusing eyes. "Yes, I've been having you followed by one of my Secret Service contacts."

His voice was low, but harsh: "I told them you might be a part of the forgery ring. I wanted you checked. You arrived at a pretty convenient time, didn't you? You wanted to search her room, then look at the body. You knew the body wasn't Nancy. And never mind that business about the tooth."

"But why would you think I was mixed up in this? I've been in Europe for the past four years!"

"I know that now," he snapped. "You were cleared. I got the report this morning. After the agent lost you today, he telephoned me. I called him off and told him to forget you. But how could I have been sure until I had you checked? Nancy had one vulnerability. That was you. How did I know if you'd been back in this country when I didn't know about it? How did I know what she might have told you...." He closed his mouth. His eyes shifted.

I stared at him. "What do you mean, how did you know what Nancy might have told me? Did she know what you were doing?"

"Yes!" he said angrily.

I felt the anger turn my face warm. I tried to control my voice: "Why didn't you tell me that from the beginning? For God's sake, Rollins! If she knew what this was about, then—"

He shook his head. "What does it matter now? It's all been done. I'd cut my hands and legs off if I could turn back. But I can't!" He hunched his shoulders, as though the wind were icy. "I never should have brought her into it. But the job was taking too much time. I couldn't explain that to her mother. She's been neurotic lately. Change of life, I guess. She thought I was neglecting her. I finally told Nancy what I was doing. I had to, to keep my marriage. She helped keep her mother calm. It was much easier. And Nancy was of tremendous help to me. She was the one who first discovered those specks on the documents. Without that, we might never have started breaking this. She understood how important it was that those documents never get to South America. She was a wonderful daughter. No man could ask for more in his life than to have had a daughter like Nancy. She—"

"Stop talking like she's dead." I wanted to hit him, to snap him back into trying. But I knew even that wouldn't help now. I told him, "This makes a difference, Rollins. If Nancy knew everything, she could have told someone."

He stared at me angrily. "Impossible."

"How about Doctor Curtis Cornell? She was in love with him."

"No."

"She was going to marry him. Maybe she—"

"She never would have told him anything. Even if she had, it would have stopped there. He has an absolutely untouchable background. Nancy met him after I got into this. So I had him checked out, just as I had you checked out. He's above reproach. A truly brilliant surgeon. They put him in *Who's Who* two years ago."

"All right," I said. "But that doesn't mean anything. Politically, he could be—"

"He's a staunch conservative. He hates everything communism stands for. You can forget Curtis Cornell."

"Who else could she have told?"

"No one. There was simply a leak somewhere else. And that means you can't trust anyone. Not even life, because she's dead, I tell you!"

"Rollins, you're going to have to trust somebody—me." The sailors got into their convertible and drove off. The people from Nebraska wandered into the lower part of the tower. I knew I had to take over completely now. "Did you bring the binoculars?"

"In the car," he said uselessly.

"The pistol?"

"In the glove compartment."

I walked to his car and slid the pistol from the glove compartment under my belt beneath my jacket. It was a small-caliber Walther, easy to carry concealed. I picked up the binoculars and went back to him. "Have you got a pistol?"

"In my pocket."

"This is up to you and me alone now, Rollins. You think there's a leak somewhere with the government people. So keep them out of it from now on. Just stay up here and keep watch on that house. If they bring

Nancy back, you call in the police, the fire department, the Coast Guard and anybody else you can think of."

He looked at me dully. "What if someone calls my house about her?"

"There's a public telephone over there. You can call home every hour."

He turned and looked down again at that yellow house. Small craft skimmed over the water beyond the piers. The water was dark now; the sun had gone under clouds. "She's dead," he whispered.

I left him and went down the hill on foot, back to the International Settlement where I'd left my car, buying a newspaper on the way. In the car I looked at the paper's sailing schedule for ships in port. There were none sailing that day. But two tankers and one passenger liner were scheduled to leave the next morning. The luxury liner's name was the *S.S. Belmont.* It was to sail at 11:00 a.m.

I drove downtown and walked into the sales office of the shipping lines owning the luxury liner. A very young-looking girl with a sophisticated manner asked me to be seated. She looked at me archly and asked very politely if she could help.

"I'm a friend of Miss Grace Sing," I said. "She's booked a passage on your ship, the *S.S. Belmont.* I'm sure that's the ship." It was a wild shot, but it was all I could do.

"The *S.S. Belmont?* For the South Seas?"

"I think that's it. Miss Sing is very busy packing. But she wasn't certain of some things. She asked me to check on them. If you don't mind."

The girl looked at me skeptically. "You're certain it's the *S.S. Belmont?*"

"I'm almost positive."

She turned in her chair and ran her finger down a passenger list. "Miss Grace Sing?"

"That's the one," I said, and now I knew.

"What was it Miss Sing wasn't certain about?"

"Clothing. You know how it is with a woman."

This girl was dressed in superb taste. She nodded. I smiled. "Aboard ship," she said, "informal dress is the order of the day."

"But isn't dining formal?"

"Semi-formal, if she wishes, starting with the cocktail hour. Cocktail dresses and/or short evening dresses. But not on the evening of departures and arrivals. It's informal then, even at cocktail time."

"That's wonderful. That's exactly what worried her. And she was told the purser is the answer to everything. Where does she find him?"

"On the main deck. The chief purser wears an oak leaf over three gold stripes." She was cool and efficient and extremely polite. "I think all of this information should have been given to Miss Sing in our pamphlets."

"It's just possible," I said, "that she lost them."

The girl gathered up a collection of pamphlets and handed them to me. "Of course, the ship is staffed with a physician-surgeon and two registered nurses. I noticed Miss Sing is traveling with an elderly companion. I believe I remember, now, taking care of Miss Sing when she bought her passage. It was her grandmother, I think? Who's partially paralyzed?"

I nodded quickly, letting that information register. "Her grandmother."

"There'll be excellent facilities for her."

"I'm certain of that. And it's all right for me to see them off?"

"You can board the ship at nine tomorrow morning. The ship's whistle will tell you when to go ashore."

I thanked her and carried the pamphlets back to the car. I checked the route of the ship. It went down the coast to Los Angeles, then to Tahiti, to New Zealand, Australia, back to New Zealand, to Fiji, Samoa, Hawaii and back to San Francisco.

I thought back to my talk with Lawrence Rollins. He'd told me those forged documents were post-dated January 19th. That was the day after tomorrow—all the time the people who had Nancy needed ...

I looked again at the sailing schedule of the *S.S Belmont*. The first stop would be Los Angeles Harbor, at the southern edge of Los Angeles, at San Pedro. The ship docked at 8:00 in the morning. It didn't leave the harbor until 11 that night. Then it would be at sea for eight days, when it arrived at Papeete, Tahiti.

I rubbed my mouth, then drove back to Coit Tower. Lawrence Rollins stood defeatedly beside the heavy wall, staring down in the direction of the yellow house. The air had turned sharply cold.

"Did anyone come back?" I asked him.

"No." There was no life in his voice.

"I just checked with the sales office of the shipping lines. Grace Sing is sailing on the *S.S. Belmont* tomorrow. With her grandmother. The ship docks at San Pedro the next morning. Down the coast from Malibu."

He turned and looked at me. I knew my words were registering in his mind. But he was like a man only semiconscious now. He had become too dependent upon his devotion to Nancy. Without her, he was badly crippled.

"Malibu," I said. "Where the documents are to be delivered."

He shook his head. "What's the use?" He turned his eyes from me and stared down at that house. He'd given up so completely that all he could do now was stare at that last place we'd known Nancy to be.

I took the binoculars from him and looked along the piers. I found the *S.S. Belmont* in its berth, a compact, gleaming-white liner just visible in the dimming light. What did that ship have to do with Nancy? Where was she now? And where would she be ...?

It was a long, cold night. I spelled Rollins watching the yellow house. I slept a little in my car. Rollins kept telephoning home, returning to his vigil with the shuffling gait of a beaten man. He refused to talk. I drove down and brought back sandwiches and coffee. He refused to eat. Dawn arrived. The sun came up on the other side of Golden Gate Bridge, seeming to put its superstructure in flames. I told Rollins:

"Stay here. If I find her, I'll telephone your house and leave a message. If I don't, I'll come back. If I run into trouble—" I shrugged. He did not respond. I drove down the hill to The Embarcadero in the freshness of the morning. At nine o'clock, feeling my pulse begin to hammer faster, I climbed the steps leading to the waiting room for the *S.S. Belmont*.

The room was reached by a wide hallway bordered by colorful paintings of brown maidens dancing on South Sea shores. There were several chrome-framed sofas and a large bulletin board upon which was placed a passenger list by stateroom numbers. There was no one in the room except an elderly uniformed guard standing near the door which led to a long glass enclosed ramp that would take passengers and visitors to the ship.

I looked down the columns of names on the bulletin board. I found Grace Sing, paired with the name of a woman the sales clerk had told me was her grandmother: Mrs. Y. Sing. They were assigned to stateroom 334.

An elevator led up from street level and opened into the room to my left. The sales girl had told me the grandmother was partially paralyzed. She might then, I thought, come aboard in a wheelchair. That would mean they would have to take the elevator, if they came this way.

I crossed the room toward the two glassed sides facing the inside of the cavernous pier building. I could look down at the vast high-ceilinged interior. As I watched, a Yellow Cab ran along the interior to the mouth of a canopied gangway. A couple got out, and a porter took their hand baggage. All three disappeared, moving through, I knew, the bulwark of the ship to the main deck. I had a view both of the passengers boarding from automobiles and those who would take the route through this waiting room, to walk down the ramp on foot to that gangway.

I had carried with me the pamphlets the sales girl had given me. I got out the room plan for this ship. Grace Sing's stateroom was on the main deck, just off the foyer, on the outside. I rubbed my jaw and put the folder back in my pocket.

The traffic increased, by car below, on foot through the waiting room. The passengers were mostly elderly; it had taken most of them a long time to make the money to enjoy a cruise like this. By 9:30 I had not discovered Grace Sing.

At 9:32 the elevator door slid open. I stared at two figures coming out.

The girl I'd seen leaving that Telegraph Hill house was pushing a wheel chair. She was now wearing a sashed kimono made of blue flowered silk. She wore a kerchief and dark sunglasses and a beatific smile, as though she had just had a glimpse of heaven.

Then I examined the figure in the wheel chair. She sat motionless, a shawl over her shoulders, a light blanket over her lap, hatted, so completely veiled that no part of her face was visible. I looked at the small white-gloved hands resting limply against the blanketed lap. I looked at the small, tapered ankles visible below the blanket. My nerves jerked. I knew. It was Nancy.

The Chinese girl wheeled the chair across the waiting room to the long ramp leading to the gangway. I was ready to rush across the room. Then sensibility came back to me. Two men in dark suits were coming down the hall. I slipped a hand inside my jacket against the pistol.

The men went by. I followed. We stayed behind Grace Sing, who pushed the occupied wheel chair swiftly and gracefully down the ramp.

Below, cars were bumper to bumper now, moving toward the gangway. We went along the ramp and down, then Grace Sing was pushing the wheel chair onto the gangway.

I followed, into the foyer of the main deck. Elevator and stairway were to my left. A dining room was to my right. People rushed past me, chattering with excitement. Over that sound came brightly tempoed music from loudspeakers.

A white-jacketed steward came up to Grace Sing, spoke to her quickly, then led her down a passageway to my left. I looked at everyone moving through that foyer, letting Grace Sing go out of sight. A young girl with deep red hair caught my eye and smiled, sliding her eyes away from me and heading up the stairway to the promenade deck. I let three minutes go by. No one remained in the foyer who had boarded with us. The steward who had let Grace Sing away reappeared.

I stepped from the bulwark and went down the passageway. I stopped at the first narrow passage running off the main one, looking back and forth. Then I moved into the smaller passage. The stateroom numbered 334 was at the end. A "Do Not Disturb" sign had been hung on the door.

I rapped against the metal.

There was no answer.

I rapped again. A thin, precise voice said from the other side:

"We do not wish to be disturbed."

"The Junior Third Officer, ma'am."

"My companion is very old and not feeling well."

I put one hand flat against the door. "I'm afraid there's a mix-up about your stateroom. I'm very sorry."

There was silence. Then I heard the lock clicking. The door gave against my hand. I slammed it open and went in fast. I got a hand over her mouth. Then I kicked the door shut. She wriggled furiously in my grasp, amazingly strong for her size. I was not polite. I ripped the sash from her waist and knotted it tightly against her mouth.

She tried to kick at me. I put a hand against her throat and whispered, "I'll kill you ...!"

My voice was trembling. She stopped struggling. I saw an open case a porter had delivered ahead of her arrival. There were nylons in it. I used a pair to bind her wrists.

"Sit down over there."

She sat down on a chair and stared at me with dark, savage eyes. All of it had taken only seconds. I turned toward the sofa below a pair of portholes facing the wooden side of the pier building. Nancy lay on a couch, face down, quite nude, quite motionless. Sunlight came in from the portholes and shone against her bare white skin. The clothing she had worn coming aboard was piled in the wheel chair. Straps were attached; they'd been used to hold her in the chair.

I snapped the lock on the door, went across the room and kneeled beside her. She was dead, I was certain of that.

I put my head against her bare shoulders. I felt a jolt of relief. She was breathing. I looked around the room. There was a dressing table in front of a wide mirror. A small medical kit rested there, with a hypodermic syringe beside it.

I looked at her body. There were fresh needle marks in her right arm. My stare traveled down the graceful swell of her hips along her legs to a point just back of her right knee; there were similar marks there, but older. She was drugged, I knew.

I heard a movement behind me. I looked in the mirror. The Chinese girl had gotten to her feet and to a table bordering the opposite side of the room. Her handbag was there. She'd got it open and, her back to the bag, was pulling out a small revolver. I dove across the room and slapped the gun out of her bound hands.

I picked it up and pointed it at her, motioning her back into the chair. Staring at me with hating eyes, she sat down. I got another pair of nylons from her bag and bound her ankles.

I was suddenly aware that light, bouncy music was coming in softly from a loudspeaker. There were two closets to the side of the door, a large bath opposite them. I checked all three rooms, to make certain they were empty. Then I looked again at the Chinese girl, who continued to murder me with her eyes.

The music stopped. A deep male voice announced, "All visitors ashore." There was a deep-throated blast of the ship's whistle. I stared at the Chinese girl with the same hate she was feeling for me. She might have help aboard, I thought. If she did, I couldn't afford a single mistake. I made up my mind. When this ship sailed, I was sailing with it.

I kneeled beside Nancy again. The ship's whistle sounded a second time. Music was again pouring gaily into the room. The whistle finally sounded again. The last time, I thought.

I stared at Nancy's motionless face. It was the face I had tried to picture so many times. Now all of her real beauty was formed in front of me. But she was still separated from me, this time by another invisible thing, gotten from that needle....

At last I heard and felt the engines starting. The hawser lines would be freed from the bollards on the dock, I knew. Then we were moving. The tug would help the ship back from the pier until it could turn, reverse engines and begin the journey south. The tug would cut free. And they would slide out the wings of the gyro-stabilizers. I thought of Lawrence Rollins standing atop Telegraph Hill. You would be able to see him with glasses from the bridge of this ship, a small figure, lonely-looking and defeated, waiting for sight of his daughter, who now lay motionless before me.

"Nancy," I whispered.

Slowly she opened her eyes. They looked very dark. Then she found me. A soft, slow smile moved her lips.

"Tony?" she whispered.

She turned face up and lifted her arms languidly, holding them out for me. I put my arms around her.

"Where are we, Tony?" she whispered lazily.

"On a ship."

"Where is it going?"

"The South Seas."

She moved her lips to my ear and kissed me. "I've always wanted to go to the South Seas. I'll go anywhere with you, Tony. Why don't you kiss me?"

I kissed her. She whispered:

"How did we get together again? You were in Europe, and I—"

She pushed me away, staring at me. Her eyes looked more normal now. She was beginning to look angry.

"You can't kiss me," she said. "You threw me over, Tony Kirk, damn you!"

"Nancy, listen to me—"

"What's going on!"

I tried to keep my arms around her, but she pushed away again.

"You were kidnapped," I said. "I flew back from Europe to attend your wedding. Everyone thinks you're dead but your father. He knows you were kidnapped, and I know it. You've been drugged. I broke in here when that so-called lady over there wheeled you aboard in a wheel chair. Now we're sailing."

She looked down along her body, blinked, drew in her breath and said with great indignation, "You've taken off my clothes!"

I picked up the blanket she'd worn over her knees boarding. She grabbed it from me, covering herself.

"How long were you looking at me before I woke up?"

"Nancy, you've got to wake up completely. You're in great danger."

She looked at me with indignant eyes while I quickly explained how I'd found her in the Telegraph Hill house, lost her, then found her again. She was coming back to total consciousness, I knew. She must have remembered seeing me through that window now. But there were still traces of that drug. She said:

"I was going to marry Curtis Cornell."

"I know that. But it doesn't matter now."

"Not to you, I imagine. You had a lot of nerve to want to come to my wedding."

"Nancy, you've got to tell me all you know about this." It was like trying to reason with someone who'd had an extra drink and had decided to be faintly difficult. I tried to keep the tension out of my voice and said to her, "Do you know why they brought you aboard this ship?"

"How would I know?" She finally sat up, keeping the blanket pulled primly around her. "Don't you have a cigarette?"

I lit one for her. She continued to stare at me accusingly. I had broken things off between us, and she was not forgetting that now. "Didn't you hear anyone say anything?" I insisted.

"Where?"

"In that house on Telegraph Hill."

"I didn't even know where the house was. They blindfolded me when they took me there, then kept me almost all the time in that bare room. Then Daddy—" She blinked slowly. "Where's Daddy?"

I explained. "He's all right, but he's nearly lost his mind worrying about you."

She frowned a little. "And Mommy and Curtis think I'm dead?"

"Yes. And you never heard any plans discussed when you were in that house?"

"No." She smoked her cigarette.

"What happened after I saw you in that house? They took you away. Then—"

"Why does everyone think I'm dead?"

"Because a body was found in your car, burned. They had your funeral yesterday."

"Who was in the car?"

I motioned at the girl across the stateroom. "She could tell us, I think. But right now I want you to think and tell me everything you can."

She looked at the tip of her burning cigarette. "When they blindfolded me and took me out of that house, they drove me to some kind of place that looked like an old warehouse. I don't know where it was."

"You mean they took off your blindfold there?"

"Yes. There were three men. I don't know who they were—the same two who took me out of the house and one other."

"Any of them Chinese?"

She shook her head and pointed to the girl across the room. "She was there. But the men weren't Chinese."

"Did they say anything?"

She shrugged. I took the smoked cigarette from her fingers and put it out in an ashtray on the cocktail table. "She," Nancy said, nodding toward the Chinese girl, "had a medical bag. She got out a syringe. They put me into that wheel chair, and one of the men told her to make certain I was kept drugged until we got to Los Angeles. Then she injected the needle. I don't remember anything after that."

Apparently her clothes had been removed as a precaution against her trying to get away, if she found a chance. They had obviously intended to keep her alive at least until the ship reached Los Angeles. It wasn't much to go on, but it was something.

"How are you feeling now?" Her eyes looked more clear now; she was sitting more erectly.

"All right, I think."

"Can you stand?"

I helped her to her feet. "I'm a little woozy," she said, "but not too much."

I showed her my gun. "Can you handle this?"

She held out her hand. I gave her the pistol, shoving off the safety. She held it, slipping one small finger over the trigger, clutching her blanket with her other hand.

We crossed the stateroom to the Chinese girl. "Put the gun against her right temple." Without hesitation, Nancy did. I said to the Chinese girl, "I'm going to take off the gag, and you're going to speak only in a whisper. If you cry out, she'll pull the trigger." I looked at Nancy. Nancy nodded.

I took off the gag and said:

"Where were you taking her?"

The Chinese girl looked at me. She was quite beautiful, with a fragile facial bone structure and flawless skin. But her eyes were fierce. She did not answer.

"Have you got help on board?"

She did not answer.

"I would co-operate, if I were you."

She finally talked. She talked in a low whisper, and she delivered a long, inventive, emotionally charged string of profanities the match of which I'd never heard. I put the gag back on and took the gun from Nancy. I asked Nancy to sit down again on the sofa. I sat beside her.

"We can pick up that telephone on the table, Nancy, and sound the alarm. We can ask for five ship's officers and twenty seamen, and it's over. Or we can sit tight and try to finish this off, once and for all. You know everything I know. The documents were being brought in through Los Angeles. This ship will dock in Los Angeles Harbor tomorrow morning at eight o'clock. The delivery point was to be Malibu, just up the coast. The odds are pretty good, I think, that nobody connected with the ring knows anything has gone wrong yet. That's our advantage. But it's up to you."

I watched her eyes. They seemed very clear now. She blinked once. "I didn't go through this for nothing."

I nodded. I picked up the Chinese girl's handbag and went through it. I found her passport, containing her picture, visaed for ports of call along the route. There was also a vaccination certificate. And there was a driver's license. I was ready to put them back when I looked again at the small picture reproduced on the white California license. The name on the license was the same as on the passport: Grace Sing. Both license and passport gave the Telegraph Hill address. But there was something wrong with the picture on the driver's license.

I handed it to Nancy.

She looked at that, then at the girl across the room. She shook her head. "Not the same."

"The passport has her picture. I think they had a phony made up. But the license looks real. And it doesn't belong to this woman."

"Whose is it? I mean, if—"

"After they took you out of that Telegraph Hill house, I broke in and searched it. I found pictures of the girl who lived there. I thought she'd changed with the years. But I was wrong. The girl pictured on the driver's license is the same one I found pictures of in that house." I motioned toward the Chinese girl "I don't know who she is—maybe a friend of the girl who owned that house. But I think I've got an idea what happened to Grace Sing."

Nancy met my eyes. "They murdered her."

"And buried her in your place. You came aboard disguised as Grace Sing's grandmother. Only I think she's in the same place her granddaughter is—dead and buried." I looked coldly at the Chinese girl who stared back at me with venomous eyes.

Nancy drew her blanket closer around her neck. She was nearing complete realization of reality now, and with it was coming a greater awareness of the danger.

"Do you still want to go through with this?"

"All the more."

There were four lightweight Samsonite bags in the stateroom; the extra luggage, if there were any, would be in the baggage room, I knew. I went through one bag, then another, hoping half-heartedly that I might find written instructions which would give a lead about what was planned when the ship reached Los Angeles Harbor. I found only personal possessions, mostly expensive clothing, obviously belonging to the Chinese girl. I found nothing of help until I pulled a thickly packed manila envelope bound with a heavy rubber band from the third bag.

Inside were four papers: a birth certificate, a sailing permit, a diploma, another passport. I looked at the picture on this second passport. This was her real passport, I was certain—it contained her picture. I was also certain that the other papers truly belonged to her.

Her real name was Helen Woo. She was resident of Hong Kong, born in 1933. But she had obviously been in the United States before. The diploma had been issued from St. Mary's in San Francisco, in 1955, when she'd graduated as a registered nurse.

I handed the papers to Nancy. "The diploma explains her ability with a needle anyway."

"Yes. But it doesn't help very much otherwise, does it?"

"I think it might." I was finding a thin thread to hang onto now. I sat down again beside Nancy. The ship was moving down the coast, and you could see the water graying with descending fog. There was a faint rolling motion, held to a minimum by the fins of the gyro-stabilizer. Music kept coming softly into the room from the loudspeaker. Metal doors clanged shut against other staterooms. "These people found out what your father was doing, Nancy. We know that. So we know there was some way they found it out. But just you and your father knew how much information he had. Did you tell anyone about it?"

"Of course not!"

"I've got a small, needle-sized hunch. I'm going to follow it. And I'm going to have to leave the stateroom."

She looked immediately concerned. I hoped she was concerned for me, as well as for her own safety. I had been stupid in London. I was going to try to make up for that. "It's too dangerous, Tony."

"I don't think so. Even if Miss Woo's got friends aboard, I don't think they know me. But if they do—I'll have to take the chance."

"But you don't even have a ticket."

"It won't matter. They checked those at the sales office before the ship sailed. Nobody's going to look at papers now until this ship reaches Tahiti. There hasn't been time for the stewards to count heads. I think I can move through the ship right now, and nobody'll question it. I'm only worried about you."

"If you can go out there, I can stay here."

"All right. I want you to put on that girl's clothes. Then we're going to put her on this couch, under the blanket. If you put on that kimono, the kerchief and the dark glasses, you can pass reasonably well for her, in case. You're almost the same size. You both have black hair. All right?"

Nancy nodded.

She unbound the Chinese girl. I held the pistol. The Chinese girl continued to hate us with her eyes. Nancy got her clothes off and redressed her in a robe from one of the bags. I gave the gun to Nancy and performed the job of retying her ankles and wrists. I was certain that if this girl had half a chance, she would tear loose like a wildcat coming out of a sprung trap. I re-gagged her with a towel from the bath. Then I picked her up and carried her to the couch.

"I'll put these on," Nancy said. She carried the Chinese girl's clothes with her into the bathroom, reappearing a few minutes later, looking very much as the Chinese girl had when they had boarded. She handed me the blanket. I put it over the Chinese girl. I also put the veil Nancy had worn aboard over her face.

"Take her gun," I said. "And don't let anybody in here. If anyone tries before I get back, shoot."

She nodded. I got out the room-plan pamphlet of the ship. There was a library on the promenade deck. I would have to get out of this stateroom unseen, then down the passageway toward the stern and climb two decks.

I fitted my own gun under my belt and buttoned my jacket. I looked at Nancy. She took off the dark glasses. Time and distance disappeared. We were in London again, in Piccadilly Circus. I could see the look in her eyes, and I could feel the same emotion I'd felt that night when I'd kissed her. But then a self-consciousness intruded, and time and distance came back, like an invisible explosion. I wanted to kiss her, but I did not. I smiled at her instead.

"Be careful, Tony."

I nodded and went to the stateroom door. I placed my ear against it and listened. I heard footsteps moving along the larger main passageway. Then they diminished. I opened the door and walked swiftly toward the main passageway.

I went down it at a quick, even pace. Midway I met a steward. He was a very tanned blond man with a strong look. I knew him. He was one of the two men who had taken Nancy out of the room in that house on Telegraph Hill. I tensed, forcing a smile. He smiled back and moved on down the passageway.

Near the rear foyer, I looked back. The steward turned abruptly into a small off-passage. It was the one leading to Nancy's stateroom.

I went back down the passageway at a trot. He was not the steward who had led the Chinese girl to the stateroom, but he still might very well have a key for it. I turned into the small passage leading to the stateroom.

The steward was not in sight. I ran toward the door, hoping he had not had time to lock it behind him. He hadn't. I kicked it open, and saw, in one frozen second, the steward advancing toward Nancy. She was pointing her gun squarely at him, her finger tightening on the trigger.

I chopped the side of one hand hard against the back of his browned neck. He dropped to his knees as though tripped. I knocked the door shut, locked it and came back swiftly.

"Tony," Nancy said. "I was ready to—"

"I know. It's all right now. You didn't have to."

The steward shook his head stupidly and lifted his hands as though trying to find something upon which he could climb back to his feet. "Don't do it." I put my pistol against the back of his head.

"He's one of them," Nancy said. "At the house, and then in that warehouse —"

"I know." Then I told him, "Get up and hold your hands toward the ceiling."

He did as I ordered. I slapped his pockets. He wasn't armed.

"Over there and sit down on that bench facing the mirror."

He sat down on the backless bench in front of the dressing table. I was able to keep the gun against his head and at the same time watch his face. Nancy had removed her dark glasses. He knew the situation had been reversed. I could see flecks of rising fear in his eyes.

"You're mixed up in this," I said to him. "I know that. And I want to know something else. Who else, on this ship?"

He looked at me through the mirror and said nothing.

"Your friend lying on the sofa has gotten off easily so far. But it isn't going to bother me to get rough with you, friend. Who else is helping you on this ship?"

The flecks of fear in his eyes became more obvious. But he didn't answer. I didn't want to do it, but I had no time to waste with him. I flicked the barrel of the pistol against the back of his head. He gasped. Nancy gasped.

"Who else?" I snapped.

"Tony—" Nancy said.

I snapped the barrel against his head again, harder.

"No—" he said, bringing up his hands.

"Next time I'll really put something into it."

"I'm the only one!" he said. His tan had gotten a painted look as he paled beneath it. "I was to check with her." He bobbed his head to indicate the girl on the sofa. "Nobody else. Just the two of us."

I was reasonably certain that he was frightened enough to tell the truth. He was familiar with the tactics of his own kind. He expected everyone else to use the same methods. That was working for me. "What were they going to do with her?" I motioned my gun toward Nancy.

"I don't know," he wailed. "I swear it. I just take orders."

"You were at that Telegraph Hill house. You helped move the girl."

"I had orders to do that. We took her to a warehouse in the produce section. Then I was told to check with her." Again his head bobbed in the direction of the Chinese girl. "They told her to keep the Rollins girl doped until we hit L.A. That's all I know!"

"You're a communist?"

"I get *paid!*"

I was certain he was telling the truth. They needed a type like this. They could find him. He was one of the many links in the whole chain. But we had broken two of those links now, and I hoped that we were weakening the chain enough to break it finally.

"Get more nylons out of the bags, Nancy. And tear a blouse so we can make another gag out of it."

She did as I asked. I told her to put her gun against the back of his head. I told her to fire if he so much as twitched a muscle while I bound and gagged him. I bound his wrists and gagged him. He didn't twitch a muscle.

"Get up."

He stood up. I motioned him into one of the closets, ordering him not to budge an inch.

I closed the door almost shut, leaving him air, and returned to Nancy, out of his sight now. I took her in my arms. I whispered, "I'm going out now. Keep that gun ready. I hope you don't have to use it. But if you have to—"

"I will," she whispered.

I looked down, into her eyes. "I was a damn fool," I said softly. "I can't say anything else."

I kissed her. Everything stopped for that brief moment. Then I went back to the door leading to the passageway, listening. I heard nothing—the decks and bars and lounges would be getting most of the passengers now. I stepped out quickly. That steward was going to be missed pretty quickly. And I would have to do something about it. But not before I checked out my thin lead ...

I could see no one in the main passageway this time, except the back of a steward working in a linen closet as I passed. I thought about that linen closet. Then I reached the far end and went up the metal steps, past the upper deck to the promenade deck. The library was a glass-enclosed room. Bordering it was the large promenade lounge, filled with people starting new friendships.

I stepped into the library and crossed the deep carpet to smile at a pretty uniformed girl seated behind a desk. Her expertly arranged hair was the color of an ocean sunset. I was the only customer. The others hadn't had time to think about reading yet.

"I'm looking for a book," I said.

"Then you've come to the right place." She smiled at me steadily, and the smile was meant to be comforting and reassuring. I had a feeling that most of the people who made these cruises regularly were so used to being cared for by servants and managers that the crew tended to treat everyone as though he were slightly child-like.

"I'm looking for an American *Who's Who*."

"I'll bet you want to look someone up, don't you?"

"That's it," I admitted.

She plucked the book from a shelf. "We keep the book just for that very reason. There're ever so many of our regular passengers who have earned their way into the pages of this volume. It's of great pride to us."

I sat down and opened the book. I found what I was looking for, thanked her and left.

I went down the stairway, back to the main deck. I bought two fifths of a medium-priced blend in the auditor's office and paid cash to avoid signing. Then I returned down the passageway, ambling slowly. The linen closet door was closed now. When I reached the narrow off-passage, I dodged into it and rapped sharply at the stateroom door. "It's Tony, Nancy."

She opened the door. I went in quickly, gun in hand, and locked the door behind me. "Are you all right?"

"Yes. But what did you find out?"

"I'll tell you pretty quickly. But first we've got to take care of these two. That steward has probably already been missed. And what we don't need is to have the crew start tearing the ship apart searching for him."

"What can we do with him?"

I opened the closet door and motioned him out with my gun. He came out with fear in his eyes and sat down obediently. I bound his ankles. Then I told Nancy to hold her gun at the back of his head again. I untied his wrists and pulled the gag off.

"We're going to have a party now," I told him. I opened one of the bottles I'd bought and filled a water glass with bourbon. "Bottoms up. It's a party for one. You. Start drinking."

He blinked in confusion.

I said, "Don't try anything with us, or she'll squeeze that trigger and we'll redecorate this room with your blood. Just drink."

I looked at Nancy. Her face was determined. She did not know what I was doing, but she was willing.

The steward took the glass with both hands. Then he poured it down. His Adam's apple bobbed. Tears went into his eyes. But he kept drinking. He was all for it. He killed the glass faster than I had thought possible. I refilled it and handed it back to him.

He leaned back. His eyes were already glazed. I hoped he wouldn't drink it so fast he would kill himself. But the thought wasn't disturbing. This time he went slower. His eyes grew filmier. He leaned back, carelessly, unmindful of that gun against his head now. He finished the second glass. I filled it for him again.

He looked at me with a sly, cunning grin. He winked at me, then drank again. Suddenly the glass clattered on the floor. He started up. Nancy looked at me. I waited. When he got half to his feet, he pitched straight forward and lay on his face, unmoving.

I untied his ankles. Then I picked up the bottle and rinsed my mouth with bourbon. I got one of his arms around my shoulder and lifted him. He was heavy, but I was enthused about getting rid of him.

I asked Nancy to go to the door and listen until she thought the main passageway was clear. She did that, then nodded to me.

I dragged him across the stateroom, outside, to the main passageway. No one was in sight. I lugged him to the linen closet as fast as I could, slung him in, then came in after him, shutting the door behind us. I turned on a small light, as he slid down to a sitting position against shelves of linen, eyes closed, a stupid smile on his mouth.

I pulled a pillow case from a stack and shoved a corner of it into a pocket. Then I switched off the light and opened the door slightly. I could see, without being seen, down the passageway in the direction from which I'd come. I watched a dozen people go by before I found the one I wanted, hoping another steward would not want to use this closet.

She was alone, about eighteen. She was probably sailing with her parents. She was extremely poised for her age, not very pretty but tastefully dressed to bring out her better features. I decided that, despite her sophisticated bearing, she had seen very little of life. Now she was going to have her chance, and for a good cause.

When she had just passed the door, I stepped out behind her. I clamped one hand around her mouth and yanked her, back into the closet. I kept her faced away from me and booted the door shut.

She struggled like a frightened colt. I put my mouth against her ear and blew my whiskey breath at her. I whispered, "Ah, come on …"

I pulled the pillow case from my pocket and got it over her head. I let go of her and stepped out.

She screamed and whooped and bellowed. A steward appeared suddenly, down the passageway. I tried to look bewildered. "Shocking thing," I said to him. "That steward just grabbed the poor girl!"

The girl came flying out of the closet, trying to tear the pillow case off. The steward ran toward her, looking desperate. I ducked into the small passage leading to the stateroom. Nancy had the door open a crack for me. I went in fast and locked the door behind me again.

"What in the world happened?"

I explained. She looked at me with flashing eyes. "That poor girl."

"That's what I said to the steward. And poor us if I hadn't done it. If they'd just found him drunk, they would have simply sent him to his quarters to sober up. Now he'll sober up in the brig. If he has any contacts on this ship, he isn't going to reach them from there. They'll throw the book at him."

I walked across the stateroom and removed the veil from the Chinese girl, whose eyes had turned no kinder. "Now we take care of this one."

"What are you going to do to *her?*"

"Put her in the wheel chair." I pulled off the blanket and put my gun in front of her eyes. "Can you get her wrists untied?"

The Chinese girl stared at me while Nancy worked the nylons off her wrists. Then I said to Nancy:

"Do you want to pick up that hypodermic and see if you can figure out how to use it?"

I watched the Chinese girl's eyes. They switched from hate to panic. She watched Nancy pick up the syringe.

"There must be enough stuff in the syringe, plus what's in the medical kit," I said, "to keep her in a blue cloud until we reach Los Angeles. That's what they had figured for you. That's what we'll do with her. Then strap her in the wheel chair, shawled and veiled."

Nancy met my eyes and nodded. She moved toward the Chinese girl, syringe in hand. The Chinese girl flailed wildly, trying to knock it out of Nancy's fingers.

Nancy stepped back quickly. I put the pistol flush against the Chinese girl's head. Then I said, "Go ahead, Nancy."

"What if I do it wrong?"

"We'll find out when it happens."

The Chinese girl wagged her head violently.

"Or maybe you'd like to inject yourself?" I asked her. She kept wagging her head.

"Take your choice," I said.

She lay with hands clenched, staring at that needle. Finally, defeat in her eyes, she nodded. Nancy swabbed her arm with alcohol.

I said to the Chinese girl, "Don't try anything with that needle. Just use it on yourself. Otherwise—" I kept the pistol tight against her forehead and nodded to Nancy, who handed her the syringe. The girl injected herself, and Nancy took the syringe from her hands. The stuff worked fast. Her eyes darkened. Her lids dropped. She was out.

I lifted her into the wheel chair and strapped her in. Then we arranged the shawl over her shoulders, the blanket over her knees, and fitted the veil over her face. "When she wakes up, she can refill the syringe and do it over." I took a long breath. "Now let's sit down, for God's sake. We need a rest."

I lit cigarettes for both of us. I asked Nancy if she wanted a drink. She didn't. We were getting well down the coast now. Fog was thickening, so that all you could see through the portholes was a gray, ghostly mist. The ship's whistle sounded periodically. I could hear a bell buoy now and then, and the horn of a lightship somewhere.

There was a sudden peace about that room, as though we had, with the Chinese girl asleep, been shut off from the world. I would have liked to have relaxed with that feeling, but I was thinking about Lawrence Rollins still standing in the chilling air beside Coit Tower, certain his daughter was dead. Nancy's mother, right now, would be submerged in the gloom of grief. And the ship was slipping down the coast, bringing us closer and closer to that harbor at San Pedro—and whatever awaited us there ...

"Nancy, I've got to ask you some questions."

She nodded, looking at me with eyes that revealed she was trying to find sense in all of this, to discover what she really felt about me again.

"Dr. Curtis Cornell," I said. "What was your relationship with him?"

Her eyes changed. She looked at me darkly. "I don't think that's any of your damn business."

"Do you love him?"

"Why else was I going to marry him?" Her voice had turned crisp. She met my eyes coolly.

"I've got to level, Nancy. I went up to the ship's library and checked Cornell's record in a *Who's Who*. I wanted to know where he was practicing in 1955. He was a resident surgeon at St. Mary's." I motioned toward the sleeping figure in the wheelchair. "That was the year she graduated from that hospital as a nurse. They must have known each other."

Nancy frowned in confusion.

"Nancy, were you ever asleep in his presence?"

"I don't like the implication," she said, her cheeks flushing faintly.

"I'm not trying to imply anything at all. I just want you to remember. Were you ever asleep in his presence?"

She took a breath. The flush remained in her cheeks. She turned her cigarette out in an ash tray swiftly. "Once, yes. But I don't see that it's any of your business whatever."

"When?"

"About a month ago."

"Tell me about it?"

"Why should I?"

"Because everything depends on this! Damn it, I'm not trying to do anything but get this thing solved. What happened?"

"I got drunk." She turned her face from me, looking angrily across the room.

I was the one who was bothered now. I did not like the idea of her getting drunk with Curtis Cornell.

She suddenly lost her anger. She brought her eyes back to meet mine. "I was so unhappy."

I touched her hand. Her fingers came around mine tightly. "Okay,"

I said softly. "Tell me about it."

"We were having dinner in his apartment. I thought about the wedding. I thought about you—" Her small hand gripped mine even tighter. "We usually never had more than two drinks before dinner—Curtis is very conservative. But he seemed to be feeling very jolly that evening. I was melancholy and sad. Curtis kept mixing drinks for me. I guess I passed out. I woke up on a couch in his living room, very late. Curtis had telephoned Daddy and told him I'd suffered a touch of food poisoning. He would take me home in the morning. I had a furious hangover the next day."

"But maybe it wasn't just from the drinks. Do you ever look at the backs of your legs, behind your knees?"

She looked at me puzzledly. "When I'm wearing hose, to check the seams."

"Bare?"

"I never thought about it."

"There're needle marks behind your right knee. They're not fresh. They might be a month old."

She slid the kimono above her knees and looked. She turned to me again, surprise in her eyes.

"I don't think you got that drunk," I said. "I think you were drugged. He probably put something in the drinks. Then, later, he used a needle. You talked then. About the forged documents. About everything."

"You mean he used truth serum?"

"Yes."

"But I can't believe that Curtis would have anything to do with this. He's—"

"Above reproach. I know. But maybe he isn't. And it's the only thing that makes sense, isn't it?"

Slowly she nodded.

I handed her the telephone. "Ask for the radio room. Tell them you're Grace Sing, in this state room—it's 334. Send a radiogram to your father. He'll still be at Coit Tower, but he's checking home by phone. Tell him you're safe aboard the *S.S. Belmont*. You're with me. Ask him to come with help to Los Angeles pier at arrival tomorrow. But tell him not to reveal his presence until I straighten my tie. Tell him it's imperative he do it this way."

She lifted the telephone and delivered the message. "Now?"

"We wait."

I looked at her eyes. They darkened. "I didn't love him," she whispered.

I reached for her and held her tightly. She tipped her head back. I kissed her. It was a gentle kiss, and then it became something else. There was a sudden shift of emotion, into something as deep and wild as the water we were above …

The ship slid through thick fog. We talked. We planned. The future was in sight, but just beyond touching. We tried, in that long night, to make it more real by talking of it. I was weary of travelling, I told her, of being rootless and unresponsible. I would like teaching—more education, then a quiet campus somewhere, using my experience to strengthen what could be learned from books and instructors. She liked the idea.

We grew intensely hungry after midnight. The Chinese girl had awakened, coming out of the drugged sleep pliable and without antagonism. She put herself back to sleep on my instruction. We decided to take the chance. Nancy telephoned room service and ordered two dinners. I moved into the bathroom. The night steward arrived with the food. Nancy re-explained the delicacy of her grandmother's health and asked that the dishes not be picked up until morning. When he left, we ate greedily.

Near dawn we went over again the plan I had worked out to use when we reached Los Angeles Harbor. Then daylight spread over the sea, though the sky was lightly overcast as we approached the harbor. Again the Chinese girl awoke. Again she delivered herself back to sleep with her instinctive skill with the hypodermic. I saw land, then a white company launch ran out to meet the ship. A tug, to feed us into the berth, appeared.

I felt myself tensing. We had owned a night of our own. That was over now, but the danger was not. I kissed Nancy once more and asked, "Scared?"

"Yes. I've got too much to lose now. I know it."

She stood on tiptoe and hugged me. Then she put on the dark glasses and rolled the wheel chair to the door. I rechecked my pistol. I slid it beneath my belt and buttoned my jacket.

We were in the harbor now; the ship was sliding to the berth. I examined the dock through a porthole. They were securing the lines. The engines stopped. The pier building, a sand-colored structure of Spanish design, was perhaps fifty yards from the bulwark of the ship. A white gangway with a blue canopy running above it was fitted through the door of the main deck. There was an open space of 25 or

30 feet from the end of the gangway to the ramp leading into the pier building. Two men in business suits leaned casually against the white picket fence closing off the area to the left. Two others, similarly dressed, were on the other side, next to the building. I could not see Lawrence Rollins.

The ship's whistle sounded the all-ashore signal. Passengers began streaming down the gangway for their day in Southern California. I looked at Nancy and nodded.

I moved into the bathroom, leaving the door open a crack. She opened the door leading to the passageway and pushed the wheelchair out, looking almost exactly as the Chinese girl, shawled and veiled in the chair, had looked when she'd boarded in San Francisco.

I didn't want to let her out of my sight, even for seconds. But I couldn't risk being seen leaving with her. I waited just ten seconds, hoping that a bellboy would not appear for those dishes. Then I stepped out of the bathroom and checked the short passageway leading to the main one. It was empty. I went out of the stateroom fast and joined the passengers moving along the main passageway toward the main-deck foyer.

The foyer was full. I saw Nancy ahead in the throng, waiting to file out over the gangway. I felt a jab of panic. I was a dozen feet from her, with a wall of people in between; anyone near her might be someone assigned to help the Chinese girl. If they examined her closely, saw that she was not the Chinese girl, it could mean a knife, used expertly …

I put my hand inside my jacket around the pistol. Nancy was moving toward the gangway. Someone stepped aside to let her go ahead with the wheel chair.

I pushed past a half dozen people and reached the gangway five passengers behind her. Outside, Nancy neared the end of the gangway. I looked at the two men in business suits to the left, the two to the right. Two were watching Nancy intently, two were watching me.

Then from the pier building he came: Dr. Curtis Cornell, in dark suit and hat, striding swiftly in his awkward manner, face looking strained and nervous. He was looking straight at Nancy; he didn't see me.

I pushed past the people ahead of me. Cornell reached Nancy and said harshly, "I'll take over now." I knew, in that instant, that he believed he was talking to the Chinese girl and Nancy was in the wheel chair.

Nancy stepped back and removed her dark glasses. "All right, Curtis."

He had started pushing the wheel chair toward the pier building. He stopped, turned swiftly and stared at Nancy. He blinked very slowly. I touched my tie. The men on either side of the gangway came in, fast. Lawrence Rollins appeared out of the pier building at a run.

Cornell wheeled slowly, staring, mouth moving silently. I motioned toward him as one of the men came toward me. Cornell took a half-dozen steps away from the gangway as though he were going to attempt to run. But his arms were clamped tightly and he was moved toward a gate in the picket fence. It happened so swiftly that none of the passengers moving off seemed to have noticed.

Lawrence Rollins had reached Nancy and put his arms around her. I came down to them. A man with hard gray eyes looked at me. I nodded to the figure in the wheel chair. "She goes too. She's drugged, but she'll come out of it." The man wheeled the chair toward the gate in the fence, following the two who had Cornell.

Lawrence Rollins hugged Nancy, then held her away, staring at her with unashamed tears in his eyes. "Are you all right?"

"I'm fine, Daddy."

He turned to me. I grinned at him. He smiled crookedly and pressed a hand hard against my shoulder. Then we moved together into the pier building. The world was suddenly all right.

KILL HIM AGAIN

Night had settled over the California hills. Fog, pushed by a strong breeze, fingered through the valley from the coast, spreading and wiping out a clear sky which had sparkled with stars and a white moon. The great house stood in solemn gloom. Light from a dozen windows glowed through the fog filter. Marshall Reed, 81 that summer, had given up active control of his ranch years ago and had leased out his wide spread of land to other cattle owners. But the cattle were still there.

Sitting in the giant living room, gaunt and patrician, he could hear them: cows bellowing to calves through the mist, a live sound through the night. And the other sounds: the distant hum of cars on the highway, a hated sound; the on-and-off grind of the pump in the water shed, a welcome sound of self-sufficiency; ten minutes ago he'd heard the wild sound of coyotes—a pair of them, he thought, probably treeing a raccoon south of the barn—also a welcome sound, because it was the sound of the primitive and the primitive was of the past. A man 81 years old, he thought, twice a widower, twice a millionaire, could only enjoy the past and somewhat the present, but almost never the future.

Except now. And now, for the first time in many long months, he was looking forward to something that was going to happen. Patrick was coming home. Patrick, ace newspaperman, missing, dead in Vietnam. And then found, alive again. By God, he thought jubilantly, Patrick was coming home!

He looked across the room and smiled at the bitter looks they could not hide. Son George, half-brother to Patrick, half a man in comparison. Stocky, flabby, flaccid George, who'd gotten onto him like a slug. That was a good description of George, when you got down to it: a slug. He laughed aloud, a jumping cackle that made both of them jump.

The woman looked at him and asked, "What is it, Father? Is something funny?"

And Clair, he thought. Wife of George, daughter-in-law to himself. Handsome, with an extraordinary body; but super-dramatic, super-ambitious and super-selfish, whose main accomplishment had been to cook his meals and kow-tow to him, sitting now beside her slug of a husband, hating it because he was laughing. Neither of them, he thought, could see anything to laugh about now. Not with Patrick coming home. "I was thinking of a slug," he said.

"I've always hated slugs," George said.

"I would imagine."

"I don't see what could be funny about them."

"I don't suppose you could, George," Marshall Reed lifted a blue-veined hand. "What time is it?"

Clair looked at a slim watch. "Ten after ten, Father."

"He'll be here soon, won't he? Gael would have picked him up at the airport at nine. They'll want to say hello and get acquainted again. But my granddaughter said she'd drive him right up here. My son Patrick."

George looked at him across the room. "I'm your son too, Father."

"Did you think you had to remind me of that, George? You've lived in my house all these years just because you were my son, haven't you? Doing nothing?"

"Father," Clair said, "that isn't fair. George has worked very hard helping you. I've tried to do my best too."

"I know what you've both done," he said shortly. "I prefer to think of what Patrick has done. He did something with his life, didn't he? Now he's come back from the dead. You should try to do something impressive one of these days, George. You might surprise yourself and succeed."

"Why are you trying to hurt us? What have we done?"

"Nothing," he said. "Except hope that someday something might happen to Patrick and I might write over most of what I own to you in my will. Well, we thought something did happen to Patrick, didn't we? I did change my will. I did give you most of what I own, and just a little for Gael, because she's independent and doesn't want any more. But now Patrick is alive, after all. He's coming back tonight. That's why you two are so gloomy, isn't it?" He was enjoying himself. "Why don't you touch up the fire, George? The fog's turning it cold as winter in here."

George walked woodenly to the large fireplace. He picked up a heavy poker and pushed listlessly at two fir logs smoldering on blackened irons.

"That's a good boy, George."

George turned and stared at his father. "You always said I was the good one. When we were young, you said over and over that I was the good one. You said Patrick was wild and scatter-brained and would come to no good end. You threw him out of this house a half dozen times. But you said I was steady and right. You said you could always count on me. Now all you think about is Patrick. Why did you change, Father?"

The old man smiled. "When Patrick was younger and I was younger, I saw myself in him. Years ago that didn't please me. But I'm 81 now. I don't hate myself so much anymore. I realize all we can do is do the best we can. I did that. Patrick did that. I accept myself. I accept Patrick. But you, George. The trouble with you is that not only didn't you do the best you could, you never did a damn thing. Except live off me. Hang around and run errands. You and Clair." He turned his head toward Clair, his aged eyes glistening with enjoyment.

"I think you are being very spiteful this evening, Father," Clair said. "We both love you very much."

"Then you won't mind doing what I ask, will you, George?"

"I'll do anything for you, Father."

"First thing tomorrow morning, call up Horstram and tell him to get out here."

George blinked slowly. "Horstram?"

"My lawyer, George. In case you've forgotten."

"Why do you want to see Horstram?"

"I'm going to change my will back to the way it was."

George's face had become ashen. He held the poker tightly. His knuckles had whitened. "You can't do that."

"George, you are shouting, aren't you?"

George's voice rose, singing through the large room. "Not after all I've done for you. You can't do that!"

"Well," the old man said, "scream, George. Shout! But I'm going to do it. You'll still get something. Not all of it now. But something. Maybe Patrick'll be kind, after I've gone. Maybe he'll give you something too. A nickel? How would that be?"

Cheek muscles shivering, George moved toward the old man, who had begun cackling. Tears blurred his eyes. "A nickel!" the old man said. "Wouldn't that be wonderful! For both of you. From Patrick—my son!"

The poker rose, then came flying down. There was a brutal cracking sound. The old man pitched forward out of his chair.

George stood frozen. The poker fell from his hand. He stared down at the crumpled form of the old man. "My God," he whispered. "Oh, my God!"

He stooped swiftly and flung his arms around his father, sobbing.

Then someone was pulling him away, guiding him roughly back to the chair. He looked up at the hard face of Felix Argon, his father's ranch manager, who had come running in when Clair screamed.

Felix, a tall, muscle-heavy man in his mid-thirties, said, "What happened?"

"He ..." Clair began, thrusting a long-fingered hand at George.

George looked through his tear-blurred eyes at his wife. She was not in grief, he thought, only panic. He looked at Felix, moving across the room to bend beside the body of his father. Felix's shoulders were wide, his waist was slim; his thigh muscles pushed against tight Levis cloth. Jealousy poked through his own grief and burned like a small flame.

"Dead." Felix's voice was flat, but penetrating. He straightened and looked at George with cold eyes. "Why?"

George ran his tongue along his dry lower lip. He shook his head slowly and couldn't stop doing that.

"He was changing the will," Clair said. "He was mean about it. He said now that Patrick was coming back, Patrick was going to get most of it again."

George was finally able to stop shaking his head and stare with a returning detachment at Felix. Felix's face had stiffened. "Had he changed it yet?"

"No," Clair said.

Felix's hands closed so tightly that the muscles of his arms thickened.

"He was my father," George said, hearing his voice breaking. "I loved him! I always loved him!"

Clair was suddenly under control again. She came across the room, her handsome face furious. "You are so stupid! You have always been stupid! A fat, stupid—"

"Shut up," Felix snapped.

She stared at him.

"Call the police," George said, and pushed his hands against his face.

"We're not calling the police," Felix said.

"I killed him! My own father!"

Felix looked at Clair. "When does he get here?"

"Who?"

"Patrick!"

"Any minute. But—"

"Call the police!" George wailed.

Felix grasped the back of George's jacket collar and snapped him upright. George looked into the chilling blue eyes, frightened of the man even in his grief. "We're not calling the police. We're not doing anything now, but what I say. Do you hear me, George? Fat, stupid George?"

Gael Reed sat with Dean Powers in the lounge of San Francisco International Airport. "How much longer?" she asked. Her voice was crisp, though it could turn soft and husky. She almost always spoke quickly.

Powers looked at his watch. "Twenty-two minutes, on the nose."

"It's not late?"

He shook his head.

Her slim fingers fumbled into her bag. He quickly brought out a pack of cigarettes from his jacket. She took one, and he lit it, watching it tremble with her fingers. She inhaled deeply. "I'm shaking more inside than out."

"I don't blame you."

She looked across the lobby toward the large window which faced the complexity of runways. The lights out there were myriad. He could hear a plane taking off with a muffled roar. There was bright laughter coming from the nearby bar. She said:

"It isn't real, somehow. When I saw him on television this noon, I thought it was a film. I thought it's something they took a long time ago, and he's still out there, dead in that mountain country. I was almost getting used to it these last weeks. There wasn't a grave here, but I took flowers to my mother's grave and put them down for both of them. Now—"

"I know," he said softly.

He knew she was feeling the emotional jar of knowing her father had returned from the dead. Patrick Reed's daughter had idealized her father. But she resented his long absences abroad. That was why, Dean thought—and no matter the strong attraction between them— she constantly put up a shield between them, because she could never allow herself to fall into an emotional involvement with someone who wished to emulate her father's career. And Dean Powers, he thought, was one who wished to emulate Patrick Reed's career.

"How much longer now?" she asked.

"Fifteen minutes," he said. "Don't try to feel and think too much right now, Gael. He's been through a lot. Let him get his bearings again. That's enough, isn't it? To know he's alive? To let him get used to being home again?"

"Yes," she said softly.

Ten minutes later they walked down the tunnel which legged out to receive the passengers of Patrick Reed's plane. There was a smaller waiting room at the end, but they didn't sit down. She seemed, he saw, in better control with the reality of her father's appearance drawing closer. He looked out of a window and saw the large plane moving in toward the ramp.

She wouldn't look out the window. She waited at the top of the escalator. Pretty soon the passengers stepped onto the escalator and rose toward the lobby. Then Dean saw him.

He'd seen photographs of him. He'd seen him on television earlier in the day. But he was much smaller than he'd expected. His bright red hair, with very little gray, also surprised him. But the gaunt look, the lines in the freckled face, the look of the eyes, none of which had come through clearly on the television screen—that didn't surprise him. He's been through it, he thought.

He felt Gael's hand going into his, her fingers tightening, as though holding desperately to him for reassurance just before diving from a very high board.

Then she broke as her father reached the lobby level. She ran to Patrick Reed, tears in her eyes, and put her arms around him, calling him by the name she'd always used, "Paddy, Paddy ..."

Patrick Reed held his daughter for several minutes, then she wiped swiftly at her eyes and introduced him to Dean. Dean felt the man's hand limply in his. The eyes looked at him remotely. "My pleasure," Dean said. "I've admired your work for a long time."

"Thank you," Patrick Reed said, and no more. They walked back along the tunnel. Dean offered to get his car from the parking lot while they waited for the bags to be unloaded from the plane, to let them be alone together. But when he walked outside and got his Chevrolet from the lot and drove it back up the ramp, he was certain that no matter if she were alone with him or not, Gael was not going to find a quick communication with her father. He'd been out there too long, he thought. He'd been through too much.

He loaded Patrick Reed's bags into the car, then the three of them got in the front seat. He drove the car down the ramp and out to Bayshore Freeway, then south, toward Palo Alto. Finally Gael said, "We can stop at my place, Paddy. Or we can drive straight out to the ranch. Whatever you want."

Patrick Reed was silent for several seconds, then he said, with more life in his voice, "I'd like to go to the ranch, I think. If Father—"

"He's dying to see you," Gael said quickly. "He was so pleased when you telephoned him. When we found out you were safe—we all ..."

Dean could see Patrick Reed's hand move and touch his daughter's. He could almost feel Patrick Reed relaxing, and then he heard him laugh softly and said:

"I should tell you, Dean ... it's Dean, isn't it?"

"Yes, sir."

"My father and I have been battling for years. We were too close. Too much alike, I guess."

"You love each other too much," Gael said. "That's all."

"I guess," Patrick Reed said. "But I wasn't a prize son. George, my half-brother, always did everything right. Almost. He tried very hard to please Father. But I helled around too much. He kept kicking me out. Five times, I think it was. He wanted me to stay home and run the ranch. I wanted to see the world. I saw most of it. I wrote about what I saw ..." His voice trailed away, and once again Dean could feel the atmosphere tightening.

"It's all right now," Gael said softly. "It's going to be fine."

Patrick Reed nodded slowly, then said, his voice carefully polite, "I haven't heard of you before, have I, Dean?"

"I wrote," Gael said swiftly. "I kept hoping you'd be found and so I sent the letters."

"They're probably stacked up somewhere. I'll try to send for them. I'd like to read them."

"We'll talk instead," Gael said. "About everything."

"That's right," Patrick Reed said. "What do you do for a living, Dean?" His voice was cool, and he was not truly interested, Dean was certain. But he answered:

"Sports reporter for a Peninsula daily. I graduated from Stanford a couple of years ago. The job was open. I took it. But I don't plan on doing that the rest of my life. What you've done—that's what interests me."

He felt a sudden self-consciousness, knowing that he was demonstrating almost a boyish eagerness to tell his ambitions to this man whose work he'd admired and been influenced so much by. But he was certain, as he turned the car west and drove toward the hills, that Patrick Reed was not faintly interested. He kept talking, to keep the silence from enveloping them into an uncomfortable vacuum; but he knew, as they climbed those hills, that Patrick Reed had finally stopped listening altogether.

The road descending from the highway was rock and dirt, narrow, and curled in tight curves. Dean saw Patrick Reed lean forward, his frail body tensing. The fog had shut out the moonlight they had travelled through below, on the Peninsula, and he was watching the dim shafts of light sent forward by the headlights.

"Yes," he whispered. "I kept thinking about it ..."

The car's tires bumped over the steel rails of the cattle guard, then the buildings of the ranch came into ghostly view. "Here we are," Gael said softly.

The front door of the large house swung open as Dean stopped the car.

Clair, whom Dean had met a month ago, was the first to greet Patrick Reed. She put her arms around him in a show of emotion that Dean had not thought she possessed. Then George, blinking back sudden tears, gripped Patrick Reed's hand.

Dean followed them into the living room and watched Patrick Reed search the room swiftly—for his father, he was certain. But only Clair and George were there to greet him.

"Sit down, Patrick. Use Father's chair."

Patrick Reed nodded and sat down. "He's moved this chair, hasn't he?" he said. "Just a foot or two, but he always kept it right there. Is he all right?"

"Gael and Dean, you sit down over there. Isn't this wonderful! Oh, Patrick. It's so good to see you. George, you sit there. Let Patrick relax. You'd like a drink, wouldn't you, Patrick? Can't we fix you a drink?"

"My father," Patrick Reed said. "He's all right, isn't he?"

"Of course," Clair said. "But—"

"Why isn't he here?"

"I'm so sorry. But you know how he can be sometimes."

Dean watched the disappointment and weariness return to Patrick Reed's face. "I think so. He isn't here, is he?"

"No, darling. He went down to the retreat." She turned to Dean with a swift, forced smile. "Father has a house down the coast where he goes to hibernate now and then. He calls it his retreat, and—" She turned back to Patrick Reed. "Don't be upset, Patrick. He'll just look into his soul, then he'll be back."

"I thought—" Patrick Reed began. Then finally he said, "He sounded fine when I talked to him on the telephone."

"Of course! He's delighted you're back. Your own father? But you must remember, Patrick—he thought, we all thought, that you'd ... well, it's a shock to him. He was quite emotional about all of this. He got to feeling the old resentments, thinking about how you'd left home those times, and—" She took a breath and lifted her chin. "He'll get over it. Felix—that's his new manager—drove him down this evening. Tomorrow he'll be calling for us to come and get him. Then everything'll be fine. Won't it, George?"

George sat unmoving in his chair. He looked at his hands. He didn't answer.

Patrick Reed's eyes were dark and bitter-looking. "Back from the dead, and he couldn't stand the sight of me."

"Patrick," Clair said, "don't do that."

Gael sat down on the chair arm beside her father. "It isn't like that, Paddy. He's old, you know."

"Patrick," Clair said, "can't we fix you that drink? George, you know what Patrick likes."

But George didn't move, and Patrick didn't answer. Finally Clair said:

"You must be tired, Patrick. We've fixed up your old room so nicely for you. Maybe you'd like to go up and get some rest. Don't you think so, Gael?"

"Would you like that, Paddy? I'll come see you tomorrow afternoon. About one?"

Slowly, Patrick Reed got up from the chair. He moved across the room and mounted the stairway without another word.

Patrick Reed had been almost asleep, when the sound had come into his ears. His ears opened wide and he listened to the far-off barking. He felt himself trembling and sweat turned his body damp beneath the sheet. Then he remembered. He was home. And those were wild dogs, somewhere out in the hills.

He took a deep breath, fighting to keep his mind from spinning back to that narrow coastal plain edging the South China Sea, the chopper coming down, forced down by stray bullets from the Viet Cong moving mercurially back and forth into the jungles like phantoms. He'd looked at the wounded pilot and known the boy was dead when the blades stopped rotating. Then he was out and moving through that mountain country, a hundred miles above Saigon, above where the rice paddies and the rubber plantations thinned out, until the dogs got his scent, the Montagnards behind them...

No, he thought. Not tonight. I am home. Those dogs are not the dogs of the Montagnards. They are only the raiders of my father's ranch. And my father's ranch is my home.

My father, he thought, hands opening and closing in that sweated heat of his bed. My father, who could not bear to greet me …

Downstairs, in the large living room, George again sat motionless, looking dully at his wife, then at Felix Argon. "Call the police," he repeated, his voice whispered and whining.

"Shut up," Felix snapped.

"But what good is this doing?" Clair said. "We can't go on this way."

"We can," Felix said. "We are."

"Where did you put him?"

"In the right place."

"But—"

"You listen to me, both of you. I'm running this now. We're not calling the police. We're not going to do anything but what I tell you. There's an answer, and I've got it. You saw him, didn't you? You heard him. I did, through a window. Patrick. He's a squirrel, and he's the answer."

"That's my brother," George complained. "And I killed my father. Pick up the phone, won't you? Call them and tell them what I've done!"

He watched Felix move toward him threateningly. All at once fear overpowered his grief. He licked his dry lips and managed, "I know what's been going on." He jerked a shaking hand at Clair. "I know why she's insisted you stay on this ranch all along."

"That's right," Felix whispered. "And there's nothing you can do about it."

"I'll turn myself in. I'll tell them exactly what happened."

"All right," Felix said. "Do that. Get up. Pick up the telephone. Tell them to come out. I've got that poker now. They'll find your fingerprints on it. Any second-rate lab technician could do that. Clair saw you do it. She'll be glad to tell them that, won't you?"

Clair was seated with her hands on her lap. She nodded, staring at George darkly. "Yes," she whispered.

"You see, George?" Felix said. "I'll tell them I saw you do it too. How's that? That'll fix it for good. That's what you want, isn't it, George?"

George sat rigidly, feeling the fear growing. The stunning guilt he'd felt earlier was fading away.

"Come on, George," Felix said, moving toward Clair. "Pick up the phone. Tell them you killed your daddy." He grinned and came around Clair's chair to stand behind her. "Why not?" He waited. George stared down at his lap, not moving. Felix laughed and put his hand against Clair's cheek. "No guts. Is that it? Lots of talk, but no action. What's the matter with you, George? You killed your poor daddy, now you just sit there. And you say those things about me and Clair. If you think something like that, you ought to do something about it." Slowly, Felix moved his hand down from Clair's cheek toward the swell of her breasts. "I wouldn't take it, George. Do you hear me? Fat, stupid George?"

George stood up and walked slowly across the room. He stumbled once at the foot of the stairs, then climbed them, like a weary, aged bear. In the bedroom, he stripped his clothes off and dropped them listlessly. He climbed into bed and waited for Clair to come.

She did not.

Pretty soon he heard the sound of a car starting, then rolling out of the grounds. He thought: I'll get up and go to the telephone and call them. I'll tell them about my father.

But he didn't get up and he didn't call anyone.

Morning came with summer warmth. Sunlight flowed through the pine and scrub oak and the red-trunked madrone to the east, lighting the hills to the west with a golden glow.

Patrick Reed came down late and sat at the familiar kitchen table, waiting for the breakfast Clair promised with exuberance. She worked at the stove, pouring batter, while bacon curled on the grill. Good smells, he thought. Good home. But he could not find the reality of it. It was as though he were watching himself from somewhere afar, as though he had some kind of special power to be one place and see himself in another. He wasn't here, he thought; he was still in that mountain country ...

He pushed that feeling away and looked at George across the table. "You look fine, George. Little heavier, maybe?"

George nodded silently. And George, he thought, seemed as distant as he felt himself. Well, it's strange: to think someone's dead, then find him across the breakfast table from you as though nothing had happened. But something had happened, he thought. Down deep, in himself.

"There," Clair said, and placed a large plate of hotcakes, bacon, eggs and potatoes before him. A good ranch breakfast, he thought, but he would be able to do no more than pick at it.

When he'd finished, the man came in the kitchen door: a work-slim man in Levis and checked shirt, whose muscles pushed against cloth as he moved, his eyes quick and searching in a hard, handsome face.

"This is Felix Argon, Patrick. Father's new manager."

Patrick shook hands briefly, thinking of his father again, not really caring about this man. But Felix, taking a cup of coffee, sat down and said:

"Glad to see you back, Mr. Reed."

Patrick Reed nodded mechanically.

"Tough going out there, wasn't it?"

"Pretty tough, yes."

"What was it they called those people?"

"Montagnards."

"That's right," Felix said. "Head hunters. Right?"

"Felix," Clair said, "maybe Patrick would rather talk about something else."

"I was thinking," Patrick said, "I'd like to see my father. I'd like to go down there this morning. If you've got a car I could borrow, why—"

"Patrick," Clair said quickly, "I know how you feel. But maybe it would be better to wait. Let him make up his own mind. He said he didn't want to be disturbed by anyone. It'll be all right, Patrick. You wait and see." She nodded positively. "I've got a wonderful idea for you. Why don't you go out with Felix? Let him drive you around the ranch. You haven't seen the new lake down by the creek Father put in, have you? Isn't that a marvelous idea, dear? Don't you want to do that?"

Listlessly, Patrick climbed into the Jeep with Felix. Felix kicked the Jeep forward and drove swiftly down the dirt road leading toward the creek toward the south. "Real glad to see you back, Mr. Reed. Heard a lot about you. I've got an idea what you had to go through. I was in the Korean war myself. You saw some of that, didn't you?"

"Yes."

Felix nodded. "That was a war, all right. I don't care what they called it otherwise. I was working on a ranch up in Oregon when they called me up for that. Infantry. D Company. That's a lousy company to be in."

"Yes," Patrick Reed repeated.

"I found it out. I found out something else too." He looked at Patrick Reed, then at the narrow road again. "People at home get these ideas about what some man in combat feels. They think when he comes home he doesn't want to talk about anything." He shook his head. "I think a man should talk about it. Get it out of his system. What do you think about that, Mr. Reed?"

Patrick Reed tried to estimate him, to keep his mind from returning to that vacuum state. "D Company?"

"Fourth platoon."

"Platoon sergeant, I'd guess."

"That's it."

"You had something to talk about then, didn't you?"

"It wasn't a picnic."

"Well, I've written about what I've seen. Talking isn't a lot different."

"That's right," Felix said. He glanced at Patrick Reed again, then said, "What happened out there anyway? How'd they get you in the first place? Chopper, wasn't it? Shot down?"

"Yes." And now he sensed that this man would know what he was talking about. He was hard, tough, and he'd been in a war. "Stray shots. We were heading toward the South China Sea. We came down in the mountain country. That's Montagnard territory."

"Wild people."

"Most of them. They're descendants of the Malayo-Polynesian peoples. They were driven from China into those hills hundreds of years ago. They're transients who live off slash farming. They come to a new hillside, set fires, burn off the trees and use the ash for fertilizer. Then they plant rice seeds, build their bamboo-stilt village, harvest the crops and move on. Their methods aren't popular with the Vietnamese economy. They cost millions of piastres every year, with those fires." He felt himself relaxing a little again, talking this way.

"Mean, aren't they?"

"Primitive. The Rhade, Sari, Bahner, all of the tribes. The Katu come out of the hills every February. The young ones have to make a kill, because they have to dip their spears in blood before they can marry."

"But that's South Viet Nam, isn't it? That isn't communist there, is it?"

"No."

"What did they have against you then?"

He was tightening again. "The people in the villages where I was had some bad luck. The Viet Cong had only killed a few district chiefs. The tribesmen didn't like them anyway. But a loyal Air Force raid had put a few napalm bombs into the village a few weeks before they found me. They thought there were communists hiding there. It was a personal thing for the Montagnards, against the government. They thought I represented the government...." He became silent and tried to concentrate on the fields lying ahead and the trees below, where the stream cut through loco banks. There were cattle grazing along the west edge of the creek.

"How did they get hold of you?" Felix said. "After the chopper went down?"

He closed his eyes, telling it, and living it too in his mind, all over again, just as it was:

Crouching, running, ducking, with the barking behind him, the breath burning out of his lungs. And they kept coming, armed with crossbows, spears and machetes, to drag him with savage joy back to the stilted huts. Brown-skinned bodies in loin cloths. The women bare-breasted. The men with long, matted hair. And that big one, chanting them into their pagan sacrifice, oriental face gleaming, ivory earplugs swinging, a white cross drawn on his forehead. The earthenware jugs going from one brown hand to another. The long reed straw passed from one brave to the next, as they sacrificed a bullock to their gods. He'd been certain, when he'd seen the jaws of those dogs snapping against tossed meat, that he would follow the bullocks....

"Yeah," Felix was saying. "Better to talk about it though. Right?" He nodded emphatically, and Patrick Reed suddenly realized that the man did not care, could not feel how it had been, and was not attempting to project to it. "Goddam dogs," Felix said. "Driving us crazy around here too. Got a pack of wild ones out here. Did you hear them last night?"

"Yes. I heard them."

Felix reached back and slapped the leather cover of his rifle. "I'm shooting every one I see." He suddenly braked the Jeep. "Speak of the devil."

"What's the matter?"

"Saw one of them. Over that rise. You wait here. I'll see if he's holding up over there. You had your fill of dogs anyway, right?"

Patrick Reed watched the man climb the rise to disappear at the crest. Minutes went by. Then Patrick heard the sharp crack of the rifle. He jumped with the sound, then rubbed an unsteady hand across his mouth. *I went over the Ron River when they had every gun in the world exploding,* he thought. Now...

Felix walked back with a victorious spring. He shoved the rifle back into its cover and slipped easily back of the steering wheel. "One less to chew up the calves." He started the Jeep, and Patrick said:

"That's Sid Blake's property over there, isn't it?"

"Yeah, but we're all in it together. I've got a dog of my own. But if I ever caught him taking a chop out of a calf, I'd give him the same thing I gave that one. Your old man's leasing now, you know. But I'm responsible just the same. It's in the contract. Too bad about the way he went down to that retreat. That's no way to treat a man like you." Felix shook his head. "But he'll come out of it. He's just stubborn, that's all." Felix drew out a cigarette from his shirt pocket and lit it. Smoke whipped back from his thin lips. "What kind of dogs were they anyhow, that finally caught up with you?"

At the house, Patrick Reed moved slowly inside. George and Clair were waiting in the living room. Clair smiled at him brightly. "Did you have a nice tour, Patrick?"

"It was fine," Patrick Reed said listlessly.

Twenty minutes later, Felix Argon drove a station wagon to the highway. Well, he thought, he was taking the long chance. And it felt good down deep inside, because it was going to work. He knew that. His strong hands gripped the steering wheel. He thought of how, after Patrick Reed had gone back to bed, George had demanded to know where he and Clair had driven last night.

He laughed aloud, pushing the station wagon faster along the highway. He'd known the day he'd gone to work for the old man what it was all about between Clair and George—nothing, except that Clair wanted that money. And it hadn't taken him any more time with Clair than it had with any of the others in his life. Then it had looked absolute. All they'd had to do was wait until the old man gave out his last breath.

But Patrick Reed had turned up alive. And stupid George—fat, stupid George, with a poker in his hand ...

He shook his head abruptly. It was done. But it wasn't lost. He licked his thin lips and thought of that period he'd liked best in the Army: when he'd worked the stockade. He'd found out how to do it to them in there. Now he was going to do it to someone else, because it was the only way. If Patrick Reed had come back from the dead, they would simply have to kill him again.

He turned in at a gate in front of which stood a battered mailbox with the owner's name drawn laboriously in black paint. Felix grinned. Sid Blake owned two thousand prime grazing acres, but he wouldn't spend a penny for anything he didn't have to. A month ago, kids had knocked down his mailbox and driven over it until it was flattened. Typically, Sid had carefully hammered it back in shape, then repainted his name on it.

Felix stopped in a small valley beside a plain, white house. He tapped the horn button. A thin white-mustached man in ancient work clothes came out.

"Hello, Sid," he called, and thought: Sid Blake was not only stingy, he was also talky; if you told it to Sid Blake, you told it to the entire area. "Listen, Sid," he said, "you're not going to like this, and I don't blame you. But I want to be fair about it. It just happened ...”

Twenty minutes later he was back on the highway, speeding in the direction of San Francisco, knowing he had started it now.

At one o'clock, Gael stopped her red Renault at the entrance of her grandfather's ranch. Clair, in riding clothes, was waiting beside the open metal gate. A horse was tethered to an old-fashioned hitching post driven in nearby. She smiled at Gael. “I thought you'd be coming along about now, dear. I wanted a ride, so I decided to meet you here.”

“Fine,” Gael said. She got out and stood beside Clair, admiring her cool, handsome appearance. She had always admired Clair's poise and good looks, ever since Clair had married her uncle nearly ten years ago. But she never found a warmth in her presence, despite the cheerful, engaging way Clair delivered almost everything she said. She could not, somehow, think of her as an aunt, and had never been able to call her that. Yet she was the wife of her uncle, and had seemingly been devoted to that position for all of these years. “How's Paddy?”

“Oh—” Clair's smile lost its brightness.

The familiar panic returned; Gael could feel a pulse beating in her throat. “Something's happened.”

Clair touched her arm gently. “Now he's perfectly all right, physically. It's just—”

“It's just what? What's the matter, Clair?”

“Well, he's—disturbed.”

“Disturbed.”

“He's not himself, dear.”

“I could see that. But he's going to be all right. I'm going to help. I'm going to drive down now, and—”

“No, dear.” Clair shook her head. “He doesn't want to see you.”

Gael stared at her.

“I'm so sorry, darling. I didn't want to tell you that. It's just the way he feels today. He'll get over it.”

She kept staring at Clair in astonishment. “You mean he actually said he didn't want to see me?”

“I'm sure he meant just for today. In a few days—”

“I just can't believe that.”

“He was so upset when Father wasn't here to greet him. It doesn't take much, after all he's been through. We're all being so careful. But the slightest thing and he gets terribly angry. Then he lapses.” Clair shook her head.

"I want to see him," Gael said.

"We've all got to be understanding," Clair said patiently. "I don't think you should do what he doesn't want you to do. That's just going to disturb him even more. Isn't it, darling?"

Gael spread her hands in frustration. "I don't want to disturb him. But I'm his daughter."

"Dear," Clair said smoothly, "let's just let him rest. And try to do things the way he wants them right now. Everything's going to be fine before you know it."

Reluctantly, Gael returned to her car. She sat there, feeling the hurt. Then Clair carefully closed the gate and locked it. Clair mounted her horse and disappeared down the road. That gate, Gael thought—it had never been locked for as long as she could remember....

The sun had gone over the highest hill west of the house. Cattle were grazing at the top, black shapes against the reddening sky where the sun was descending swiftly. It was suddenly very damp-cool.

Inside the large living room, Patrick Reed watched his half-brother fire the paper beneath the small pieces of kindling beneath the two large logs in the fireplace. The edges of the torn newspapers caught and burned slowly. George, staring down, saw that there was not enough air to let the flames grow. He hesitated, then lifted the poker and pushed at the paper to make more space and let the air through to the fire. The flames grew and spread, and the small timber caught fast. George put the poker back in its iron holder, as though it were too hot to handle.

"That's a new one, isn't it, George?" Patrick Reed asked. "That poker?"

George turned and looked at Patrick. "The other one was broken."

Then Clair appeared. "I've just about got it done, Patrick. Just the way you wanted it."

"What was that, Clair?"

"The roast you asked for this morning." She examined Patrick carefully. "Well—anyway. It's your favorite. And we'd better have a cocktail, hadn't we, George?"

George got up to make the drinks at a long oak table. While he was doing that, Patrick said, "I think I'd better call her."

"Who, Patrick?" Clair asked.

"Gael. She said she was coming this afternoon. I know you said not to worry about it. But I am getting worried."

"Patrick, I don't think you should be worried."

"But she said she was coming."

"Well—she did, Patrick."

"She did?"

"I was riding up near the highway just after noon. Gael drove up."

"And what?"

"I'm sorry, Patrick. But she said some very mean things."

He frowned. "What kind of things?"

"I don't want to repeat them. You'll simply have to try to understand. You've been away, and everyone thought you were lost. But now you've come back. People have suffered for you, Patrick. You can't blame them for that. Oh, I know. You've always felt a dedication to your work. But you've hurt people too. I'm sorry to say that. But it's true. I know you didn't mean that to happen. But it did. You've been away so much of the time. Gael resents it, that's all. She feels you deserted her and her mother, and—well, Patrick, you have to admit you've lived your life rather selfishly, when you get right down to it. Father wanted you to stay here and help. George and I did. But you didn't. You've hurt him. You've hurt Gael too. You can't blame them."

George handed him a drink. Patrick looked down at it and said nothing.

"I had to say those things," Clair said. "Patrick?"

"It's all right," he said softly.

"Darling," Clair said, and came over to touch his cheek tenderly. "It *will* be all right. Just be patient. Try to understand. George and I will help every way we can. *We* understand. Father and Gael—they'll get over this. Now drink your drink and have George mix you another. I'm going to finish that roast, just the way you like it. Relax, Patrick."

He finished the drink swiftly. George smiled at him and hurried to get him another. Then he sat down across the lamp table from him again.

"Patrick?" George said. "Look at this."

Patrick turned his head slowly and looked at a new ballpoint pen George held in his chubby hand.

"It's a new pen," George said, and Patrick, with detachment, could hear the boy that had once been, in George's fifty-year-old voice.

"Where did you get it, George?"

"From Clair. I've always liked pens. Wait a minute. I'll get some paper." He got up and got a note pad from a desk. He brought it back and ran the pen over the top slip of paper. He looked at Patrick. "It won't work."

Patrick studied him, remembering vividly every word Clair had delivered about Gael's visit. No, he thought; he hadn't given his daughter the attention he should have, but ...

"It's a new pen," George said, "and it won't work."

That lake, he thought. How could I have missed seeing it? And when did I ask for a roast for tonight? Now George, sitting here with that pen, acting and talking as though he were a child again. *Something is wrong*, he thought. "It has a seal, George. Most of them do." His voice was hard and his words were short.

George smiled eagerly. "You try it, Patrick."

Patrick took the pen and held it over the paper.

"Write your name, Patrick," George said. "I like to see you do that."

"Why, George?" Patrick asked bitterly, irritated with everything at this moment, including George. "Why is that?"

"Because I know you've done something with your life. Father told me that, you know." He nodded. "And it's true. I never did anything, really. But you did. You're a celebrity. I saw you on television, and I knew, then, that you were. I knew people would ask you to sign your name for them, just like I'm doing."

"I'm no celebrity, George."

"Yes, you are. Weren't there newsmen to meet you when you flew in last night?"

"No."

"But they didn't know you were coming, did they? They didn't know what plane you were on?"

"I tried to keep that a secret, yes. But I'm not a celebrity."

"What if they find out you're home? They'll want to come out and interview you, won't they?"

"I would rather they wouldn't."

"Shall I tell Clair that?"

"Yes. Please."

"Sign your name, Patrick, just as though I were somebody you didn't know. Just because I want your autograph."

Patrick signed his name, pushing the pen hard against the paper. "The pen's all right, George."

George tore off the top slip. "Sign again, Patrick. Right there. I like to see you do that. It says you've done something, and I never have."

"I wish you wouldn't talk like that, George," Patrick said. "It's nonsense."

"Let me get you another drink while you do that." Again he hurried to the table and fixed a fresh drink. He brought it back and picked up the pad on which Patrick Reed had signed his name the second time.

"I don't want to talk nonsense, Patrick," he said, and now Patrick could hear the years going back into his voice. "I guess everything works out. I was one thing. You were another. But Father loved us both, didn't he? Equally?"

"I don't know. I wouldn't put it in the past tense, though. He's still alive, even if he won't see me."

George's smile flickered away, then returned. "Yes," he said quietly. "And he won't see you, will he, Patrick? But he was mean to me sometimes too, even though he loved me. I wouldn't worry about it, Patrick. Don't you worry about it at all."

He drank the drinks George kept bringing him. The evening blurred into a hazy montage. Felix came in; he could remember that. He could remember Felix urging him to talk again about how it had been in Viet Nam. He barely remembered eating dinner. He did not feel himself just getting drunk; there was another heavy, detached feeling. When the Montagnards had finally been convinced by a U.S. liaison team, who had found him in that native village, that he should be released, he'd been given something by the doctors; he had felt this way then.

But he drank hard, and he was getting very drunk too, and he didn't care.

He talked. He told them how he'd made an escape midway in his imprisonment, certain he was going to make it, and how again the dogs had trailed him and found him, so that he was finally dragged back, screaming....

Then he realized that his words had become too thick to be understood. He stood up, weaving. The last thing he remembered was being helped up the stairway to his room by Felix and George.

It was the sound that awakened him. He opened his eyes, mouth dry, head still swimming, and heard it: high-screeching birds. His eyes widened. He stared up, with only a shaft of moonlight from a window to relieve the darkness. Birds, he thought—like those from the jungle, below where he'd been forced down in the helicopter.

Then he heard something else: music, oriental instruments, playing in the pentatonic scale ...

He pushed himself up, fright running through him like electrical current. "No ..." he whispered.

Then, into the shaft of moonlight, they stepped. Shadowy figures, ghostly in the pale light. There was a tall man with oriental features, large ivory earplugs swinging from his earlobes, a vivid white cross drawn on his forehead, naked except for loin cloth. Beside him came a woman, her oriental face passive, bare breasts gleaming.

His breath was coming hard, as he stared at them, feeling some small thing snap deep down in the back of his brain. He gasped, then yelled. The figures slid silently from the room. He forced himself out of the bed, falling, then getting to his knees. He crawled to the door and pressed himself against it, to hold them back, yelling ...

Finally, as though surfacing after a long drive through terrible waters, he realized that the sounds of the birds had stopped; the music had stopped. All he could hear was Clair calling to him from the other side:

"Patrick?"

He kept his palms and a shoulder pressed against the door. "Patrick, what's the matter?"

Slowly, he moved from the door. He got to his feet and went back to the bed and sat down on it, weakly.

"Patrick!" Clair called.

"Yes," he said finally.

The door opened. They stood in the light of the hallway: Clair in a robe, George in pajamas. Patrick blinked against the light, then bent his head.

"Patrick," Clair said, coming in, followed by George, "what in the world?" She touched his shoulder. "Are you all right, darling?"

"I'm all right."

"But you were yelling, dear."

"I guess I was."

"Did you have a nightmare?"

Patrick sat with his hands against his thighs; he knew that if he lifted them they would be shaking badly. "I heard—" He shook his head.

"Patrick," Clair said soothingly. "You must have had a terrible nightmare. But it was just a dream, darling. Everything's all right now. You're home. With us."

He closed his eyes, trying to shut out everything.

"Darling," Clair said, and put her palm gently against his cheek, "it was only a very bad dream. You just lie down again and go to sleep. There won't be any more bad dreams. Will you do that? You'll have to promise, or we just won't leave you. Will you promise?"

He took a breath and nodded.

Clair patted his cheek, then they were gone. Slowly, nerves throbbing, he lay back in bed. He pulled up the covers to keep off the sharp night chill, because he was shivering all over. But that didn't help. He kept on shivering. He tried to will himself back to the ultimate comfort of sleep. But sleep would not come, and he could not even close his eyes again. He simply lay there shivering, staring up.

Gael handed Dean Powers a cup of coffee. Late morning sunshine played a bright pattern on the rug. She said:

"I'm glad you could get away."

He smiled at her. "I'm ahead of it anyway. You want to go out to the ranch?"

"Yes. But look at this first." She handed him a small envelope. "It was mailed late last night. I got it this morning."

He looked at the typewritten address; there was no return.

"Open it."

He opened the envelope and read the short typewritten message on a small oblong piece of paper:

"Do not bother me anymore. I never cared for you anyway, and so let us go our separate ways. Leave me alone." Beneath the typing was the signature of Patrick Reed.

He looked up at her.

"Yesterday I went out and they said he didn't want to see me. They sent me away. But Paddy could never have written that to me."

"It doesn't seem right that he would. But—is it his signature?"

"Yes."

"Wouldn't he sign it Paddy?"

"He's always signed his full name. It was his touch of humor." She shook her head swiftly, pacing the small room. "As soon as I got it, I called the ranch. George answered. I asked to speak to Paddy. George said he'd get him. Then he came back to the phone. He said Paddy wouldn't talk to me." She closed a small hand tightly. Then she came over and pointed at the note. "He said let's go our 'separate' ways. Paddy may be one of the greatest reporters in the world, but he's always been a terrible speller. He always spelled 'seperate.' Always!"

"You think somebody else wrote the note?"

"I don't know—how could I?" She paced again. "But it's possible. Wrote it, then got him to sign it. But why?" The small hand doubled again, knuckles whitening. "I don't want to believe it, but maybe he did ask somebody to type it for him, then signed it. I don't know. But it's wrong, all of this."

"Yes," he said. "It's very damn wrong. Let's go out there. Right now."

He ran his car onto the graveled turn-out just in front of the metal gate and stopped. He looked at the large padlock secured at the steel catch. She said, "Clair locked it yesterday. That gate's never been locked before."

Barbed wire fencing ran from either side of the gate; bordering the highway, squaring in the grazing fields. "Well," he said, "we'll crawl through the damn fence and walk in, that's all."

They left the car on the turn-out. He helped her through the wire, then walked with her. The grass was dry and yellow on the slope of the hill, then the green of trees was beyond; they grew along the creek, which wound down toward the ranch house with the narrow road following it. They crossed the field, went through the barbed wire again, then followed the road toward the house.

They crossed the metal rails of the cattle guard and stepped onto the grounds. They heard a dinner bell ringing, but it stopped as soon as they had finished coming around the final curve. Dean had not seen who had rung it. All of the buildings lay in hot noon sunshine. A hawk, with a dozen smaller birds, floated very high against a white-blue sky. Dean saw the man coming up a path through a thicket of trees.

He came forward toward them quickly, and Gael said, "Hello, Felix."

Felix smiled, but Dean could find no warmth nor welcome in that smile. "Hello, Miss Reed."

"This is Dean Powers, Felix. Felix is Grandfather's manager, Dean. I don't think you've met before, have you?"

Dean shook the man's hand briefly.

Felix nodded coolly and then said to Gael, "You must have walked in, Miss Reed."

"The gate was locked," Dean said. "We didn't have any other choice."

Felix looked at him with hard eyes. "Orders," he said.

"To lock the gate?" Gael asked.

"Yes, ma'am."

"Who ordered that?"

Felix touched his thin lower lip with his teeth. "Your father, Miss Reed."

"But why?"

"He doesn't want to be disturbed."

"Which means by me?" she said, her voice tensing.

"I'm sorry, Miss Reed."

"So am I, Felix," Gael said, the tense sound turning to anger. "Because there is something very wrong about this. My own father?"

"Yes, ma'am," Felix said firmly. "But I can't help that. I wish I could. He's been acting, well, nervous. I've never met him before, but I'd say he's been acting nervous."

"Which is why I'm going in and see him now."

"No, ma'am."

"Felix," she said, "I respect the fact that you're my grandfather's manager. But that doesn't mean you're to manage me, nor my father."

"I look at it this way, ma'am. Your grandfather hired me to manage this place. Now he's gone down to his retreat. Your father's here. Your father is the same as your grandfather, in a case like this. I have to take orders from him. His orders are that he doesn't want to see anybody. I have to respect those orders."

"May I please talk to Clair then, or to George, if you don't mind?"

"I don't mind. But they're not here. They went riding about a half-hour ago."

"George and Clair?"

"Yes, ma'am."

"That's very odd, Felix. I don't remember seeing George on a horse in years."

Felix smiled tightly. "You'd have seen him on one if you'd been here about a half-hour ago."

"Somebody rang the dinner bell when we got into sight of the house."

"Yes, ma'am."

"It wasn't you."

"I was down in the far corral."

"It wasn't George or Clair."

"No, ma'am. They're riding."

"I haven't heard that dinner bell rung since Grandfather leased out his land."

"I guess that's true," Felix said. "Until lately."

"Lately?"

Again his teeth flashed against his lower lip. "I don't know why he does it. But every once in a while, he steps out and rings that thing."

"My father?"

"Yes, ma'am."

"Felix, I simply have to see him."

"I know how you feel. But not today, Miss Reed. Those are his orders."

"Felix, if Paddy's acting so peculiarly as all this, including ringing that damn bell for no reason, then maybe you should listen to somebody else about this. Perhaps he isn't responsible, and—"

"Miss Reed," Felix said, his voice carefully controlled, "it was like when I was in the Army. I was a sergeant, and when the company commander gave me his orders, I had to obey those orders. I'm sorry to put it this way. But I thought two, or three, or maybe four times, that captain was crazy. But I couldn't let somebody else tell me what to do. I had to take his orders. That's the case now. I have to listen to your father."

She was silent for a few moments, then she said, "All right, Felix. I hope, though, you won't mind if I go over to the freezer and pick up those cuts of venison Grandfather told me he'd put away for me?"

Felix's face stiffened. "You and Mr. Powers go over and sit in the Jeep. I'll get the meat and drive you back to the highway."

"I'm very capable of doing it myself, Felix."

"There's a lock on that building now, Miss Reed."

"Then just give me the key."

"I would go over and sit down in the Jeep, if I were you," Felix said harshly.

"Now wait a minute," Dean said. "We've listened to your argument about taking orders. That doesn't mean you're going to start giving them."

"It's all right, Dean," Gael said quickly. "Do you know what cuts I mean, Felix?"

"I put them away myself."

"All right. We'll wait in the Jeep."

They sat in the back seat of the Jeep, while Felix disappeared into the freezer building. Dean looked at Gael's face; it was stiff with anger. "If you want me to," he said, "I'll go up to that house, break down the door, and get to your father that way."

"No," she said shortly.

Felix returned with the meat, which he'd wrapped in newspapers. Silently, he drove them to the highway. He relocked the gate when they had returned to Dean's car and drove back out of sight.

"I'm sorry," Dean said, driving away. "That didn't do much good, did it?"

"Not much good," she said, "except that now I'm very certain something's going on in that ranch. Whatever it is, they're trying to keep me from seeing Paddy. Why?"

"If it's what they say it is   "

"I'm sure it isn't just that."

He shook his head, then noticed that his gas gauge showed his tank to be nearly empty. "After what your father's been through, it's hard to judge anything."

They came into the small junction at the top of the hill, and he turned into a service station. As the tank was being filled, Gael said:

"First Clair meeting me to keep me from going in. Then locking that front gate, which has never been locked. Then the note. Now, this morning, that dinner bell being rung when we came in. Like a signal. Next, Felix rushing up. When I tried to get more time in there, just in case Paddy would see us from the house, I asked for that venison. Did you see Felix's face? And a padlock on the freezer building. There was never a lock there before. I don't like any of it. It's wrong, wrong."

Then Dean saw a man duck down beside Gael's window. He was a thin man in faded overalls who wore a white mustache. "Howdy, Gael."

"Hello, Sid. How are you?"

"Fair. Maybe better."

"Dean, I'd like you to meet my grandfather's neighbor, Sid Blake."

Dean shook the man's hand extended through the car, then the man said, "Now I just wanted to tell you, Gael. It's like you say. I'm a neighbor of your granddaddy's. Have been for forty-three years. And I've known your daddy ever since he was born. I watched him grow up and make something of himself in this world. And I say it's all right. As far as I'm concerned, anyway. When a man's been through what he has, we've all got to try to understand it. I wanted you to know. I'm not holding any grudges over it."

"I'm afraid I don't know what you're talking about, Sid."

"That calf."

"Which calf."

"The one Patrick shot."

Her eyelashes flickered in surprise, then she said, "Calf? Paddy shot a calf?"

"Your granddaddy's manager came over and told me about it. Yesterday."

"You mean he accidentally shot one of your calves?"

"I don't know it was accidental. Felix said him and your daddy was taking a ride around your granddaddy's ranch. Your daddy seen this calf over on my property. There was this rifle in the Jeep. So your daddy just stood up and shot it."

"But *why?*"

"Well, maybe that's something we'll never know. But don't you worry about it. Felix came over right away and told me. Went out and picked it up. Nothing touched it yet. It was like getting it fresh for butchering, paid for to boot. You know how it is, Gael. A rancher sells off all his animals and eats deer meat himself until he's about to grow horns. So a little veal's going to be all right, for a change. I just wanted you to know there's no hard feelings on my part." He nodded. "Glad to have met you, Mr. Powers. I'll be seeing you, Gael."

The man ambled back toward his truck. Dean paid for his gas, then drove away, down the winding, narrow road which led to the Peninsula below.

"Now this," Gael whispered. "Why would Paddy do that? He was brought up on that ranch. One of the first things he learned was never to harm the cattle."

"Gael," he said, "I don't know how completely your father was examined when he was released, but this is serious."

She looked at him with dark eyes. "He's not crazy, if that's what you're trying to say. Not Paddy!"

"I'm not saying that. But I think he should be examined again."

She shook her head.

"There're too many things," he said. "I think there's just one thing to do right now. Do you have a family doctor? A man you can trust?"

"Dr. March. In Palo Alto. He's practically a member of the family."

"Call him. Tell him your father's been acting strangely. Ask him to go out to the ranch and see him. If we can't get in there, maybe he can. Find out what's going on. Will you do that?"

She was silent. Then she nodded. "Yes," she whispered.

"George?" Clair said, laughing gaily. "What's the matter? Patrick's glass is empty again."

He sat watching them: George, Clair, Felix, all three seated in the large room with him, the night fresh, but his vision badly blurring already. George got up and refilled his glass. He watched him do that. He watched Clair tip her own glass up. He looked at Felix, across the room, also drinking. Clair was a little tight, he thought; but how could a man swiftly becoming wholly drunk know that for sure? Practice, he thought. He'd had plenty of drinking practice in his years. Plenty.

"There now," Clair said. "Everything's comfy. And what were you talking about, Patrick. Those natives who were drunk that time?"

"Drunk, yes," he said loosely. "Very good drinkers. Like myself." Oh, yes, he thought. Like himself. Always a good drinker. But tonight, as it had been the night before, there was something else: a heavy, drugged feeling, more than the liquor-feeling.

"What in the world did they drink?" Clair asked. "Out there in a place like that?"

"Rice beer."

"And that just made them insane, didn't it?"

He stared down at his new drink, then lifted it. Drink hard, he thought. Drink heavy. Find the blessed darkness that way. Shut out the words and the memories.

"I wonder if they fed beer to those dogs?" Felix said from across the room. He was smiling when he said that, Patrick thought. Or perhaps I am not seeing clearly. Not at all. The room is turning. And Felix is blurring. Is he smiling? I don't know. I don't want to know. Those dogs—did they give them beer? No. They gave them Patrick Reed.

"Don't talk about the dogs," Clair said. "Don't do that, Felix."

Her voice, far away, coming in like a voice carried on waves over water, dimmer, dimmer.

"Patrick? Are you all right, Patrick?"

Lift the glass, he thought hazily. Drink the kind and comforting nectar. Then the glass was no longer in his hand. He heard it smashing distantly against the floor. He was far away....

"Catch him, Felix," he heard from a very long distance.

The screeching birds woke him. Then he heard the music: that same oriental sound rolling in to him through the night. He sat up in his bed, heart pounding.

The door burst open. A dog leaped in, a large shape in the shaft of moonlight, jaws snapping. He felt the scream come up in his throat.

Behind the dog, holding a rope to which the dog was attached, came the man, his oriental face marked by the white cross on his forehead, ivory earplugs swinging. The woman appeared, bare breasts gleaming in the moonlight, shrieking with laughter. Fear wrenched him out of the stupor of sleep. He saw the dog lunging, teeth flashing. Then he threw himself out of the bed. He scrambled, the scream finally coming out of his mouth.

He heard the dog's teeth snap inches behind him. And a hand of the man with the white cross on his forehead was chopping down, sideways, across the back of his neck. Again he plunged into blackness.

He came awake with his cheek against the cold wood of the floor. He lay curled, legs spraddled, palms flat against the wood. He opened his eyes and stared along the wood of the floor, seeing the rug, then the bed, all in the faint glow of moonlight.

He held his breath, his heart hammering so that the pulse in his temples also hammered. But he could hear nothing.

He touched his dry lips with a thick-feeling tongue. No sound, he thought. No sight of them. No music. No birds. No man. No woman.

No dog.

They are in my mind, he thought defeatedly.

He pushed himself to his knees, then to his feet. He fumbled the door open and found a light switch and walked, weaving, down the hallway and down the stairway, to the large living room. He walked over to the table where the liquor was. He was tipping up the glass when Felix stepped in.

"Is that you, Mr. Reed?"

Patrick did not answer. He drank.

"I saw the lights go on," Felix said. "Thought maybe something was wrong. Thought I heard somebody yelling too, earlier. That wasn't you, was it, Mr. Reed?"

He finished that glass. He poured another.

"I thought maybe you had another one of those nightmares," Felix said. "I sure hope not, Mr. Reed?"

He stepped over and caught Patrick Reed as the small body slumped.

Minutes later, Felix stepped into the bedroom down the hall from Patrick Reed's room. George, a record player in his hands, paused in front of a closet and stared at him sullenly. He was dressed in pajamas and robe. Clair, also in a robe, was seated in front of her dressing table mirror. She turned to smile at Felix. Her eyes were shiny. There were two rubber masks on the bed. One of them was a female oriental face. The other was a male face, with a white cross painted on the forehead. George put the record player in the closet, shut the door and again looked at Felix.

"Did you put him to bed, Felix?" Clair asked.

Felix nodded, smiling faintly.

"You're enjoying this, aren't you?" George said. "Both of you."

"What's the matter, George?" Felix grinned.

"You like it!" George said, his face flushing. "You actually like it!"

"Now, George," Clair said. "Let's not be hypocritical, shall we?" She turned back toward the mirror and admired herself in the reflection. "I do rather like myself as a Montagnard. George, give me my mask again, won't you?"

"You're drunk," George said angrily.

"Drunk?" Clair said, laughing. "I am drunk? Patrick's drunk, but am I drunk, Felix?"

"I wouldn't say that."

"You see, George? Felix wouldn't say that. Felix, you give me the mask."

Felix handed the mask to her.

She fitted it over her head, then looked at herself carefully in the mirror. "Yes. I do like myself this way." She suddenly slipped her robe from her shoulders, baring herself to the waist.

Morning came with a chill. Low fog had come in with the first light, and now the grounds were gray. George sat in the living room with a cup of late-morning coffee at his elbow, cold and untouched. Clair sat across the room, a satisfied smile on her mouth.

"Poor George," she said.

"Shut up," he whispered.

The telephone rang. The smile disappeared from Clair's mouth. She got up quickly and picked up the telephone. "Yes?"

George watched her eyes tighten at the corners. "Yes, Doctor. The gate is locked, but—"

She stared across the room at George with anger visible now in her eyes.

"Yes," she said, "he has been acting peculiarly. But I think most of it's just a family matter. I know Gael must be upset. But even if she called you. I don't think—"

She held her hand more tightly around the telephone, then finally said:

"All right. You can drive down and talk to him. But you've simply got to leave family matters out of this. Come down from the junction, and I'll send Felix up to open the gate."

She hung up. George felt fear returning, obliterating the rage and jealousy that had enveloped him since Clair had left their bedroom last night. He wagged his head. "It's over now, isn't it? It isn't going to work after all. If Doctor March is coming—"

"Yes," she said harshly. "Dr. March is coming! And it isn't going to hurt a thing. You get hold of yourself, do you hear?"

She walked through the house and out. In a moment the ancient dinner bell was ringing.

Dr. March, a tall man with a deeply lined face, white hair, and a body that had once been forty pounds heavier, mounted the stairway with surprising speed. He knocked lightly on Patrick Reed's door.

"Yes," Patrick said finally. The doctor stepped inside and shut the door gently behind him.

"Hello, Patrick."

Patrick lay in bed, red hair tousled against the pillow, a fringe of white whiskers showing across his unshaven jaw. The covers had been disarranged, as though he had tossed for hours.

"Hello, Doctor." He stared at him with frightened, red-rimmed eyes.

"I'm glad to see you home, Patrick. How are you feeling?"

"I'm all right." But his voice was hollow and unconvincing.

The doctor drew a chair to the edge of the bed. "Patrick, Gael phoned and asked me to come out."

"Gael?" Patrick said. He shook his head against the pillow. "Worried about me? She doesn't even want to—"

"Patrick, I don't want to get into anything personal. I came for just one reason. To see how you're doing. I'm going to be honest. I've been told that you've been acting strangely."

Patrick took a breath, then let it out. "I see."

"That calf, Patrick. What happened there?"

Patrick had been looking at the ceiling. He turned his head and met the doctor's eyes. "What calf?"

"The calf that was shot. You don't remember that?"

"No. I don't remember that. What calf? Where?"

"It doesn't matter, Patrick. All that matters is that you don't look well. I'd like to ask you again. How do you feel?"

Patrick stared at the ceiling again.

"What's bothering you, Patrick?" the doctor insisted softly.

"Dreams. I—"

"Dreams? What kind of dreams?"

"Nightmares."

The doctor nodded, watching him closely. "You've been having nightmares. Do you want to tell me about them, Patrick?"

Reluctantly, he told him. Then he fell silent. The doctor rubbed a palm across a row of bony knuckles. "They seemed that real."

"Yes," Patrick whispered. "That part when I was struck across the neck, I—" He lifted a trembling hand and touched his neck. "My neck feels bruised."

The doctor leaned forward, touching Patrick's neck, looking at it. "It looks bruised, all right." He straightened. "Have you been drinking since you got home, Patrick?"

"I was drinking before I got home, Doctor. I've been drinking most of my life."

"I know that. I remember a couple of times—"

"All right. Yes, I've been drinking."

"How much?"

"Quite a bit."

"I never have told you how to live your life, Patrick, because, for one reason, I knew you wouldn't listen to me. But time has a way of catching up with a man. You've been through a hell of a lot. What you used to do, maybe you can't do anymore. Too much liquor—" He shrugged. "I think you've been drinking too much. And I think you've been having nightmares because of it. Maybe you got up and don't remember it and fell down, Patrick. Maybe that's why your neck's sore. Have you been blacking out?"

"Yes," he said quietly, "of course."

"All right, Patrick. I'm going to give you some advice, about how to live, and for the first time. I'd cut down on that drinking. I'd try to relax without it. You've been through more than any man should, and I'm aware of that. But still it's a personal battle for anyone, always, and a man has to fight back the best way he can. Try it my way, will you, Patrick? I think it'll be the best way for you."

Patrick turned away and stared at the window where late-morning sunshine had finally broken through the fog. But it brought him no cheer.

"Patrick?"

"All right," he said, with no conviction in his voice. "I'll try."

The doctor had stepped out of the house and was walking toward his car when Felix came up from the lower corral, moving angrily, muscles bunching. "I'm not taking any more of it!" he said loudly.

Clair and George came out of the house immediately. "What's the matter, Felix?" Clair asked.

Felix shook his head. "I'll go along so far, but not this far!"

"What in the world's happened?"

"I'll show you," he snapped.

He led them down past the barn and through the grove to the lower corral. He stopped at the gate and pointed across the corral. A dog was lying beside the fence, motionless and bloody; there was a heavy branch-cutter nearby. "He beat it to death!"

"Who did?" the doctor asked.

Felix turned on him, glaring. "Patrick! Who else? He picked up that cutter and went to work on him!"

"Did you see him do it?"

"I didn't have to. Who else would do a thing like that? First he shoots that calf for no damn good reason. Now this. I loved that dog!"

"Felix—" Clair said sympathetically.

George stared at the dead animal, then turned away, face gray, and gazed silently into the trees.

"Felix," Clair said, "I understand. We all do. But we can't blame Patrick. He's been through such a terrible lot. He's a *hero.* Now we've got to stand by him. We just can't let him down!"

Felix stared at the dog. "Let him down! Look what he did to my dog."

"Clair, George," the doctor said, "I'd like to talk to you, please."

They left Felix standing at the fence staring at his dog and went back to the drive where the doctor's car was parked. "Do you really think Patrick did that?" he asked.

George said nothing. Clair looked sadly toward the house where Patrick lay in his bed in his room. "I'm afraid so, Doctor."

"Then I'm afraid something's got to be done about him."

She looked back at the doctor swiftly. "I know what you're thinking. But he's George's brother, my brother-in-law. Having him committed—"

"I'm just saying he should have a complete examination. My God, Clair. A calf! Now that dog!"

"Doctor, I promise you. George and I will take perfect care of him. We're not afraid of him. He just needs rest. He'll be all right. I know it."

The doctor shook his head angrily. "Goddam Marshall Reed anyway. Gael told me he'd gone down to that retreat of his, that he wasn't here when Patrick got home. That isn't helping, you know."

"I know, but—"

"That kind of stubbornness is ridiculous. I can cancel my appointments and go down there. Talk to him. Get him back up here."

"No," Clair said quickly. "He won't listen to you. He'll get even more stubborn, if you go there."

"I'll phone him then."

"There isn't a phone down there. You remember. But don't complicate it, Doctor. Father just has to make up his own mind. I'm sure he will. Then he'll come home to see Patrick. If he doesn't, in the next two or three days, we'll drive down—George and I—and talk to him. We'll get him back somehow. Patrick will be so pleased. He'll rest better then, and pretty soon he'll be all right. I just know it, Doctor."

The red Renault was parked down the campus street. Dean came out of the athletic building, moving past a long line of ticket-buyers, and saw her standing beside it. He went down the street, past tall palms, and stopped beside her. In the hard sunlight, the fine lines of tension were visible in her handsome face.

"I didn't want to call you away again," she said. "But I had to phone. I had to talk to you."

"Sure," he said smoothly. "It's all right."

"Are all of those people buying tickets for the meet?"

He nodded. "Nobody thought there would be this much response. They're figuring 80,000 people for each day now. Don't get a U.S.-U.S.S.R. meeting every week."

"I shouldn't be taking you away."

"I've covered all the pre-game stuff I'm going to. All I have to do now is be there when they fire the first starting gun tomorrow."

"I'm glad." She smiled wanly. "The doctor called. He saw Paddy."

"What did he say?"

"Let's get in the car. You get back of the steering wheel."

He helped her in, then got behind the wheel beside her. "Okay. Now."

"He said Paddy's been drinking heavily. Having terrible nightmares. He asked him to cut down on the drinking, to try to relax without it. Then, when he came out of the house, Felix came up from a corral, angry. His dog had been beaten to death. Apparently Paddy—"

Tears were in her eyes. He put an arm around her. He could feel her hurt down deep in himself. "They think your father did that?"

"Yes," she said in a small voice. "The doctor said he should have a complete mental examination. But he said he's an old friend too. He doesn't want to be responsible for having Paddy committed. He said Clair didn't want that either. He knew I wouldn't want it. So he said maybe we should just see if Paddy won't get better. He was terribly angry with Grandfather, for not being home now. But he said that Clair insisted that he couldn't talk Grandfather into anything. He said the only thing he could think of to do would be to check on the examination they gave Paddy after he was released. But that's going to take days...."

Her voice drifted away. Her hands clenched. She shook her head abruptly.

"Something is terribly wrong out there. I know it." She turned toward him. "I want to see Grandfather. I've got to talk him into going home. He's old, yes. But he's always been wise. He'll know what to do, when he hears about how Paddy's been acting, and about all the other peculiar things going on out there. Will you drive me down? Right now?"

His arm tightened around her. Then he started the Renault and drove it through the campus, west, toward the coast.

As they crossed the peninsular hump of the Coast Range Mountains and came down on a new blacktop through heavy growths of pine and redwood, she described the retreat to him.

It was a rustic cabin centered in a hundred acres of rolling coastal land. There were trees, because it was up from the flat of the beach. And there was a continuous corrugated iron fence running around it. At the front gate was a small caretaker's house manned by a Mr. Jimson, who took care of the cabin and the grounds in return for the use of the house, hunting the acreage, growing a small field of artichokes and receiving a small monthly remuneration from her grandfather. Mr. Jimson, she said, was as gloomy and bitter as the fog that usually enveloped the place. But he had held his job for eighteen years, which was exactly how long her grandfather had owned the property.

The fog had cleared even over the ocean. When they came down the final hill onto the flatter, sandy coastal land, a high sun had turned the sea into a purple-blue, with snow-tipped waves rolling gently toward the rock beach. Dean turned the Renault onto the coast highway and drove south.

They came into the small town, outside of which the retreat lay.

The town was old and lonely-looking, with a few business buildings which had, long ago, been built with the expectation of a coastal fishing boom that had never come, plus a few drab-looking houses. They passed a littered all-night service station, a single grocery store, and another service station which had obviously been abandoned long ago. Gael said:

"Another mile south of town. Then turn left."

He followed her instructions, turning off the highway onto a graveled road which led another mile into the hills and the woods. There he stopped the small car at the entrance to the grounds: a double wire gate, with a white sign that announced, "Private Property. No Trespassing." A hundred yards on the other side of the gate was a small pine house; the graveled road continued beyond the gate, curling out of view into the trees.

"Honk," Gael said.

Dean did and waited. Nobody appeared from the small house.

"Again," she said. "Mr. Jimson's stubborn. He's gotten to think he owns this place."

Dean honked the horn again, and finally a bone-thin man in gray work clothes came out of the house and looked down the road at the Renault. He stood there for a few moments, then he came forward without hurrying. He unlocked the gate and opened one side just enough to get through, then came on to the car. He wore heavy twill trousers and a thick turtle-necked sweater under a heavy jacket. He also wore a faded brown knit cap. It was cooler here near the ocean, but not cool enough, Dean thought, for those kind of clothes.

The man was small, and he did not have to bend to see who was in the car. When he looked at Gael, he showed no recognition.

"Hello, Mr. Jimson," she said.

Mr. Jimson did not answer.

Dean put out his hand and said, "I'm Dean Powers, Mr. Jimson, a friend of Miss Reed's. We've come down here to see Miss Reed's grandfather. I wonder if we could drive through?"

The man looked at him as though he had just uttered a string of profanities. He shook his head abruptly, without taking Dean's hand, and Dean thought: he looks exactly like a badger somebody had dressed in those clothes and taught to stand on his back legs. Unkind, he thought, but accurate. "Nobody goes through that gate."

And his voice, Dean thought, sounds like a fog whistle.

"It's important," he said. "Miss Reed has to see her grandfather."

The man shook his head again. "Nobody goes through that gate."

And then he thought: *there is something wrong, all right, wrong to the core; but I don't know what it is.*

"This is Mr. Reed's granddaughter, Mr. Jimson."

"I wouldn't know that."

"Mr. Jimson," Gael said. "My father's ill. And I have to see my grandfather."

Mr. Jimson shook his head a third time. "I've got orders. Nobody goes in—strangers, family, nobody."

"Well, who gave you those orders?" Dean asked, feeling himself turning angry.

Mr. Jimson looked at him with disdain. "I don't have to answer to you, do I?" He shook his head a fourth time. "No, sir."

"Mr. Jimson," Gael said, "did Grandfather give you those orders?"

"Same as."

"What is the same as?"

"Your grandfather's manager, Mr. Argon, drove Mr. Reed down the other night. Mr. Reed was asleep in the back of the car. I saw him there, just the way he rides about half the time since he got a little older. All covered with his coat and his hat down and sleeping. And Mr. Argon said to me, 'Mr. Reed wants a few days of rest here, and he doesn't want to be disturbed by anybody. That includes you and anybody else who wants to see him.' That's what Mr. Argon said to me.

I said, 'That includes family too?' And Mr. Argon said, 'That includes everybody in this world, including Mr. Reed's family.' So he drove Mr. Reed in to his cabin, then drove out, with Mr. Reed left back there. That's where he is right now. I'm not disturbing him. Nobody else is either." He pinched his turtle neck higher under his throat and said, "That's more than I figured to say, and that's all I'm going to say. You better get on now, because what Mr. Reed wants is what he gets."

He walked back through the gate, shut and locked it, and went back to his house.

Dean said, "I don't think I particularly like Mr. Jimson."

She sat looking forlorn. He put his hand on hers and said, "And I don't think I particularly like the story he gave us either. I want to check something." He smiled at her, and he was certain that he saw a little more determination go back into her eyes.

He drove back into town and swung the car in front of the single grocery store. "What are you going to check?" she asked.

"Just a feeling. I'll be right back."

A few minutes later he returned to the car. "You know more about your grandfather than I do. It does seem very damn peculiar that he'd go into that kind of seclusion when your father just got home. But I just checked with the grocer. He says he sold enough supplies weeks ago to Mr. Jimson, to stock your grandfather's cabin, so that he wouldn't have to come out in weeks. He says your grandfather does go in there and not come out this way. Often."

She nodded, looking worried again. "Yes, I know. But—"

"I know." He drove down the street and stopped in the all-night service station. He ordered the tank filled and asked the operator, a thick-shouldered man with a ruddy face, "Do you know Marshall Reed?"

The man nodded. "This is his granddaughter, isn't it?"

"She wants to see him. But he's given orders to his caretaker not to let anyone in. We're a little concerned about him."

The man grinned. "Sounds like Mr. Reed, all right. Sounds like Jimson too. He looks after that place like he was a guard dog. Not much better tempered either." The man nodded again. "The old man came in, what? About three nights ago? Early in the morning. Car stopped here to get gassed, then went on."

"Did you see him?" Dean asked.

"Not me. Harry—that's my night attendant—did. Car stopped, Harry said. Somebody driving it for him, the old man's foreman or whatever he is. But he came down, all right."

"I wonder if Harry talked to him."

The man looked at Dean with new interest. "Something wrong?"

He looked, Dean thought, like a man who would give more if he thought something were wrong. "We don't know. But we're trying to find out."

"I could call Harry. Right now, if you want. He lives out there on the edge of town. He ought to be up by now. He ought to be home, if he didn't go fishing. I don't think he did."

"We'd appreciate that. Ask him if he sure saw Mr. Reed, please. And if he actually talked to him."

"Yes, sir," the man said eagerly. "I'll do that right away."

As the man walked inside to his telephone, she said, "What are you thinking?"

"I don't know. I just want to check. Let's see what he says."

She was silent until the man came back and said, "Harry was home, all right. He says the old man was in the back seat, asleep. Covered up with his coat and his hat pulled down over his face."

"But he didn't actually see his face?" Gael said. "He didn't talk to him?"

"I guess not. He talked to the foreman, or whatever, that's all."

"Thank you very much."

As they drove out of the service station, Gael said, "I don't like this."

"I don't either."

"Where are you going now?"

"Back to the retreat. Is there any other way to get into it, from the side or back?"

"You can drive down a mile further, then take a dirt road in that comes around to the south side of the fence. But that fence runs all the way around."

"All right," he said, and drove swiftly down the highway toward that turn-off.

"But what are you going to do?"

"Get over the fence and into that cabin. I want to see if he's really in there."

She looked at him, frowning. "Then I'm going with you."

He shook his head, then turned off the highway and rolled the car along the narrow dirt road leading to the south fencing of the retreat. "I don't trust Mr. Jimson. Is the house straight in from here?"

"Yes. And I don't trust Mr. Jimson either, but I want to go with you."

"No," he said, stopping. He looked at the iron fence. It was perhaps eight feet high; there were strands of barbed wire on top of that. "You couldn't get over that anyway."

"Dean," she said softly, "be careful."

He turned toward her, then kissed her. He got out of the car and strode to the fence. He estimated it again, then jumped upward, catching the iron near the top. He scrambled up, using the traction of the rough fencing against his soles. Then, carefully, he crawled over the barbed wire and dropped to the grass on the other side.

In the small house near the gate, the caretaker held the telephone and finally heard the hard, flat voice: "Hello?"

"Mr. Argon?"

"Yes."

"Mr. Jimson, Mr. Argon. I've been trying to get you for twenty minutes. Called you right away, like you told me to do. But they said you were out on the ranch somewhere."

"What's the matter, Jimson?"

"They came down here and wanted to see Mr. Reed."

"*Who* did?"

"This fellow name of Powers and Mr. Reed's granddaughter."

The caretaker listened and heard nothing. He said:

"Mr. Argon?"

"Nobody's to go in there!" Felix exploded. "I told you that!"

"Well, they didn't!" Mr. Jimson shouted. "I kept them out, just like you said. They're not in there!"

"What did they want?"

"Said the girl's father was sick and wanted Mr. Reed to know. I said they weren't going in. They drove away then."

"All right, Jimson. You make sure they don't try it again, because Mr. Reed absolutely doesn't want anybody monkeying around in there. You. His granddaughter. That Powers. Absolutely nobody. Do you understand me, Jimson?"

"I did right along! I was calling to tell you. On your orders. That's what I'm doing. Following orders! What's wrong with that?"

"Nothing, unless you quit following orders. Nobody's to go in there, and I don't care how you keep them out. Phone me if anybody tries it again. Do you hear me, Jimson?"

"Yes!" the caretaker said, and slammed the telephone down. He paced angrily around the room, then went outside to fill his lungs with fresh air. Then he heard it: somebody moving through the woods inside the fence. He went inside, picked up his rifle, slammed a bullet into the chamber as he came out, then hurried toward the sound.

Dean, moving toward the center of the grounds, found a walking trail and followed it. Minutes later he came into the clearing where the cabin stood. It was made of aged redwood and was rusty with reddish moss. It was surprisingly small, and he circled it swiftly. All of the windows were closed and shaded. He rapped on the door. There was no response.

He tried the handle. The door was locked. Again he circled the house, trying to lift windows. There were no screens, but they were locked. All right, he thought. I'll buy Marshall Reed a new pane. He found a rock in the sandy soil beside the house, chose a large front window and smashed the pane. Then he reached inside and turned the lock. He shoved the broken window up and crawled inside.

There were three rooms, all bare-floored, furnished with simple inexpensive pieces. Marshall Reed was in none of the rooms.

He unlocked the door from the inside, and went out that way. He looked around toward the trees again. The grounds were large, and it was possible Marshall Reed could be out on them somewhere. But that cabin did not look as though it had been recently used, he thought. It was that, if the old man kept everything in perfect order. And where is that caretaker? he thought—did he hear the car or me coming in?

He decided to go back to Gael and moved across the clearing. When he'd reached the edge of the woods and the trail he'd used to get there, a shrill whine of a bullet went over his head. He heard the cracking echo of the rifle, then dove into the brush. He lay there, listening. There were no more shots, but he was certain that he could hear someone moving through the woods.

When she heard the shot, Gael got out of the small car quickly. Heart pounding, she looked through the fence. She saw only the trees of the woods and the brush, and there was no more sound after that. She waited tensely. Minutes went by.

Then she heard and saw him, coming fast out of the woods.

"Are you all right?" she called.

"Yes." He came to the fence and put his hands on the wiring. "Somebody shot at me. Jimson, I think."

And then he heard: "Far enough." The fog-whistle voice sounded from the woods, and Dean turned around to see the caretaker step out with his rifle in his hands. "Trespassing," the caretaker said. "I warned you."

"Listen to me, Jimson."

Jimson walked forward until he was just in front of him and pointed the rifle at his stomach. "I'm not listening to anything," he said. "I'm turning you in. Breaking into private property."

"Mr. Jimson," Gael said from the other side of the fence, "I'm Mr. Reed's granddaughter!"

"I don't care about that. I've got orders."

"And there he is," she said. "My grandfather—coming through the woods."

Mr. Jimson's head swiveled around. Dean, looking past him, could see no one. Then he knew what she was doing. He stepped forward swiftly and yanked the rifle from Jimson's hands. The caretaker swore and pawed after it. But Dean stepped back and said, "All right, Jimson. You've got your orders. But you're wasting your time. Mr. Reed isn't coming through the woods. And he isn't in that cabin either."

The man blinked slowly. Dean jacked the ammunition out of the rifle. He put the shells in his pocket and the rifle on the ground. Then he clambered over the fence and dropped on the other side.

"Let's get out of here."

They got into the small car and drove off. Jimson, eyes furious and confused, picked up his rifle and went back through the woods at a trot, directly to his house and the telephone there.

In the ranch house, Felix listened to the caretaker's rasping explanation and felt fury turn his face hot. George sat on a large chair and watched him sullenly. Clair stood nearby, tensely. "All right," Felix said angrily. "You had a simple job to do, and you couldn't do it, could you?"

"I did my best!" the caretaker complained.

"And that wasn't good enough."

"Well, it has been for the past eighteen years! Mr. Reed never complained in all that time!"

"He's going to this time, Jimson."

"I don't know what that damn Powers meant—saying Mr. Reed wasn't back at his cabin. I didn't take time yet to get a look. I came right back here and phoned, straight on your orders. But if you're going to talk to me that way, I'm going back there and find where he is and tell him!"

"You'll tell him nothing—because I told you! He doesn't want to be disturbed. By you! By anybody!"

"Well, maybe nobody's going to, if he isn't back at the cabin!"

"You left your place unlocked when you heard Powers and went after him, didn't you?"

"I never lock my place when the gate's closed. I never have in eighteen years."

"Well, that's how he got into your house and used your phone."

"Who did?"

"Mr. Reed. He must have phoned me while you were out there running around after Powers. He heard somebody tramping around. And he walked up to your place and phoned me to come down get him, just because he isn't getting the peace he asked for. Now, you try to do what I tell you this time. You stay in that house of yours, and don't leave it. I'm coming down to get him. Right now. And if you can't do it right this time, Jimson, you're out of a job!"

Jimson slammed the telephone down. He whirled and then began pacing his cabin.

At the other end of the line, Felix also put his telephone down hard. He glared at George and Clair. He rubbed the back of his hand over thin lips.

"What are we going to do now?" Clair said.

"Finish this." He jerked his head toward George. "Go up and keep Patrick occupied. Play tiddlywinks with him if you have to."

George remained sullenly in his chair.

"Go on!" Felix snapped.

George got up and moved heavily up the stairway.

"Felix," Clair said, "do you still think we can—"

"I know it! Now go get that stuff we used before. I'll get the car. Let's move!"

Dean drove north on the coast highway, and Gael said, "I knew something was terribly wrong. We found that out absolutely, didn't we?"

"I didn't have a chance to look for him in the woods, Gael. Maybe he was out there somewhere, and—"

"No. I know what's happened."

He looked at her and saw that her face was pale. "You've got to be doing better than I am then, because—"

"Grandfather's dead," she said in a peculiar flat-sounding voice.

"Dead?"

"Dead! Because somebody killed him. And I know who. *My father*."

He swung the car off the road and braked it to a hard stop. He stared at her. "You don't know what you're saying."

"Yes." Her eyes were dark. Her voice trembled. "Grandfather must have gone down to that retreat before Paddy got home. But then he finally went back to the ranch. When he did, Paddy killed him. The way he killed the calf. The way he killed that dog! Because he's crazy!"

"Damn it, Gael."

She was crying now, but the words kept tumbling out:

"They know it at the ranch. And that's what they've been doing— trying to protect him. That's why everything seemed so peculiar. My father killed his own father, because he's *insane*."

He took her shoulder and held it in a tight grip. He spoke to her harshly. "Goddam it, Gael, listen!"

"No!" She shook her head, blind with tears. "No!"

"You've already got him tried and convicted. And you don't even know if something *has* happened to your grandfather. Why such a damn quick judgment?" He closed his fingers more tightly. "All right. I'll tell you. It's because you don't trust your father. You never have. Oh, yes, you've had the big hero-image of him. But that's only been half your mind doing that. The other half, that's been condemning him. You told me how your mother was always so patient with him. Maybe she was, on the outside. But how about inside? Down deep?" He shook his head. "Maybe not, that way. Maybe she honestly resented him. And how much of that rubbed off on you? It was bound to, if she felt that way. So that now, without proof even of anybody being dead, including your grandfather, you're accusing your father of being insane and of having killed him! That's really fast judgment, isn't it?"

She was crying against her hands, steadily wagging her head.

"All right," he said. "What do you want to do? Drive back to Palo Alto as fast as this little car will go and call the police? If your father's crazy, if he's murdered somebody, that's the only thing to do. Call the police. Call the mental hospital. Let them go get him. Put a straitjacket on him. Chain him for good measure!"

"No!"

He watched her, then he said, "All right." He slid his arm around her gently. "I'm sorry. But you were running down that wild alley too fast. I had to stop you somehow."

Finally she turned to him, face against his chest, and cried softly as he held her. After a time, he said:

"I don't blame you for thinking any damn thing by now. Something is wrong, yes. And I think we *should* report it. But—"

"No. I can't do that."

"What do you want to do then?"

"Everything," she said, "for Paddy. But I'm not thinking well now. You're right. And I've simply got to. I've got to get things straightened out in my mind. I will, tomorrow. Let's go back now. I need the night, by myself. You have to go to that meet tomorrow. When that's over, we'll decide."

"Good," he said. "Nothing until tomorrow. Will you promise?"

"Yes," she said.

He started the car and drove it down the highway. He had missed seeing, as he'd held her, the station wagon which had gone by, speeding in the direction of the small town, near the coast where the grounds of the retreat lay.

Felix stopped the station wagon a half mile from the small town in the deserted parking circle of a small beach. "Did they see us?" Clair asked. "We were right on that car before—"

"No! Now get in back and stop worrying."

"Felix, we have to do this. We *have* to. This is everything. All those years with George?"

She got into the back of the car and curled on the floor. He covered her with a blanket. Then he drove back to the highway.

He went through the town and took the road leading to the retreat. He stopped in front of the double gate. The caretaker swung open both sides. He drove in and stopped beside Jimson.

"Did you manage to do what I asked this time?"

The caretaker's eyes were bright with indignation. "I never left this house one minute since I talked to you."

Felix drove on without answering, through the woods, to the empty cabin. He pulled the blanket from Clair, then followed her inside, carrying a black leather bag.

Inside, she said, "That broken window. Powers must have done that. And gotten in. He *knows* this house was empty."

He didn't answer her. Instead, he opened the bag and pulled out the dark, old-fashioned suit, the topcoat and the hat. "Get into these."

Minutes later, dressed in Marshall Reed's clothing, her hair pulled tightly beneath the hat, Clair got into a rear seat of the station wagon.

"Tip that hat forward more," Felix said. "And don't look at Jimson's house when we go out."

He drove back out of the retreat, passing the caretaker's house swiftly.

The caretaker watched them pass from his open doorway. Then he walked out and slammed the gate shut. Damn old Marshall Reed, he thought—wouldn't even nod goodbye to him. Bad as his manager, he thought. And if he'd had to deal with them more than a few days out of every year, he'd quit. He walked back into his house and slammed that door shut behind him. When he realized that he was wholly alone again, he felt better immediately.

Patrick intended to follow the doctor's advice that evening. When Clair had first offered him a drink, he'd refused. But when she kept insisting that he should relax and at least have one, he'd given in. He'd had one. Then another. And finally he was going at it steadily, hoping to escape the nightmares that way, but knowing that he was only finding his way back to them again.

Finally had come the familiar blurring. He had made an attempt to hang onto a small flame in his mind, to keep from diving into the complete darkness and the terror there. But the small flame went out, and he was in the darkness once more....

He awoke with the same suddenness, mouth dry, sweating. The music. The birds. He lay in his bed, trembling. Then the door slammed open. In the dim moonlight in the room, he saw the tall man in loin cloth striding toward him, the white cross on his forehead almost phosphorescent. The woman followed, laughing, bare breasts jutting....

He tried numbly to twist away when the man reached for him. But it was no use, and he whimpered as the man pulled him from the bed. "No," he whispered. But he was dragged from the room and yanked brutally down the stairway. Then he was pushed outside, and through the trees, to where the bamboo frame was waiting, its yellow wood pale in the dim light.

"No, no," he whispered, as he was lifted bodily against that frame, his arms forcibly spread, his wrists and ankles tied. Christ-like, he thought, his mind seeming to tear apart in his skull.

The man was laughing now, with the woman, and she came dancing toward him, a small bush in her hand. She thrust it at his middle. *Kpung*, he thought wildly.

He struggled desperately against the cords that bound his wrists and ankles. The woman kept thrusting that bush at him. And then he felt the cords give. He came off the bamboo frame and scrambled away from it. The tall man leaped in front of him, making a vicious sound. The woman darted toward him from the other side. He plunged forward in the only direction open to him, and ran. He crashed through the brush, hearing them shouting behind him. He plunged into a tree, ripping the side of his face. Then he bounced away and ran again, until he found a road.

He ran along that road, until the rise of it slowed him. Then he walked as fast as he could, panic jumbling his thoughts. His breath was searing his lungs. But he kept going, to get away from them, away, forever....

With a hammer and a small axe, Felix tore down the bamboo frame. George, who had stepped from the woods when Patrick disappeared, said, "You've gone too far this time. You're drunk. Both of you!"

Clair was seated now on a tree stump, her nearly bare body lighted softly by the moon. She laughed.

Then Felix lifted the bundle of bamboo and said, "Let's go. I've got to go get him."

"I swear you'll pay for it!" George said.

Felix passed him without a word. Clair stood up and smiled at him. "Good night, dear."

He watched them moving back toward the house. She was going with him again, he knew.

Tears of rage, fear and hopelessness blinded him. He leaned against a tree and beat his clenched hands uselessly against the rough bark.

Minutes later, fully dressed, Felix left Clair and his quarters. He got into the Jeep and drove toward the highway. George was right, he thought. He was drunk, all right. But not too much. Not too much to foul this up now. Not too much not to enjoy the thought of Clair waiting for him back there.

Well, he thought, Patrick Reed wouldn't have enough steam to get too far. Maybe the highway, if he stayed on the ranch road and kept climbing. Maybe the highway.

He got out at the gate and opened it. Then he saw a lone car coming down the highway and in its headlights the wild-looking figure standing in the middle of the road, waving his hands, yelling like a banshee.

The car screeched to a halt. Patrick Reed pawed at the door, yelling.

Felix trotted down the highway. A small, bald, white-faced man sat frozen behind the wheel. Felix said, "That's all right, Mr. Reed. Everything's all right."

Patrick whirled, looking at him with wide, fear-staring eyes.

"It's me, Mr. Reed. Felix." He grinned at the driver. "Sorry.

Everything's all right here. He's just a little confused. You go ahead now." He took Patrick's arm. "It's all right, Mr. Reed. I'm going to take you home now."

The driver swallowed, then moved his car on with a roar. Felix guided Patrick to the Jeep, thinking: better this way, even better; maybe he'll report it.

He pushed Patrick gently into the Jeep, then locked the gate and got behind the wheel. "Little nightmare again, right, Mr. Reed?" He grinned. "Got you up and really moving this time, didn't it?" He drove down the road, back toward the house. "But don't you worry, Mr. Reed," he said. "Everything's all right now."

Midday sunlight lighted the hills, so that the trees cast almost no shadows. A herd of does and fawns, supervised by a lone buck, heard the crack of a young boy's rifle as he shot at and missed a tall-eared jackrabbit; they bolted down the side of the gulley, while the buck looked back, holding his guard in quivering tension. On the road bordering the back of the ranch there was a sign: "Coast Hills Stables."

The red Renault was parked beside it. Down, beyond the small house, in the stable, the keeper was tightening the cinch of a gray gelding.

"Yes sir," he said, "you'll like this one, Miss Reed. Bought him off your grandpa in the first place. Do you remember?"

"Yes," she said, listening to him vaguely.

"Let me help you up."

Dressed in riding habit, she mounted the horse easily. "Have a nice ride, Miss Reed."

"Thank you."

She walked the horse across the road. Then she put him into a trot, moving north, along the smooth, dry-grassed bank. She rode without effort. And she thought about how she had barely slept the night before, not in more than scattered intervals. The last time she had awakened, she had escaped a chilling dream: her grandfather was lying upon a flowered bier, face waxen in death, a crimson pool over his heart; her father stood over him, grinning, eyes lighted with the flashing exultation of the insane....

That had been her last effort to sleep. She'd gotten up and drunk cup after cup of coffee. Late that morning, she'd decided what she was going to do. She had promised Dean to do nothing until he could join her late that afternoon. But she couldn't wait, she knew. She had to go out there. And she knew how she was going to get in. She knew what she was going to look for when she got there. And where.

The back entrance to the ranch was a simple barbed-wire gate with a loose post fixed at bottom and top with wire loops. She dismounted and hooked an arm around the stationary post for leverage, then pulled the loose post toward her, in the way her father had taught her years ago. Paddy, Paddy, she thought. She slipped the top loop up and free. Then she lifted the post from the bottom loop and dragged the fencing clear of the opening.

She walked the horse through, then fixed the gate again. She rode on until she reached the old cattle trail which led toward the house and stayed on it until she was a half mile away. There, she tethered the gelding in a small grove and walked carefully toward the buildings.

She came up past the lower corral and stopped finally beside the barn. She saw no one. The grounds were silent. There was not even a cat in sight. She looked beyond the barn, along the quarters used by Felix and the adjoining tool shed, and across the open space to the freezer building. That was where she was going, she thought, stomach tightening. If it were still locked, she was going to try to get unseen into the tool shed, where she could find something to break that lock open.

There was perspiration on the back of her neck, and a faint breeze turned it cold. She shivered. Then she moved forward, running. Nobody was going to stop her this time. Nobody—because she was going to find out the truth, no matter how horrible.

She reached the freezer and turned the corner. The padlock was hanging loose on the door, not locked. She looked at the house and saw no one yet. She put her hand on the handle of the freezer. She took a breath, fighting a sudden light-headedness. Then she pushed the door open and stepped inside. The door swung gently closed behind her.

As it did, Felix Argon came out of his quarters and walked quickly toward the house. He wore leather work gloves. In his right hand he carried the heavy fireplace poker, holding it at the end opposite the handle.

In the house, upstairs, Clair tensely repaired her make-up, trying to keep her hands from trembling. It's all right, she told herself. It's nearly finished, and everything's all right. We've done it exactly. And it's going to work perfectly.

Downstairs, in the living room, Patrick Reed sat motionless. His hair was a tangle. He had not shaved in days, and the white stubbled beard had aged his looks heavily. The vivid red mark where he had run into the tree the night before was plainly visible beneath the whiskers. His eyes were vacant and staring. George sat across the room, looking at him.

Felix walked in and George turned to stare at him with hatred. Felix held the poker in front of Patrick. "Mr. Reed?" Patrick seemed to see nothing.

"Mr. Reed!" Felix snapped.

The vacant, dark eyes moved.

"Do you recognize this, Mr. Reed?" Felix asked.

Slowly Patrick nodded. "Yes," he whispered. "The old poker. The one we always had in the house."

"Take a good look," Felix said, motioning with it.

With a trembling hand, Patrick took it and held it. "Yes," he said.

"Did you hide it?"

Patrick looked up, staring bewilderedly at him. "No," he said. "No, I—"

"It doesn't matter," Felix said abruptly. He took the poker and strode outside.

In the freezer, Gael switched on the light and looked swiftly around its interior. On hooks were hung frozen sides of venison, a skinned calf, a lamb, and nothing else. Again, she took a long, quivering breath. I was so certain, she thought. But Dean was right. I haven't trusted him—my own father. And yet ...

She turned and pressed the door open slightly, just in time to see Felix striding across the grounds toward the barn, poker in hand. She watched the way he moved, with a certain stiffness, as though he were very tense. He opened the small door to the barn and stepped inside.

He came out almost immediately, without the poker, and moved back into his quarters. Again, she looked around the grounds; there was no one else in sight now. She came out of the freezer and ran toward the barn.

In the house, George had watched Felix walk away with the poker in his hand. He had watched the muscles moving beneath his shirt, the angry, nervous spring of calf beneath Levis cloth. An animal, he thought. A bull. A stud. And that was all Clair had ever wanted ... and money.

As Felix disappeared, George again looked across the room at his brother. Not brother, he thought, but half-brother, whom he'd always resented. Until now.

Grief welled up in him, just as it had when he was a little boy and his mother had died. It was grief not just for a mother lost, and now a father lost, but everything lost. He grieved for all of his life, and for himself, and tears came into his eyes. All he'd ever wanted was a little love, he thought, and now he sat in the hollowness of nothing.

He walked slowly across the room, feeling weak and vacant. "Patrick?"

Patrick sat there, not seeing him.

He dropped to his knees beside him. Tears ran out of his eyes now. He rubbed at his nose. "Patrick, listen to me."

Slowly Patrick turned his head and looked at him with dark eyes.

"I can't go on with it." He wagged his head, looking at Patrick imploringly. "Listen to me, Patrick."

When George finished speaking Patrick Reed knew what he must do.

Gael opened the barn door slowly, an intuitive feeling of disaster strong in her now. Sunlight cast down from the doorway across yellow straw spread on the floor, moving forward as the door opened wider.

Then the light was on him. She made a low, moaning sound. He hung from a pulley, his shoes just above the straw and the poker lying there. She looked at him, horror stopping her breath. His body was stiff, his ancient face a death mask, his skull cracked and gleaming with thawing blood.

She drew her breath in with a hiss and spun around, stomach lurching. She saw nothing for a moment. Then she saw him coming out of the house moving as though in a dream. She stared at the maniacal-looking figure with the tangled hair and bearded face. He motioned a hand at her. She screamed and ran.

She ran for the Jeep parked in front of Felix's quarters, and she didn't stop screaming. She saw the keys in the ignition and scrambled behind the wheel. She heard the hollow voice behind her calling, "Gael? Gael ...?"

She hurtled the Jeep out of the grounds, up the road, toward the highway, as Felix plunged out of his quarters, a small pistol in his gloved hand.

The Jeep disappeared around the first bend, and he shouted across the grounds. Patrick Reed blinked in confusion. Clair came running from the house. Felix jerked his pistol at the station wagon in front of the house and called to her, "Get in there, behind the wheel. Gael found him!"

Clair ran to the station wagon and got behind the wheel. Felix moved swiftly to Patrick Reed and grasped his arm, hard. "You too. Hurry up."

He pushed Reed into the second seat of the station wagon and got in beside him, snapping to Clair, "Move!"

Clair sent the station wagon out of the grounds and up the narrow road.

"Now you listen to me," Felix said to Patrick Reed. "You killed that calf. You killed that dog of mine. Now—you went and killed your father, just as soon as he got back up from that retreat. Do you hear me? You killed your father!"

Patrick sat stiffly, staring ahead.

"You went out in that barn and clubbed him over the head with that poker," Felix said harshly. "I found him out there, hung on the pulley. What did you do that for?" He shook his head. "It doesn't matter. All that does is that somebody else found him out there too. Your daughter. Gael. Do you understand me, Mr. Reed?"

Patrick Reed said nothing.

"You'd better," Felix said. "Because you're in real trouble. But we're going to help you. Because we know you don't know what you're doing. But your daughter, she's running scared now. And she's going to report what she saw. Then we can't help you anymore. So we've got to stop her. Do you understand me, Mr. Reed?"

Still Patrick Reed said nothing.

"All right," Felix said to Clair. "Speed it up!"

In the Jeep, Gael reached the gate at the highway. She made her decision quickly. She slowed, then slammed the front bumper squarely into the gate. The lock snapped and the gate flew open. She skidded onto the highway, tires shrieking. She drove north with the accelerator all the way down, in the direction of the small junction.

There were the usual slow Saturday drivers on the highway, and she passed them wildly as she caught up. She was almost to the junction when she saw the trailing station wagon in the rear-view mirror. Panic welled up again, and she thought: stop at the junction and scream for someone to call the police ...

But when she reached the junction, she knew she could not do it that way. Not the police. *Dean,* she thought. *I've got to get to Dean.*

She took the sharp turn onto the road that descended to the peninsula below, the Jeep careening dangerously, then drove the sharp curves hard. She passed slow-moving tourist cars, engine roaring, swinging back just in time from blind curves and oncoming traffic.

In the station wagon, Clair said, "She'll kill herself. And us too!"

"Shut up," Felix said. "Just stay behind her!"

When Gael reached the flat below, where the highway widened and led into Palo Alto, she was cars ahead of them. "Move this damn car!" Felix said brutally.

She was still ahead of the station wagon when she came to the edge of Palo Alto. She ran the signal light there and speeded toward the Stanford campus beyond. The station wagon gradually closed the distance between them.

Heavy traffic for the track meet had piled parked cars bumper to bumper to the edge of the campus. They were lined along the street bordering the east edge approaching the stadium. Then she saw that a barrier had been put up, stopping all traffic, and she came to a skidding stop. She leaped from the Jeep and ran for the large sand-colored arena. There was an echoing, muffled roar of the crowd as she moved. But she thought only of escaping that following station wagon, and of reaching Dean....

Behind, Clair rocked the station wagon to a stop. Felix opened a door and said to her, "Stay here." Then he pushed the numb Patrick Reed out. He grasped the man's arm again. "We've got to follow her. We've got to stop her. It's your only chance. Do you understand that?"

He jerked Patrick Reed ahead, following Gael through parked cars onto the concrete bordering the gates of the stadium.

Gael turned and saw them coming. Then she ran through a gate, past a protesting attendant, and up one of the narrow stairways which led to the top row of seats. He's mad, she thought; *Paddy's mad...*

She reached the top. The inside of the stadium was an oval of 80,000 people. Four 10,000-meter athletes were moving around the track in the calculated pacing of long-distance runners; a slow roar of the crowd followed them. In the green of the field, enclosed by the track, a broad jumper left the ground, skimming flatly through the air, then landed, rolling in a cushion of sawdust. In the center of the green a strong-muscled Russian girl ran with a javelin, then stopped and sent it spearing through the air to plunge quiveringly into the ground 180 feet away. A slim American set himself, pole in hand, then trotted forward. He drove the pole down and pushed himself into the air, floating over the bar and landing on the other side with practiced abandon. There was an individual cheering for the feat. And the other roar steadily followed the long-distance runners like the moving sound of a large wave. Cameras flashed. Newsmen sprinted.

Microphones were held before breathless competitors. Television cameras played silently over the field while a commentator talked high above, unheard by the crowd.

She saw him from that top row: he was just beyond the javelin throwers, talking to a smiling girl who had just won the 100 meter dash.

She ran down the narrow aisle between seats.

Patrick Reed found himself pushed to the top of the stadium. They stopped there. He saw his daughter running down the narrow aisle toward the track. He felt as though he were coming out of another dream, using that small thread of hope very carefully, because this time he had to find reality, he knew.

Then, as though that thread had thickened and straightened, he knew that he was climbing out—hand by hand, with thread becoming rope.

Felix pushed him down the steps, and he went. Halfway down, he saw Gael go over the short ramp bordering the track to cross behind the smoothly kicking runners. An official turned suddenly and waved a cane toward her. Then Felix's gloved hand came up with the pistol. The gun kicked and the report went unheard by the crowd, as the whole stadium picked up the cheers for the runners sprinting out their last leap. He saw the bullet kick into the grass just behind his daughter's heels, as she dashed across the inner green.

Then, using that rope that had become strong and thick, he yanked himself completely back to reality. He knew what Felix was doing: if he could hit her with that pistol, he would then place it in Patrick's hand ...

With a final strength, he put a foot sideways and pushed Felix forward, tripping him. Then he ran past him, down the stairway, leaving him sprawled behind. At the bottom, he went over the ramp and crossed the track just ahead of the finishing runners.

Across the field, Dean saw her coming. He turned from his interview, staring in amazement. She came, tears on her cheeks, arms spread. Then he had her, holding her. "Paddy!" she whispered.

He saw Patrick Reed crossing the track onto the green center field. He came in a weary, weaving run, hair flying, whiskered face taut. Then he suddenly stopped. He picked up a javelin. He turned as Felix came over the ramp, his gun in hand. Gael screamed. And Patrick Reed hurled the javelin. The crowd saw it.

The javelin arched through the air. Felix's pistol jerked, and the bullet slammed uselessly into the ground. The javelin drove through his side, jerking him back with it as it struck into the ground. There was a shocked gasp through the stadium. Then officials were running toward the impaled man, toward the wild-looking Patrick Reed.

The hospital was busy. Dean sat waiting at the end of the corridor and read a newspaper account of it. They found Marshall Reed's body where it hung in the barn. They found George in the house; he readily told them everything. Clair was found in the station wagon, waiting. Felix's wound had been clean and he was repairing. All three had been arrested and were awaiting trial. He put the newspaper down carefully and waited until she came out of the room down the corridor.

She came to him and smiled at him.

"He's all right?" he asked.

"Better each minute, I think. If all of this had happened to anyone else—"

"I know. He's tough. Tougher than he knew himself, I think."

"He'd like to see you. Alone. He wants to tell you something. And so do I. Before you go in."

"All right."

She put a hand in his. "I think, all of a sudden, I know him. All of a sudden, he's very real, a human being, like the rest of us. Not a myth. Not a dream. He's just a man who's got his weaknesses and his strengths. He's simply human. And you're human too. And if you want to do what he's done, I won't try to stop you anymore. You have to do what you want to do. I know that now."

He held her hand. He said softly, "Thanks."

When he stepped into the room, Patrick Reed, clean-shaven and with his hair neatly combed, sat propped in his bed and looked at him with clear, alert eyes. There were newspapers on the bed beside him. He motioned a hand. "Sit down."

Dean sat down and said, "How are you feeling?"

"Good," Patrick Reed said crisply. "I should be out of here in another day or two."

He was certain that he could see hints of the old strength, as he must have had it, coming back in him. He said, "I wish I knew the right thing to say about all of this. I don't. Except to say I'm sorry."

"Yes," Patrick Reed nodded. "I'm sorry too. Sorry as hell. My father. George." He shook his head abruptly. "It happened. It can't be fixed now." He was silent for several moments, then he tapped the newspapers. "I've been reading your stories. You do it all right. I mean that's the way I say it when I think it's the best. It's all right."

"Thank you, sir."

"I didn't ask to have you come in here to listen to my sage advice. But I want to say something anyway. About Gael. She loves you, you know."

"I hope she does."

He nodded. "She does. And ... love. That's all George said he wanted. A little love. He was all twisted up over that. Maybe he was so twisted that he wouldn't have recognized it if it had knocked him down. But maybe he never had it, and knew that, and that was what twisted him. I don't know. I thought I loved him, the way you do a brother. But that isn't what he needed. He needed more than that. We all do, you know. I know that now more than I ever knew it before. I know it, because I passed the real kind and the good kind by."

Dean watched him and saw the reflection in his eyes and knew he was hearing Patrick Reed speaking of a truth he knew completely.

"I never had any time," Patrick Reed said. "I always kept going. I went to the far ends of the earth, searching out the wars and the killings and the butcherings, and—that's what you get when you do it my way. That and not much more." He looked at Dean. "If you want to try it my way, do it. Don't let anybody stop you. But make sure it's what you want. She'll go on loving you, all right, no matter how you do it. But you'll kill a part of it, doing it my way. I know." He put out his hand.

Dean shook hands with him and said, "Thank you, sir." Then he got up and went out. He looked at her waiting for him at the end of the hall. He thought about what Patrick Reed had just told him.

Then he walked toward her, knowing, finally, how he was going to do it.

THE END

www.ingramcontent.com/pod-product-compliance
Lightning Source LLC
Chambersburg PA
CBHW071728190726
48292CB00003B/664